The Special

Betrayal

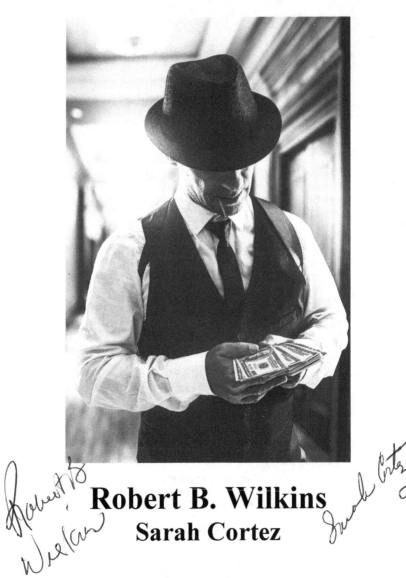

Robert B. Wilkins
Sarah Cortez

2021 White Bird Publications, LLC

Copyright © 2021 by Robert B. Wilkins and Sarah Cortez
Cover by E Kusch

Published in the United States
by White Bird Publications, LLC, Texas
www.whitebirdpublications.com

ISBN 978-1-63363-531-9
eBook ISBN 978-1-63363-532-6
Library of Congress Control Number: 2021943068

PRINTED IN THE UNITED STATES OF AMERICA

To all those who have stood by us.
To Mary Ann, the love of Bob's life.
To Gabino, the love of Sarah's life.

With deepest gratitude to Carol M. Wilhelm and Lourdes Venard, whose careful shepherding of this project has resulted in the goal being accomplished. With deep appreciation to those fellow authors who have believed in this project from the beginning: Johnnie Bernhard, Stephanie Jaye Evans, Germaine Welch.

The Carlucci Betrayal

**White Bird
Publications**

CHAPTER ONE

Jakesberg, Mississippi
Population: 2,240

Frank Carlucci slapped down the New Orleans newspaper he was holding and began talking before his dozing brother fully opened his eyes. "Look at this headline, Vince. 'Tabbaracci Opens Lavish Club.'"

Vince's head jerked up as he bolted from the creaky barber's chair, beefy hands already tightened into fists and ready for a fight, any fight. Vince was always ready.

He grabbed the paper in one thick hand, read for a moment, and tossed it aside. "It's time to leave."

"What do you mean?"

Vince sat heavily, facing his brother. "I'm leaving, Frank. I hate it here. The only reason I came back was you said to. That we had some money to make, big money. Big plans. But Uncle Mario opened that club, and he'll rake in the cash. We're falling behind sitting in this dump town. Prohibition ain't going to last forever."

"I haven't figured everything out yet. What's your rush? We only been back from boot camp a few months."

Vince just sat.

In the brief silence that followed, the faint music of a radio drifted in from down the street of dusty storefronts and vacant lots.

"You can't leave without me," Frank insisted, his wiry frame focused and taut. "I'm older."

Vince's chin lifted. "Yeah, that makes a lotta sense. You got twenty-one years of bullshit, and I got twenty. Don't worry—I can make it alone. Uncle Mario taught me everything I need to run some rackets. You know that."

"What you learned from him, yeah, you're good at. No question. And I could hold my own...if it was just me. But we need each other, Vince, to make it in another city, to make it big. Together, we're unbeatable. You know that." A quick smile crossed his face. "Me, inside; you, outside—like always. I just need more time to plan."

Vince scowled and didn't answer. Frank leaned close, his hands on his brother's shoulders, his eyes intent on Vince's. "Big money, I'm talking big. Bootlegging, gambling, dames. We can do it in Zapata, but we need to talk to Uncle Mario. I've got to make sure I have it all figured out right." In his enthusiasm, he gently pushed Vince into the back of the chair, oblivious to his brother's suddenly hardened face.

Holding his hand up where both could see it, he rubbed two fingers against his thumb as if massaging a thick wad of bills—a promise to both of them. A promise of the respect that always came with cold cash.

Vince pushed away and walked toward the plate glass windows at the front of the shop. "All I've done my whole life is wait for you, Frank. I'm not waiting any longer."

Frank punched his newspaper, his voice rising. "Goddammit. You always go off half-cocked."

"We hate this town, and it hates us, just like the military hated us. So what are we fucking waiting for? The name Tabbaracci carries enough respect wherever we go."

Raising two blunt fingers in front of his brother, Vince spoke slowly, emphasizing each syllable. "Frank, you got two days. That's all. In two days I leave, with you or without you. You're the thinker, so think. Think fast."

Frank exhaled heavily, slim fingers absentmindedly combing through his black hair. "And what about Mom?"

Vince, so unlike himself, answered softly. "No matter what we do, we can't take her with us, Frank. She's made her bed." Bitterness crept into his voice. "She'll have to lie in it."

They threw their crumpled white coats across the barber's chair, put on their hats, locked the dusty shop, and left in silence. Without any relief, Frank's clothing stuck to his sweaty back. He had a feeling that his dreams tonight would circle around Vince's two upraised, uncompromising fingers.

CHAPTER TWO

New Orleans, Louisiana
Office of Don Mario Tabbaracci

"No way in hell," Mario Tabbaracci said softly.

His meaty palm slapped the desktop. *Just to get the point across to this skinny, overdressed little upstart.* Drops of sweat flew across the stacks of paper onto Don De Lasso's face.

De Lasso, dapper and unflappable as ever, wordlessly flicked off the offending drops while raising a single eyebrow as if to say, "That the best you can do?"

A whiff of the nearby seafront restaurant drifted into the room, mingling with Tabbaracci's cigar smoke and the fainter odors of formaldehyde, stale air, and even the less pleasant but unmistakable traces of things no longer living.

Tabbaracci's respected funeral home was the setting for their meeting. His massive bootlegging and extortion empire—with all its revenue—was at stake and had kept them at it for over two hours. That, and respect. The funeral home merely served as the legitimate front.

They stared at each other with no hint of weakness or

4

compromise. Tabbaracci finally rubbed his oversized, sweaty palm across his face as his expression slowly hardened. He leaned forward. "Fine," he spat through clenched teeth. "Keep the fucking territory, you son of a whore." He leapt to his feet, knocking over a chair and shattering an engraved ashtray. "Now get the hell out."

De Lasso, still immaculate and unperturbed in his elegant white summer suit, rose. "By all means." He calmly walked out to his car and waiting men.

Two days later in the quiet predawn of a late New Orleans summer, two men crouched among the thick oleanders and azaleas outside De Lasso's sprawling house, watching as he stepped out.

"One whack," whispered the taller one. "Fast and quiet."

De Lasso, in tan silk pajamas, robe, and slippers, stretched and walked to the end of the driveway. As he slowly bent to get the morning paper, the powerful smash of a bat turned his skull into bloody mush. The two men slid his limp body into the back of a black van. They covered the corpse with a blanket and left the quiet neighborhood, driving to the rear of Tabbaracci's tranquil funeral home on rue d'Bella—the one equipped for "special deliveries."

"Don Mario always says the best way to get rid of a rival is to have him disappear from the face of the earth. I guess this is one of those days," the taller man chuckled as they unloaded the body.

New Orleans, Louisiana
One day later

Don Mario's wife, "Big Lena," as she was nicknamed, was found dead in her own bed, drenched in blood from a shotgun wound to the back of the head. Few felt sorry for the ex-Miss Louisiana, who'd been drinking herself to sleep for years, trapped in an unfulfilling marriage and an ever-increasing girth.

She made her bargain early in life—let her live with it, people said, sitting on their porches and shaking their heads in an "I-told-you-so" smugness. *Shows what happens when you try to buy happiness.* Her husband's illegal money bought her everything—every expensive bauble, piece of furniture, pricey meal, and Paris fashion, including the hand-stitched, bias-cut ivory satin nightgown she'd died in—all three hundred and fifty miserable pounds of her.

In Jakesberg that evening, Frank and Vince sat in their parents' kitchen as their mother, Olivia, broke the news of Lena's death and where they'd all be for the next twenty-four hours. "Lena's funeral Mass is in New Orleans," Olivia gulped, barely able to control her voice. "We leave in the morning." Her face matched the sickly whitish-green walls; all the energy seemed to have gone out of her body. But Olivia always looked that way. She'd once been almost as beautiful as Lena, the baby sister she'd adored. Now she was a faded, almost flinching remnant of the woman she'd been.

Her husband, Coleman, worn out and washed up after decades of disappointment and failure, feebly patted her hands across the kitchen table. As usual, he could think of nothing to say.

The next day Coleman drove the long miles while his family sat in silence. Frank whispered across the tattered back seat to Vince, "Perfect timing. We'll talk to Uncle Mario while we're there."

Vince said nothing. His face showed nothing. He simply raised his index finger to remind Frank that only one day remained before Vince left—with or without Frank.

CHAPTER THREE

During the last few hot, twisting, dusty miles before they finally popped up on the outskirts of New Orleans, Vince twisted and turned in the back seat of the family's beat-up black Ford as it rattled down the rough road. Frank's mind was on how Aunt Lena's funeral would drive his mother into hysterics. Neither Vince nor their father seemed bothered to think about it.

"Hurry up, Dad," Vince snapped. "I'm going crazy in this cramped car. I gotta take a leak." He crossed his legs, stretching the fabric of his already tight suit across his heavy thighs.

Frank rolled his eyes. They could all die with Coleman behind the wheel, and Vince could only think about his damn bladder. Frank had no trouble detecting the smell of booze on his dad. Holy Mother of God—he was drinking from his flask as they drove. *What if he kills us all?* The old man was a careless, whiskey-dribbling fool.

Eventually, the car sputtered into the parking lot of the St. Louis Cathedral, backfiring and spewing smoke. As

7

Coleman parked behind a shiny sedan, Vince growled, "For God's sake, Dad. Can't you afford a halfway decent car?"

"Damn it, Vince, keep quiet," Frank snapped.

Vince shoved open the back door and disappeared into thick bushes at the perimeter, where he relieved himself, the sounds painfully clear to the rest of the family waiting by the car.

"For heaven's sake, Vince," Olivia fussed. Her face, already blotchy from heat, now flushed deep red.

Vince, walking back to the car, merely slid his belt back into place.

They walked behind a small group of mourners moving through the hard-dirt parking lot toward the cathedral. Olivia squeezed Coleman's hand.

"Let's wait out here till they all go in." Coleman slid a flask from his suit pocket and took a long swig, wiping his mouth on his sleeve.

"Christ, Dad," Frank muttered, combing his hair and straightening his dark suit jacket. It was his most recent splurge, and he was secretly proud of it.

"Look at all the expensive cars," Coleman whispered to his wife. An almost visible cloud of alcohol escaped his mouth.

Vince smirked. "I know whose cars those are. Uncle Mario's the top dog in this city. Everybody knows it, and they all better be here to show some respect." No one argued. His smile widened. Fists shoved in his pants pockets, his walk turned into a swagger.

Frank ignored his brother. Instead, he admired the cathedral's moss-covered bell tower, rising several stories tall, the great carved doors. Outside, the archbishop, tall in his mitre, stood with several priests and altar boys at the head of the granite steps. He leaned slightly on his bishop's crosier while he spoke in low tones to the others. The solemnity of their vestments and their quiet dignity were impressive. The contrast to Vince's idea of respectability struck Frank.

The hearse bearing Lena Tabbaracci crept into the circular drive at the precise moment the massive bells began to chime. Don Mario's limousine followed; behind it were four black Cadillacs. The procession stopped in front of the church. The archbishop lifted his right arm in blessing.

The immediate family, clad in heavy, solemn black from their hats and veils to their shoes, emerged from the Cadillacs and stood outside the cathedral apart from the other mourners. They held onto each other in silence, their white faces registering the shock, the disbelief. And the fear. *Who might be next?*

Frank overheard whispering about the mysterious disappearance of Don De Lasso two days before. He watched the pallbearers haul Aunt Lena's large coffin from the rear of the hearse. Beside him, Olivia bowed her head to make the sign of the cross. She slowly turned to her husband and murmured, "He killed her; I know it." Choking, muffled sobs shook her, her face pressed deep into Coleman's sloping, unsteady shoulder.

"Hush, now," Coleman whispered.

Frank put his arm around his mother.

Two burly security men, scanning the surroundings, preceded Mario Tabbaracci out of his limo. Mario did not so much as put his foot outside the vehicle until the men gave him the okay. The guards hurried up the steps and into the church, pushing past the assembled clerics without a word of greeting. Uncle Mario walked to the back of the hearse with bowed head, a signature red rose in his left lapel.

"You bastard!" someone shouted from the back of the crowd, followed by the staccato pop-pop of two gunshots. At his mother's side, Frank saw Vince jerk his head around and scan the people behind them. A hush of fear briefly engulfed everyone. Olivia abruptly stopped her sniffling, staring wide-eyed toward the growing disturbance. Another shot followed as cries arose from the now-fleeing crowd.

Frank grabbed his mother's shoulders and shoved her to the ground.

Instinctively, Vince turned toward the sound of the shots. "Over there," Frank yelled, pointing to an unshaven man waving a gun.

Mario's bodyguards rushed out of the church, but the hearse blocked their view of the gunman. They shoved through the screaming, stumbling mass toward their boss.

The man with the gun fell, regained his feet, and staggered toward Mario. "My daughter was good 'nough for you to play aroun' with, you bastard, till you k-k-killed 'er. Now iss your turn." The half-shouted, half-sobbed accusation was slurred. He aimed at Mario and fired, but the shot went wide.

Mario, still behind the hearse, pulled out his own weapon, moving quickly for a line of sight that would let him shoot. He couldn't find an angle.

The guards continued their fight to get through the terrified mob. For Frank, what took place next seemed to be happening in slow motion, though it was over in seconds. The pallbearers dropped Lena's coffin and fled. The coffin smashed on the hard-baked surface, and its lid sheared half off. Two of Mario's men rushed to the casket, crushing the top down hurriedly, then running for cover. Olivia had lifted herself free of Frank just long enough to look toward the commotion. She looked briefly at her sister's ruined coffin. Her entire body went rigid. There was no grief on her face now, only horror. She screamed and buried her head in Frank's chest.

"Ma, Ma! Stay down!" Frank pushed Olivia flat, covering her torso with his own body. *Oh God, not here. Not like this.* A few feet away, Coleman whimpered uselessly in the dirt.

The crowd finally scattered. Frank lifted his head, looked around. The sharpest-dressed men in attendance hadn't panicked, hadn't run. They'd pushed their own loved ones to the ground, looked around for the source of the shooting. From under suit jackets and out of waistbands they pulled guns always in reach, even at a funeral...maybe especially at a funeral. Don Mario had moved with the pallbearers to the side of the hearse sheltered from the crazed shooter lurching their way. Even as he struggled to stay upright, the man's eyes held Mario's with a chilling, intense hatred.

Frank searched for his brother, caught sight of him. *Oh shit. He's headed straight for that wacko.* "Get down, Vince," Frank yelled, but his brother never even hesitated. He ran right at the guy.

Olivia again cried out, grabbing for her son, her husband, any safety or comfort in the sudden insanity.

Vince tackled the man, and both grappled for the gun. They rolled, cursing and flailing at each other. A couple of shots rang out, driving the terrified people cowering nearby into greater hysteria. One bullet shattered a window on the hearse; another hit a fleeing pallbearer in the shoulder, knocking him to the ground. Vince, his muscular girth atop the drunkard, grabbed hold of the gun with both hands and shoved it square in the man's face. "Gotcha, you bastard!"

"Don't kill him!" Frank yelled.

He hovered over his parents, keeping their heads down. People around him tripped and fell, running in all directions. Police cars skidded onto the scene. Officers pulled people out of their way, then cuffed the crazed man and took him.

Peace, of sorts, returned, but most of the people had fled. Olivia was still hysterical. Frank and his father consoled her and took her to the Ford, but she couldn't talk. She gagged and choked while clinging to the two men.

"Please, baby," Coleman said, holding his wife tightly, "Vince is all right. Everything is under control." He killed the whiskey and slipped the flask inside his coat.

Frank patted her face. "Mom, things are quiet now."

Olivia's words wouldn't come out. Her pale face was greenish, and she turned to retch her breakfast onto the grass.

"Most everyone has left," Frank said. "Maybe it'll be peaceful at the gravesite. Here comes Vince now, thank God."

Coleman rushed to Vince and tried to hug him. "You're a hero, son."

Vince shrugged and let his father's arms fall away. "Let's get the hell out of here."

At the cemetery, a white-faced archbishop and one altar boy hurriedly rushed through the ceremony before they buried Lena's coffin in the family plot under a huge oak tree.

After the brief service, Don Mario ambled to the family and put his arm around Vince. "I owe you. You're more than family now. You need me some day, and I will be there."

The jittery Coleman and his sobbing wife ignored Don Mario and walked to their car. She was still trembling uncontrollably. Threads of yellow bile stained her dress. Neither of them looked back at their sons.

Vince hugged Uncle Mario. "Soon I'll be leaving home. For good. You know—to make use of what you've taught me already."

Mario's black eyes bore into Vince's eyes. "Lots of money to be made." He shifted his gaze to Frank. No words were necessary. The question hung in the steamy air. *What about Frank?*

The ghost of a smile crossed Mario's face as his gaze swept both brothers. "Let's talk before you go. Remember, anything, anytime," he said, hugging Vince and kissing him on his pudgy cheek. Mario turned to walk away, then stepped back to Vince, grabbed his shoulders, and spoke into Vince's right ear. No one else heard the words, and no one dared ask Vince—not even Frank.

The family started the long drive back home. The barbershop would be open tomorrow, and the men had to work. A sobbing Olivia kept reaching for Coleman's thin arm as he tried to drive.

Frank, in the backseat, broke the silence. "Aunt Lena was the one who got me and Vince jobs with Uncle Mario. He treated us like sons."

"Yeah, him and me got along. He treated me with respect too," Vince said. "But right now, I'm just a dirty Italian barber in a hick town, for Christ's sake."

Frank scowled. "Shut your yap, Vince."

Vince wasn't done. "Maybe Uncle Mario was just plain tired of being married to a hog."

Olivia yanked around, focusing for the first time in hours. "How can a son of mine say things like that?"

"Have some goddamn respect for your mother, at least," Coleman said.

"Dad, you're a drunk barber in a stupid white coat. I've stuck around because Mom begged us to."

"Vince, how can you?" His mother turned to face him squarely. "Your Uncle Mario is a gangster, a murdering mobster." She choked, paused, then continued in a strangled voice, "There was another person in the coffin. I saw him—a man."

"Oh, Mom, come on," Frank said, reaching up and placing his hand on her shoulder. "You're imagining things. Please."

His mother's lips thinned, but she just looked out the window.

After a short silence, Vince said to his parents, "I'll get this all out now. Here in the car when no one can walk away from me. I want a different life. Money. Respect. I want to be somebody. Is that too much to ask?"

No one answered.

CHAPTER FOUR

Back home in Jakesberg, the next day was a Saturday of haircutting. After the last customer walked out, Coleman locked the glass door and sat in his barber's chair facing Frank and Vince in the customers' chairs. This time, the boys didn't display their usual casual disdain.

Coleman swallowed, and then began. "Okay, I want to hear more."

Vince spoke, large, blunt fingers at rest for once, clasped in his lap. "I'm sorry for what I had to say yesterday. I learned from Uncle Mario what money can buy. You won't miss me."

"When are you leaving?"

Vince paused and looked at Frank. Tomorrow they both would know if Vince would leave alone or not.

Frank stood and began pacing. After getting no sleep, he wasn't at his best, but maybe his dad really was interested. "We don't need to join Uncle Mario—we're gonna do it on our own. On Zapata Island—off the coast. Uncle Mario calls it 'a gold mine waiting to be worked.'

Yeah, it's a tough place, but we'll survive. Right, Vince?"

Vince's only reply was a knowing smile—small, but knowing.

"We'll probably start out as barbers, but we won't be barbers long. We can outdo Uncle Mario. We want to run Zapata, the whole damn place, like he runs New Orleans."

Coleman ran an unsteady hand through his thinning hair. "Gangsters? That'll kill your mother."

"Tomorrow, I leave." In the small room, Vince's voice rang with finality.

Coleman got up, put his arms behind his back, and walked to the front of the shop, looking at the setting sun.

The boys glanced at each other but stayed quiet.

Coleman finally turned to them, his face dissolving into tears he couldn't hold back. "You know, I really don't blame you."

He paused and turned to look out the window again. A whole life of moustache wax, Brilliantine, and cutting hair. A thirty-year-old rented duplex with peeling paint. One son who spent every last dime on fancy clothes with nowhere to go; the other son who couldn't be bothered to shut the bathroom door—he never had.

He turned back and walked closer to them. "I'll miss you, but get the hell out of here while you are young." In an uncharacteristic embrace, he held each of them tightly. "You're men now. You make your own decisions."

That night they both went together to tell their mother about leaving. Frank had expected Vince to argue while they walked there, to badger Frank into the decision to leave that Frank wasn't sure he was prepared to make. To ask for details. But nothing happened as they walked through the sleepy dusk. Vince acted as if they hadn't argued about leaving, as if he hadn't issued the ultimatum to Frank, as if Frank didn't matter. Didn't he remember raising his two blunt fingers in the air?

As always, Olivia sat, wan and silent, in a darkened front room while Coleman drank in the kitchen alone.

"Goodbye, Mom," Frank began. "Tomorrow, we're moving out of town."

Olivia looked up as if seeing ghosts. Since her sister's funeral, she had been halfway in another world. "No, no, don't do this, please," she moaned.

They embraced her.

She didn't relax in their hugs but remained rigid and unbending. Her dark hair, tight against her skull, looked almost painted on.

Her eyes searched theirs, and she finally yelled, "Go, go."

They hugged her one last time and then quietly left, not looking back at the small house containing so much misery. Frank could feel the same misery they had eaten, drank, peed, and spit for all their stupid lives. That was gonna change.

Vince turned to Frank. "You coming, then?"

Frank flinched. "You thought I wouldn't? What kind of older brother you take me for?"

Vince, silent, looked away into the darkness. In this neighborhood, there were no streetlights, no stars, no gleam of brightness to reveal what best should be kept a secret.

CHAPTER FIVE

Zapata Island, Mississippi

All night Frank lay on the hard boxcar floor sweating. September had only brought a moist, warm breeze with a faint saltiness from the Gulf. Voices drifted on the wind along with the stimulating aroma of coffee and bacon. Who was he kidding? He wasn't ready, but here he was anyway. Could he control Vince? What would happen if Vince ever stopped listening to him?

Frank sat up, gazing out the open boxcar door. The fog hindered his sight but small fires burned alongside the tracks. He grasped a leather strap on the wall for support and stretched.

"Hey, Vince, we're here. Get up."

The train continued forward, passing small warehouses and other buildings. Rusting metal shades covered dim outside lightbulbs. The train slowed again, creeping forward.

Long piers extended into a bay. Oceangoing vessels

were tied to each pier. In the haze, Frank could make out gangs of men tossing large burlap sacks onto conveyers that took them up to the ships' decks and down into open holds.

"Come on. The train's going to stop."

There was a sudden shrieking of brakes followed by a series of loud metal-on-metal screeches as each car bumped the one in front, the whole train then coming to an abrupt stop. Frank fell to his knees and rolled on top of Vince.

They both grabbed their bags and jumped, one after the other.

In the distance, beyond the tracks and a wire fence were buildings: the small city that would make their future. Picking up their pace, they reached an intersection. A few blocks away, a flashing "City Diner" sign illuminated the corner. White seagulls flew overhead, squawking. Frank's skin prickled with the sun's increasing warmth. At this rate, the shirt he had so neatly hung up in the boxcar would soon be wilted.

As if reading his mind, Vince glanced over at Frank. "You know, you look pretty good, older brother. That is, for sleeping in a boxcar. Hell, you're the most pretty-fied tramp this side of the Mississippi. Combed hair and all."

"Yeah, well, at least I shaved before I left town."

Frank stopped their forward progress to the diner with a hand raised to Vince's chest. "Hold it," he said.

Frank's heart raced, and sweat beads dotted his forehead. "Something's going on in there. Maybe we should move on."

Two sedans were parked out front, with two suited men guarding the cars.

"To hell with that," Vince answered. "That's the closest place to eat, and I'm starving." He removed Frank's hand from the front of his chest and moved toward the diner. Frank held him back once more.

"Let's think, Vince."

"You wanna come?"

Vince walked toward the diner, and after a few seconds Frank followed. The suited men had moved to the street side, where they occupied themselves lighting cigarettes, talking and laughing, constantly scanning the traffic and sidewalks.

Frank opened the glass door to the diner. Vince barged toward a four-top and sat. Every head turned their direction. After a few moments, a waiter in a long white apron approached. "What'll you guys have?"

Vince didn't pick up the menu. "Two eggs, over easy. Bacon, crisp. Bread, light-toasted. Hot joe."

Frank ordered, and the waiter returned quickly with two thick china cups and saucers stacked in one hand and a full pot of coffee in the other. Vince held his cup up, one finger curled around the handle. Steaming coffee splashed out in a burning arc over Vince's fingers, hands, and lap. Vince jerked the cup up in reaction, accidentally splattering the face of an expensively suited man with a hatchet face at the next table. The man jumped up with a roar of pain. His pals—all dressed the same as the guys watching outside— stopped talking.

"What the fuck?" yelled Vince, waving his fingers to cool them.

Hatchet-face at the next table grabbed a glass of cold water and poured it over his head, rubbing it on his face.

Vince grabbed the hapless waiter, who was still gaping at the mayhem with an almost full pot of hot liquid. "You need to watch what you're doing, asshole."

"Yessir, yessir," the waiter breathed before scurrying away.

The man put one hand on Vince's shoulder, "You need to apologize." He tried to spin Vince around.

But Vince wouldn't be moved and instead spun the opposite direction. He laid a solid roundhouse into the man's left jaw. "Nobody puts their hands on me."

"Just apologize, brother," yelled Frank.

The suited men from outside rushed in, ready to defend the man at the table. "Cops on the way," someone yelled. "Get out of here."

Frank pulled at Vince's jacket. "We gotta get out of here."

With a final lingering look at the coffee still steaming in his cup, Frank hurried Vince along as everyone ran out of the diner before the cops arrived.

"I got a good look at his face," Vince said. "I won't forget that nose. He's gonna pay."

"Pay? For what? Your coffee? C'mon, Vince," Frank sighed. "You fucked this up good."

CHAPTER SIX

Frank and Vince moved into the haircutting business with relative ease. Vince handled a job at Adcock's Pier, enjoying the barbering, often ribbing with the gangsters who came to the shop. Vince also kept his eyes peeled for any luscious-looking dames strolling among the hordes of pleasure-seekers shopping at the pier, eating at the cheap lunch counters, or chomping gum in the pier's beauty parlor.

Frank worked at the luxurious Cortez Hotel, a much classier location. The gleaming wood detailing, the wide porches with white wicker chairs, the manicured palms in the hallways—the elegant venue fit Frank perfectly.

One of Vince's favorite customers was Mr. Mitcheletti, who spoke in a thick Italian accent that exceeded even Vince's. "Come on down to the wrestling matches tonight, Mr. Vince. We got a couple of midgets in the program." Mitcheletti bit a Baby Ruth candy bar every chance he could, while Vince's scissors did their magic. "The toughest little guys you ever saw. I'd hate to tangle with one of them."

Vince's eyes rose momentarily to a curvy blonde strolling by in a starched pink cotton dress. "I don't need midget wrestlers. I need a looker with a friendly attitude." Vince inspected his handiwork from all angles, and Mitcheletti did the same, their reflections sharp in the floor-length mirrors of the shop. Mitcheletti's pudgy face inclined slightly toward Vince. "Miss Marie usually has two or three of her best girls there from Backbay Street."

He elbowed Vince in the ribs and winked. He pushed a large chunk of Baby Ruth out of its wrapper and devoured it in one bite. "We'll see if we can find you one."

Vince chuckled as he carefully brushed Mitcheletti's shoulders with a horsehair brush. "The cat houses? I'll tell my brother."

Mitcheletti stood and reached for his wallet. "Come about ten o'clock. That's when everything gets going." He gave Vince an extra half-dollar as a tip, then walked to the glass door. "I think one of the new girls has your name on her," he said before he disappeared into the thick crowd.

Vince called Frank on the shop's telephone. "Come over after work. We're invited to a midget wrestling match."

"A midget what?"

"Yeah, a midget match. One of my older customers runs the thing. He says lots of girls show up. Should be fun. I'll wait for you here."

The night was warm, and the welcome Gulf breeze brought only slight relief as Frank and Vince, chewing on toothpicks, rushed out of Bart's Seafood Restaurant.

"Hurry up. Looks like we'll be fighting a crowd tonight," Vince urged as they followed the masses of mingling tourists toward Adcock's.

Frank surveyed his brother's pressed slacks and

starched shirt, slicked-back hair, and freshly shaven jaw. "That's the best I've seen you look in weeks," Frank joked. "Got something in mind, brother?"

Vince scowled a wordless reply. Both brothers' white shirts gleamed in the humid night as the heat brought sweat glistening to their foreheads. The crowd bumped and pushed each other. While others ate pink cotton candy, ice cream, or popcorn in greasy paper bags, Vince savored his Cuban cigar.

Frank scanned the crowd. He had been wary since their first day in town. "No sign of those guys from the diner."

"Uncle Mario called me afterwards and told me they work for Jimmy Jack, one of his longtime associates. I still watch my back, though. He also told me he had talked to the other bootlegger—DeLuca. Jimmy Jack and him hate each other. Old, too. Maybe close to retirement, brother." He winked. "One way or another." He chuckled and punched Frank in the ribs with his elbow.

"When did you talk to Uncle Mario?"

"A couple of days after it happened."

"Shit, Vince. How am I supposed to figure out our new business when I don't know what's going on?"

"You worry too much, Frank."

"Most of my worrying is about you."

"Well, dammit. Most of my worrying is about you, Frank. Shut up, and let's enjoy the evening. I ain't in the mood to talk."

They passed the darkened barbershop that Vince had only recently locked up tight for the night.

"I'm glad to pass you right on by, baby," Vince said, patting the brass doorknob of the shop.

As they neared the arena, bright flashing bulbs emphasized the words on the marquee: "Mitcheletti Presents Big Benno vs. Mean Moe. Tonight."

Vince laughed as they plunged toward the arena's door. When they tried to pay, the ticket man said, "Mr.

Carlucci?" Then he retrieved two tickets and handed them to Vince. "Have fun."

Vince and Frank looked at each other and grinned. This was going to be a great night.

They entered the smoky arena. The roar of the crowd was deafening, as hundreds of people filled the place to capacity.

The usher pointed to their seats at center ringside. After squeezing past jutting knees and bulging backsides, they made themselves comfortable.

"Best seats in the house. If we were any closer, we'd be right in the ring," Frank said.

Mr. Mitcheletti was on the opposite side of the ring holding court between two slender young women in sheer cotton eyelet tops that were made to trap the slightest summer breeze but also to cause men to be distracted by what might be viewed through the small holes. Mitcheletti waved with a big smile.

Vince pointed to Mitcheletti. "How does an old man like him get such good-looking dames? Ain't fair."

Frank looked around the arena. "Look at all the booze flowing. What about Prohibition?"

Vince shifted his eyes off the dolls with Mitcheletti.

"Holler at the beer man," Frank suggested.

"Hey, guy. You got two dry sponges over here needing a cold one quick."

The man acknowledged them with a wave while making change for another customer.

"There is even a cop at the door. What the hell?" Vince said. "I thought this was illegal."

Frank punched Vince on the shoulder. "Look over there. Aren't those guys the ones from the diner we saw our first day?"

"No, but they sure do look like them. They dress the same. Classy."

One of the men noticed Vince and Frank staring at them. He pointed across the crowd at Vince and patted a bulge in his jacket, then smiled. Vince, smiling even broader, opened his own jacket displaying no gun.

"I guess he was just kidding around," Vince said. "Maybe the word is getting around."

"Could be. But we're just like them. Best seats in the house. Looks like they could be running this place. Let's keep our eyes open."

The beer vendor finally sent two cold ones their way, and Vince downed his as the vendor watched.

"Damn," Frank joked, "you must be thirsty." The vendor threw back his head and laughed, moving on through the crowd.

Frank, lost in thought, said, "Those guys over there are bootleggers. He's patting his gun to tell us we are protected. That's where the booze comes from. Maybe we can learn something from them, but let's leave it alone for tonight."

"I'm not looking for trouble. This is a fun night." Vince followed the beer man's slow progress through the crowd before yelling, "Don't go off too far, beer man."

A slow smile came over Frank's face. "Now I know how we are going to get out of the barbering business. Tonight is the beginning for us."

The beer vendor, carrying a restocked box, rushed back in response to Vince's hand gestures.

"Tell me tomorrow. Tonight, let's enjoy the fight. I'm grabbing us another beer before the match starts."

The lights dimmed, and an immaculate tuxedo containing a thin, gray-haired man climbed into the ring. The crowd hushed as a spotlight came on, bright and blazing, for the introduction of two well-muscled, but very short, men at the announcer's side.

"Ladies and gentlemen, Mitcheletti Interests presents our main event tonight. From Canada and undefeated in two hundred matches, Mean Moe."

Mean Moe glared his animosity toward the crowd as he strutted the ring in black satin trunks. His oiled arms and

Robert B. Wilkins and Sarah Cortez

torso radiated strength. A large scar across his left cheek pulled skin away from his eye into wrinkled flesh.

The announcer continued, "His opponent from Jackson, Mississippi. Big Benno."

Clearly the crowd's favorite, Benno taunted Moe by dropping his red satin shorts and mooning Moe, then skittering away across the ring when Moe advanced toward him. Benno slapped his own chest, pointing to the elaborate tattoo on his right shoulder. Crude black letters surrounded by red roses spelled "Benno."

Frank saw Vince visibly relax as he downed his fourth beer. What a relief.

The wrestlers ran to their corners. The crowd hushed again. The bell rang, and they darted to center ring, grabbing each other by the arms in a sudden display of brute force. The crowd exploded into a roar. Frank and Vince stood cheering with everyone else.

Benno slammed Moe to the mat, but Moe jumped up and gave a hard forearm to Benno's chest. Benno bent forward, and Moe put a knee in his face, knocking him backward. Moe grabbed Benno by the wrist before Benno could recover and swung him into the air and over the ringside ropes.

Benno landed directly in Vince's lap, spilling beer and crushing Vince's chair, sending wood, beer, and beer bottles in every direction. Frank backed away, laughing at Vince's flailing arms and legs.

"Goddammit," Vince yelled, going down on his back in the spilled beer, the wrestler on top of him. Vince grabbed at anything for support to get up. He managed to get halfway up only to slip again on the wet floor. The crowd howled with laughter as his fury built.

"For Christ's sake," Vince screamed, his feet sliding on the wet floor. Benno, still dazed, grabbed Vince to try to right himself, but Vince couldn't get his footing on the wet floor and slammed down again. He slid on his back across the floor in front of the ring.

The crowd loved it, screaming for more as though this were part of the show. The more they laughed, the angrier Vince got. Several spectators sprayed their beers on Vince and Benno while hooting uncontrollably.

Then Moe came out of the ring running to grab Benno. Vince got himself upright, though he was having a hard time seeing with beer streaming down his face.

Frank bent over with laughter. "Get 'em, big Vince," he yelled. "Shoot them a moon."

Vince struck out at the blurred movement that was Moe and caught him flat on the nose, sending him sliding across the floor to land under ringside seats. Moe was knocked out cold on the floor. Vince fell to his knees and used his sleeves to get the beer out of his eyes. He went for Benno but was overpowered by three huge bouncers in tight white T-shirts. Vince cussed and fought them, his clothes soaked with beer and his hair hanging wet and limp.

Mr. Mitcheletti and Frank found him in a small dressing room, held in a chair by the bouncers.

"What the hell's going on here? One damn minute I'm sitting, enjoying a beer, and the next I've got a nasty midget sweating on me and people throwing beer. What the shit kind of place is this?"

"Calm down. It was all an accident." Frank handed Vince a thick towel.

"I'm so sorry, Vince," Mr. Mitcheletti chimed in. "Please, we never intended this. You are my special guest. I'm really sorry."

"That's the damndest thing I could even imagine," Frank said between muffled chuckles. "You coldcocked the poor midget, and he's still out. Couldn't you pick on someone your own size?"

"You made the show," Mitcheletti said. "The crowd liked you better than the match. Can you come back tomorrow?"

"Big joke," Vince said. "Real funny."

The bouncers loosened their grips. "I want to see that midget, Benno, that was thrown on me. The other guy can go to hell," Vince continued.

"Moe was taken to the hospital, but Benno wants to see you," Mr. Micheletti said. "I think he wants to apologize. You know, people say Benno's a murderer, but he never did time."

Someone brought Vince a dry shirt. He stood up to put it on. It had "Adcock's Pier" embroidered over the front pocket with a smiling porpoise above the letters.

"What the hell is this laughing fish?"

"That's probably all they had," Frank said. "Put the towel over the fish."

"It just gets worse and worse," Vince said.

Frank burst out laughing, quickly stepping back from his brother to avoid being hit. Instead, Vince finally joined in the laugher and sat down again.

Benno came into the room dressed in a coat and tie, his head held high. "I'm sorry, Mr. Carlucci," he said. "Mr. Mitcheletti should have warned you about the front row seats. We frequently get thrown out of the ring. Please let me know if I can do anything for you." With that, Benno halfway smiled and pulled the door open. He turned back before leaving, one hand still on the doorknob. "Nice shirt. I'm told porpoises never stop smiling." He scooted out, laughing and slamming the door.

Mitcheletti, Frank, and even Vince joined in laughing. The crowd had dispersed after the match's unexpected finale, and the room was quiet. A lone lightbulb hung over the chair where Vince sat. Someone brought him a cold beer.

Frank turned to Mitcheletti. "Who were those guys ringside with the Manhattan jackets and splashy jewelry?"

"The older guy with the lavender shirt is Tony DeLuca. Tough guy. Most people leave him along. He's a bootlegger—makes lots of money. Biggest on the island."

"Lots of money?" Frank said.

"You should leave him alone," Mitcheletti said with a shake of his head. "Those other guys with him watch his back."

"I want to meet that guy," Vince said.

Mitcheletti headed to the door and put his hand on the knob, then stopped and looked back. "They're bootleggers, and killers. People here in Zapata steer clear. They also stay away from the other gang—the Bayou Bunch run by Jimmy Jack. He's a real mean one. Good night, boys. Shut the door when you leave."

CHAPTER SEVEN

Frank and Vince slowly walked onto the now-deserted pier, past the closed shops on the darkened breezeway. It was after midnight. The brisk breeze blew warm air in their faces. In common accord, they sat on a wood bench facing the sea. They said nothing for several minutes.

Frank looked around. They were alone but for a drunk guy sleeping on a nearby bench. He leaned into Vince. "Are you thinking what I am? We've now run into the two biggest gangsters in town."

Vince turned toward Frank and put his arm on the backrest. "I'm thinking they are running *our* business. *Our business.*"

"We've got to think smart, Vince. Keep that iron fist in check. First, we try it my way."

"What's your plan?"

"We cozy up to both sides. Find out their distributors, their buyers. Then, we pick which side we want."

"Why shouldn't they bump us off first?" Vince asked.

"We got Uncle Mario's protection."

"You sure about that?"

"You ought to know. You fucking talk to him all the time."

The guy on the bench sat up and looked at them.

Frank turned to Vince. "Who is that fucking guy? He heard everything."

The man fired one shot at Vince, who dropped to the ground and reached for his ankle gun. Frank sped after the man as he raced away. When he was close enough, he tackled him.

Frank's grasp was desperate and fueled by fear. The man scrapped at Frank's hold on his torso and arms. They rolled across the weathered lumber, and all Frank could think about was getting shot. Vince raced toward the fight. He couldn't shoot for fear of hitting Frank, so he fired into the air.

Vince threw himself at the man's shoulders, knocking his gun hand hard into the splintery wood again and again, until the man's knuckles were a bloody pulp and his hold on the gun gave way. The weapon slipped between the boards of the pier into the ocean.

Up close, they could see the man was tall and muscular. He used this advantage to get up, but the brothers clawed him back down, grabbing his clothes and belt in desperation. Their feet slipped on the moisture of the night mist, but Vince and Frank fought him as long as they could. Frank's mouth began to swell from the hits, and his nose clogged with blood. The man smashed Frank's head with his fist, momentarily stunning Frank. Leveraging both legs, the man pushed Frank over the rail into the dark ocean waves fifteen feet below the pier, then he ran.

Vince pumped two shots at the running man, who stumbled and threw himself into the roaring water below.

Vince scrambled to the edge of the pier. He couldn't see either man. He bounded down two sets of stairs to the sandy beach below. He desperately scanned every set of waves and cursed the darkness. He had to find Frank. The whitecaps loomed ghostly in the bottomless ocean. *Was Frank alive?*

Late-night strollers joined him.

"My brother. Help me find him," he pleaded.

Before long, a dozen or more bystanders were searching the waves from shore, one with a weak flashlight.

"I see something white!" someone yelled. "Look over there."

Vince ran into the surf and pulled a panting, choking Frank from the water.

A small group had gathered on the wet sand.

"Let's get out of here," Vince said. He helped Frank struggle up the stairs to the concrete seawall. It was a long walk, but they made it. They didn't talk much. Vince choked out only a few words. "I tried to ice him. But I don't know for sure. He's in the water."

Frank calculated the risk of the unknown eavesdropper escaping death. Surely, his wounds had weakened him enough so that the current had pulled his bullet-ridden body far out to sea. Dead men didn't squeal.

CHAPTER EIGHT

Frank and Vince waited and planned their next steps. The game was deadly serious. Was the guy who heard everything on the pier dead or alive? Had he talked to anyone? Sometimes Frank's skin crawled as if somebody were about to attack him from behind. He would force himself not to turn around. If it came, he didn't want to see it coming. And Vince? Vince didn't seem to be affected by anything—just like always. His rough laughter and slow eyes hid everything he felt.

On this particular morning, the barbershop at the Hotel Cortez hummed with conversation. Frank cut as fast as he could while the men sipped their complimentary shots of hootch purchased from Tony DeLuca's runners. The golden-brown liquid fired all their conversations into raucous rounds of laughter and bawdy comments about the girls in swimming suits who strolled through the hotel lobby. The radio was turned to opera, Frank's favorite, and the men teased him about it.

Frank snipped while he circled the chair holding Bill

Johnson, a banker from Zapata National Bank. They were talking about the weekend's close game of semi-pro baseball when Tony DeLuca walked in with three of his boys. His boys eyeballed everyone as they walked around the shop as if they owned it—one of them dropping his lit cigarette on the floor and grinding it out with his heel. Despite the situation, Frank found himself admiring the careful tailoring of their three-piece suits and the Chinese silk of their ties. No one in the state could cut a suit like that.

Frank held the razor over the lathered face of Johnson. Frank's waiting customers had already thrown down newspapers and magazines. The door wasn't wide enough for all of them to leave as quickly as they wanted, muttering excuses and grabbing hats from the rack.

Johnson took a hot towel and cleaned his own face. "I just remembered. I got an important meeting. Catch you later, buddy." He grabbed his coat from the rack and darted out the door.

DeLuca stood still as a rock in the middle of the shop, smiling as if amused. "Boys, we must smell bad. You smell anything, Mr. Carlucci?"

Before Frank could reply, DeLuca walked over to the barber's chair recently vacated by Johnson. He climbed into the chair, large hands clasped in front of him, completely at ease. Shifting his weight, he brought up a cigar from his front inside suit pocket, which one of his boys lit for him.

"No, Mr. DeLuca, I smell nothing," Frank said. "Maybe my sniffer is not as good as theirs. What can I do for you, gentlemen?"

"I hear you have interest in my business. You're asking too many questions. And talking big." DeLuca paused. "You're asking for trouble. You don't even know how much trouble, sonny boy."

"Your hair needs a little trimming." Frank slowly lowered the razor onto the marble countertop. "I don't see that you need a shave right now."

"Your brother fucked up your first day in town. You both should've taken the next train out."

"My brother and I are always looking to better ourselves."

"Your questions are beginning to bother me, Mr. Carlucci"—he pointed his finger at Frank's chest, punctuating his low voice with a light tap on every syllable—"and you don't want me bothered."

Frank reached up to his chest and moved DeLuca's manicured finger to the side. "I hear you don't mind listening to a business proposition."

"Business? With you and junior?" DeLuca's snort of cigar smoke underscored his derision.

"We've worked for Don Mario Tabbaracci. We've very close to our uncle, Mr. DeLuca—I've heard you are too." Frank paused. "He taught us the business."

DeLuca's face betrayed no reaction.

"Vince and I could help you. You heard how everyone on the island comes to me for haircuts now? It's because I've made them like me—I can make anyone like me. Vince is the guy no one likes. But his fists and gun can get any job done. No one pushes Vince around, not even me."

"Are you threatening me, Mr. Carlucci?" DeLuca said, scowling. "I respect your uncle, but we're talking about you, not your uncle."

"If you didn't want to add us to your business, you wouldn't be here," Frank said. "We are smart and tough. We're waiting to put our talents to work. I assure you we have abilities that will up your profits."

"You're a cocky bastard," DeLuca said. "How the hell do I know who you are and how you think? Why should I want you in my organization?"

"What did our uncle tell you about us?"

"Why should I tell you?"

"Then let me tell you what he said. He said to give us a chance. That we're part of the family. That we're two halves of the same apple—Vince, the maniac; me, the planner."

DeLuca smiled for the first time. "You're a self-assured smart-ass, kid."

Frank picked up his scissors and whipped out a white cutting cloth that he draped around DeLuca's body. "Let me give you that little trim, Mr. DeLuca. An important businessman like you shouldn't go around needing a trim."

Frank picked up his cutting comb and began working at DeLuca's rear hairline. "I know there are two bootlegging crews: the Harbor Gang that you run, and the Bayou Bunch that Jimmy Jack runs."

DeLuca grunted, and Frank's scissors continued their snip-snip.

"We like your organization, Mr. DeLuca. Your class, your type of life. Your boys are classy. Every one of them dresses in New York City-tailored suits. We will up your profits so much you can buy ten New York suits for each of your guys and make a big donation to the cathedral here. Your gross every week is eighty K. We will expand your distribution through trucking in the Midwest. We'll use variable networks that'll only demand one percent instead of the five percent you're paying right now. We can double your weekly gross. We'll show you how to expand into Canada. We can bring you so much more money that you'll need bigger buckets for the nightly deposits into Zapata National Bank. I guarantee that."

Frank walked to DeLuca's side and began trimming a sideburn.

DeLuca, after a pause, turned to his boys. "Leave me alone with the barber. Wait outside."

They left slowly, eyeing Frank on their way out. Frank waited until they had closed the door. He sat in the customer chair nearest to DeLuca's chair. "It seems to me that it might be helpful to your business expansion if a certain impediment were to decide to retire. Wouldn't this be advantageous to a three-year expansion plan, Mr.

DeLuca?"

DeLuca's expression didn't change. "Maybe."

"Planned expansion of your business interests, Mr. DeLuca, is something that my brother and I can furnish."

"Continue."

"We don't come cheap. It's going to be dangerous. We expect a significant bonus."

"What the hell do you have in mind? You're damn pushy for a guy outgunned four to one right now."

"Kill me here in the hotel?" Frank stood and approached DeLuca so that their noses almost touched. "I'm not asking you for anything that Jimmy Jack wouldn't give us if we went to him first with an appropriate business plan."

DeLuca puffed on the now-dead cigar and looked at the cold tip as if surprised. "You drive a hard bargain. We could ice your ass right now, right here. In the Cortez lobby. It wouldn't be the first time."

Frank turned the chair and looked at DeLuca's sideburns in the wall mirror with satisfaction. "Now they're even, Mr. DeLuca. Someone should tell your regular barber that his eye is off. A successful businessman like you deserves a perfect haircut."

Frank whipped off the white cloth and picked up a thin horsehair brush. As he lightly brushed stray hair from DeLuca's shoulders and neck, Frank said, "You may kill me, but then you would have to deal with my vicious brother. He's ruthless, and he would follow you into the grave if he needed to. That's how he is—loyal, fiercely loyal to me and to whoever he works for."

Frank stepped to the counter and opened a small round can of pomade. "Would you like some pomade, Mr. DeLuca? It's straight from Paris, France. The girls like it a lot."

DeLuca shook his head. "You make things very interesting. You had better be as smooth as you talk because if we deal, you've got to deliver."

"Let's all three of us talk—you, me, my brother," Frank suggested.

"You talk to your brother first. See what he says. If he agrees, let's meet tonight at Miss Marie's in the District. Back room at eleven. If you're not there at eleven, I'll know your answer. I got some thinking to do myself."

Frank walked behind him to the exit door. DeLuca turned as if something had just occurred to him. "Watch your loud mouth. What you said at Adcock's Pier after the wrestling match could have landed you floating in the bay. It still could. Oh, yeah, thanks for the trim, Mr. Barber."

Frank watched DeLuca and his boys stride across the hotel lobby and leave before he allowed himself to expel a sigh of relief. He picked up the phone at the rear of the shop.

"Vince, get over here now. Just stop what you're doing. Yes, it's that damn important."

Frank locked his own shop and stepped outside to the front plaza of the elegant Hotel Cortez, where he waited under the stucco porte cochere. He made himself sit on the bench, but his nervous energy soon had him pacing back and forth. Finally, Vince appeared about a block away. Frank ran to him and placed both hands on his shoulders. "This is our day. Listen to what just happened."

Vince's reaction was a slow smile that Frank knew to read as excitement. "You done good, brother. Let's make our plans and go to that whorehouse to start our new life or die trying."

"You think it's a trap?"

"It could be, but we don't have a choice," Vince said. "We've got to go."

CHAPTER NINE

On the long Gulf Stream evenings, Frank had seen how the island became everyone's playground: sailors on leave with broad grins, hillbilly tourists from the Delta farmland, beautiful girls looking for a handsome guy for the evening or for life, and more than enough guys to fill the bill. Dance music filled all the downtown and seafront streets.

Tonight, Frank and a grumpy Vince had hired a taxi to take them to the recreational part of the island, Backbay Street. Here, two-story wooden Victorian houses crowded each other on both sides of the old brick streets that were jammed with slow-moving cars.

At nightfall, each house's expansive porch had a glowing red light that gave an attractive gleam to the shoulders, bosoms, and long legs of the many girls lounging on the front porches. Scant bedroom attire clung to each girl's body, showing more than it concealed.

Vince sighed, and Frank wasn't surprised at the exasperation in Vince's voice: "These damn cruising cars. We'll never get there in time. What's wrong with these saps? Can't they make up their minds? One set of tits is the same as any other."

"C'mon, Vince. Sure, we got business tonight. But look at that blonde dish over there," Frank said as they pulled up to Marie's. "Classy."

That same slender blonde came up to Vince as he stepped out of the taxi. She grabbed his forearm and pressed it into her. Slightly taller than Vince, she was willowy next to his muscled bulk and graceful next to his heavy-footed lumbering.

Damn, thought Frank. How did Vince get so lucky? I'm stuck here paying for the cab, and he's already scored with the prettiest girl here. Short, black satin pants and a prim white blouse. Man-oh-man, those long legs. White high heels.

Almost as if she could read his thoughts, the girl turned back toward Frank and smiled. "Come on, honey child. You don't want your friend here to start without you, do you?" she said with a laugh.

Frank couldn't keep his eyes from her pert little ass in the tight satin as she walked ahead of him toward the house. Something in her nervous giggle rang a slight alarm in his head. Meantime, another girl—this one dark-headed and heavy-chested—grabbed Frank's arm and pulled him up the walk to the house.

They all four walked up the porch steps into a well-preserved Victorian entryway. Vince had overcome his irritation as his thick hands descended to the blonde's ass.

"Wish we didn't have business here, tonight," Vince moaned as his hands moved to unbutton her gauzy white blouse.

"What do you mean 'business'?" she asked as she removed Vince's fingers from her blouse and stepped away.

"Oh, nothing," he murmured.

"Shut up," Frank cautioned. *Damn that Vince. Always a loudmouth. Never thinking.*

She looked inquiringly at Frank. "You a businessman too?"

Frank grasped at the first thought that popped into his mind. "What's your name?"

"Lisa."

"Where you from?"

This simple question seemed impossible for her to answer. Instead, she teared up. "Not here. Not anywhere near here."

Vince found the exasperation that Frank thought had been left in the taxi. "You're the first whore I ever met who got shy when she was touched."

Lisa's cheeks flared red, and her light blue eyes flamed. "Listen, you may wind up paying your twelve dollars, and if you pay it, I got to go upstairs with you. But I'm not a whore, buddy. This is my first night here, and you're not making it real easy."

Frank's girl had departed at the first mention of "business," and Frank found himself standing alone with Lisa as Vince strolled off, saying he needed a stiff drink.

The girl's intensity drained away, and Frank didn't know what to say. He wondered what sad story had brought her to Marie's.

Finally, she seemed to rouse herself, focusing her baby-blues on him. "What's your name, handsome?"

"Just call me Carlucci, baby. But you got another guy interested—he'll be back once he finds a drink. He might not like you talking to a guy like me."

"You think he'll be back?"

"I think he likes you."

She sighed and looked at the heavyset piano player, tinkling away on an out-of-tune piano. "That's Marie. She runs this place."

Couches around the room were filled with giggling girls in pale satin and lace. A few smoked cigarettes in long ivory holders. The street noise was kept out by heavy, dark red drapes that fell from a twelve-foot ceiling in front of the only two windows in the room.

Frank wanted to ask Lisa more questions, but Marie's piano music seemed to grow louder as the laughter grew louder. Vince returned with a couple of heavy glasses containing rocks and liquor. He handed one to Lisa. "Drink up, doll. This is going to be a good night."

Lisa gave a tight smile and sipped slowly, turning to Vince. The neon-framed sign proclaiming "Marie's Place" shed its warm glow over the crowd. Lisa's smooth cheeks called to Frank's fingers for a caress in a way that made him uninterested in anything else. *What's wrong with me?* he thought. *One set of tits is just like any other set.*

Marie got up from the piano and left the room. Five minutes later she returned in a pink satin housecoat with her white hair falling to her shoulders. The multicolored wooden beads hanging between the back room and the parlor sounded like rain as she walked through them.

Marie approached Vince and Frank. In a husky smoker's voice, she said, "You guys are here for business in the back. Go through this door." She pointed behind her, then winked and smiled. "Those stairs over there go up to the rooms for fun. Fun is our specialty."

Vince looked at Lisa. "I've got some plans for fun—"

Frank interrupted, "Business first."

Vince snapped, "I meant for later."

Marie intervened. "No one says you can't do both tonight, but Mr. DeLuca is waiting. Just go through the door. Follow the hall back to the last room with the open door."

Vince drained the rest of his drink. "I'm ready," he said, abruptly turning away and striding off.

Lisa leaned toward Frank. For a moment, Frank stared into her eyes, lost in their intense sadness. Then he had to leave. Damn Vince, always rushing. Vince had already burst through the curtain of beads, but Frank caught him by the arm in the dimly lit hallway.

"Slow down," he whispered. "We are going to listen

and learn. If we play our cards right, I promise we will be running this show before long. Let me do the talking. DeLuca is a tired has-been. He needs us. You, listen. Don't let them know how smart we are. We want them to think we're a little smart, but not too smart."

From outside the room, they could see that DeLuca sat on an upholstered leather chair with a small wooden table on his right. Smoke curled up from a cigar in a glass ashtray. There were two other men in long-sleeved shirts straining over biceps. Shoulder-holstered guns were prominently displayed in a casual ease that bespoke habitual wearing. The men sat across the room from DeLuca in straight wooden chairs. One of them had a chair turned with its back in front of him as he straddled it; the other slouched with his legs crossed at the ankles. They were smoking with drinks in their hands.

As Vince and Frank entered the room, the two men stopped laughing and stood. The brothers paused just inside the door.

DeLuca stood, smiled, and extended his hand. "Welcome, Vince—may I call you Vince? —and Frank."

"Sure, why not," Vince said without cracking a smile, extending his hand to DeLuca.

"Have a seat." DeLuca waved at a couch positioned directly across from him. "You guys want a drink?"

"Water with ice," Frank said.

Vince followed. "Scotch. No ice."

One of the boys yelled out the drinks. Footsteps ran down the hallway.

"Sell me," DeLuca said.

Frank quickly took control of the conversation. "I see two selling jobs tonight. We sell you; you sell us. We have been watching and studying you. Same for Jimmy Jack."

Frank emphasized points with his slender index finger, looking straight into DeLuca's watchful eyes. "We could go either way, Mr. DeLuca, except we like your methods and your people. We have lots of ideas for working with you when Jimmy Jack is gone."

"How are you going to get rid of Jimmy Jack? He's got four or five goons with him at all times. I can't get close to the guy."

Frank moved closer to DeLuca and lowered his voice. "As I said, we watch him. We know where he goes and when. We know some of his men. We've been thinking about this. We like you. We admire you. We like your operation, and you are highly recommended by our Uncle Mario. So here we are."

DeLuca turned his focus elsewhere. "What about you, Vince?"

Vince leaned forward in his seat, ignoring everything and everyone else in the room. He looked into DeLuca's eyes. "I ain't seen anybody in Zapata that my brother and I can't outsmart and outgun. You have class and the smarts we're looking to join. I can see a great future if we develop mutual respect." Vince sat back, but kept his eyes glued to DeLuca.

A thin guy delivered the drinks then hurried out. The brothers sipped as Vince's statement settled in the air.

"Well, you seem confident, or should I say cocky," DeLuca said. "I do know your Uncle Mario. Known him for years. He told me to look out for you boys. What have I got to lose?"

He looked hard into Vince's dark eyes. "If things don't work out, no one can prove that I had anything to do with this meeting. People, a few people, will just wonder what happened to you guys." He leaned back and took a drag on his cigar.

Everyone paused.

Frank knew he had to get to the numbers. "Vince and I are the only ones with anything to lose. If all goes well, we get a thirty percent ownership in the combined business of you and Jimmy Jack. If we prove ourselves and you like the way we operate, fifty-fifty partnership six months later."

The breathing in the room almost stopped. DeLuca coughed and then burped. He didn't reply.

Frank continued, "If things don't work out, you've lost nothing. But I can tell you it will work out. We don't fail."

He stopped talking, sat back, and waited.

"I see what your uncle meant. You're smart. Maybe too smart," DeLuca said.

Frank could feel his heart sinking. Had he played his cards all wrong tonight?

DeLuca picked up his cigar and took a long drag. "I think we could have a deal, but you need to prove yourselves to me, and that involves Jimmy Jack. You know what I mean."

"Damn, that was easy," Vince said. He chuckled, lounging back on the couch. "We should've asked for fifty-fifty upfront."

The tension flowed out of the room as everyone laughed, and DeLuca said, "Don't get greedy. Your time will come. You guys are fresh blood with balls and ambition."

DeLuca turned serious, studying Vince's face. "How you guys going to do it?"

"Just leave it to us," Vince said. "We won't rush things. He just simply won't be here one day. Maybe tomorrow, maybe a couple of months."

"Meantime, we won't see you again till it's done," Frank said. "Just be patient and wait. Count on it."

"Then our business for this evening is concluded," DeLuca said, standing. "I'll see you when I see you, and we'll toast with Scotch and another cold glass of water."

"We'll steer clear of each other," Frank said. "We don't want anyone suspicious."

"Remember, Jimmy Jack knows what you want. Courtesy of your loud mouth on the pier. You better get him before he gets you."

Vince shrugged. Frank's hands went numb. The two

brothers left the room the way they'd come in—through dimness and the stale-smelling corridor. Tinny piano music led to the room of flirting baby-dolls, cheap liquor, and easy-come, easy-go.

CHAPTER TEN

The bright lights of chandeliers and the blaring noise of carousing sailors and their chosen escorts greeted the two brothers as they returned to Marie's high-ceilinged parlor. Lisa stood alone by one of the velvet-cushioned couches. Before Frank could intervene, Vince approached her from behind. "Hey, kitten, glad you waited for me," he whispered in her ear.

She turned her head quick as a bird and jumped as Vince's thick hands pinched her ass. Frank bit his lip. *Damn you, Vince. You're always an animal.*

"You want another drink first?" Vince's lips began a long trail from her ear down her neck.

"Maybe your pal here could buy me a drink," she said, looking at Frank.

"Oh no, he can't." Vince placed one of his thick fingers under her chin, forcing her gaze to meet his eyes. "I claimed you before the meeting. You're mine for the night, and I don't share with no one."

For a moment, Frank thought she might slap Vince,

but she controlled herself, lapsing into the vacant gaze of a china doll. Vince took her hand, pulling her toward the stairs. "Upstairs, right now, baby-doll. What did you say your name was?"

"Hey, Vince, wait a minute. Let me have a quick word with you," Frank called.

Vince walked back to Frank, pushing the girl toward the staircase. "What the hell?"

"Let's talk about Jimmy Jack. He's your customer. He might give us a better deal. This DeLuca is competent but older. We can play his game for a while and see where it leads."

Vince glared at Frank. "All you're saying is fucking obvious, brother. I've got a kitten already purring over there, and you stopped me for this?"

Vince started back toward Lisa, dropping words to Frank over his shoulder. "We'll end up dead or successful. Right now, I don't care. Get lost."

Frank's cheeks went warm and sweat beaded on his forehead. "Don't push me, Vince. Don't you dare push me."

A loud blast of noise from outside interrupted everyone. Police whistles and scuffling sounded on the porch.

A small man burst in the front door with blood streaming down his face. He made a beeline for the velvet couch and ran behind it. Three towering police officers swinging billy clubs chased him.

"Hold that guy," one shouted. "Hold him."

The entire room quieted, all faces turning to the dwarf, bleeding and breathing heavily behind the maroon velvet. Vince had stopped on the stairway, turning back toward the commotion. He ran down and across the room, yelling, "Benno!"

A policeman had raised his nightstick, preparing to strike, but Benno thrust his head into the officer's belly.

"You son of a bitch," the officer choked out. The two

other officers behind him rained down blows from their own nightsticks. Benno thrashed and lunged, kicking and snarling, but he was no match for the big-armed officers. He fell to the ground, rolling and twisting.

Frank and Vince had reached the fight by this time. "I know this man," Frank shouted. "Leave him the hell alone." He pulled one of the officer's shoulder from behind.

The officer turned and swung his billy club in a fluid motion into Frank's chest and stomach. Frank heard Lisa scream.

The boisterous crowd of sailors had sobered up quickly and were squeezing out the front door as fast as they could. Most of Marie's girls had retreated to the stairs and seemed to be enjoying the free entertainment as they laughed and pointed.

Vince yanked the officers off Benno, punching and yelling, "Get the hell off this guy. You're killing him." Vince cracked one of the officers behind his neck with his forearm and brought him to the floor. With this, three more officers arrived and dived at Vince, holding him to the ground with the few remaining patrons' help.

"Let me go, goddamnit." Vince kicked and twisted. At one point, Vince managed to stand up and walk with two huge guys on his back. But they soon subdued and cuffed him.

"How can anybody beat up a little guy like that, for Christ's sake," Vince yelled, drops of sweat flying off around him. Every single inch of him was sloppy wet, his trousers were torn, and he had lost a shoe.

Benno was dazed and lying on the floor. Blood covered his shirt, the right sleeve of which had been torn off in the fight.

Things quieted when a tall, heavyset police lieutenant arrived. "Get both them laddies out of here," he shouted in a thick Irish brogue. "If anyone else wants to go with 'em, just give us some trouble."

Frank couldn't believe his eyes. For an evening that had started out so well, it sure had gone to hell. He walked to the front porch to watch the police lights blink red-and-blue down the now quiet street before turning off to the right. *Now I've got to bail out Vince. Dammit.*

He became aware of someone behind him on the porch and turned. Lisa was holding a tall glass of something.

"I bet you need some cold water," she said, offering him the glass.

He gulped it down. "What the hell happened? I was going to help Benno when all hell broke loose."

"Can we sit?" she asked, pointing to a wooden porch swing.

The chain squeaked as they sat. A breeze came up, and Frank felt peaceful for the first time in a long time. She used her feet to rock the swing gently, then stopped and looked at him.

"I'm getting you some ice for your face."

She returned with cubes of ice in a bar cloth. "Here, turn toward me. This should help with the swelling."

Her hands were cool and delicate as she held Frank's jaw. Gentle.

"Why did you come here tonight?" she asked.

"Why does anyone come to a…" He couldn't bring himself to say "whorehouse" and instead said, "We had business. You heard."

"Why didn't you stop that other guy from grabbing me to go upstairs?"

"You've got a lot of questions, doll-baby."

"I want to know." She said it with such sweetness, instead of the anger Frank expected, that he decided to answer. Crazy, the effect this girl had on him. Besides, her hands never wavered in holding the ice to his sore jaw. Her touch soothed him. That was the word. Soothing. She touched him as if he mattered.

"Nobody stops Vince. Not even me. You saw what he

did to those police officers. It took about five guys to even slow him down."

"Is that really why?"

"He already put his claim on you."

She sighed. "I'm leaving here. I'll never see you again, but I had to know."

"You're leaving?"

"I don't know why I tried it. Guess because I had no money, no family, nobody at all."

"Where will you go?"

"I'll find something, but it won't be this." She placed her hand, palm side down, on Frank's leg—the one closest to her. The heat seared his muscles despite the lightness of her touch. "I would have liked to have gotten to know you."

"Would you let me know where you go?" Frank asked.

"Why?"

"I don't know. Just to be sure you're okay."

She smiled a bit, almost as if remembering another time. A better time. "I'll send you a note through Mr. Micheletti. I think we both know him. That's where I first saw you."

Frank thought about Vince's uncontrollable anger and wondered if Vince would care if she wrote him. *What the hell. Neither of us will ever see her again.*

"I got to go, babe. Vince will be crazy at the police station. I got to bail him out before he kills someone." He picked up her hand and placed it on the wooden swing's slats. "Send me a letter in care of Micheletti. He'll give it to me."

She lowered the icy towel from his face and ran her fingers lightly across his cheek. Her touch was as sweet as her voice. Something Frank couldn't decipher filled her eyes before she stood to go back inside.

CHAPTER ELEVEN

Frank had called Mitcheletti before arriving at the police station. Now as he waited for him, the sun rose, turning the sky a pale pink and then a faint orange. The clear sky promised a thousand new beginnings. Frank remembered Lisa's slender frame and the way her body seemed almost too thin until the beautiful swell of her hips and chest filled her out. What would she be doing right now? Was she watching the sunrise from one of Marie's porches? Was she still sitting on the swing deciding where to go next? He could almost feel that last caress across his cheek. Her touch had felt like a whisper between lovers, a secret that couldn't be repeated.

His aching tiredness drained all thoughts from his mind—even pleasant thoughts of Lisa's long legs. Where was Mitcheletti? How long could it take to get dressed?

He finally saw Mitcheletti's black Cadillac easing around the corner. Mitch rolled down his window.

"What the hell happened?"

"We were at Marie's. A big fight with the police.

Vince and Benno were arrested."

Mitcheletti frowned and grunted. "Let's go see what I can do. I know Judge Hanson. You work your magic on your brother. Tell him to keep his mouth shut."

"I'll handle Vince," Frank said as they rushed up the concrete steps of the police station.

The elegant cast-iron balconies on the top floors of the police station reminded Frank of the elegant buildings in certain quarters of New Orleans. But the yellowish-brown bricks were the color of bile.

They entered a high-ceiled room and approached a wooden counter with peeling brown paint and an old wrought-iron enclosure above it. A half-asleep police officer slouched behind the counter.

"Officer, I'm Mitch Mitcheletti, an old friend of Judge Hanson. Is it possible to see the judge right now?"

The officer forced his eyes opened, yawned, and stretched inside the heavy blue uniform.

"The judge was leaving when I last saw him," the officer drawled. "I can see if he's still here, Mr. Mitcheletti."

"Please hurry."

"Judge," the officer shouted toward a dark hallway as he strode toward the back of the building, "a friend here to see you."

"Frank, I may be able to pull this off, but I can only do it once," Mitcheletti warned.

The blood drained into the front of Frank's head and brought on a throbbing headache. *Vince, your timing always fucks me up.*

"I know, Mr. Mitcheletti. Vince and I will never forget this. You have my word of honor—it won't happen again."

"Something tells me big things await you two, but you need to keep Vince in line. Hot tempers get people killed, you know."

A short, plump man with a half-eaten donut in one

hand and a steaming cup of coffee in the other bounded out of the dark hallway behind the counter.

"Why, good morning, Mitch. It's a fine day when the first thing my eyes lay on in the morning is a good friend like you."

Mitch beamed from ear to ear. "Good morning, Judge. I was hoping you might like an old friend's company for your first cup of the day."

"You come on in my office, and sit a spell. I have a whole pot of hot coffee just brewed."

Mitcheletti turned back to Frank. "You stay put."

The two older men, talking and laughing, disappeared down the hallway. Frank looked at the meager furnishings and walked back and forth until his legs demanded he sit on one of the hard, inhospitable benches lining the room. He put his throbbing head into his hands. Vince's fuse was shorter than it had been in Jakesberg. Why? Didn't Vince realize how much better off they were here? Here, they had chances to go big-time. Here, they could make some money. Here, they could, at least, look at beautiful women. Hell, Vince had almost scored last night with the most beautiful woman Frank had seen in forever.

Frank rested his head against the wall behind the bench, eventually dozing off. Vince's throaty growl awoke him.

Mitch burst from the hall's darkness with Benno and Vince in front of him.

Frank jumped up and crossed the room to them. "Thank you, Mr. Mitcheletti. This is the only time, I promise."

Vince's face and shirt were crusted with blood. The beginnings of bruises made his face puffy and discolored. Vince—for once—was uncharacteristically quiet. He walked with a slight limp, as if in pain.

Before Frank could speak to him, Vince said, "I'm okay, you hear? Leave me alone, brother."

Mitcheletti drove them away from the police station.

Vince's cool reception, layered on top of Frank's headache, made for a quiet ride. They dropped Benno at his rooming house.

"I'll fix some breakfast, and you can tell me what happened," Mitch said. "I'll talk to Benno tomorrow. He's too beat up to talk."

Frank thought he might be able to eat a little now that his headache had subsided, although he wasn't surprised when Vince said he felt sick to his stomach as they pulled into the driveway.

"Go ahead upstairs," Mitch said. "Don't get sick in the car. Front door is unlocked."

Vince quickly opened the car door and limped up the steps to the house's porch. An envelope with sloping cursive in blue ink rested on the doormat. "Please deliver to Mr. Carlucci," it read.

He slid one swollen finger under the flap. A small locket-sized tinted photo fell out—a picture of a beautiful blonde. That same girl as last night—what had been her name?

He opened the page:

Please come help me—if you get this. At the bus station.

Lisa

"Hey, Frank," Vince tried to yell through swollen lips as he shoved the note into his trouser pocket. "That girl found me."

Vince went down the hall and looked into one of Mitcheletti's homey guest bedrooms. Every bone in his sore body urged him to lie down.

Frank, standing in the kitchen, didn't know what Vince's slurred words meant, but he knew Vince was exhausted and suffering the effects of a meeting with five or six beefy Irish cops.

"Hey, Mitch," Vince yelled. "Can I borrow your car for an hour or so?"

Mitcheletti poured Frank a steaming mug of coffee and gestured toward the chairs at the kitchen table. "You better drink up and wake up, Frank. Don't you start work in another two hours or so?"

He turned to Vince as he came into the room. "Where you going?" Mitch asked.

"None of your business."

"Promise you won't beat up the rest of our local police force?" Mitch said with a twinkle in his eyes.

Vince grabbed the keys from Mitch's countertop and left without another word.

CHAPTER TWELVE

A day later, Vince sat in his sparse room in the boarding house. Could he have found the woman he'd always wanted—a classy doll? A woman who gave him what he needed? He combed his hair with thickened fingers and wished his hip didn't hurt. Crossing the room, he flipped on the radio and turned the volume up.

An insistent pounding on his door made him curse under his breath. Damn boardinghouse. Someone was always offended by his radio.

"What?" he shouted.

Frank walked in, already dressed in perfectly pressed dark slacks and a white shirt with stiff creases and French cuffs. Vince fell back on the bed and propped up his head with one of the flattened pillows. "You look like a fucking pimp. Why you always dress up for work?"

"What's going on?" Frank asked. "I thought I heard you talking, then the music began."

"Nothing," Vince said. "Nothing I can't work out for myself."

"Listen to me," Frank began. "We gotta talk serious. We just made the deal of our lives with DeLuca. Not even ten minutes later you get into a fight. We don't need this kind of problem."

Vince flexed his fingers.

"You're not handling problems; you're causing them," Frank continued.

"What was I supposed to do? It was unfair odds—those bohunk cops and little Benno—"

"He's a professional wrestler. He can handle himself."

"Not against those odds."

"Look, this conversation isn't about Benno. It's about you and me working together. I can't do this alone and neither can you. Remember? We're together in this. What I do can hurt you, and what you do can hurt me."

Vince raised himself to a sitting position. "You're not going to tell me what to do, Frank."

"Yes, I am. I'm telling you what you can't do anymore because it could blow everything. You can't go crazy and fight the cops."

"He's just a little guy."

"I don't care if he's an Irish elf or a Russian bear. Dammit, Vince. Mitch might not be able to get you out of jail next time. If you want to fight, fight Jimmy Jack's boys or someone else trying to keep us down. Don't fight the cops. We got more important things to do."

Vince put his huge hands over his face and took a deep breath. After a long exhalation, he said, "You don't get it, Frank. You don't get it at all. I was tiny—a little boy. At home, one day. You weren't there. Dad was passed out drunk. They locked me in a closet—some neighborhood toughs. They slapped Mom around for a while. I could hear their hands hitting her.

"Then they threw her on the bed. For a long time, all I could hear was the springs squeaking, and her yelling, 'No, no, please no.'"

"You got to be kidding."

"When they broke in, I didn't fight them like I should have done. I could've kicked. I was big enough to kick damn hard. But I didn't."

"Vince, you can't blame yourself."

"After that, I made sure I was strong. I made sure that every time I heard the sound of bed springs squeaking that I got up and did pushups. No one ever is going to hurt someone of mine again."

"Did you ever talk to Mom about it?"

"No reason to. She burned her bloody clothes. She pleaded with me never to tell anyone, and I never did— until now."

Vince removed his hands from in front of his eyes and sat up straighter. "But you got to understand. Sometimes I see red. I gotta destroy everything in front of me."

Frank stepped back and turned away from Vince's heaving shoulders. "But Vince…"

Vince grabbed Frank from behind and wound his thick forearm around Frank's neck too tight for comfort. Vince's heavy, warm breath was on his left ear. "Don't you ever tell me what I can't do, Frank. You hear?"

"Okay, Vince. Okay. But remember, we're on the same side. I'm all you got, and you're all I got."

Vince's heavy forearm eventually loosened.

After a long day of barbering, the brothers visited Benno's rooming house. They huffed their way up to the third floor to find Benno's room in a converted attic.

Frank and Vince bent over and walked in under the low ceiling. The walls were old brown boards. Benno sat in an upholstered chair with one of his legs elevated on an ottoman, an ice bag on one knee.

"Good to see you. How ya doing, Vince?"

Vince shook hands with Benno. "Guess I'm doing better than you, guy. You need a doctor?"

"This stuff's not as bad as what happens in the ring. I'm just swollen. Let me turn off the radio. Sure am happy to see you guys."

Frank felt loneliness written all over the place—in the piles of folded laundry stacked on the floor, on the thin pallet that passed for a mattress, in the blood-crusted clothing that Benno had worn home from jail, still bunched on the splintery pine flooring.

"Pardon the mess. I can hardly move, so I said the hell with it." He laughed, but his breath was cut short, and he had to hold his chest. "You got quite a brother, Frank. If it hadn't been for him, those cops might have killed me."

"I couldn't get along without my little brother."

Benno's face took on a watchful look. "You know the big guys are watching you both, right?"

Frank studied Benno's face.

"I want to be part of what you do—whatever you're planning," Benno continued. "I'd do anything for Vince—you know that, don't you?"

Frank eyed the dirty bowls and a thick china coffee cup on the floor.

"Benno, we've thought a lot about starting our own business, if you know what I mean," Frank said.

"Vince helped me last night. I don't know anyone else who would do that for me. To them, I'm just a joke. To make enough money, I got to wrestle. I've got to eat and pay for this dump—"

"What do you know about the mobs here?" Vince interrupted.

"Mostly, I work for Sunset Concrete Company. Road, walkways, public projects—you know. I dig and spread concrete. Got my own crew. The work helps me maintain."

Vince laughed. "Maintain what? Your lovely penthouse?"

"Hey, my image, goddammit. What do you think I'd be if I didn't have my physique? What would I be without muscles? Besides, I can outwork most of the guys at the plant."

"Tell us what you know about the mobs," Vince said.

"I didn't say this, but I help Jimmy Jack and his gang unload the hooch when it comes into West Beach. I know when it's coming. I know how many men they got down there and where everyone is hidden."

"So, they trust you," Vince said, eyes unmoving.

"You get more valuable all the time," Frank said. "But here's the important question: do you want to be more than a laborer walking through sand with heavy boxes?"

Benno shifted the ice bag on his knee and sat up straighter on the stained chair. "I want to work with Vince. We had the same kind of dads—remember us talking in jail, Vince?"

Vince pointed at a faded photo in a corner. "That your family?"

"I don't let many people see that. My mom and dad, and a sister."

Frank noticed that Benno's thoughts had gone to a very different place. "Where'd you grow up?" he asked.

"My mom died young when I was a kid. Before that, we were really close."

"How about your dad?" Vince asked.

A quick tear came to Benno's eyes. "I wouldn't be talking about this if I hadn't been manhandled so much by those cops, then sitting here all alone—no one besides you guys has even come over to check on me. Not even Mitch."

"That's okay, Benno. Talk all you want," Vince said.

"My dad was regular-sized—like everyone else in my family. Plus, he was a real outdoorsman. He wanted a real son—not me. Someone he could be proud of. Athletics, fishing, you know, all the standard stuff. I tried so hard." Benno now looked as if he might bawl.

"What happened?" Frank and Vince simultaneously said.

"One night he came home after he'd been drinking—he was zozzled. He came into my bedroom. I was hoping for once he'd call me 'son.' He began hitting me. He just kept hitting me. When he finally stopped, he just said, 'Why were you ever born?'

"I screamed back at him, 'What about me? What about me?'"

"Benno's like me," Vince said. "We both got a loser dad."

Frank turned to Vince. "We don't have to look any further for the one person we'll always be able to trust."

"You won't be sorry you found me," Benno said.

"Right now, we need you to sit tight," Frank said. "Keep doing what you're doing, and wait. Keep your ears open, and we'll meet from time to time."

"I may need someone to watch my back and help me with some of the outside work," Vince added. "You up for it?"

"I told you I've done it all. Don't worry—I've never killed anyone unless they needed killing. "

Frank eased himself up from the hard seat of a sturdy wooden chair. "I think we understand each other."

"Remember, Benno," Vince said, "there are now plenty of reasons to get rid of you—from us, if you tell about this conversation; from them—if they find out what you've told us. Understand?"

"I'll never let you guys down," Benno said.

For the next several months, all three went to work as usual. Frank and Vince barbered in stiff, starched white jackets every day, and Benno did the grueling work of laying cement. Benno was even promoted to senior supervisor.

They met every week. Shipments of liquor had increased in frequency with the beach patrol paid off to look the other way on West Beach, Benno reported. Jimmy Jack watched the nighttime arrivals from a pickup truck through binoculars about a quarter mile away, in case a quick escape became necessary. Tip-offs from one of the secretaries in the Jackson, Mississippi police headquarters whenever the state troopers were coming ensured that Jimmy Jack's operations were largely safe. DeLuca, on the other hand, had shipments brought by small motorboats into Mason's Bay, a large inland area known mainly for great trout fishing and flounder.

As spring approached, Frank told Vince and Benno that the time was at hand for them to get serious.

"Finally," Vince grumbled.

Benno rubbed his hands up and down his formidable arms. "I'm ready."

"I've got everything in place," Frank said. "We're going to be rolling in dough."

CHAPTER THIRTEEN

In the intervening months of long preparation for Frank and impatience for Vince, girls never came up. Frank had learned from years of experience that Vince didn't like questions about his love life and never mentioned it. For Frank, meeting other girls was easy—they liked his smart clothes and trim build. But something was missing in Frank's life. Was it the sweetness in Lisa's pale face during that brief talk on Marie's porch swing? Was it the almost desperate longing in her face when she had asked him why he wanted to know where she was going when she left Marie's? And her touch, her whisper-smooth touch—like she meant it.

Jimmy Jack had become Vince's customer at the Adcock shop on the pier. His large girth and red satin suspenders became a predicable sight every Thursday morning when he showed up for his haircut.

One Saturday afternoon, as the last customer was leaving, Jimmy Jack and his ever-present five boys appeared.

"Come in, my friend," Vince said with a laugh as Jimmy Jack walked in, the door opened by one of his muscled goons.

Two of the suited boys stayed outside the shop. Jimmy Jack hoisted his ample body into the barber's chair while one of his boys opened the back storeroom door, turned on the light, stepped inside, and looked around. He signaled to the others that all was okay.

Vince stood silent and out of the way. "Don't mind me," he said, standing against the wall with his arms stretched out in an exaggerated pose of surrender.

"Come on, you know I have to do that," Jack said. "I always love the smell of that brilliantine. Use some on me—it makes me feel young."

Vince picked up a black comb and walked around the chair, combing Jimmy's hair from all angles before he picked up the shears to cut.

"To anyone else, I would be closed. But to you, my good friend, I am always open. Let me turn an ugly turnip into a beautiful onion."

Vince began to cut, and the shop's silence was accentuated by the precision scissors' snip-snip. Vince tried not to think about why Jimmy Jack had broken from his usual Thursday timing. "I hear you've got a great new act at your club, Mr. Jack. Where do you get those dolls?"

"Come over—maybe next week. My treat. Bring your brother. I'd like to get to know you guys better," Jack said with a small grin.

Oh, shit. Does he know? Vince's mind ran out of control, but the snip-snip continued in the regular pattern already established. "You know, I think we will just do that."

"Good, then it's a date—say Wednesday or Thursday. I'll call you. First show is at nine."

Vince continued circling Jack's bulk, his hands steady at their precision task. "You got something to eat over there at the Moulin Rouge?" This was calculated to bring a laugh since the place served excellent seafood. It was famous for its huge platters of steaming food delivered by white-coated waiters.

"Just for that comment, you only get one fried shrimp and one oyster. Then you'll have to beg for more." Jack's huge bulk shook with humor.

There was a sudden sound of loud voices and scuffling at the front door. The three men who were inside ran to investigate. Jack stood, his white cover sheet falling off, and reached inside his jacket for his shoulder-holstered gun.

Vince ran to the door. "It's my brother, Frank. Back off, guys—he's okay."

"He's a friend," Jack yelled. "Let him in."

Frank stepped into the shop, brushing himself off and retrieving a comb from his hip pocket to tidy his hair. "Mr. Jack, I thought your guys knew me," he said.

"They are doing what they get paid for," Jack said. "Come in, we're just talking about eating good seafood, having fun, talking a little business, maybe." Jack looked intently at Frank.

"Three of my favorite subjects." Frank smiled. "Combine that with good-looking dames, and you've got my idea of a party."

Vince finished the haircut, reached for a long brush, and cleaned Jack's shoulders.

"Well, Mr. Vince, you put on the Ritz for this old man. I brought you a nice tip." He nodded to one of his boys, who took a bottle of Crown Royal bourbon from a paper bag and handed it to Vince.

"Wow, that's good hooch," Vince exclaimed. "Where would a kindly, law-abiding Christian gentleman like you come across a gem like this?"

Jack smiled. "I want to talk to you guys next week at the Moulin Rouge about my business. You guys impress me, and I'm not getting any younger." He rose from the chair, paid the bill. With his boys both ahead and behind him, he reached into a pocket and flipped Vince a silver dollar.

Vince caught the coin and winked a thank-you to Mr. Jack. *This is it. He's made his first move.*

Mr. Jack paused at the doorway and looked back at Vince. "I'll call you one night this week. I'd like to show you what kind of night fishing I do."

Holy shit. He knows all about us.

After the door closed resolutely behind the entire group, Vince stopped his sweeping of hair and looked over to Frank. "Well, brother, are we biting off more than we can chew? Now we've got the two biggest, richest, meanest guys in town after us."

Frank answered with a slow smile. "They may be the biggest, richest, and meanest, but they're not the smartest. Let's go and see what he has in mind. If Mr. DeLuca hears about it, he'll just think we're looking for the right opportunity to move in on Jimmy Jack."

"Yeah, but remember the last thing he said."

"You mean about night fishing?"

"What do you think that means?"

"You got me. Mr. DeLuca might actually have a surprise waiting, but so could Mr. Jack, or so could you, on the other hand. Be prepared for anything and anyone."

Vince lowered the shades to the shop, leaving the rest of the sweeping for another day. "I gotta go now, Frank. Hot date."

"Hot date?"

"Yeah, you need to find yourself a girl, Frank. Take some of the edge off. See ya."

At a small beach cottage across the seawall from the Gulf, Lisa greeted Vince with a warm kiss. He had rented the cottage for Lisa, but it had been days since he'd seen her. Tonight seemed like a good night, though. Who knew what would be coming down the pike later in the week? Yes, tonight would be a good night to ease off a little bit.

Lisa whispered in his ear that it'd be a good night for him to stay the whole night—something he didn't normally do.

He suggested they sit on the porch, and she brought out two Scotch and waters on the rocks. He grabbed her hand as they sipped the drinks. "I want to make you happy, Lisa."

"How was your day?"

"Pretty good. But I was planning to see you tonight, so I was thinking of you."

"Hey, that's what a girl likes to hear—that her guy was thinking of her."

Vince didn't reply or smile, but instead focused on the cresting waves beyond the seawall's height.

"What are you thinking about, baby?"

"Why do you want to be with me?"

She put her drink on the porch railing and took both of his hands in hers. "Don't you know, Vince?"

"If I knew, I wouldn't ask."

"You make me feel safe. You treat me good. It makes me happy when you hold me and tell me you like me."

"Do you love me?"

Lisa's voice cracked, and tears welled up in her eyes. "Vince, I—"

He interrupted quickly. "I know I'm not great looking. I'm rough and tough, and don't care what most people think. But you, Lisa. I care what you think. You're the only one I care about—"

"You treat me real good. You know I'm grateful."

She dropped Vince's hands and picked up her drink.

"Don't ever stop loving me, Lisa."

"Don't worry, Vince. Everything's going to be okay. We're happy now. That's all that counts."

"Let's go inside, honey." He tugged her hand to get her up from her porch chair.

They left their drinks to sweat in the humid evening's heat. The wooden screen door slapped in the painted doorframe behind them. Neither of them turned on any lights inside; neither of them spoke a word.

CHAPTER FOURTEEN

Frank stood with his silent brother outside one of Zapata's most notorious good-time dance clubs as they waited for Benno to appear.

He eyed Vince's new shoulder sling. "What's wrong with your arm?"

Vince responded with a morose glare. "I told you to mind your own business."

"I'm your brother, aren't I?" Vince's resentful glare did little to lighten Frank's mood. "Besides, we're here to give Benno a good time tonight. Ease up on that bad mood."

Before Vince could reply, Benno appeared, dressed in a gray pinstriped suit with matching leather shoes, a gray fedora, and a starched white shirt. "Boy-oh-boy, I'm looking forward to this."

"Yeah, from the name of this place and the front door, I can see why." Frank gestured to the sinuous neon that read "Omar Khayyam Club."

Laughing and joking, they walked to a covered

entryway resembling a shallow, dimly lit cave. A life-sized burlesque queen with a large fake ruby in her navel was painted on the door.

Benno's smile grew even wider when Vince pushed a doorbell and the ruby was replaced by a blue eye with long, black eyelashes. After an unblinking inspection, the door opened.

The first of the night's gorgeous ladies stood in a pale green gown flowing to the floor. Her husky whisper greeted them. "Come in, boys, and welcome to the Omar Khayyam Club." Behind them, she shut and bolted the door. The sounds of laughter, conversation, and clinking glasses washed over them. In the background, a band played "The Sheik of Araby."

Vince eyed the place. "Talk about atmosphere, huh? Special place tonight for our special friend. Right, Frank?"

"This is our treat tonight, Benno. Anything you want. Tonight we're all in Arabia with a thousand and one beautiful girls—all Shebas."

Benno's wide smile showed both appreciation and anticipation. "Good place to turn thirty—what a birthday!"

Another girl led them to a wide table with plush chairs atop thick carpet. Two revolving mirrored balls hung from the ceiling. Scattered shards of light illuminated the guests' faces and bodies.

Frank eased himself into the comfortable chair and surveyed the room. *We could do this. We could do even better than this.* We could hire musicians, bartenders, beautiful girls. Soon we'll have all the liquor...

"What are you dreaming about, brother?" Vince asked in his deep growl.

"Nothing."

"The girl is waiting for your drink order."

Frank smiled at the girl. "And I never keep a beautiful girl waiting. I'll take a seltzer. Lots of rocks."

As the girl swayed back to the bar, Frank roused himself. "Man, look at that waitress. What is she wearing?

Ain't nothing holding up all those sequins!"

Benno made appreciative noises. "I don't know what you call it, but it doesn't leave much to the imagination, does it?"

Vince leaned in toward the table. "I thought you guys would like this place. Look at those white couches." He pointed to the curving white expanse close to the bar.

"Yeah, can you imagine the mess it'd make if all those bottles got broken?" Benno pointed to the shelves of fancy liquor bottles and faceted glasses above the bar.

"Well, my favorite thing here is those right there." Vince pointed a thick finger to the colorful posters of fan dancers and burlesque queens in provocative stances on the walls. "I love this place. I love those damn musicians over there. Hell, they got piano, bass, guitar, sax—this is a classy joint even without the dames."

"Happy birthday, Benno," Frank said. "This night is yours."

Vince assumed a serious face. "We'll be moving on with our plans this week. So tonight is the last partying for a while."

Anticipation reached every nerve in Frank's body. "Don't talk here. The walls have ears. Catch us up later."

Vince simply stared at Frank, his face a blank slate. "I've got a big fucking surprise. You won't believe it."

"A surprise?" Frank said, smiling. "Have you cooked up something for Benno?"

Vince continued staring. "Not just Benno. For all of us."

Frank remained silent. It had been a hard day in a series of weeks of hard days. Vince had been harping that he was tired of waiting for Frank's preparations. Frank's feet hurt from standing all day cutting hair, and he felt his own exhaustion. Tonight he just wanted to relax and forget about the future. "Okay, Vince. Tonight let's keep it happy. This is Benno's birthday. End of discussion."

Vince winced as he adjusted his shoulder sling, but he

quit talking.

Their waitress returned with the drinks—Scotch on the rocks for Vince, Benno's bourbon, and Frank's seltzer. With a toast to Benno, they began the evening by watching scantily clad harem girls gliding through the room selling cigarettes and cigars. As the club filled with smoke and more laughter and talking, a sudden drum roll interrupted the crowd, and a spotlight hit the stage, showing an announcer in an immaculate tuxedo. "Ladies and gentlemen, the lovely Candy Sweet, America's foremost burlesque queen."

The musicians played an unmistakable bump-and-grind as a beautiful young lady peeked from behind a heavy velvet curtain beside the band, then ducked back in the first of her taunting movements. A perfectly shaped, unusually pale leg slowly thrust out from behind the curtain, the foot flexing back and forth. The crowd roared in appreciation, and even Frank felt a stirring.

Candy Sweet slinked out in a colorful get-up resembling Cleopatra, with a glittery snake-like costume covering a few vital areas of anatomy. As she made her way through the tables on the floor, she stopped in front of Benno and flounced her silk drapery, asking Benno to help her adjust the sequined snake across her breasts, then lowering her bottom to his lap while kicking her feet up in the air.

Benno hit Vince on the back and crowed, "She loves me," as the crowd went wild.

She went from table to table, sometimes letting customers adjust her snake, sometimes revealing other body parts by coy movements with her silk shawl across men's faces. Eager customers laughed and applauded, whistling and catcalling. After minutes of seductive play with the crowd, she returned to the dance floor, and quickly did a series of breathless spins. Abruptly, she stopped and pointed to one man in the crowd with a provocative look and pouting lips. Then she disappeared back behind the velvet curtain. Vince, Benno, and most of the crowd stood and yelled for more.

"Miss Sweet will be back at eleven thirty tonight. She thanks you all."

The crowd booed, then hissed, then laughed. As the band members left on break, the crowd quieted to a low rumble. Frank felt like everyone, including him, needed a break after the titillation of Miss Sweet and her music.

"You got your hands close to some vital spots when she was on your lap, Benno," Frank laughed. "The last time I saw you panting was when those big Irish cops had you on the floor at Marie's."

Drinks continued, round after round.

Frank gestured to the waitress. She walked to their table and sat on Frank's lap. "How about letting Louise get you guys another round? Looks like you need it."

"Make them doubles and fast," Vince said, laughing and patting Benno on the back. "Listen, guys, you won't believe it, but—"

Before he could go further, the front door of the club opened, and Mitcheletti burst in. Mitch paused and looked around the club before rushing over to their table, nearly knocking the drink tray out of the hands of a waitress.

"There could be a war here in Zapata," Mitcheletti whispered as he wiped perspiration from his brow. He had already sat in a chair, but now looked over his shoulder toward the front door and continued with a slight tremor in his voice. "The Feds found Jimmy Jack—dead. Shot on the beach."

When the round of drinks appeared, Mitch, not looking up, spoke to the girl. "Honey, bring me a martini."

She left, and when she was a safe distance away, he spoke again. "There was a big shoot-out on West Beach. Feds, state troopers, even the sheriff's boys. They must've been watching him. His guys scattered—some to the Gulf in small boats."

Through all the news, Vince retained a poker face.

"Interesting. Quite interesting. Mitch, we never told you anything, but we're not the kind of boys who're going to cut hair all our lives."

Mitcheletti smiled. "If I was a betting man, I'd say that the time has come to bet on you guys."

"I guess DeLuca will be making big moves now," Mitch continued. "He's bigger than Jimmy Jack ever was. Besides, I know—"

A low, musical woman's voice broke through their conversation. "Mind if I join you?"

Frank's heart skipped a beat. The lovely young woman named Lisa from Marie's was standing behind Vince with those intense blue eyes boring into Frank's.

What was she doing here?

"Where the hell have you been?" Vince asked. "I thought you'd forgotten."

"Sorry, baby, but I'm running late."

All the men stood while Vince pulled out a chair from the table next to him and made her comfortable. "Sit right here, baby. You know I can't trust these guys around a beautiful girl like you. Hey, guys, this is Lisa."

She sat carefully, lowering her shapely figure onto the plush upholstery.

Oh, shit. Why did Vince invite her tonight?

As if hearing Frank's thoughts, Vince awkwardly grabbed her hand and brought it to his lips in a rough kiss. "Meet the girl who is making me happy."

Frank was stunned. First, the news about Jimmy Jack. Now this. His eyes were drawn toward her sweet, intense face and the curves of her tight outfit. Her softness against Vince's rough fingers and split nails—every night? Frank wanted to throw up.

He cleared his throat. "Can I order you a drink, Lisa?"

She raised her eyes to his face. "That would be very nice."

Vince snorted and lifted his hand from her dainty one to point a finger at Frank. "Don't be trying to poach my girl, big brother. Not with your fancy manners and expensive suits."

"I wouldn't dream of it, brother," Frank said with a laugh. "Besides, you get your suits tailored at the same place, so we're even."

Everyone laughed.

The band returned and played a slow number for close dancing. Vince had removed himself from the conversation about Jimmy Jack and then excused himself as he got up to go to the restroom.

Frank made his decision. "Mind if I ask your girl to dance, Vince?"

"Go ahead, brother, but mind where you put your hands."

The waltz put them together on the dance floor, although Frank carefully held his body a safe distance from Lisa's slender form.

"Why didn't you come after we talked at Marie's?" she asked.

"What are you talking about?"

"You said you wanted to get a note from me." Lisa's whisper became more plaintive. "I was counting on you."

"It looks like you've done okay with Vince."

The muscles in her back stiffened, and the anger poured out in her carefully controlled soft voice. "I had no money, no friends, no nothing. I wrote you a note, and you didn't come. Vince came. I had no choice."

"Listen, this has gone to the dogs. I wanted you. But Vince put his claim on you. You know that."

"Yes, but—Frank, I really wanted you. I sent you a damn note like you said. Just like you said. But you didn't come help me; Vince came."

"And he's paying your rent and bills?"

She pulled back and looked into Frank's eyes. "But I don't love him."

"Vince is walking back. We can't talk anymore now."

"Meet me on the beach at Seventeenth Street

tomorrow before work. Seven-thirty. We'll talk."

Before Frank could reply, he felt Vince's heavy grip on his shoulder. "Mind if I cut in, brother?"

Frank thought about a quick quip about Vince dancing with only one arm, but refrained when he saw Vince's glowering face in the dim lights. "No problem, brother."

Frank was drained. "Hey, guys, I'm calling it a night." He threw money on the table, wished Benno a happy birthday once more, and waved as he walked to the front door through the well-dressed crowd. The Gulf wind blasted his face as he walked home. He thought about Lisa's intense blue eyes. In private, did she look at Vince the same way?

CHAPTER FIFTEEN

Frank walked alone on the beach. Cool breezes tugged at his hair the way he imagined Lisa's small fingers might. The sun rising over the horizon reflected the promise of the big money he and Vince would soon be in a position to earn. Bootlegging, gambling—these rackets would buy him the life he'd always dreamed of. Even the wind's fishy odor didn't bother him—it was the stink of his and Vince's opportunity. It was the stink of Zapata Island—the only place in the U.S. where bribes could raise the bridge and seal off access from the mainland. Other bribes could get them adequate warnings when state troopers or the Feds were on the way. Big money was going to be coming their way—new cars, huge houses, servants, everything. Just like Uncle Mario.

It was almost too perfect. Just like a dream come true.

As the sun rose higher, streaks of sunlight danced across the Gulf while small, rippling waves rolled toward the white sand. Clusters of shells lay scattered across the beach. Frank looked through their scattered patterns as he thought about Lisa. She'd been bought just like any other whore. Why did it bother him that his brother had done the buying?

He should leave without seeing her. But his legs wouldn't let him walk back to his car. He kept trudging forward, his legs growing heavier as he walked to the rendezvous. By the time he reached Seventeenth Street, he had convinced himself to forget Lisa and tell her he couldn't talk with her ever again.

She was already standing at the appointed spot. A floral dress of light fabric swirled around her slender frame, and a sun parasol kept her face out of the sun's rays. She twirled and almost ran to him, grabbing his shoulders and pressing her body against his. "Oh, Frank. Thank God you came! You came."

Her sweet voice, her delicious smell, her smallness next to his taller frame, the way the sun made her face and hair luminescent—it all literally made Frank's heart skip a beat.

"I've looked forward to seeing you again—you don't know how much."

"Hug me, Lisa. Hug me and don't let go—just hug me."

And she did.

Then, he took her hand and continued walking. The steady crunch of their shoes on the firm sand sounded surreal.

"I can't see you again. You know that."

"Oh, Frank, don't say that."

"I can't betray Vince. He's happy with you. I got to let him have his happiness."

"Frank, don't discard me. I'm a better fit with you. I could tell that from the first night—couldn't you? You have class." Her eyes filled with tears.

"I can't go against my brother. It would destroy him. It could destroy me—and everything we're building together."

As the sun rose higher, the breeze calmed. As the day heated up, they headed for the seawall and a vendor of cold drinks.

Frank bought two tall lemonades, and they sat in wooden chairs under a striped awning. Lisa had stopped crying, but her eyes were still watery.

Frank looked around before he reached for her tiny hand and cupped it in his. "Lisa, I shouldn't have come to meet you. No good can come from this. We barely know each other."

"Oh, Frank—I've thought of you so many times since we talked at Marie's. Our time on the porch. And now we are together."

Frank brought her fingers to his lips and brushed them against his cheek. Their softness burned a thousand memories into his nerves. Never had a girl affected him this way.

"Listen, Lisa—you're one beautiful dish. You know that, don't you? But I can't ever see you again. It's not right."

Lisa withdrew her hand from his. She stared out to sea and shrunk into herself, the smile gone from her face. "It's okay. It's really okay. I can make it alone. You don't even have to walk me back to my car. Just go ahead and leave."

Frank heard the defeat in her voice. No more was she the luminous woman in the sunlight and beautiful swirling dress of printed pink flowers.

"There's one thing we can do before I leave," Frank picked up her hand, stood them both up, and walked back the same route until Tenth Street. Then he guided them into the neighborhood.

Frank tried the door of a small rental cottage and pushed it all the way open with his foot. "You're too beautiful not to make love to."

He guided her to the bedroom after wedging the door shut.

Lisa turned to Frank. "This is all I am to you?"

"I want to give you something of me. This is the only thing I can give to you now," Frank said, already unbuttoning his shirt and jerking it off.

"This is what you think of me?" she said softly, standing by the bed fully clothed. "I thought you were different."

Frank undid his belt buckle and lowered his trousers to the sandy floor. "Lisa, I want to remember you in my arms the rest of my life. I want you to remember me inside of you the rest of your life. I can't give you what Vince gives you. But I can give you this today, and it's all I have. Please, it's all I have."

She sat on the bed and mechanically pulled off her clothes. Not once did she look at him. Frank wrapped his arms around her and whispered in her ear, holding her a long time. He entered her, and she shuddered; by the time they were finished, Frank didn't know if the wetness on his face came from her tears or his sweat. If only life were this simple: a beautiful girl, a bed, sunlight everywhere. A girl who touched his face with kindness.

"You are the most beautiful woman I have ever dreamed of," he said as they dressed. He didn't hear her answer, but she let him hold her hand as they walked back to the beach then parted without a word in the burning sunshine.

That same day after work, Frank went to Benno's dilapidated rooming house.

"I didn't know if I'd find you here," Frank said. "Can you talk?"

"What's up, Boss?"

"With Jimmy Jack gone, his boys will be scattering. Everyone is probably still wondering who did it. I heard today at the shop that his two top guys, Piero and Rick, are in jail. Some of them will be picked up by DeLuca. It's time to move forward."

"We've been waiting for months," Benno said, flexing his forearms.

"Aren't you putting up the statue of Bernardo de Cortez next week?"

"The Father of Zapata is fixing to be able to wave at the ships coming into port," Benno said with a laugh. "A pretty spot, but deserted."

"Can you make a hidden compartment down there? Pretty big. I'll give you the dimensions."

"Sure, Boss, that's easy to do."

"Good. You do just that."

Frank drove home and walked to Vince's duplex for a brief meeting. They found out that DeLuca had called both their shops and asked that they meet with him the following day. They agreed to go together. Frank left as quickly as he could, pleading exhaustion from the Omar Khayyam club.

Going to sleep should have been easy for Frank. After all, it had been a strenuous day with not too much shut-eye the night before. Instead, he tossed and turned. He couldn't forget Lisa's soft white flesh and sweet blue eyes. Every time he closed his eyes, the image of her sadness and the hot trickle of her tears haunted him. The memories they had made today would have to last him a lifetime—this much he knew, and this is what he pounded into his pillow all night long.

CHAPTER SIXTEEN

Frank kept a nervous ear cocked for any gossip among his customers about Jimmy Jack's death. DeLuca had specified an afternoon meeting, so he and Vince made excuses at work and closed their respective shops.

"Tell me what else I should know about DeLuca," Frank asked Vince in the car on the way to the meeting.

"Grew up here. Left for sixteen years and worked as a seaman. In his day, had a reputation for never losing a fight and never backing down from one either. He looked for them."

"I heard he joined Fat Kelly's bootlegging gang here."

"Oh, yeah, the guy they found buried in sand up to his neck on West Beach." Vince smiled. "Head was inside the tide line."

Frank stared out the window as they passed the sheltering limbs of old oaks in the wide expanses of front yards in one of the finer neighborhoods. For weeks, he'd been calculating DeLuca's profits from bootlegging. His customers repeated the local legends about DeLuca—the liquor he smuggled onto the island was from the Caribbean, Cuba, and even Canada. The best there was—high-quality hooch.

Frank's nervousness ramped up as they got closer to DeLuca's house. He pressed Vince for more information. "You started to talk at the Khayyam. What do you know about Jimmy Jack's last night on the beach?"

"I'll tell you soon."

"I want to know now. Before the meeting, Vince."

"Well, big brother, practice your patience. You know, that same 'patience' you've been telling me to practice for months."

"Vince, I'm—"

The car pulled up in the circular driveway of DeLuca's house, and Frank muttered his last few words to Vince, "Just keep your mouth shut. Let me do the talking."

The sound of the car doors slamming all but obliterated Vince's growled reply, but Frank caught enough: "—you always say—".

The two brothers walked to the huge wooden front door with its beveled glass inserts. Before they could knock, a tall man in a butler's jacket stood before them. Frank got the impression of a solid wall of muscle topped by alert eyes of steel.

The man spoke first. "The boss is expecting you. Walk in front of me to the front parlor on the right."

DeLuca was not yet in the parlor, and the boys sat on the upholstered red silk furniture. Vince pointed one stubby finger at a full-length portrait of a wide-eyed young beauty with long, dark hair. "Probably the current Mrs. DeLuca."

Before Frank could reply, DeLuca burst into the room, flashing an exuberant smile and extending his hand. "Glad you were available for a meeting, boys. My new wife insists that I'm free to spend evenings with her, so I'm confined to afternoon meetings."

"Beautiful room," Frank said, hoping his voice didn't betray his nerves or his envy.

"We do enjoy it." DeLuca crushed his cigar out in a crystal ashtray. He took a deep breath. "It's been a long time since we met at Marie's. Oh, forgive me. Would you like a drink?" He gestured to the white-coated man to advance nearer. "This is Spoon. He knows my business. All my business."

"No alcohol for me," Frank said, wishing he had an excuse to stand up and move around to dispel some of his nervous energy. He forced his tailbone into the upholstery and sat up straighter.

"Fine," DeLuca replied. "You know, since hitting seventy, I rarely drink myself."

"Not thirsty," Vince said.

DeLuca leaned forward from his perch on one of the couches. "It's been a couple of days since Jack got it. Vince, your name comes up most often."

"Me?"

Frank could feel the sweat trickling down his backbone.

"Yeah, people say you were in Jack's truck that night." DeLuca inhaled repeatedly to pull the flame from an ornate silver cigarette lighter into his fresh cigar.

Vince bared his teeth for one moment, then leaned forward and looked straight into DeLuca's eyes. "Your cigar smoke is bothering me, Mr. DeLuca. Could you wait a few minutes before you light up again?"

DeLuca paused as if considering the request. Maybe DeLuca would just have them killed right there on the spot. Spoon could do it easy—those big, rawboned hands around Frank's throat. Of course, he'd kill Frank first. Then, three or four slugs into Vince. The carpet could be replaced later.

DeLuca put the lighter down on a small table as if it were a time bomb. "I consider myself to be a perfect host, Mr. Carlucci. If my smoke bothers your delicate sensibilities, then by all means, I will graciously wait until our business is completed."

"Yeah, I killed Jimmy Jack. He made it easy because

he took certain things about me for granted." Vince looked at both Frank and DeLuca. "For him, a fatal mistake."

Frank's lips tightened with all that he wanted to tell his dumb-ass brother.

"Jack invited me to see his setup for the arriving liquor. We drove way out West Beach around three a.m.— just the two of us. No road, just ruts in the seagrass."

"He always had two of his boys with him," DeLuca sputtered.

"Yeah, well, his first mistake was trusting me," Vince said.

"We drove forever down the island. Then he stopped the truck. Out to sea, there were lights from two big cabin cruisers. There were lights going back and forth from the beach to the boats. These big boulders everywhere—half as big as the truck."

DeLuca shifted his weight. "I know that spot."

"They had a system of signaling with headlights from truck to truck. Finally, he parked behind a boulder about a hundred yards from all the activity. He told me to stay in the truck and wait for him. He walked away, and there I was getting my ass eaten alive by those damn mosquitoes."

Vince's breathing was coming quicker, he waved one arm, and sat forward. "I couldn't see my hand in front of me—that's how dark it was. A perfect spot, and he'd already told me that two more boats would be delivering.

"So I just waited. I found a gun under the driver's side seat and decided to put it in my pocket. Couldn't hurt, right? When Jack returned, I was slapping my face so hard trying to kill mosquitoes that he said I was like a frigging windmill. He suggested we go to a place on top of the boulders where the wind would keep away the mosquitoes.

"Once there, it was actually better, and I stopped slapping. We had a drink of bourbon from his flask and just watched the lights go back and forth down on the beach."

Vince turned to Frank. "You may not want to hear this part, big brother. All of a sudden, Jack pulled a gun on me and said, 'You son-of-a-bitching traitor.' I turned away from the beach and found him standing about six feet away from me with his handgun pointed directly at my head. Guess I'm lucky he didn't bump me right on the spot."

DeLuca clasped his dead cigar in his thick hands. "What did you do?"

"He had me wedged in on both sides. Those boulders. I couldn't run, I couldn't do nothing. Fortunately, he wanted to scream at me for a while." Vince smiled. "Another mistake.

"He said he knew I was fucking him around because that guy I shot and pushed off Adcock's Pier survived and went straight to Jack."

Vince became serious. "He fired his gun, but the adrenaline must've screwed up his aim because all if did was power-burn my arm.

"He ran to me and forced his gun into my mouth screaming 'eat it, you bastard.' I thought I was done for, but on the beach behind me—something happened. It must've been an explosion and a flare because I saw Jack's face all lit up in blinding white light. It caused enough of a pause in Jack's grip that I threw him off of me, grabbed my own gun, and shot him. He went down like a ton of lead. Head shot. Lucky shot. No fucking chance of recovery.

"Down on the beach, everything was chaos. A bunch of guys ran out from the dunes and boulders. Two phosphorus lights floated down on little parachutes. It was like daylight. More boats, with searchlights. Finally, I saw that the men running toward the beach and boats were wearing police uniforms. It was a raid. Everyone ran; some grabbed their guns and tried to shoot it out."

"I don't believe this." DeLuca rubbed his hands slowly down his fleshy face.

"I got into the truck and drove back to town. No headlights the entire way. Got to a nurse friend who did wonders. Then I got a change of clothes and went to my social engagement for the night. Remember, Frank?"

Frank could only nod. There was no going back now.

DeLuca rose and gave Vince a strong bear hug without touching Vince's injury. "I can't believe this! You don't even realize what this means." DeLuca circled the small room, rubbing his hands together and smiling. "This seals our partnership, boys. But we don't have time for a drink to celebrate."

He turned to Vince. "You need to get out of town. They'll find you and kill you. Piero, Jack's top man, is already out of jail and asking too many questions."

Frank began pacing himself. "We got to keep Vince safe."

DeLuca raised his penetrating gaze to Frank's face. "Vince needs to go to Cuba."

"Cuba?" both brothers chorused.

"Yes, Cuba. There you'll talk to one of our suppliers who is making noise about raising my prices for his product. You'll deliver the message that we're good for Jack's deliveries and that increased volume will mean we need a decrease in price."

Vince asked, "What's our leverage? Volume alone won't do it."

"Tell him that there's plenty booze coming out of Canada. If he doesn't like our deal, then we'll get all our booze from Canada, or even the Bahamas."

Vince thought for a moment, scratched his head, and looked at DeLuca. "I've got business to tend to: the shop, my job, my girl. You know—things."

DeLuca sat and picked up his cigar. Then he looked down at its unlit end and placed it in the ashtray. "Word will be getting out that we met at Marie's and that you came here today. Nobody will tell the cops, but they'll talk among themselves. Piero will be salivating for revenge. He'll also be looking to take over or partner with me or someone else from the outside. There's also Rick, Jack's other top guy, who telephoned me today and asked for a meeting. It's getting crazy fast.

"It's not helped by the Adcock pier fiasco you pulled, because that guy has been throwing your names around also. Everyone has just thought you were too small-time to pull off a big hit like this and survive."

DeLuca rubbed his face and looked weary all of a sudden. "And if you don't go to Cuba, you may not survive."

Frank put his hand on Vince's good shoulder. "You need to go now, brother. I'll take care of everything for you. I'll figure out the right things to say."

Vince simply shrugged. Frank knew this meant acceptance. Grudging acceptance.

DeLuca made a few phone calls and found out the schedule of departures for the night's sailings to Cuba and beyond. A few terse sentences confirmed the man Vince would find in Cuba and the details of the business he would conduct.

Vince and Frank strode out the front door as DeLuca and Spoon saw them out. As the brothers turned to say goodbye, two shots rang out. Frank and Spoon fell. Vince jumped behind one of the porch's heavy pillars, and DeLuca disappeared into the house.

Across the wide lawn, a lone man sprinted to a waiting Packard. He grabbed the door handle, and a shot rang out. Frank was dimly aware that the sound of the shot came from Vince's spot on the porch. More of DeLuca's boys ran from the side of the house and fired at the departing car.

Frank felt rather than saw Vince's strong hands turn him over. "Brother, you okay?"

"Yeah, it doesn't feel too bad. More like it just grazed me. Burns like hell."

Vince examined the wound and patted Frank on the back. "It's nothing much. You can go to that nurse friend of mine."

They heard sobbing behind them and turned to see DeLuca holding a bleeding Spoon in his arms. "We were together most of my life. Like brothers."

DeLuca raised his face to Vince. "Those bullets were for you. Somebody is watching us close."

A sob rose in Frank's throat. This was the first time he had been scared in a very, very long time. If the bullet had been twelve inches to the left, it'd be Frank with the open chest wound, not Spoon.

He swallowed the lump in his throat. "You must go before they try again," he told Vince.

Vince turned to the street and the wounded shooter on the ground that DeLuca's men held. Frank walked over as well.

"Hey, Vince," Frank said, "I recognize this guy. He's the one in the diner our first day—you remember?"

"This couldn't be better. I'll take care of him before I leave. Tell Benno to meet me at the duplex, Frank."

DeLuca told his men to keep the wounded shooter in his basement. "They may come after you too, Frank. I'll have a couple of my men stay with you for a while."

The two brothers drove away in silence. DeLuca's men had placed two worn suitcases in the trunk of the car. Each contained twenty-five thousand dollars. There wouldn't be any stopping point now—Frank knew this. One day he would own a house in this beautiful neighborhood; one day he would have huge oak trees whose branches swept gracefully across wide lawns. Maybe, one day he would even have a beautiful wide-eyed wife, whose portrait stared across a gilt frame, and who invited him into her arms nightly.

In the middle of the night—a few hours before Vince's departure—Vince, Benno, and one of DeLuca's men motored away from a private pier toward one of the huge piers of Zapata Island. On the floor of the boat under a tarp was the man who'd killed Spoon that afternoon—alive, bound and gagged.

At the pier, they removed the tarp. They had carefully planned to arrive at low tide. They fastened the gagged man to the piling so that when the tide came in he would gradually be covered with salty water. Small crabs and fishes would consume his corpse until someone found him.

The conscious man couldn't even struggle against them.

As the small boat puttered away, Vince turned to the guy, whose eyes pleaded eloquently above his gag. "You showed me Zapata hospitality my first day here. Now you get my kind."

CHAPTER SEVENTEEN

As Frank watched Vince's ship nose its way into the Gulf of Mexico, there was a sudden lump in the pit of his stomach. *Settle down, Frank. Your brother will be back soon. You can make it until then.*

"How were DeLuca's boys to work with?" Frank asked Benno as they drove away.

Benno answered. "Young guys—respectful. After I gave them the cash, they were even more respectful."

They pulled up to Frank's and left the car in the driveway. As Frank opened the door he heard the phone ringing and ran to grab it.

Uncle Mario's voice came loud and clear to his ears. "Frank? You listen to me, boy. Drive here right now. We need to talk. If you don't come immediately, you'll be dead. You understand?"

Frank swallowed. "I'll come right now."

Uncle Mario gave a few more particulars, then ended the conversation abruptly.

Frank turned to Benno and said slowly, "Uncle Mario

has word that remnants of Jimmy Jack's gang are going to kill me since they can't find Vince. I've got to drive to New Orleans."

Benno looked grave. "Don't worry, Boss. Things will go our way—we just got to be patient."

Frank left Zapata within hours. Two of DeLuca's men in a dark Buick followed his car. The drive to New Orleans was only a few hours, and Frank drove directly to Uncle Mario's waterfront office. His uncle greeted him at the door with a frown creasing his high forehead and a new cane at his side.

Mario held Frank at an arm's length. "You guys have really started something big. I knew you were ambitious, but Christ, man. You knocked off one of the top men on the Gulf Coast."

Frank didn't know what to say. In Zapata, everything had made perfect sense.

Uncle Mario's stern demeanor changed to a sly smile. "Good work, so far, but you have some business in Zapata to take care of before Vince can come back."

Frank's stomach dropped.

"And," his uncle continued, "I have the perfect person to help you." Uncle Mario gestured to a silent shape sitting in a darkened corner. "This is Sal Maneli Urso. We call him Sal."

A tall, bulky man rose from a chair and walked to him. His dark gray suit was perfectly pressed and creased, his white shirt almost glowing in the dim interior office. His huge jaws worked over a piece of gum. Steel-blue eyes shone with an intensity Frank had never seen.

Sal extended a huge hand toward Frank. "How you doing?" he said as they shook in a grip that almost crushed Frank's bones.

"Let's talk. All three of us." Uncle Mario pointed to a table. Outside, a boat plowed down the river, the salty smells of the riverfront rose and entered through the open windows.

"Sal is my best man," Mario said. "He taught Vince everything. We've been together thirty-five years. He was your age when he started to work for me."

Sal chewed his gum and adjusted his muscled bulk to fit in the chair.

"I have complete trust in him," Mario said. "Like a brother. He's going back to Zapata with you to watch your back."

Frank was speechless. Things were moving too quickly.

"You guys are my sons. My sons. You've replaced my real son. Sal will see to it that I don't lose you. Use Sal and his expertise. You need it."

Frank looked at Sal, still moving restlessly in the chair, crossing and uncrossing his legs, chomping his gum, but smiling as though he knew something no one else knew. "What do you think of all of this?" he asked Sal.

"Territory problems are my specialty," he said and almost laughed out loud. "Remember Wart De Lasso?"

"I remember," Frank murmured, thinking of his mother's hysterical reaction, the gaping coffin, and a dead man's hairy arm.

Sal moved closer to Frank, scrapping his chair across the floor. "Seems like you got a serious problem, but it's just starting. After Mr. Tabbaracci called me, I called some people. There are two guys we got to recruit or eliminate: Rick Lazaro and Piero Cucci—two of Jimmy Jack's boys from a long time back."

"I know them."

"They will kill you and never look back," Sal said. "They don't know me, and that's our ace in the hole."

Mario stood. "Okay, you guys. Work out your plan here before you drive back." He turned to Frank and hugged him once more. "I've not forgotten the funeral and what Vince did for me."

Mario shook hands with Frank, and then turned to Sal. "Frank and Vince will be bigger than me some day. Help them get the respect they need—they're already tough."

"Don't worry, Boss," Sal answered. "I will get the job done."

Mario turned and grabbed the cane that had so surprised Frank when he'd arrived. Frank watched his uncle walk to the door using his cane to propel him forward. How had Uncle Mario aged so much in such a short time?

As Mario left the room, Frank turned to Sal. "Vince is out of town for a while. Maybe we'll have all this resolved before he returns. What do you think?"

"You're the boss," Sal said, "but I can give you some things to think about. From what I know, Jimmy Jack's organization is in disarray. Piero and Rick are watching each other hard. They hate each other and have for a long time. Each wanted to be the top man under Jimmy Jack. It never happened. If one of them kills you, he'll whop the other and take control."

Frank could almost feel the warmth from a bullet in the middle of his back.

"Lucky for us they hate each other so much," Sal said. "Also lucky for us they're so suspicious of each other. It'll be simple to use that to defeat them. I'll slip into Zapata and then contact you. Stay out of sight—inside. Use the two men DeLuca gave you."

Frank and Sal took notes and drank several pots of coffee in the next two hours as they finalized their plans. Finally, they shook hands, and Frank left to drive home with the dark Buick, still a silent but welcome escort.

As Frank's car idled in a long line waiting to drive onto the ferry, it suddenly hit him. *That's it. What if we can get both Piero and Rick to a nighttime meeting on the ferry? That's it!* DeLuca's men could control the ferry by paying off the employees. The meeting would be on the higher deck. Both those bozos would come—they would be afraid not to come and join forces.

On the appointed night, Piero arrived at 1:00 a.m. sharp, as agreed. No other cars were on this early-morning ferry ride. Piero parked and walked upstairs to Frank.

"Sit down, my friend." Frank gestured to one of the humid seats in the second-deck interior cabins. "Let me pour you a Chivas."

Piero rubbed the palms of his hands down his pants legs and perched on the edge of the seat. "I need one, partner."

Frank and Piero clinked glasses and toasted as the ice knocked against the heavy glass tumblers.

"What you got in mind?" Piero asked.

"Cuba."

"Be specific."

Frank set his glass on the table. "You'd be perfect to run operations in Cuba."

"Hotter than hell, ain't it?"

Where the hell was Rick? Frank picked up his glass to keep his hands from shaking. "But the lovely señoritas more than make up for it—you'll see."

Piero inserted one pale finger into his glass and swirled the ice. He shifted on the seat and reached inside his jacket.

Frank winced. He waited for the blue gleam of a revolver to emerge.

"You always so jumpy, Mr. Carlucci?"

Piero extracted a cigarette from a package of Lucky Strikes.

The door burst open, and Sal shoved a stumbling Rick inside.

"What! What's going on?" Piero dropped his glass and stood with palms out in front of him.

"This guy's got a gun in my ribs," yelled Rick. "You did this, you bastard!"

Frank's fingers closed around the .38 in his right jacket pocket, but before he could pull it out, Sal put two slugs into the chest of each of the men.

"C'mon, Frank," he grunted. "Help me lift these guys and carry them down the stairs. We don't have all night."

Frank grabbed thick arms still warm inside suit jackets, while Sal tugged at the feet and knees. Together they hoisted the bodies onto the dolly Sal had placed at the foot of the second-deck stairs. The bodies were thrown into the Gulf.

"You're sure the bodies won't rise?" Frank asked as Sal heaved the dolly overboard also.

Sal smiled. "Like I said before, my specialty is making people disappear. I know the Gulf very well, and I know its sharks extremely well. Nobody will even find skeletons."

The ferry horn blew to signal its approach to land. Frank's legs wanted to give out under him, and the Scotch tasted bitter in his mouth. Brownish tongues of kelp reached through the salty water as the ferry slowed.

Sal clapped Frank on the back and turned back toward the ocean. A small smile creased his smooth jaws as he worked his chewing gum. "People will just wonder where they went. No one will ever figure it out."

CHAPTER EIGHTEEN

Sal stayed with Frank to provide instruction and additional security. Frank's days slipped into new routines as he quit his barber's job and stayed up all night with Sal and Benno to receive the liquor shipments from Cuba. Everything had an eerie feeling of unreality as Frank advanced deeper into the business, often transporting huge amounts of cash for quick payments and bribes, and always carrying at least two holstered firearms. Somehow he couldn't bring himself to hire another full-time bodyguard to be with him when Sal slept.

One early morning Frank felt himself drawn to Lisa's small bungalow. After all, he had promised to check on her for Vince. It had taken him quite a while to fulfill that promise, though. Frank had been fighting his deep desire for her. Finally, he thought he had it under control. They could be friends—no romance.

He parked in front of the wooden bungalow and ran up the wide cement stairs. He'd explain that he was running between meetings and could only talk a minute.

He knocked on the painted doorjamb. Lisa appeared behind the screen door. Her mouth dropped open, and she pulled her robe closer. Was she trembling?

"Hi, Lisa. How you been?"

A soft flush of pink climbed up her face.

"Can I come in, Lisa? It's so great to see you." Frank stepped inside the door and gave her a quick hug and a peck on the cheek. He was surprised to feel her stiff body, so different from what he remembered.

She backed up from his hug, but let him continue into the small living room. "I have something important to tell you, Frank."

"Gosh, I have a lot to tell you too. It's been a wild ride. I want to tell you all about it. I had—"

"You didn't hear me. This will change your life."

Frank heard the pleading underneath her hard-edged voice and stopped talking. He rubbed his eyes and tried to focus on what he had to do next.

"Change my life? My life has changed ten times over since I last saw you, Lisa. Something is always changing our lives, for God's sake." A long night on the beach counting wooden cases and squinting at lights through the fog while slapping mosquitoes had tired him.

"It's too big to talk about when you're exhausted." Tears spilled down her cheeks. "Leave. Just leave, Frank."

"Listen, I've been up all night, and I'm not in the mood to talk about something serious."

Frank stopped talking and looked at her again. Her clear blue eyes were cold.

"Lisa, I'm not going to leave until you promise we'll talk later. Besides, I want to invite you, Mitcheletti, and Benno to eat tonight. We can all come here and be safe and together—right? We're all under a lot of stress. We need some home cooking and a place where we're not going to get shot in the back. What do you think? Would you do that for us?"

"Only if you promise we can talk after. If you

promise, then I'll make sure you have a wonderful evening—just as if Vince were here."

Frank was too exhausted to argue. He just nodded as she pushed him gently out the door onto the porch. Tonight would be better. He'd sleep all day and be able to think clearly tonight.

Part of him wanted to pound on the door and yell, "It's not fair," but another part of him told him to go home, sleep as much as he could, then show up later with some nice hootch. Maybe some flowers too.

Frank and Benno arrived at Lisa's door at the same time—eight on the dot. Frank had dressed in new slacks and slapped cologne across his chest and shoulders. His shirt was starched and clean—he knew he looked sharp.

"Look what I got here, Boss," Benno said with a flourish of a bottle of Jack Daniel's.

"Even I like Mr. Jack sometimes." Frank thought that it had been a long, long time since he had laughed.

Lisa opened the door. She stood in front of the lamplit backdrop of rooms in a light-colored dress that displayed all her gorgeous curves underneath heavy fabric. Not for the first time Frank felt a sharp stab of envy toward Vince.

"Hey, guys, come in. Oh, boy, my favorite." Lisa took the gift bottle from Benno and gave him a quick hug and kiss. "Mr. Mitcheletti will be here soon. He's bringing a chocolate cake."

"Good," Benno said. "He needs to hear all the conversation tonight. I got news from Vince in Cuba."

Frank and Lisa looked at each other quickly. Frank's stomach dropped. Couldn't he have one single evening away from business? Away from the burning realization that Lisa belonged to his brother?

Benno took the bottle into the kitchen to fix highballs.

Frank put one arm around Lisa's waist, then held her

at arm's length. He looked at her face and smiled. He longed to envelop her in his arms and kiss the length of her pale neck. The last time they'd made love, she had cried. This time he would make sure she didn't cry. This time would be different.

"What was that earlier today about something important for us to talk about?" Frank said. "Surely, there's nothing more important than us being here right now."

"It'll just have to wait. I'll need your full attention, Frank." Her voice broke, and he thought he saw her fighting back tears. She broke away from his grasp and turned her back to him while walking to a front window.

Benno entered with the drinks in colorful peanut-butter glasses. They all took one, even Frank, and raised them in a toast. Benno said, "Here's to you, Vince. We miss you, old man."

Next they toasted the new partnership with DeLuca. Each raising of the glasses contained more talk of the wonderful future of wealth, power, and excitement they all anticipated.

Frank turned to Lisa. "Hey, I was almost knocked down by the fantastic aroma when we opened the door. Reminds me of my mama back home."

Lisa dimpled prettily. "Oh, Frank, I'm so nervous. Italian food for Italians, and I'm not even Italian. I want it to be special. The recipe is from Mama Siro."

"Well, it smells fabulous."

Frank looked at the dining table set for four. White tablecloth, basic white plates, plain stainless flatware. How much he wished he could buy crystal and silver for her. Hand-painted china from Europe with tiny red rosebuds. She deserved beautiful things.

The doorbell rang, and Mitcheletti was ushered in. He had beautiful red roses, two bottles of Chianti, and a white box that Mitch said held the best chocolate cake on the island.

"What do I smell?" Mitch asked. "Man, my mama

must be here. Come down straight from heaven." He pretended to look around the room. "Where are you, Mama? I miss you!"

"Bless your soul," he said as he grabbed Lisa into a bear hug, planted a loud kiss on her cheek, and whispered, "Thanks for having me. I haven't been to a friend's house for dinner in years."

Benno fixed another drink for everyone. "Easy, everyone. These are all doubles," he said.

Seated on the dark brown upholstered couch and chairs, they all drank, laughed, and chatted. Frank kept looking at Lisa, but she was careful not to make direct eye contact with him.

Finally, when everyone was at the point of slurring their words and trying to talk over each other to tell the funniest story, Lisa said, "Let's go eat while we can still stagger there. We have the wine to go yet. I could serve hillbilly food tonight and call it Italian, and y'all wouldn't notice."

Benno and Mitch took their places at the table. Frank opened the wine and poured for everyone. Lisa brought out the steaming pasta, meatballs, and vegetables.

Before she sat down, she glanced at everyone. "Let me pray. My dear God, bless my dearest friends and protect Vince on his journey. May you see fit to allow us to celebrate again like this—together—in the future. Bless us all as we go with you on each of our individual journeys in life. Bless this food, we ask."

Frank tried to figure out what she meant, but decided to brush if off. He raised a fork to his mouth. "The pasta is the best—cooked with lots of love." He smiled at Lisa, but she still wouldn't look at him.

Mitcheletti looked up toward the skies. "Forgive me, Mama, and let me burn in hell for saying this, but this is the best pasta I've ever had."

Frank paused in his eating. "You guys are my closest friends. Vince and I have big plans, and we need each of you to pull them off. What we have now are just a few gold coins falling out of the pot at the end of the rainbow. Before we finish, we're going to own the whole damn pot."

Frank stood and walked to the back of Mitcheletti's chair and slapped both his hands on Mitch's shoulders. "You are our senior member. You know we're walking on the edge. You don't need these risks at your age. But you keep supporting us in every way."

Mitch nodded. "I once had a dream of a life, but I never lived it. I'm sixty-eight years old, and I've never taken a risk. My wife and son left me because I had nothing. I want to live my life before I die."

Everyone clapped.

"That's how we all need to think," Frank said. "Mitch summed it up for all of us. The money and success is out there. Let's go get it. The bootlegging won't last forever. We need to think beyond it—maybe gambling."

"I'll drink to that," Benno said. While everyone toasted, Benno added, "How about casinos?"

"Well, it's all on the table," Frank said. "A few more years bringing in the booze, then on to bigger and better. We'll see how Mr. DeLuca plays into all of this."

After more discussion over cake, Mitch finally got up, staggered over, and kissed Lisa goodbye. Benno followed shortly as well. Frank stayed behind and, after closing the door, walked over, hugged Lisa, and held her close until her arms closed around him. His lips found hers, and he gave her the kiss he had wanted to give her all evening. "Now what's all this you need to tell me?"

The sobs shook her body uncontrollably before she whispered, "Oh, Frank, all these wonderful plans may fall through. I am so dreadfully sorry." She ran into the bedroom.

Frank stared at where she'd been, too drunk to think of questions or to follow. He staggered a few steps to the couch and passed out.

CHAPTER NINETEEN

Havana, Cuba

Vince had enjoyed his peaceful cruise to Havana—safe from Jimmy Jack's boys. As the ship arrived, Vince leaned on the ship's railing, looking over the busy Havana harbor at sunrise. Rusting warehouses lined the waterside. Dozens of overall-clad workers scurried along the waterfront driving tractors, pushing carts, and pulling huge ropes. Behind the ship, porpoises broke the slick surface of the water as white pelicans dove, scooping up bills full of small fish and shrimp stirred up by the ship's massive propeller. A Cuban band played as the ship was secured.

The early morning was quickly becoming warm, and Vince threw his linen jacket over his shoulder and chewed on a cigar. As he disembarked, a young man approached him. "You are Señor Vince?"

"Yeah," Vince answered. "What about you?"

"My name is Ricardo, señor, but please call me Rick. I pick you up and take you to hotel. This here is for you." He handed Vince a large white envelope.

Vince reached for the envelope while shifting his jacket to the other arm, but dropped the envelope and bent quickly to pick it up from the dusty street. A shot rang out just as he bent over, striking a steel barrel behind him. He dove to the ground and crawled behind the steel drum as he drew his own gun. Two men ran through the crowd. Vince raced after their fleeing backs, and Rick followed with his own gun drawn. The two men darted into narrow back alleys and disappeared.

Vince stopped, panting and red-faced, unwilling to expose himself to a possible ambush. He and Rick returned to where Vince had dropped the white envelope. He picked it up, as well as his now-dusty jacket. They crossed a busy street to a clean, older-model black Ford. They jumped in without a word—Vince in the back and Rick in the driver's seat.

"What the hell was that all about?" Vince asked.

Rick's white shirt was drenched in sweat, and his hands clasped the steering wheel tightly. "It is not for me to tell you, señor. I am sure that Señor Carlos will tell you what you need to know."

Vince placed his gun barrel against the back of Rick's head. "I'll choose my own hotel. Give me his address and phone number."

Rick took a card out of his front shirt pocket and handed it to Vince. Handwritten numbers were penciled in.

"Get me to a taxi now, goddammit."

Rick drove to a corner with six cabs lined up against the curb.

"You tell your boss that I'll contact him when I'm damn good and ready." Vince slammed the car door.

As Rick sped away, Vince jumped into the third cab. "You speak English?" he asked.

"Poco, poco, señor."

"Take me to a hotel. Hurry up!"

A sly look came over the cabbie's face. "Sí, señor. A

good hotel with very beautiful señoritas."

Vince watched the streets behind his cab with his gun drawn. After winding through traffic on the main roads, and chickens and children on the back streets, they arrived at an old stucco hotel with chipped yellow paint on the exterior. A young girl in a skintight red skirt and an even tighter black lace top sat outside.

Vince turned around after paying the cabbie; the girl was beside him, showing off her breasts to full advantage. She smiled at Vince and said in a breathy voice, "Señor, my name, Violette."

Vince didn't even respond. He turned and entered the rundown hotel. A clerk, looking almost as rundown as the old hotel, looked up at Vince with a bored look.

"I want a room with a telephone. Comprendo? I'm in a hurry."

The clerk didn't appear to know the meaning of "hurry."

"Move, goddammit. I need a room."

The clerk raised his eyebrows and murmured, "Most of our guests are in a hurry, señor."

"Yeah, well, then you should be in practice."

"No phones in rooms." He pointed to a phone booth in the street. "Only in front."

"Then just give me a room. I want a street view. You got that?"

The clerk passed Vince a key and directed him to a second-floor room.

"You want company, señor?"

"Hell, no."

"Girl part of room price."

"For Christ's sake, how much am I paying for this room?"

"For you, señor, only fifty US dollars per night."

"I'll give you twenty dollars. No damn more."

"Very well, señor. No girl. Pay now."

Vince put the money on the counter and walked to his

room down dim hallways of intricately colored tiles. His footsteps echoed loudly, and he thought how hard it would be for someone to sneak up on him.

The interior of the room was less than basic, but good enough. As he stretched across the bed he remembered that DeLuca had told him that word would get to Cuba that he was coming. Someone here was unhappy Jimmy Jack got murdered. But who? Vince decided to wait until dark to phone Frank.

A car honking outside his window woke up Vince in early evening. He jumped out of his bed and checked out the street. The lone streetlight farther down barely illuminated the street.

Vince walked to the sink in one corner of the bedroom and threw water on his face, drying it with the thin towel. Now was a good time to call Frank.

Vince paid a different clerk to make the long-distance call for him outside.

"Man, things are happening down here," Vince said when Frank answered. "I need some backup and quick."

"I know all about it," Frank said. "Carlos called DeLuca. Carlos thinks the shooter works for his brother, Javier, who used to do business with Jimmy Jack. Now with Jimmy Jack dead, Javier has no one to sell to. Carlos and Javier have been in some kind of war for the business."

"I'm having to hide the fuck out. I have no idea who to trust."

"Get to Carlos. Short guy, pencil-thin moustache. One ear. His code word is 'Jean Lafitte.'"

"Okay, but send Benno. I need someone to watch my back."

"I'll get him on a boat tonight. He'll be there soon."

"Tell him to get a room at the Hotel Sevilla. I'll be in touch with him there."

"Be careful, little brother," Frank said. "I've got things covered here."

Vince hung up. The street remained relatively

deserted, but the growing darkness brought out people who lived in the neighborhood. Shabby, barefooted men strolled while women sat outside small houses nursing babies. Garbage had been thrown in the street, and chickens pecked at it while a pig or two rooted through the piles.

Vince walked back to the hotel's lobby and asked for assistance making another call—this time to the penciled digits on the small white card that Rick had given him.

A deep male voice answered, "Bueno."

"Who is this?"

"It is Carlos, my friend. Who are you?"

"Vince Carlucci here. Do you know someone has been using me for target practice?"

"Please accept my apology, Señor Carlucci. That was regrettable. I was most distressed that our meeting today was postponed."

Vince bit his tongue to keep from saying what he really wanted to say as the smooth voice continued its honeyed words.

"May I send my driver Rick to pick you up in the morning, Señor Carlucci?"

"No, send him right now. I'll wait thirty minutes at the address I give you, and if he doesn't show up in a car alone, then I'm moving to a different location."

"Well, Señor Carlucci, you give me no choice, do you? Where is your location?"

"Lady Bird Hotel."

Vince walked upstairs to retrieve his jacket and the envelope, which he folded and tucked in the small of his back. The last thing he needed now was reading material.

As was his custom, he checked his spare gun in the ankle holster and the gun he carried in his pants pocket. After verifying that they both were loaded, he left the room.

Down the block, he sat in a bench partially obscured by banana leaves and waited. Exactly twenty-two minutes later, the same black Ford drove up to the front of the hotel.

The clerk walked to Rick and handed him the note Vince had left with a hefty tip. Vince waited as Rick drove off, tires squealing. Five minutes later Vince met him at the corner of a small square several blocks away. He opened the back door and slid in, his drawn gun visible to Rick. "Let's go see Carlos."

They raced through the crowded, dusty streets of Havana. In another very different neighborhood, men in tuxes and women in long gowns laughed as they got out of polished cars and walked into elegant hotels and restaurants. Massive, well-lit billboards in English advertised liquor, girls, and slot machines.

Rick pulled into a secluded driveway under a porte cochere and stopped in front of a gold-colored glass door. Ten thousand lights lit the front of the large building, but this driveway was darker, and Vince wondered what the darkness might hide. A doorman in a long, green topcoat with matching hat and white gloves opened the back door for Vince.

A barrel-chested, short man with a thin moustache and only one ear grabbed Vince's hand. "Welcome, welcome, at last. Señor Carlucci, my friend, you are here at long last."

Before Vince could reply, a car nearby backfired, and everyone twisted around. "Holy crap... I feel like I'm in a war zone."

"Please come inside. You have a meeting with Jean Lafitte tonight."

"What are all those lights on the front of this building?" Vince asked.

"You will see, my friend. Once we go inside, you will see. Hundreds of people come here every night to my beautiful Casino de Cuba. They gamble. They make me rich. Those lights are to make them happy."

"Looks like a glorified whorehouse."

Carlos responded with a beatific smile. "My casino makes people happy. You and I, my friend, will meet in a private room upstairs, talk some business, eat our famous fish caught just hours ago. We will relax."

"The hell I hope so. I haven't relaxed since I got here."

They walked through room after room, finally entering the largest room Vince had ever seen. There were hundreds of slots. Carlos guided Vince through the jostling crowd to an elevator flanked by guards. The elevator rose to the top, depositing them in an executive's office filled with leather-covered chairs and couches.

Vince flopped into a chair. "That racket down there was making my ears hurt."

Carlos remained standing and looked down at Vince. "That is the sound of money, Mr. Carlucci. You interested in money, señor?"

"Yeah, I'm interested in money, but I'm even more interested in my own hide. They nearly knocked me off before I left the dock."

"Please, Mr. Carlucci. Remember that I'm on your side. You know that from Mr. DeLuca and from your own brother."

"You haven't told me what that shooting was all about."

"We want to do business with you, señor."

"Who was shooting at me?"

"I see you have a one-track mind, Mr. Carlucci." Carlos smiled, gesturing for Vince to join him at a heavy wooden table in the center of the room.

"The person who tried to kill you is my brother, Javier. He also supplies the product that I supply— premium-grade liquor, the best our part of the world has to offer. Javier, was, shall we say, 'in bed with' Jimmy Jack. He is understandably offended that Mr. Jack is no longer with us."

"Yeah, well, I'm offended that Javier is trying to put me in the same position as I put Jimmy Jack."

"Of course, I understand, Mr. Carlucci." Carlos

looked Vince in the eyes. A cold energy replaced the polite veneer. "Trust me, Mr. Carlucci. I have plans to eliminate my brother—today's incident proved to me that these plans will have to be, as we say, muy pronto."

Carlos gestured to one of his boys, who had stayed close to the elevator's doors. "Bring me a Chivas on the rocks, Luis. Will you join me, Mr. Carlucci?"

Vince felt a little more at home after seeing Carlos's harder side. In fact, the tension was draining out of his body. "Sure, I'll join you."

Vince leaned forward and placed his arms on the table. "Okay, let's talk business."

"There are two men in Havana who supply all the liquor to the southern U.S.," Carlos said. "My operation is the biggest, and Mr. DeLuca is my biggest customer. I want to keep it that way. The other supplier is Javier, and he supplied Jimmy Jack."

The drinks were delivered, and Carlos raised a toast. "To Jean Lafitte's business with the Señors Carlucci."

"I'll drink to that, but you can call me Vince."

Carlos inclined his head in a brief bow of agreement. "Yes, by all means, Vince. And you, of course, may call me Carlos."

After a few swigs of the fiery Scotch, Vince continued with his questions. "So, how often do you currently deliver to DeLuca? And how often could you deliver if we doubled the inventory we need?"

As both men lapsed into a detailed discussion of the practicalities, Vince's amazement grew. The shipments already encompassed millions of dollars with distribution to the Midwest through Chicago. It was midnight by the time the men finished talking, eating a dinner of red snapper, and consuming several more rounds of drinks.

"So do you think you can handle it?" Carlos asked.

"Handle it? That and much more. In fact, I could get used to this kind of life—good food, people waiting on me, the sound of money rolling in."

"I hear your brother, Frank, is a smooth character. A great front man is vitally important to handle the authorities. Do you think he would be interested in putting a casino in Zapata?"

Vince turned around from the large two-way mirror above the gambling floor that he had gotten up to inspect. He wasn't smiling. "Mr. Lafitte, one thing is important that you understand. Frank is not in charge. We both make all the decisions. Do I make myself clear?"

Carlos paused before replying. "Yes, of course," he murmured.

Vince turned back toward the mirror and the throngs of people below. "This is a great idea. It sure pays to know what's going on behind your back, doesn't it?"

Vince quit gazing at the happy crowd and looked at Carlos. "I'm going to think about all of this. We haven't talked money yet, and there may be other bidders."

"The people who are following you for me could just as easily kill you as protect you, Mr. Vince. I suggest you do not talk with Javier. I suggest that you trust me."

"I never limit my options. If your bid is right, then we'll do business with you. I guess it's all up to you, isn't it?"

Carlos appeared lost in thought. "Wait a minute. What do you really want, Señor Carlucci?"

"I want a good night's sleep, Mr. Lafitte. I'm a simple guy."

Carlos's thin moustache stretched across his taut lips. "I won't be riding back to the hotel with you, Mr. Carlucci. I will be solving a little problem."

Carlos motioned for his boys to call the elevator, then rose from the table to shake Vince's hand as he left.

Vince had the car leave him at a new hotel, Los Ambos Mundos, then retired to his room, bolted the door, and wedged a chair against it. He slept with a holstered gun across his chest.

Later the next day, at a secluded table in a fine

restaurant, Benno and Vince reconnected.

Benno's concern was written over his face. "What's going on, Boss?"

"Thank God you're here. I need you." Vince squeezed Benno's shoulder. "We've got two people who want our business or our lives. I want a deal from both of them. Then they can fight it out, and we'll make peace with whoever is left."

"Sounds like our kind of business." Benno leaned forward toward Vince.

"They are brothers, but they don't get along. I want to see who is the strongest." Vince rubbed his face. "It's a good thing Frank and I get along. It'd be hell to kill a brother."

CHAPTER TWENTY

In the next several days, as Frank and Vince planned by telephone, Benno contacted Javier, saying that he represented DeLuca and the Carluccis. Benno requested a meeting.

At first Javier was reluctant, but after a week of dilly-dallying he finally agreed to a short meeting at a busy restaurant. Benno revealed that Vince was talking to Carlos but that the business would go to the top bidder. At that point of the conversation, Javier paused and stroked his own thin moustache. "Why should I trust you?"

"Why should I trust you?" retorted Benno.

"I could have you killed at this table, señor."

"Yeah, that'd do you a lot of good in getting our business, wouldn't it?"

Javier's lip twisted into a broad smile. "So, you count on my lust for money, is that right, Mr. Benno?"

"We are counting on your desire to make millions of

dollars. Yes, this is true. And this is what we can guarantee."

Naturally, Javier bid extremely high. When Vince heard the deal, he rubbed his hands slowly. He was really playing with fire. Could he get out alive? Carlos's bid had the added advantage of a promise from his experience to bring casinos to Zapata after Prohibition ended—which it probably would one day. That would bring in much more profit than just running liquor.

Vince called Carlos, telling him to come to Vince's hotel that night at ten. An hour beforehand, Carlos's guards secured the street and hotel lobby, and at ten, precisely, a limousine arrived at Vince's hotel. Vince met Carlos in the lobby and ushered him up to his suite.

Vince began without formalities. "My partners and I are concerned about your ongoing feud with your brother. We don't understand why you haven't iced him already."

Carlos rubbed a sweaty forehead. "The hell with my brother. Even as little children, we battled. My mother always takes his side. We partnered up in the business for five years but split after he killed one of my best men and his wife."

"Why haven't you taken care of him? Sounds like the brotherly love left long ago."

"I've tried twice; he's tried once. We both have too much protection."

"We can't put all our business with you and have you go down. Then we will only have your brother as a potential supplier."

"Have Mr. DeLuca call Javier and demand he and I talk and work a deal," Carlos said. "Javier will do anything to get DeLuca's business. The meeting can be at my casino."

"Why would Javier come there?"

"He's desperate to keep me from getting both DeLuca's and Jimmy Jack's business. If I do that, he has nothing. But here's the deal, my mother will be at the meeting also."

"That's brilliant. Nothing would ever happen in front of your mother," Vince said. "Everyone will be patted down, no pieces."

"He can search the room before the meeting, and we can both have our men at the elevator pat down everyone before the meeting—even me and Javier."

"Sounds like a good plan."

The two men shook hands, and Carlos left with his boys, the black limo gliding smoothly into the tropical night.

That same night Benno told Javier, "Mr. DeLuca says he'll only deal with one of you. He said get it together or the deal leaves Cuba and goes to the Bahamas."

Javier got out of his comfortable leather chair, took a draw on his cigar, then walked to a window overlooking the city and thought for a long, silent moment. "I have to talk with my esteemed friend Mr. DeLuca myself before I decide. I will call you after I talk with him."

Hearing this news later, Vince grew some appreciation for Javier. "You think he suspects a trap?"

"Don't know, boss," replied Benno. "We done all we can for now."

"Yeah, too bad we can't find some friendly señoritas."

After days with no answer from Javier, Vince directed Benno to go pay a visit. "Tell him I'm tired of working on my frigging tan. Either he talks to Carlos and they work it out, or I leave Cuba."

When Benno approached Javier, he delivered the news as if it was a done deal.

"Carlos wants us at his casino tomorrow night at ten," Benno said. "You can have all your boys in the casino, but only two of us can go up to the office. Your mother will be there to supervise."

Javier smirked. "If that's what it takes. I'll face the scared dog in his office with Mama protecting him. Set it up."

Javier arrived at the casino the next night with much fanfare—a huge limousine, a voluptuous girl on one arm, and his mother on the other.

Javier, cigar in mouth, wove his way through the people to the elevator as he escorted the two women. They were all searched for weapons before they got into the elevator. His mother got into the elevator first. Javier waved to the crowd and his girlfriend as the door closed. "You're a good man for setting it up," he told Benno.

As soon as the elevator door opened at the top floor, Benno and Luis grabbed Javier from behind, forcing his arm up to the back of his neck, to the point of almost breaking. They ran straight ahead, pushing Javier ahead of them.

He screamed as he was pushed faster and faster across the room toward the two-way mirror. "You're killing me, you no-good sons of a bitch."

His mama stepped off the elevator, falling to her knees screaming and crossing herself.

The three men sped up as they neared the mirror. With a massive heave, Benno and Luis pushed Javier through the window. He screamed and clawed the air as he fell into the floor of slot machines and people below. Glass shards rained down with him as people ran to get out of the way.

A stunned silence overtook the room. His sightless eyes stared upward. People continued to stampede toward the exits, some falling over others as they panicked. Crowds jammed the doors. House security guards stayed out of their way.

Within a few minutes, uniformed medics removed Javier's body from the room on a stretcher.

"My baby, my baby. What have you done?" Carlos's mama screamed as she ran to him and beat his broad chest with her fists.

"Get her out of here," Vince yelled.

Carlos turned to Vince. "Did you see him jump through that mirror? What came over the fool? My God, was he that drunk?"

Carlos and Vince smiled and brushed themselves off before getting into the elevator.

"How did the ambulance get here so fast?" Vince asked.

Carlos smiled again. "That's our ambulance. It goes to only one place—a secluded beach of perfect darkness. People will wait a long time for Javier at the emergency room downtown."

As the elevator doors opened on the first floor, they were greeted by Javier's sobbing girlfriend. She pointed an accusing finger in Carlos's face, yelling words in Spanish that Vince could only guess at. Carlos slapped her hard across the face. She stumbled in her high heels and fell against the plants in the lobby.

"You want her for the night?" he asked Vince. "A little unexpected reward for my American partner."

The long-legged beauty climbed out of the foliage and adjusted her ample cleavage, which tumbled out of her skintight dress. Mascara streamed down her face, but her exotic beauty was unmarred.

"I got other plans, Carlos," Vince lied.

Carlos chuckled. "Oh, my new Americano friend. You don't yet understand how we do business here, do you?" Carlos grabbed the girl by her arm and thrust her into the arms of one of his muscle men, issuing curt orders. "Don't worry. Mr. Americano Vince, I'll keep her busy for the night."

CHAPTER TWENTY-ONE

Zapata Island, Mississippi

Frank awoke stiff and uncomfortable on Lisa's couch. The sun blasted into his eyes.

Lisa walked into the room, massaging her forehead. "What time is it anyway? I've got the world's worse headache!"

"What were you talking about last night, Lisa? Something about changing our lives?"

Her eyes teared up. She sat on another chair and pulled her robe tighter.

"I'm going to have your baby," she said as she began to weep.

"You got to be kidding!"

She lifted her eyes accusingly to his face and choked out a few words. "Would I kid you about something like this?"

Frank abruptly got up. "That's all the hell I need to worry about now. For Christ's sake, how the hell could you let that happen?"

Lisa stopped crying almost as abruptly as she had begun. "I didn't even want to make love with you. It was all your idea. Remember?"

Frank paced back and forth in the small living room. "Are you sure it's my kid?"

Lisa's face turned white. She stood up. "Listen, Mr. Frank Carlucci. I had the biggest crush on you. I thought at least we might have made something beautiful from our love—"

"I never told you I loved you."

She faced him with a stiff body and eyes blazing. For what seemed like an eternity to Frank, she simply stared in his eyes. Then she raised one hand to cover her eyes. She swayed as if to fall, and he reached to steady her.

"Get your fucking hands off of me," she yelled. She uncovered her eyes and walked away from him. Her shoulders sagged, and she began crying again. She turned to face him. "Oh, Frank, this isn't how it's supposed to be. We're destroying each other.

"You don't know about your brother, do you? He…he…doesn't like…he doesn't do intercourse. It can't be anyone's baby other than yours."

Frank's head was spinning. His stomach rose up with bile. This could destroy everything. He placed one hand on his aching head and tried to think. "Listen, Lisa, I've come too far to ever go back. I've made decisions that can't be undone now."

"What are you really saying, Frank?"

"Look, I don't know what to do. Sure, I wanted to be with you from the first moment I set eyes on you. You make me feel the way no other girl has made me feel. You're beautiful; you're sweet. But you and I never planned anything—you're Vince's girl. That's it."

Lisa's face took on a tinge of sadness—that same sadness that Frank had noticed in her before. "I didn't have anywhere else to go, Frank. I had to accept Vince's offer. I can't go back home—"

"I can't stop everything I'm doing because you're pregnant."

"Frank, I'm telling you for the last time that this isn't 'my baby'—it's 'our baby.'"

"Lisa, you don't understand. I grew up with nothing. Yards and yards of nothing. Spit was too expensive to buy in my family. All I ever heard at school, on the street, everywhere, was how dirty and how stupid we were because we were wops. I'm not quitting until I have expensive cars, fine silk suits, and engraved crystal—"

"You think you have a sob story? Well, I can top it. I left rural Georgia because I might have killed my own father in a stupid argument that he started. The son of a bitch. I'll never go back."

Each of them assumed an uneasy silence. Finally, Frank spoke up. "If Vince finds out, we're dead."

Lisa nodded and spoke quietly. "We both have betrayed him. You, as his brother and business partner. Me, as his girl." She winced as she spoke. "I guess we're quite a pair, huh?"

Frank straightened his clothes, tucking in his shirt, running fingers through his hair.

"We've got a little bit of time to think this out while Vince is in Cuba. There's got to be a solution."

"I thought I might love you, Frank. You're so different than Vince. He's all blustery and loud; you're calm and elegant. But I can tell you don't love me."

Frank looked at her. She was scarier when she was calm, harder to predict. "If you need to stay with Vince, that's okay by me. We just need to make sure Vince never finds out about us and the baby."

Lisa shook her head. "Oh, Frank, I thought you were a different kind of guy. At least Vince loves me—in his own way. He tells me so all the time. He'll know it's not his."

"I got to go now, Lisa. I need to think."

She looked at Frank and wiped her still damp face

with her forearm. "I'm going to marry Vince. I'll give up the baby."

Frank felt numb—frozen in place.

"You drove me to this. You and your love of money. Go wallow in it. I hope it makes you happy."

She began sobbing heavily. Frank walked over to her and tried to embrace her.

She pushed him away. "Shut the front door when you leave."

Frank was tired, defeated. Usually, he could talk himself out of any situation. But this time the words didn't come. He walked to the front door, his soles echoing harshly on the wood floors of the small bungalow. He opened the front door and walked slowly down the sidewalk to his car.

Despite the crazy stress of building an empire of rackets, in quiet moments, late at night or sometimes at red stoplights in broad daylight, Lisa's words haunted Frank. *I didn't even want to make love with you. It was all your idea.* She was right—he'd known it at the time. But it hadn't seemed that important. Now, look at everything it had caused. Look at what he'd done to the one girl he'd ever met who was the right kind of special. *It was all your idea.*

One night Frank cradled the phone to his ear as it rang in Lisa's house for the fifth time. Frustrated, he sighed and shifted to hang it up.

Then Lisa answered. "Hello?"

"Lisa, it's me. How are you doing?"

"Oh, Frank. It was terrible that other morning, wasn't it?"

"Well… it didn't meet my standards for a good time."

"I was emotional. Too emotional. I didn't want to fight with you."

"I got carried away the other morning too. Listen, let's

meet tomorrow morning. To talk. Do you know the Claw—way down on East Beach? If we go at six-thirty, no one will be there because the fishermen will have already left."

As a faint sunrise edged over the horizon and the Gulf waters were painted grayish-pink with horizontal streaks of small, white-capped waves rushing to shore, Frank drove to East Beach. Just as he remembered, the little restaurant was indeed isolated, built on a pier over the water. Weathered wood on the front had a colorful, peeling sign painted with "Claw."

Frank had deliberately worn a pale blue, open-necked shirt under his jacket. Hadn't a lot of women said they liked to see him in blue? As he parked, his nose picked up the fishy smell of Zapata's cool breeze. Lisa's car pulled up at the same time. As she got out a surge of unanticipated joy passed through him. Her long legs floated under a dark brown skirt. Frank walked over, giving her a light squeeze and a peck on the cheek. They grabbed hands as they walked to the front door.

"Let's sit over in that corner." Frank pointed to an isolated table. It hadn't escaped him that she had checked her hair and lipstick in the rearview mirror before getting out of her car.

"Sounds good to me."

They sat at a heavy wooden table that had been painted over many times.

"What a cute place." Lisa looked around. "I love the solitude. This is the most picturesque place I've been to in Zapata. Sorry we couldn't be here at a different time."

"I agree." He pulled his chair closer to the table and cupped her small hands in his. "What are we going to do?"

"I've given this lots of thought, but the tears are gone now." She smiled briefly at Frank. "I was heading down a path, and I thought you were with me." She took a deep breath. "You weren't even close. Now I understand."

"Lisa, that's a good way to put it. I'm fond of you—more than fond, in fact. But the timing is all wrong. Let's talk about you and me, where we are in life, and where we hope to go. Then we'll discuss the baby, okay?"

"I think I just built up things in my mind after that first night on the swing."

An overweight waitress in a white uniform, a toothpick in her mouth, ambled to their table with two glasses of iced water. "What can I get you guys?"

"Coffee for me," Lisa said, smiling. Frank ordered coffee and rye toast, dry.

Lisa took a big gulp of water. "I need to tell you something, Frank. Maybe, it will make you understand better." She gazed into Frank's eyes and reached for his hands across the tabletop. "My father was educated but a mean, hopeless drunk. We were driving to the grocery store late one evening—I was only nine years old—and my mother asked him to slow down. He slugged her so hard that she hit her head on the side of the car and started bleeding. With all that commotion—me crying, him yelling, my mother screaming and bleeding—he lost control of the car, and it rolled, hitting an oncoming car with an elderly couple. My mother was horribly disfigured. For the rest of her life, she could only open her right eyelid with her hand."

"My God, how horrible." Frank squeezed her hands.

Tears spilled down her cheeks. She cleared her throat and wiped her eyes with the napkin. "He got off in court, but he lost his job. From then on, we were poor. His drinking only got worse. My only sister, Julie, left without saying goodbye right after Mom got home from the hospital. She was only seventeen years old, Frank. You see why I have no one."

"Have you looked for your sister?"

"No, I never saw her again." She took a sip of her

cooling coffee. "She's all I had, beside my mom. And after her injury, I had to take care of Mom.

"My father called to me one afternoon when I was about eighteen and told me to bring him the newspaper from outside. I answered 'Okay, Dad, in a moment.' He yelled at me to do it now. I knew right away he must be drunk out of his mind, so I rushed outside to get the paper. When I handed it to him, he grabbed my hand and yanked me to the floor. I started screaming for him to let me go. He hit me again and again, slapping at me, then started kicking me—I curled into a ball. I thought I was going to die right there. I grabbed for anything to help me, and my hand found a marble bookend on a side table. I hit him as hard as I could, not even seeing what I was aiming for.

"He fell. I yelled for Mom. She held me and tried to console me. I told her I needed to run, that I was going out the door with her or without her. I begged her to come with me. She gave me the small bills and change out of her purse. I packed just a few things, and walked to the Greyhound station. I could only buy a one-way ticket to Zapata Island. The first night at Marie's I met you and Vince. I left there right after you and I talked on the swing. It wasn't the place for me."

Frank waited for the emotions in her face to quiet down. "I'm so sorry all that happened to you, Lisa. You didn't deserve any of it."

She raised her blue eyes to Frank's face. "Can you understand me better now? Does any of this make a difference to us?"

"My dad was a worthless drunk too. I still find myself constantly thinking 'I'll never be a loser like you, Dad. Never be a sloppy drunk. People will respect me, Dad.'"

He squeezed Lisa's hands. "We will get through this. I don't know how, but we will."

She had tears rolling down her cheeks and didn't speak. But her hands clutched his with cold fingers that felt like ice.

"I've thought about the baby every minute since you left the house days ago." She squared her shoulders and looked out the large windows toward the ocean. "I have an aunt and uncle in Oklahoma. They're kind people. They pleaded with me and my sister to stay with them a couple of times when our family drove through on vacations. They must've sensed how things were in our household. They said they'd always be there for me."

Frank heard the quiet resolution in her voice. "I can go there and have the baby. Then it can stay with them—they're childless and have always wanted a tyke."

"Are you comfortable with this decision? You don't have to do this for my sake."

Lisa smiled faintly. "I'm not doing it for you. I'm doing it for the baby, for Vince, and for myself. Maybe, one day you and I will be able to look back and see that it was the right decision for us too."

"You've come up with a good solution, Lisa."

She looked at Frank and warmed her hands on the refilled coffee cup. "Who knows? Maybe one day I'll be able to bring my baby home."

After finishing their coffee, they walked to their cars. Frank escorted Lisa to hers. The early morning mist had burned off and seagulls screeched overhead. When Frank hugged her goodbye, she held him a moment or two longer. He responded with an even tighter hug. "Please be careful, Lisa," he whispered. "I couldn't bear it if something bad happened to you."

"Don't worry about me." She rested her head on his shoulder for a few seconds. "Worry about Vince. He'll go crazy if he ever finds out."

CHAPTER TWENTY-TWO

Frank reluctantly shut Lisa's car door for her. He had the sudden urge to spend more time with her. Just to watch her long legs under the wide skirt as she walked at his side would be wonderful.

"Hey, Lisa, you want to go downtown with me? I have some business at the bank, but after that I could take you to see our new offices."

Lisa smiled. "I'd love to, but I have to meet Marie."

"I thought you said you were finished with all that."

Her smiled faded. "Oh, Frank. You don't know me at all, do you?"

"Well, how could I? I haven't hardly seen you in months."

At that, she laughed and smiled up at him again. "Boy, do I have a surprise for you!" Seeing his frown, she reassured him quickly. "This is a good surprise. Follow my car, and I'll show you."

He rushed to start the ignition. Her car was already driving away.

Damn. She always had some kind of surprise for him.

They parked at the curb in front of the large white Victorian house that had been Marie's. Frank stepped out to Lisa's car and opened her door. She pointed to a new sign that said "The Top Hat."

"Does Marie run the new place?" he asked.

"Marie runs it, but I own it."

"What?"

"You heard me. I own this club now."

"I thought you said you were finished with the business."

"Oh, Frank, you're so hopeless. This is a totally legit club—for dancing. The only illegal stuff is the alcohol. Vince gave me the money."

"No more hanky-panky upstairs?"

"Just the opposite, in fact. I set it up to help girls get out of the business. They work here at night, then go to classes during the day. You know, typing, shorthand."

Lisa tried the front door and found it open. "This isn't good."

Marie stepped into the room. The pink softness of a robe wrapped her body, and she was trying to get kinks out of her hair with a large comb. "Good morning to you, Miss Lisa. Hello, Mr. Carlucci. What are you guys doing here so early?" she said with a yawn.

An older man with distinct bowed legs walked out from the next room. Marie waved at him. "A longtime boyfriend. Say good morning, Bob."

The guy waved and rubbed his sleepy face. "See you later, Marie. I got to get going."

"Robert Stewart. Police chief. Known him for years," Marie said.

Lisa turned toward the room containing tables and chairs with the bar at the end. "Marie, this place looks like a dump." She gestured toward the empty beer bottles, wadded-up napkins, and plates with remnants of food. "You've got work to do."

Lisa looked at Frank. "Let's leave."

As they walked to the curb, Lisa sighed. "I hope I can keep Marie. Sometimes I think she doesn't understand how different it is to set a good example."

Frank nodded. "I don't understand you, but I think it's good to help these girls get out of the business."

Lisa sat in her car and looked at him through the open window. "I know you don't really know me."

"Lisa, I didn't say that…"

"Yes, you did." She grabbed the steering wheel with both hands. "I'm going now, Frank."

"Aren't you coming to the bank with me?"

"I've got other things to do." She turned the ignition and shifted her car into gear. "Frank, you just don't get it, do you? I almost killed myself all those months ago when I had no money, no friends, no family. The only voice of hope was the priest down at the cathedral but he couldn't give me a place to live or a job. I have to help other girls who might be like me—thrown out on the streets by life. Not bad girls, just unlucky girls."

Frank wished he hadn't come. Lisa was impossible to predict. Everything he said made her angry. What if he was seen in this neighborhood? He was careful about where he was seen. This wasn't respectable.

"Look, Lisa. I think it's great what you're doing. When I get a little ahead on funds I'll give you some money too."

She continued as if she hadn't heard him. "That's me—unlucky. Unlucky enough to be pregnant by someone who doesn't love me."

Frank reached into the car and gently moved her face toward him. Keeping his voice soft, he said, "Lisa, I'm sorry. Maybe I could love you—I don't know. Right now we're on one path—to keep our secret safe, to keep you and the baby safe. That's all that matters. I'll help you all I can. Please don't be so upset."

She reached up to grab his hand, then closed her eyes.

Her chest rose and fell as she took several large breaths. "Okay, I understand. It's just...it's just...I get so tired of being alone. Of not having anyone to call my own. Vince hardly ever sees me. I'm the only person I can rely on...and I get so tired."

Frank stood there and just let her hold his hand tightly. There was nothing to say—nothing that could make it better. After all, they both knew that she couldn't rely on him. And Vince? He was the most unpredictable person imaginable.

In the weeks to come, Frank, Mitcheletti, and Benno, now back from Cuba, worked hard to set up distribution for the Cuban liquor that would be arriving. Every once in a while, Frank and Lisa talked by telephone. Sometimes they met in out-of-the-way locations for coffee or a meal. She had talked to her aunt and uncle, and all the plans were in place.

Finally, Vince let Frank know that he would be returning.

Frank called Lisa.

"He's coming back, isn't he?" she asked as soon as he said hello.

"How'd you know?"

"Your voice is different today."

"Well, this means we've got to get you out of town, right, baby?"

Her voice lightened for a moment. "I love it when you call me 'baby,' Frank."

"There's a bus out tonight, right?"

"It runs every night. Can you take me to the bus station?"

Lisa looked nervous when Frank picked her up later. The radiance in her face that the pregnancy brought had now dimmed. "Are you feeling okay, Lisa?" he asked.

She sighed. "I don't know if what I'm doing is right or not. What do you think?"

He loaded up her small suitcase and opened the car door for her before sliding into his seat. "Well, I believe you told me early on that your priorities were the baby, Vince, and yourself—in that order. I don't have a right to have an opinion in all this."

She nestled one small hand in the crook of his arm. "You've grown on me since that day at the Claw."

He patted the smallness of her white hand and looked over at her. "You've grown on me too. I'm going to miss you."

She squeezed his arm.

"Don't forget to use the P.O. Box number I gave you. I don't want Vince to see any long-distance records, so I can't call you. But write to me to let me know what's going on. I'll send some money to your aunt and uncle's address."

Lisa placed a soft kiss on Frank's cheek. "Let's go to the bus station. Otherwise, I won't be able to do this."

Later, as Frank saw her gloved hand wave from the bus's window, he teared up. He sat on a wooden bench at the far end of the terminal and tried to put order to his thoughts. Was this love? Was this how it felt? Hell, it felt shitty.

Out loud, he said to himself, "I can't get dragged down—I've got too much to do. Vince will be home, and our business needs to grow fast. I don't want a family."

With that, he squared his shoulders and drove to the new office in the building he had renovated when the bank loan came through. Restaurant on the bottom floor; offices above. As he strode up the hallway, he admired the black-and-gold letters on the frosted glass of their new front door: "DeLuca/Carlucci/Mitcheletti Interests." Cash-and-carry. Soon they'd be swimming in money.

CHAPTER TWENTY-THREE

Early on the day of Vince's return, Frank drove through blinding rain to Marie's. She had called him in a panic and told him to come immediately. He had promised Lisa he'd take care of things while she was in Oklahoma, but today's timing was bad. Vince would be at the office soon and had told Frank to be ready to talk business.

Frank felt like he could've walked faster than driving in the rain and heavy traffic, but he finally pulled to the curb down the block from Marie's. The summer rains soaked the front yard and wide planks were laid across the muddy yard to the front porch. Frank saw a dozen men and women with closed umbrellas standing on the wide porch.

Marie was in the middle of the crowd in her usual early-morning, pink-satin house robe. Her hair flew in all directions, and she was thrusting her cigarette at the leader of the group. He kept pushing the cigarette away from his face.

"Get that nasty cigarette smoke away from me, madam," he roared.

"Get off my porch."

Frank stepped up on the porch and placed himself between Marie and the tall man. "Sir, you have no right to be here."

"It's Reverend, not 'sir.' I'm Reverend John Fickum, and I demand to know what kind of establishment you are running."

"You have no right to create a public disturbance. You need to leave."

The reverend's voice gained in volume as he replied. "I don't know who you are—probably another sinner supporting a sinful business—and I don't care, sir."

The reverend's high voice held his supporters captive as it swelled in volume even more. "This woman is expanding evil operations. We have watched carpenters building more rooms of sin."

Frank's anger grew hotter. "Listen, this isn't a whorehouse."

At the mention of "whorehouse," the entire group gasped.

Frank ignored them. "You should be glad because it's helping young women get out of the business."

One of the women signaled to the others by raising her hymnal, and they all formed a circle closer to Marie and began singing at the top of their voices.

Fickum raised his umbrella so that its point poked Marie's ample chest. Frank didn't even think, but reacted by shoving Fickum back. Arms flailing, Fickum fell off the porch. Frank quickly walked to the edge of the porch to see if Fickum was okay. The mournful singers stayed crowded around Marie in a tight circle. Fickum had landed in a large puddle. A holstered gun had fallen out of one of his coat pockets. Why would a reverend carry a gun?

A few seconds later, a police car skidded to the curb, and two officers jumped out and ran to the porch.

"Okay, folks. Time to break this up."

Marie and the drenched reverend began talking at

once, then Frank stepped in. "Shut up," he yelled, then turned to the police officer and pointed at the singers. "These people are trespassing and causing a disturbance. They need to be arrested."

One of the huge Irish cops looked with amusement at Frank. "Mr. Carlucci, nobody is getting arrested today. Everyone, go home. The people who live in this house have a right to be here. No one else does."

Frank thought the reverend would argue, but he didn't. Instead, he drew himself up to his full height, scowled at the officers, and told Frank, "The devil is in Zapata, and I now know who you are, Mr. Carlucci. I will not rest until—"

"Get along home, folks," one of the police officers interrupted. "Time for this to break up."

The crowd filed down the sidewalk and across the wobbly boards, singing "Jesus Loves Me."

Frank watched them go, then turned to one of the officers on the porch. "Jimmy, what was that all about?"

The cop squinted in the direction of the departing crowd. "That's the brand-new, hellfire-and-brimstone reverend from the brand-new Baptist church. He's going to clean up Zapata—so he says."

Frank turned to Marie. "You okay, Marie?"

Her weathered face was set in a scowl. "Thanks for coming over, Mr. Frank."

"Yeah, no problem."

"We haven't seen the last of that idiot—you know that, don't you, Mr. Frank?"

Frank nodded grimly. "Yes, I know."

CHAPTER TWENTY-FOUR

Frank drove through the rain to the offices above the Derby Club. Why the hell had all this commotion occurred on the one day that Frank had to have his thoughts focused on explaining all he'd done to Vince? Not on Lisa, not on the baby he'd fathered, not on whether he was goofy for Lisa, not on anything but business.

Frank parked his car and ran through the rain to the front door. One of the boys he'd hired swung the door open and spread a huge umbrella.

"Good morning, Mr. Carlucci."

"Is Vince here already?"

"Haven't seen him."

Frank tried to eye the operation the way Vince would. Was there enough door security? How far would a shooter make it before getting nailed?

He saw Vince run through the rain and ignore Bob's efforts to open an umbrella for him. Both brothers rushed toward each other and hugged.

Frank slapped Vince on the back. "It's been a long

time. How you doing?"

"Hey, brother, I been good. I even got a tan. Look here." Vince pointed one thick finger toward the back of his other hand.

"I'm glad you're back, Vince. Everybody's upstairs."

"Looks like you got us quite a place here, brother."

"I think you're going to like what I've set up. Look around." Frank gestured to the polished hardwood floors and the twenty-two-foot mahogany bar topped by thick glass.

Vince gave a low whistle as his head turned to take in the shelves of gleaming liquor bottles under the high ceiling. The wall's blackboards held race results written in thick chalk.

"We get the races phoned in from all over the country. I hired professional pony announcers to call the races as if they were live."

Vince smiled. "It smells like money to me. They trust you?"

"They know we wouldn't post dirty results. We want them to come back over and over. And they do, brother. They just keep pouring in."

Vince looked rested. Less stressed than when he had left. "Let's go upstairs. Mitch and Benno are dying to see you."

Frank punched the elevator's call button. They waited and waited. Vince kept looking back around at the layout and was deep in thought. Frank knew he should be talking more to Vince but couldn't think of a thing to say—to his own brother. Crazy.

Finally, Vince turned. "What else you been doing, brother?"

"Not too much. It's taken hours and hours to get this show on the road."

"I heard you been taking up tennis."

"Joining that country club brought us—"

The elevator arrived, and they got on.

Vince turned toward Frank. "I hear you got a lot of fancy contacts there—especially with the dames. What's it called? The White Magnolia or something?"

Frank knew it was going to be a slow ride. He'd had it installed that way on purpose. But today, it seemed even longer. "You like the slow elevator, Vince? It'll come in handy if the Feds ever show up unannounced."

Vince didn't respond. Finally, the elevator reached the floor with the offices. He turned to Frank. "Sixty-seven seconds. That's good. A lot could happen in sixty-seven seconds. Right, Frank?"

The elevator door opened into an office space. Benno and Mitcheletti got up from their chairs. Mitcheletti's big right hand held a half-eaten candy bar, as usual. Benno's smile at seeing Vince lit up the room.

After hearty back slaps and hugs, they settled around a table. A white-coated waiter came up with coffee in a silver urn and offered to pour for the group.

"Give us coffee, then get the hell out of here." Vince moved his cup closer to the waiter, who filled all the cups and then fled back downstairs.

Vince lit a cigar and spoke first. "You told me the dicks got almost every other shipment out of the Midwest last week. What the hell's going on?"

"It doesn't matter," Mitcheletti chimed in from his favorite leather chair. "We each made a hundred and seventy-two grand last month. It looks even better for this month. Sixty-eight percent of our trucks get through monthly—at different times of day or night. We switch it up constantly. The Feds don't spend enough money to stop us, and the state cops all drink, so they don't give a damn."

Vince didn't look convinced but only chewed on his cigar and remained silent.

Frank spoke up. "There's been talk about repealing Prohibition."

Benno interjected, "That won't happen anytime soon."

"Yeah, but if it does, who needs us?" Frank said. "If

buying liquor by the bottle or the drink is legal, but people can't gamble, then we have an out."

"What's that?" Mitcheletti asked.

"Private casino. But big-time, like Vince just saw in Cuba. Right, Vince?"

Vince's eyes lit up. "Yeah—just like in Cuba, except we could do it better."

"Are you sure?" Frank asked. "We need big profits. Bigger than we're getting now because the upfront expenses and the ongoing operations will cost us big-time."

Vince stubbed his cigar in a heavy ashtray. "Think about it. This is a small island. We'll fix it so that no one comes on or off without our permission. Frank, you keep up that country club membership because we'll need all your contacts on city council, county commissioner's court, city permitting, all those guys."

Frank nodded. "I've already got some people on our payroll—cops, politicos, a couple department heads. I can start working on this casino idea Vince, now that you're back. Mitch, you work on better percentages on the Midwest deliveries. Vince, you and Benno keep the beaches moving, Mitch will count the money and help me with meeting the right people. We'll look at all the angles on opening a casino especially now that we have an in-house expert—mi hermano Vince."

Mitcheletti folded up the candy wrapper and tucked it under the ashtray. Then he turned to Vince. "When's Lisa coming back?"

Vince shrugged. "When her relatives are better. Hard to know."

Mitch laughed. "For such a classy dame, I don't know how she picked you."

Vince shrugged again. "Guess I got lucky—for once in my life, huh?"

They all laughed except Frank, who forced a smile. This was going to be harder than he had imagined—much harder.

His imagination had made Lisa his all these months. But with Vince back, it was time for reality—the hard reality of an impossible love.

CHAPTER TWENTY-FIVE

As Frank slogged through the daily problems of creating an empire based on illegal booze and illegal gambling, he didn't allow himself the luxury of thinking about Lisa, much less about his baby growing inside of her. But as he fell asleep each night, or at times when he got away and sat alone inside a darkened church, Lisa's glowing face would rise unbidden in his memory. Sometimes the image was so clear that he could almost feel the softness of her hair as he bent his head down to place one cheek on top of her head. The talcum powder she brushed through her golden hair would rise to his nostrils.

He didn't give up going to the post office box each day, although she didn't write him. Every time he turned the small metal dial in the sequence of the combination, his stomach lit up with anticipation. Maybe, today?

The rainy summer turned into a humid, sticky autumn. Frank switched from white linen lined with ivory satin to tailored wool suits. The women he escorted to country club dances told him he looked "elegant" and "handsome." But

Frank didn't care—women had said that his entire life. His thoughts were elsewhere—with Lisa in rural Oklahoma.

Finally, one day when he swung open the small brass door of the postal box, a dime-store white envelope—almost too small to carry anything of consequence—was waiting for his eager fingers. He slipped it into his inside coat pocket as if it were nothing.

Once he sat in his car, he tore open the envelope with shaking fingers.

> *Dearest Frank,*
>
> *Our boy is now one week old. I named him Randall. He reminds me of his daddy. He's beautiful. Born with a full cap of curly dark hair. Black eyes.*
>
> *Aunt Rose fell and broke a hip. Poor Uncle Louis! They'll tell Randall that they adopted him late in life and that I'm his aunt.*
>
> *I think of you nonstop. I'd give anything just to hear your voice. Vince calls every day. Don't you love me? Do you love me more than Vince?*
>
> *I have to stay longer than I planned because of Aunt Rose's convalescence. Don't forget me. This is the hardest thing I've ever had to do.*
>
> *Love,*
> *Lisa*

Tears welled up in his eyes but he quickly blinked them away. Maybe he could drive to Biloxi and call Lisa from there. In Zapata, he couldn't take the chance of a long-distance operator repeating to Vince that Frank had placed a call to Oklahoma.

Yes, he'd drive there tomorrow, or the next day. Right after the meetings to square up the deal for slots in the drive-in grocery stores. If he could just get a day with no crises—that would be a good day to drive to Biloxi. A day when Vince didn't know where Frank was going or why.

Meantime, Vince continued his monitoring of the almost nightly deliveries from boats to remote beaches. Benno was his steadfast companion. They both thrived in the foggy, nighttime world of heavy surf, muffled lights, and hard physical exertion.

One night, after a strenuous schedule of liquor deliveries, they heard the bang of metal-on-metal crashing in the street outside of Vince's house. Vince dropped his Scotch on the floor, and Benno grabbed his gun. They both rolled to the floor and cautiously raised their heads to peer out the windows.

A woman's scream came out of nowhere. "Oh God, help me—my baby. Help me."

The men jumped up and ran to Vince's black Cadillac, parked at the curb. Another car had rear-ended the Cadillac. The screams came from a young woman in the driver's seat who was twisting and turning.

Vince got there first and yanked the bent passenger door open to grab a bawling infant. He handed the blanketed bundle to Benno and began to extract the young woman from the wreckage.

"My baby, my baby," she cried. When she was free from the car, she ran to Benno, grabbed the child, and held him tightly against her chest.

"Let us help you." Vince slowly removed his light jacket and placed it around the woman's heaving shoulders. "Let me take you to the hospital. That cut lip and your forehead should be looked at. I can stay with you until your family gets there."

Benno reached into his pants pocket and handed Vince the keys to Benno's car. "Take her in my car, Boss.

I'll stay and get a wrecker to clean up the mess."

The young woman sniffed back tears. "I was going to the hospital. My baby has a bad cough. I've been up with him day and night. No sleep—I guess I fell asleep at the wheel." She began to cry softly. "I wrecked your beautiful car, Mr. Carlucci. Everyone knows who you are. Please don't hurt my baby. I'll do anything you want, just don't hurt my baby."

Looking at her small heart-shaped face under a swirl of dark brown hair, Vince saw her wide-eyed fear but also her fierce love for the infant she still clutched protectively to her chest. Was this what a mother's love felt like?

"I'm not going to hurt you. And I would never hurt a little baby. I'm going to take you to the hospital, get you settled, let you call your family. When they get there to help you, I'll leave."

The young woman's eyes shone with relief, and she clutched Vince's arm with her one free hand. "My name is Linda Loreson, Mr. Carlucci. I'm out of work right now, but I promise you that I'll work hard and pay for the damages to your car. I always pay my debts."

Vince smiled for the first time. "You don't owe me nothing. I'll pay for everything—your car and mine. Don't worry about nothing. C'mon, let's drive to the hospital and see the sawbones."

A tear slowly dripped down the left side of Vince's face as he put in the clutch of Benno's car and started for the hospital. He wiped it off quickly. Later that night, as he drove home, Lisa's smiling image floated into his mind. Dames made him soft.

Dammit. When was she coming home?

CHAPTER TWENTY-SIX

Months later Lisa sat in a first-class compartment of the train. The homecoming was something she had looked forward to and dreaded for weeks. She didn't think her body would betray her—Vince shouldn't be able to tell what had happened. But would her eyes betray her when she looked at Frank? The distance and the silence had somehow tied her closer to Frank. How could that be? She didn't know and didn't care, but felt the tug of wanting to be with him much stronger than when she had left Zapata.

The train pulled into Zapata, but Lisa didn't get up immediately. Could she really feign affection for Vince much longer? The effort felt like climbing a mountain that only kept getting higher and higher. One day she'd fall off the mountain—she was sure of it.

She stood, squared her shoulders, and smoothed the pleats of a soft yellow outfit she had chosen to show off her tiny waist. An outfit that she'd love to wear for Frank so his capable hands could run down her length and caress every inch of her.

On the platform, amid the hissing steam and yelling porters, it was as bad as she had imagined. Frank and Vince stood side-by-side, waiting, Frank as elegant as always with his short hair, smooth jaw, and square shoulders—and Vince, thickly muscled as always with a scowling face and swollen hands.

Lisa forced herself to rush to Vince. She closed her eyes so she wouldn't have to witness Frank's reaction to Vince's bear hug, which seemed to go on forever.

"It was a long trip, honey." Vince placed his lips on her hair.

Lisa opened her eyes, making sure that her smile was bright and carefree. She extended a hand to shake Frank's, but allowed herself to place a brief kiss on Frank's right cheek. He still wore the same aftershave. The months she had been gone had only made him more handsome. What if Vince ever found out?

They all made their way together through the crowd as the sun started to set, collecting Lisa's bags off a trolley. "Let's get the hell out of here," Vince said. "I hate these crowds. I want to be alone with my gal."

Vince and Lisa dropped Frank at his home, waving goodbye. Frank had deliberately refrained from telling Lisa that he was leaving early the next morning to Chicago. Maybe it would be better to be gone a while. To give Lisa and Vince time alone. It still twisted his insides to think of Vince and Lisa together, but if that's what they both wanted, what could he do?

Frank worked hard in Chicago, probably harder than he needed to. Sorting out details, forcing distributors, yelling at bankers—it kept him occupied even as he pretended to himself that he could forget Lisa and little Randall, the baby he'd never even seen in a photograph.

On his last night in Chicago, Frank made the one

mistake he'd been telling himself for weeks that he wouldn't—he telephoned Lisa. She picked up quickly. He heard her soft breathy "Hello."

"Lisa, it's me. Frank. Are you alone?"

"Frank? Frank!"

"It's killing me not to see you."

"Oh, Frank. You got to get over me."

"Are you in love with Vince now?"

Dead silence. Frank willed her answer to be "no." The silence continued.

Frank jumped into the opportunity. "I'm coming home tomorrow night. Vince will be receiving shipments all night until early morning. Meet me, Lisa. We got to talk."

She sighed. "Why do you do this to me? After all this time? Why don't you just let me forget you?"

He rushed on. "Eleven p.m., St. Catherine's. Back left pew by Father Murphy's confessional. I'll be waiting."

She didn't say anything but a soft "goodbye." Frank shut his eyes against the sudden tears that sprang into them. Had he already lost her? Had he waited too long?

Frank arrived after dark in Zapata. The sweltering breeze did little to cool him down, but he walked from the train station to St. Catherine's.

The church was dim, with only a couple of candles burning on the altar. Closer to the altar, a woman's head looked buried in prayer, but it wasn't Lisa. Frank relaxed in the environment he knew so well and prayed as he had when a boy.

Please, God, I have no right to talk to you, but I know you are up there watching over me. Please bless and protect little Randall. Please guide me through this maze I have created with my life. Please don't let me lose Lisa, dear God.

Frank made the sign of the cross and opened his eyes.

Lisa sat next to him with a scarf covering her blond hair. Red lipstick adorned her lips. Frank had never seen her look so beautiful.

Tears came to his eyes. What was wrong with him? He must be going stupid.

"Lisa, how are you?" he whispered.

"I've never seen you pray, Frank."

He almost chuckled. "I sin a lot in my business. God is the only person I can talk to about that."

Her eyes seemed to darken, and he was reminded of the sadness he had seen in her from the beginning.

"Lisa, tell me about little Randall. Do you have a picture of him?"

"I miss him so much my insides ache. I can't talk about him. It's just too hard." She began to cry softly, and he embraced her, then placed her head on his shoulder.

"I promise, Lisa. No more questions about Randall until you say it's okay."

Her sobs subsided, and she straightened up.

"Are you falling for Vince? I got to know."

She smiled and inclined her head while grabbing his hand. "I waited all my life for a man like you—classy, smart, someone to talk to. It's so hard to let go."

"You don't have to let go."

"I do."

The lady praying in the dark turned around. "Please be quiet. Show some respect." Then she looked closer at them. "Oh, I'm so sorry, Mr. Carlucci and Miss Lisa. I didn't recognize you. I didn't recognize you at all."

Lisa smiled and shifted away from Frank on the pew. The woman got up and walked quickly down the aisle and out the door.

"Who was that?" asked Frank.

"She used to be Vince's housekeeper," Lisa said tersely.

"I'll think of something."

Lisa stood and turned to leave.

"Wait, Lisa. Wait longer."

Lisa turned without a word and walked out of the church. Frank grabbed his hat and quickly followed her.

"Lisa, you have to answer me. You owe me that much."

Lisa stopped and pulled the scarf from her head. "Frank, I was goofy for you. You don't even know how much. But it can't work out between us. Not now. Vince needs both of us."

"Needs us?"

"He needs you, his brother, to be there for him always. And he needs me—just for now. He needs me to keep him balanced so he can work to make all this damn money that both of you want."

Frank couldn't think of a thing to say. Was Lisa right?

She reached one gloved hand to Frank's cheek. The sadness returned to her face. "Little Carlucci, I can't carry a torch for you forever."

Frank grabbed her hand and pressed the palm, as if imprinting it into his being. "I'm not giving up on us, Lisa. Not giving up at all."

She shrugged but didn't speak. He stayed glued to the sidewalk as her heels echoed down the empty street.

CHAPTER TWENTY-SEVEN

Vince stood on Frank's rickety wooden porch barely half a mile away. His knuckles continued rapping on the sturdy door as he cursed under his breath. Frank was supposed to have arrived back in town a couple of hours ago. Where in the hell was he? On tonight of all nights...

A lone cab's headlights announced someone's arrival. Vince stepped into the shadows until he saw Frank step out of the car, pay the fare, and swing a large, striped suitcase out of the trunk.

"Where the hell have you been?" Vince yelled after the cab pulled away into the darkness.

"I'm dead tired."

"That limp mayor called. Some guys from St. Louis—Russo's boys—are coming to take us out at the beach while we unload. We're trying to find out who squealed."

"We got informers working for us?" Frank asked.

"Hell, yes. Otherwise, those poachers wouldn't know where to ambush us—I change delivery spots every few days. C'mon, Frank. Me and the boys got a nice little surprise waiting for our visitors. I closed the ferry. They gotta use the bridge. And they'll discover that flat tires don't drive real well."

Frank dropped his suitcase inside the door and raced to Vince's car at the curb. "Hey, you got a new car."

"Yeah, well... I got to do something to keep me amused on this frigging island."

Vince sped along Ocean Front Boulevard toward the causeway. He'd thought this all through countless times, knowing that one day the plan would have to be used. He looked over at Frank.

"You look tired, brother."

"Chicago was busy. I got us some good deals and better supply routes. You'll like the percentages."

"You're going to like what I do tonight," Vince said with a small wink in Frank's direction.

"Listen, Vince, do I really have to be there?"

"You won't be there long. My plans will take most of the night." Vince twisted one side of his face into what resembled a smile. "I know you need your beauty rest, brother. My job is to protect our fucking lives and our income—day and night."

Frank sat back in the seat while Vince concentrated on running stop signs and driving through red lights.

"The bridge attendant raised the bridge when I told him. There's a police barricade on our end of the bridge. It'll be a big squeeze, brother. A big squeeze for our St. Louis visitors."

Vince skidded to a stop at the Zapata end of the bridge. The dank concrete ribbon of bridge rose high in the darkness, a road leading to nowhere. The dark water slapped against the pilings—an uninviting reminder that the sea held its own secrets forever.

"Now me and my boys will find out who's left," Vince said after being informed that two empty cars had already been identified on the half-mile stretch between the Zapata barricade and the raised bridge.

After Vince gave his crew of six guys the final instructions, Frank waved him over to the side. "I don't think I need to be here. I'm going home."

"I got this under control. You can take my car. Enjoy your soft bed."

Vince, Benno, and the other boys fanned out for the walk onto the bridge. A slight mist had risen over the water, and the whiteness of their stern faces reinforced that this would be a fight to the death forty feet above the unforgiving black water.

"Now," Vince said.

Each guy hefted a black submachine gun. Their pistols rested in two-gun shoulder and belt holsters. Dead silence reigned. Burlap had been tied around their shoes to muffle any sound.

Before they had gone fifty yards onto the road of death, they heard voices coming out of the mist in front of them. Vince quickly motioned his boys to scatter to the sides of the bridge and stack into levels of waiting, black-nosed artillery.

About thirty seconds later, several dark-suited men walked slowly out of the mist with pistols in their hands.

"Drop your guns, boys," Vince ordered.

In the split second when the decision wavered and every trigger finger itched, the St. Louis guys hesitated. Too much fog, the eeriness of the salty black water of oblivion below? Lack of sleep? Who knew? But that split second was what Vince had counted on.

The clatter of steel on concrete was heard as each of the St. Louis guys dropped their guns. The biggest guy—the leader, apparently—tried to speak.

"Listen, what's this all about? We were just coming for a little visit. Heard this is a good vacation spot."

Vince didn't even pause as his boys moved in to search and bind hands and wrists with rope. Countless drills had given their actions deadly efficiency.

Vince's crew brought in the cars the men had

abandoned and roughly hoisted the burly men into the seats before driving to a remote spot on East Beach.

Benno's car, with Vince in it, brought up the rear. They stopped next to the bridge attendant, and Vince rolled down his window. "Too bad that mist closed your bridge down for a while."

"Yessir, yessir, Mr. Carlucchi. That's exactly what my log says: Bridge closed due to lack of visibility—fog."

At East Beach, the St. Louis guys were face down on the damp pavement near the Bernardo de Cortez statue. Muffled sounds of outrage came from gagged mouths, and muscles strained against secure bonds. The rhythmic screech of crickets and a lonely foghorn could be heard through the mist. The distant red, green, and white lights of huge ships glowed through the fog as they slowly passed through the nearby harbor entrance of Zapata.

Vince gestured to his boys. They tugged and pushed the men so they were facing Vince.

"We know some son of a bitch in our organization tipped off you guys. Probably issued you a personal invitation to come enjoy our vacation spot. You're going to tell us who that is."

Not a sound from behind the gags. Vince gave a sign, and each of his men kicked the kidneys of the man on the cement in front of him. Only grunts of pain were heard.

"I need one of you to sing like a canary," Vince said. "I'll take off the gag and let you walk back to St. Louis if you tell me right now."

Silence.

"I can see I don't have a choice," Vince said. "Benno, get all their jewelry and wallets. Last chance. Going, going, gone.

"Now, gentlemen. See that black expanse in front of you. One of the loveliest vacation areas on our fair island. You said you came here for a vacation, right? People come from far and wide just to study the snakes—water moccasins—and the alligators. Yeah, flora and fauna.

"It's a vacation marsh. One of you is going to run through it—only a quarter mile wide, guys. If you make it across, then you go back to St. Louis buck-naked but free."

Vince grabbed the biggest guy by the ear and stood him up. "You were the one that said 'vacation.' We're going to show you 'vacation.'"

Vince turned to his guys. "Strip him naked. All the way."

The men cut off his clothes without untying him. They carried him bound and gagged to the edge of the creepy darkness. Keeping a close watch, one cut off his gag, and extra guys cut off the bindings around his arms and legs. They all grabbed one arm or one leg and swung him back and forth until they let go at the highest swing in the direction of the swamp.

His voice rang out and cracked as he flew six feet into the air and landed in the muck. Two of Vince's guys shone flashlights on him, and everyone's attention was on the progress of his unnaturally white body in the darkness. He stumbled to his feet, and the water around him thrashed. He reached down to scrape his legs while trying to run in high steps. At one point, he reached behind him to pull off a long black snake and fling it away, but it was soon replaced by others. His screams and writhing brought the entire swamp's attention. There were a few splashes, as gators silently moved toward him. His legs were pulled out from under him, and he disappeared into the blackness. He surfaced once more as if trying to crawl, but the paleness of his body was all but covered with black creatures working their tedious business of destruction and death. His blood-curdling screaming became a watery gurgle, then ceased altogether. A huge alligator tail broke the water once, then rolled over and over. Then, nothing.

Vince turned to face the remaining St. Louis guys. "He didn't even make it ten feet. Too bad. I thought he was tougher."

"Who's ready to talk now?"

Every head bobbled up and down.

Benno removed one of the gags at Vince's command.

"I'll tell you everything. Our contact is the ex-police chief. The guy that got fired. He works with two of Jimmy Jack's boys, Billy Bob and Mango."

The man paused, breathing heavily. "If you let us go, we'll never come back. We won't tell what happened here. Promise. Not even to Sal."

Vince smiled as if considering the idea. Then he looked at Benno and winked. At that sign, each of Vince's boys put two bullets into the back of the head of a St. Louis goon.

"Benno, take them to that concrete cave under our friend Bernardo de Cortez. Leave room for three more."

"Sure, Boss," Benno said, already expediting the bodies' removal. He handed one of the boys a waiting bucket of water and a mop to clean up the blood and brains sprayed over the damp concrete.

Only thirty minutes later, Vince and his boys came back with the bodies of the three rats. It hadn't been hard to surprise them. Vince and his boys had driven to the beach in the cars of the St. Louis guys.

Back at the statue, they laid the three bloody bodies on top of the St. Louis boys. Vince rubbed his red eyes.

"You okay, Boss?" Benno asked as his strong arms churned the concrete mixture that would seal off the crypt.

"Yeah, just lots of activity tonight. Guess I'm going to sleep good."

"You got that right, Boss. We did great tonight, didn't we? Your plan went just the way we thought it would."

"Yeah," Vince sighed. "When it's good, it's good, Benno. But when it's bad, it's real bad. But right now, everything is peachy."

Two weeks later in St. Louis, Salvatore Russo was interrupted at his office. His redheaded secretary held a large cardboard box in her thin arms.

"Mr. Russo, this came special delivery." She placed it on the gleaming surface of his mahogany desk. Russo watched her pert ass as she went back to the front office and closed the door.

Russo grabbed a knife from his desk drawer and ripped open the box. When he peered in, a black snake struck out at him. Russo jumped back, and his boys, who had gathered around to see the box, grabbed their guns.

"Don't shoot my desk, you stupids," Russo hollered. "I paid thousands for that desk."

One of the men grabbed Russo's umbrella from the rack and let the snake coil around it. Once the snake was removed, Russo opened the flaps of the box. Inside was a human hand, an alligator paw, a golden police badge with square letters reading "Chief," and a pile of cheap rings, heavy gold bracelets, and worn wallets.

A large note read: "Next time we keep the jewelry."

CHAPTER TWENTY-EIGHT

Everyone important was on hand the next morning to welcome Frank home. It was just like old times—steaming coffee and freshly buttered, crusty rolls served by a white-coated waiter upstairs in the offices. Benno and Vince appeared red-eyed and unshaven. DeLuca sported a new suit and sat regally while stirring multiple teaspoons of sugar into his coffee cup. Mitcheletti reached for a Baby Ruth in an inside coat pocket. The waiter closed the door with an emphatic click as he left.

Frank began. "I got lots of good news from Chicago. But first I want to thank you for running everything while I was gone."

DeLuca brought a teaspoon of the syrupy liquid to his lips and blew on it. "We got you covered, Frank. Who knows? Maybe you can retire now. Depends how much you played the ponies up there in Chicago."

Everyone laughed. "Hey, retirement sounds good," Frank said.

Vince scowled. "Some of us have been working all

night every night since you been fucking gone, brother."

"Well, I'm grateful to everyone—especially you, Vince. I realize I stepped up the deliveries at night on the beach but that was so—"

"Benno and I are tired, Frank. Real tired. We don't sit around in an office all day and have cocktails at the country club in the evening. We haul boxes and provide protection all night, then get a few hours' sleep before we hit the beach again. In our spare time, we deal with bozos like those guys from the St. Louis mob."

Frank momentarily thought of Lisa. If Vince was gone all the time—too busy and too exhausted to see her…

"What's going on with you, Vince? This isn't like you." DeLuca tossed his teaspoon on the heavy white saucer.

Vince rubbed his eyes, then slowly ran one large hand down his face. "You guys don't even know what I've had to deal with, do you?"

The room was deathly quiet. Even Benno stopped breathing.

Frank sat and modulated his voice. "Tell us, Vince."

"Last week. Train station. Standard weekly delivery of money from the Midwest. Adder and Nyman were scheduled, plus another guy, to get the suitcases from the messenger—same as always. Except this time, there were two other guys in the crowd at the station. They ambushed our guys and took the payments. We lost Leo.

"Don't worry. We recovered the money, eventually. But we had to teach the new guy on our payroll a lesson— he was the source of the ambush. I got one more of his cronies to deal with tonight."

Vince pointed his finger at Frank. "Success breeds jealousy and greed. Those guys from St. Louis last night were just the first sharks in the pond. We are the big fat fish that every shark wants to eat."

Everyone was silent. Then DeLuca spoke in a gravelly voice, "That's the way it is. That's the way it'll always be.

The more money we make, the more some people will want to kill us. We all knew this going in. There's no backing out now."

Frank looked at the faces around the table. Vince, red-eyed and exhausted. Benno, tired but alert. Mitcheletti, rested and perfectly groomed as always. DeLuca, with a straight spine but his lips in a thin line of grim determination.

"Look, I can't answer for the rest of you," Frank said. "But I'm in all the way. We knew the going would be tough—that's what we expected. If we get ahead far enough, maybe we can all retire, but not right now, not for me, anyway."

DeLuca spoke up first. "The recent addition of slots all over the city has made the money pour in like water from a broken faucet—which we need for all the people on payroll. But I say it's time to expand—"

Explosions of disgruntled disbelief erupted from around the table. "We can barely manage what we're doing now," Frank said.

"Just hear me out. Only two things can destroy us right now. A successful attack from the outside, or the federal government repeals Prohibition."

"For the first, we got Vince and Benno—even if they are exhausted, they're smarter, better, and more deadly than anything anyone can throw at us. But for the second, we got no insurance, guys. No insurance at all."

"Go on," Frank said.

"You guys may think I'm sitting on my hands at the train station, or in church while you're unloading crates of alcohol, but I've been studying casinos. I have a plan."

Frank's insides clutched at the mention of church. Could that woman have gone to DeLuca?

"Here's the plan. When Lucy and I were on vacation last month in Cuba, I spent a lot of time with Carlos. He's a good teacher—I'm sure Vince remembers that."

Vince nodded once in affirmation.

"We can do better than what Carlos has done. We can have the first U.S. casino with dinner, gambling, and top-notch entertainment under one roof. We'll draw crowds from more than just the South. It'll pay for itself inside of six months."

Vince spoke up. "I know all about casinos from Carlos. I say go for it, but go for it big-time. Sinatra, Crosby—those top-notch Hollywood guys."

"I already have a spot picked out—on Forty-Second Street and Mississippi Avenue," DeLuca said. "A huge empty area."

"Can we get financing?" Frank asked.

"Sure, we'll go to Canady's bank. He'll finance everything."

Maybe this will be the step that will get us where I need to be, Frank thought, suddenly tired too. Tired of worrying, tired of talking to everyone who could do them a favor and then paying back the favors—large and small. Tired of never seeing Lisa. And Vince, always a jerk to Frank.

"How much will it cost to build and equip?" Frank asked.

"I got the numbers at home. I can bring them this afternoon," DeLuca said with a sudden smile. "I even got a proposed name to run by you."

"What's that?"

"The San Francisco Supper Club."

Frank raised his coffee cup in a salute. "Here's a toast to the San Francisco Supper Club." Everyone followed suit with the heavy white cups, even Vince.

The inside telephone on the sideboard rang, and Frank answered it. After a few moments of listening, he hung up.

"The governor is coming up, boys. I should handle this by myself. I think I know why he's visiting."

They all herded to the elevator. As the doors opened, John S. Sullivan paused for just a moment and nodded to them. "Good morning, gentlemen."

They all replied, except for Vince, who only crunched down on an unlit cigar extracted from a pocket.

Frank forced his face into a smile and motioned the governor to the conference table. "Let me call for some hot coffee, governor."

"Thank you, Frank. It's too late in the morning for more coffee. I sure could use some ice water, though." The red-faced man swiped one forefinger inside of his collar as if to loosen his tie's stranglehold.

Frank remembered the governor's favorite beverage in previous meetings. "I can do one better than ice water, sir. Let me get some iced champagne. Just the way you like it. I've got a special refrigerator that's temperature-controlled."

The large man sighed and raised his eyes to heaven, "Lord, thank you for giving my business associate and dear friend a good memory."

Frank guided them around the table after placing a call for the champagne. "How are Abigail and the boys?"

"She's doing great. Thanks. She loves coming here for the ponies. Good thing she wears those large hats. What would people say if they saw the first lady of the great state of Mississippi sitting at the Derby playing the ponies?"

"Governor, tell me what's on your mind this morning."

"Frank, I need big help this year. That young crusader Will Sheppard from Jackson is stirring things up so he can run against me. His main battle cry is illegal liquor and gambling."

"My associates and I are very aware of Mr. Sheppard."

"He's a smart one. If there's any trouble with Women's Temperance League or anyone else like that, he'll make the most of it in the newspapers and turn all our names to mud."

"Don't worry, Governor. We'll be careful."

"And, of course, you know, that I, you know, would

appreciate—"

"We will, of course, double our contribution to your campaign war chest," Frank purred. "It's an honor to be able to generously support those we believe in."

The governor drank too big a swig of bubbly and coughed.

Frank slipped one hand inside his jacket and retrieved a thick envelope. "This is the first of our contributions to your campaign, Governor."

Sullivan raised his glass in a toast that Frank matched.

After the governor departed, Frank sat back down at the huge table. Would Vince be able to hold himself together or was the expansion too much? But there was no other way out. They couldn't let everything they'd worked so hard for just evaporate overnight. Frank had promised the governor they'd be careful. "Careful" wasn't even a word that Vince understood. He only understood one thing—getting his way and protecting his own. Hadn't Vince mentioned one more person he had to take care of tonight? Frank sighed. He couldn't talk to Vince—especially now. What if the whole thing blew up in their faces? The newspapers were always ready to lynch someone in mile-high headlines.

CHAPTER TWENTY-NINE

Frank stayed busy all afternoon, and early evening found him still in his office. The phone never stopped ringing and stacks of banking records, purchase orders, and payroll authorizations for their legitimate staff needed his approval.

His private line rang around seven that night. *Shit, another crisis?*

"Frankie-boy," cooed Margaret, a woman he'd dated briefly before Chicago. "Time to come play for the evening. We can start with cocktails at the club. I'm here already."

Then Frank remembered that, after all, it was a Friday. He was momentarily distracted by her sweet lisp and memories of her warm, dark hair cascading down her shoulders, but knew he had to take care of business first. She clicked her tongue in disappointment, and he promised an evening soon—just the two of them.

The day faded into a luminous glow on the horizon as he finally left his office. He drove to the seawall and parked his car to watch the sunset. The smooth sand reminded him of the day he and Lisa had walked on the beach together. The one time they made love. Frank shook his head to clear those memories. Next time it would be different. Surely, next time she would come to him eager and responsive—like his other girlfriends did—full of soft invitation.

Why couldn't he get Lisa out of his mind? Her soft blond curls. How she lightly wrapped her arms around him. Did she let Vince see the sadness lurking on all the edges of her life? No, Frank didn't believe she would do that. That was one of the secrets that bound her and Frank together. Only he was privy to those hard regrets and her violent history.

Frank couldn't live like this anymore—never able to know what the future held, never able to get things resolved. Maybe Lisa would talk to him and let him win her back. Women changed their minds all the time—didn't they? Who knew why? Randall was his son too. He deserved to know about Randall. Months and more months had already slipped by kept sealed by his inaction and Lisa's silence.

Timing. Timing would be important. Tonight beach deliveries began at 1:00 a.m. Vince had said he had to take care of one other situation before then. Frank would go to Lisa's house at midnight. It should be safe.

A dark sedan waited in an alley behind the Mother of Queen Bar. Vince swore and rubbed the sweat from his forehead while Benno sat silent behind the steering wheel. The entire city was dark. A low ground fog hovered everywhere, and a stale stench from the nearby fishing docks filled the air.

"I can't believe this motherfucker thought he could get away with double-crossing us," Vince whispered.

"Boss, are we sure? The other guy we were sure about. But this one, I don't know."

Vince flicked his eyes momentarily from the alleyway to Benno. "They were best friends. That's enough for me."

Benno paused, then said almost to himself, "The other guy didn't give it up, and we sliced him up real good—we took our time. Maybe this one tonight is clean."

"Ain't nobody stealing from us, pal. Nobody. We're not taking any chances."

"Sure, Boss. Sure."

Another dark car cruised slowly through the alley with its headlights off. The interior lights flashed off and on, and Benno fired up the ignition. The back door of the other car opened, and the bulk of a man toppled out. Nyman and Adder got out of the car and roughly grabbed the other man, standing him up.

Vince walked to the group, pulled a cigar from his mouth, spit in the guy's face, then kicked him in the groin. "No one steals from us, you bastard."

The man crawled on the pavement, not even raising his head. "I don't know what you're talking about. Somebody's framed me. I didn't steal nothing."

Blood from his nose and mouth leaked onto the concrete. The man was crying and sniffling. "I swear I didn't do nothing. You got the wrong guy."

"You helped kill one of my men. I only hurt those who need it—and that's you and your buddy." Vince spat on the pavement and chomped down on the cigar again. He nodded to Nyman and Adder. "You guys know what to do."

Vince rejoined Benno and motioned him forward. "Let's go to the beach. Deliveries start in forty-five minutes."

"Sure, Boss. Sure. Anything you say."

As Frank cruised toward Lisa's house, he watched his car's headlights play on swirling shapes inside the fog. Everything looked ominous. The oleander leaves resembled witches' fingers, and bushy azaleas resembled ghouls. Man, a good night to stay inside.

He had almost talked himself out of going farther when he turned the corner and saw several rooms lit up in Lisa's house. Could Vince be there? What if she had someone else visiting—like another man? Frank had never considered that possibility. He cruised by more than once, checking for Vince's car on all adjoining side streets, then parked several blocks over.

Frank strode the sidewalks of the small neighborhood to Lisa's front door and knocked.

A gauze curtain on the front door moved slightly. He thought he heard a gasp.

"Frank, is that you?"

"Let me in."

For a few interminable seconds he heard nothing. Then the doorknob turned, and she stood behind the door with her face in the narrow crack. "What are you doing here?"

"I have to talk with you. Please. It's really important."

"I'm busy."

Frank thought about pushing in the door—it would be easy to do. But he'd pushed his way into her life enough already. "Sorry to bother you so late. Goodbye."

He turned and was halfway down the steps of the porch when the door fully open, and he heard her say, "Wait, Frank."

He faced the doorway again. She was filled with light—as he best loved seeing her. The blond curls were slightly mussed and tied up in a pink ribbon. Her slender form was barely disguised in a diaphanous gown of some kind of thin material that reached to her feet.

"Can we just talk, Lisa? It's driving me crazy not knowing what's going on."

She stood stock-still, her hand on the doorknob. "What if Vince comes by—sometimes he does in the middle of the night."

Frank moved quickly inside the doorframe and closed the door. "Turn off the lights. He won't come inside if he thinks you're sleeping, will he?"

She walked to each lamp and turned it off. "Sometimes he does, and sometimes he doesn't."

They both sat in the house's inky darkness. Once his eyes adjusted, Frank began. "Lisa, it's good to see you."

"It's good to see you too."

"I haven't been able to think of anything else but you since last night."

"Me either."

"Really?" His heart leapt in hope.

"It's not every day that a girl breaks up with her heart's desire."

Frank forced his nails into the palms of his hands so the pain would distract him from his desire for her. She was right there—almost naked already, warm and soft, sweet curves resting only an arm's reach away. His entire lower body ached to touch her.

"We didn't break up, Lisa. It was just a bad night. You know, a bad mood. There's no one else that gives me what you give me—and that's the truth."

"And what do you give me?"

Frank tore his eyes away from the silky gown flowing over her body. "I'd like to think that I give you—" And here Frank had to stop because other than some money to help her run her halfway house for girls, he couldn't think of anything else.

"I'd like to give you a future, Lisa," he found himself saying.

She remained silent.

"A future with only one guy—me."

"Oh, Frank. Are you serious?"

"I've never said that to any woman in my entire

lifetime."

"When? When can we do it? How soon?"

Frank heard the excitement in the breathy tones of her new questions.

"I don't know. As soon as I save up more money."

"Frank—it could be years, right? Years and years."

"It could be years, yes."

"Why can't you leave the business now? You've got plenty of money—everyone knows that. Look at your cars, your servants, your fucking country-club girlfriends."

"Lisa, please. I got in trouble with some gambling— just a backroom hand now and then. But I've lost big. I've got more debt than assets. I make huge contributions at the church—they had that big disaster at the port last year—I got to help them."

She didn't say a word.

"Lisa, the guys I owe money to don't play pretty if you're late. I shouldn't have borrowed from the New Orleans crowd. Uncle Mario can't protect me—the amount's too big. I got no choice. I've got to make good on the debt."

In the faint ambient light from outdoors, he saw her bow her head and knew she must be crying. He got up and sat on the padded armrest of her chair. He placed one arm around her shoulders and brought her head to his ribs. It was an awkward hug, but the best he could do. As soon as he brought her against him, she burst out crying and beat her fists against the seat of the chair. Her muffled sobs distorted her words, and he just let her cry while he held her.

"It's okay, darling. Just cry. I'm so very sorry. Everything is a big mess. Everything. I'm sorry."

Gradually, her arms moved around his waist, and her sobbing subsided. "Oh, Frank. It feels so good to be held. It's been so long since I've been held."

"I'll hold you as long as you want."

Eventually, she turned her face up to his. Frank leaned

over and softly kissed her lips. But the softness lingered and he responded until his kisses became just as urgent as hers. He was becoming so hard—he couldn't sit any longer.

"Lisa, sweet Lisa, my love. I have to leave now. I can't take this. I'm sorry, but I'm scared of what might happen, and I don't want to offend you," Frank murmured as he forced himself away and tousled her hair.

"Please, Frank. I've dreamed of your touch so many nights."

Standing up, she took his hand and led him to the sofa. Wordlessly, she pulled him toward her and fell back on the couch. Frank reached for her tiny hips and pushed her into him. Her curves were perfect for his grasp, and his lips went to her neck and her ears, then lower as he pulled down the wispy pink gown.

His lips descended to her nipples, and her entire body arched into pleasure. He cupped both breasts in his hands and whispered, "Lisa, you are perfect. Just perfect."

Her hands reached to his belt buckle.

"Lisa, are you sure? I don't want to do it, if you're not sure."

"Yes, yes, I want you—you have no idea how much I want you."

She unzipped his pants, and then he stood and lowered his boxers and trousers. She rolled to the floor and extended her long, white legs to accommodate him while moistening him with her saliva.

"You're okay after the baby, right? This won't hurt you will it?"

"It's okay."

With that, he made love to her most of the night. He didn't once think of gambling debts or other mobsters. The only thing that mattered to him was this gorgeous girl who would be his future—somehow. They'd make it work out, no matter what.

It was still dark, but close to morning, as he got up to

leave.

"I like your hair mussed up, Frank," Lisa said as he cleaned up in the bathroom. "I've never seen it like that."

"I'm going to make sure you see it like that a lot."

"Oh, good," she said with an impish smile. "If I can have a night like this, I don't mind sleeping half the day."

Frank nudged her under the chin. "You're my future, Lisa. I don't know how we're going to make it work, but we will. You have my promise on that."

Sadness filled her eyes again. "I'm trusting you, little Carlucci. Don't let me down."

Frank kissed the top of her head. "Don't worry. I won't."

With that brief goodbye, Frank walked out the back door and down the alleyway to his car. No one saw him— or so he hoped.

CHAPTER THIRTY

Frank didn't have the luxury of a good sleep in the predawn hours once he got home. Instead, he showered and shaved. The warm water running down his body reminded him of Lisa's smooth heat.

Today would be another hard day at the office, even though it was Saturday. But he didn't care. Mountains of paperwork couldn't faze him. Lisa was his. Here was one secret that he could hold in gladness. Not like the heavy, endless secrets related to business.

At the end of the long day, Frank considered driving by Lisa's cottage again. But he didn't dare take a chance.

Sunday morning dawned, and Frank awoke refreshed. He chose a navy blue pinstriped suit with two-tone wing tips. A wide silk tie finished the outfit, and a smart navy fedora angled across his forehead.

As he walked from his parked car toward the front entrance of the stone church, a hand grabbed his shoulder from behind and spun him around in the crowd.

"You bastard hoodlum," a woman screamed at him as

she pounded his chest with tiny fists.

"Who are you?"

"You killed my husband, you scum. Cut him up and stuffed him in his suitcase."

"I don't have any idea what you're talking about." Frank tried to keep her from falling down on the uneven cobblestones.

"Don't touch me, you filthy scum. God will avenge my husband. You'll pay for what you did."

The crowd stood back, mouths gaping. The two policemen hired to control the church's traffic reached the hysterical woman and calmed her. Frank smoothed his suit jacket and turned into the church's cool darkness. He had known he had a lot to talk to God about this morning, but now it was obvious he had even more than he knew. That damn Vince. What had gotten into him? Wasn't it enough to kill someone, why did he need to cut him up like a chicken? Frank could see the headlines already: CARLUCCI CUTS UP RIVALS, BLOODBATH IN ZAPATA.

Frank arrived at the office around eight on Monday morning. The mayor had already called six times. Before Frank could return the call, the phone rang again. The mayor yelled loud enough for Frank to wince, "What the hell is going on? My phone has been ringing nonstop. All of Zapata is enraged. Have you seen a newspaper yet?"

"No, sir, I haven't seen a newspaper."

Frank reached for the folded newspaper placed on his desk every morning. A large picture of a bloodstained suitcase stared back at him. Frank skimmed the article and didn't see mention of Carlucci Enterprises or their names anywhere.

"Wait a minute. I'm looking at the article as we speak, and I don't see any mention of me or my brother."

"That's beside the point, Frank. Everyone assumes that you two had something to do with this because of your business."

"Well, it strikes me that it's an awful big assumption, mayor. Awful big."

"You better do some damage control, because I can't fade the heat for you guys for long. Once that Reverend Fickum or some other of his crazies get ahold of this, it's all over."

"Understood, sir. I'll look into this."

Frank hung up and yelled for Benno. "Benno, no meeting this morning. I've got a headache. I'm leaving the office now."

Frank grabbed his hat and headed for the door. "Tell everyone I'll be gone today."

"Sure, Boss. I'll let them know."

Frank didn't know where he would go for peace and quiet, but he had to find somewhere to think. Could he figure his way out of this mess? Had he and Vince become the criminals that their father had warned them about? Had that lady yesterday been right about God's revenge coming down on them?

Frank returned to his office several hours later. The time alone had been good, but it was now time to start dealing with the mess.

As soon as he sat at his desk, the phone rang.

"Mr. Carlucci? This is Jeff Larson in the governor's office."

Frank didn't recognize the name. "Yes?"

"Governor Sullivan has instructed me to tell you to appear at a meeting in his office next Monday morning related to crime in Zapata. You'll be responding to questions from a commission investigating criminal activity. The governor suggests that you retain legal counsel."

"Will a subpoena be issued?" Frank asked.

"This is not a trial, sir. However, your attendance and cooperation are strongly suggested."

"I see," Frank said in a subdued voice. "Thank you, Mr. Larson, for your call."

Frank carefully lowered the phone to its cradle. His frustration exploded as he yelled, "Shit. Shit. Shit."

Benno stuck his head inside the door.

"Get me Vince right now."

While Frank was waiting for Vince, the phone rang a second time.

"Frank, John Sullivan here."

"Good afternoon, Governor."

"You got to get this cleaned up, Frank. What in the hell has happened? Three murders in one week? Everyone is highly agitated—a suitcase full of body pieces? The press is having a field day."

"Governor, I'll try to find out. Right now, I have no idea."

"Get your damned ducks in a row before that meeting of the commission. Sheppard's in charge of that group, and he'll be looking to hang you from a tree."

"Yes, sir. Understood."

Frank hung up as Vince ambled in. "Shut the door, Benno, and stay with us."

Vince squinted at Frank. "What's going on, brother?"

"You tell me what's going on. Everyone's on my ass. We got some big problems."

Vince ran one hand down his shirtfront. "What did the governor say?"

"He said I have to show up at the capitol for a new commission's investigation on crime in Zapata. The warrior-of-the-good Sheppard is in charge and is looking to put us out of business."

"What else did he say?"

"Three murders in one week have everyone upset. A

suitcase full of human body parts has everyone upset."

"Is that all?" Vince coldly eyed Frank across the broad mahogany expanse of desk.

"Isn't that bad enough?"

"Anybody say there are witnesses? Are there formal charges pending?"

Vince's logic wasn't reassuring. He didn't understand perception. Public perception—they had to keep the Carlucci name respected. "What are you getting at?"

"They got no evidence, no witnesses, nothing. And they won't get nothing, brother. They can't tie me, or Benno to the murders. That's the bottom line."

"You have to cool down, Vince. Way down. There's too much attention on us right now. Any little misstep can bring Sheppard and the public right down on us and close us down. We can't afford that right now."

Vince just eyed Frank.

Benno jumped in. "Don't worry. We can cool it down, Frank. You'll see."

Frank reached his right hand toward Vince. "Can we shake on that?"

With a snort, Vince extended his right hand and gripped Frank. "Don't worry so much, brother. Like we said in the last meeting with all the boys, you don't know nothing about what Benno and me do at night. No one can touch you because you're clean. All you know is that problems get solved. See, like magic." Vince snapped his fingers in the air. "It's magic—that's what you have me for."

"Okay, Vince. But don't work your magic for a while. I got to figure out how to defuse this situation, and it's not going to be easy."

On the appointed day, Frank had his taxi arrive fifteen minutes early to the governor's office in Jackson. A milling crowd of newspapermen packed the street in front of the building. Frank gritted his teeth. "Go around to the back entrance." Even that area wasn't clear of the press, but Frank jumped out anyway and strode rapidly through the door and to the freight elevator.

A secretary in the wood-paneled, high-ceilinged domain of the governor's offices barely lifted her eyes when she murmured, "Good morning, Mr. Carlucci. Please have a seat."

Frank swallowed—just weeks ago she had been friendly and flirtatious, caressing him with a light but knowing touch in the small lobby, issuing a clear invitation.

He perched in an upholstered monster of a chair. *What's going on here? What's really going on? Do they have evidence they haven't told me about?*

His thoughts were interrupted when a police officer opened the governor's office and walked toward Frank. "Come in, Mr. Carlucci."

The governor and two other men sat at a large conference table. The room was stiff and uncomfortable. The two ceiling fans didn't provide much air to combat the sun's heat streaming through the frosted glass windows.

"Mr. Carlucci, let me introduce Lieutenant Governor Gregory Smith and Attorney General William Sheppard."

"Good morning," Frank said.

"Do you have counsel?" Sheppard asked.

"This isn't a trial or deposition, is it?"

The governor pointed his glasses at Frank. "What do you know about the recent murders in Zapata?" He paused and shuffled papers in front of him. "Between May first and May third?"

"I only know what I've read in the newspapers. One of my employees was shot at the railroad station. I didn't know him personally—we have over one hundred employees. I didn't know the others."

"Weren't they your employees also?"

"I don't know."

Sheppard's face took on an expression of sharpness. "You're telling us you don't know who works for you and who doesn't?"

Frank forced calmness into his voice. "We have numerous business enterprises all over the island. There's no way I can know every employee at every location. People come and go. They get tired of the restaurant business—you know, it's all pretty much drudgery, especially back in the kitchen."

The men at the table whispered among themselves. Then Sheppard spoke again. "Mr. Carlucci, this is not a criminal hearing. We are just investigating the facts. Trying to fulfill our responsibilities to the public.

"Crime is on the rise on Zapata Island. This concerns us, and it mightily concerns our constituency. Your business enterprises contribute to crime, according to our sources."

"Sir, I am a businessman. I own numerous restaurants, concession stands, and other types of legitimate businesses. I resent your implication that I am involved in illegal activity."

Everyone at the table looked at Frank.

"In fact, if you have proof of this so-called illegal activity, then you need to provide it so we can have a legal trial and I can be cleared. I deserve the right to protect my family's name."

Sheppard warmed to the questioning. "Are you telling us that you are not involved in the movement and selling of illegal alcohol?"

"I am not involved."

"Are you telling us that you are not involved in the brutal murders of three men recently killed in Zapata?"

"I am not involved."

Questions of a more general nature continued for two and a half hours. Frank wondered if they were just trying to wear him down.

Finally, Sheppard signaled the governor. "Thank you, Mr. Carlucci, for your time today," the governor said. "You have been helpful. The citizens of Mississippi will, no doubt, feel reassured by your testimony to our commission."

Before Frank could speak, Sheppard continued, "Let me say, Mr. Carlucci, that we will be watching Zapata Island very closely. I can solemnly assure you that if we find any illegal activity, we will prosecute to the fullest."

Frank was almost too exhausted to speak, but he knew he mustn't let them see it. "Don't worry, Mr. Sheppard. You won't need to come to Zapata Island. Carlucci Enterprises runs smoothly and legally, just as we always have. In fact, you might want to come bowl in one of our bowling alleys. It's great fun."

The governor proclaimed the meeting adjourned and all three men stood.

Frank turned and walked out after shaking hands with everyone. Again, the cute little secretary kept her eyes on her typing and her small, capable hands steady over the keys. This smallest change of all the changes today told Frank that this legal mess was only beginning.

CHAPTER THIRTY-ONE

Almost a year passed, and Frank never felt the heavy weight of impending doom lift from his chest. His jaw was always clenched, his hands were as tense as Vince's had always been—curling and uncurling into fists in every conversation. Every time Frank stared at the phone and told himself he'd call Lisa that day, he didn't. And, every night when he hit the deck, he was too worried to talk nice to anyone, much less a special girl like her.

The San Francisco was close to being finished. Vince, Benno, DeLuca, and Mitch sat in Frank's office on a morning that had begun cool but was threatening to become too hot for comfort. Partially consumed coffee sat in thick white china cups, and sunlight poured in through the windows.

Frank began the meeting. "Tony, give us an update on the construction."

DeLuca looked up and grunted. "You're going to like it, boys. That fancy Spanish architect has done us proud. Four world-class carved mahogany bars—long enough for fifty people each. Wrought-iron gates and squiggles throughout. Today the workers are planting three different kinds of palms—the trucks with them are lined up for half a mile."

Vince squirmed in his chair. "We got all the security features I asked for?"

"It would be like breaking into Alcatraz to get into there—iron gates, big doormen, thick walls, multiple safes, elevators with secret codes that only the five of us will have. One safe just for guns, and one safe for ammo. We could hold off the Marine Corps from inside. Don't worry—everything you asked for plus more is there."

"More?" Vince raised his eyebrows and gave DeLuca a hard look. "What do you mean 'more'?"

"Frank asked for—"

Vince's open hand hit the table so hard that it sounded like a rifle discharge. "I'm in charge of security for Carlucci Enterprises. Not my fucking brother."

Everyone else's eyes turned to Frank. He could feel them as sharp as iron pokers. "I am not your 'fucking brother,' Vince."

Vince's face turned beet red, and he sat stock-still. When he stood, he turned away from the table. "See you guys later."

After he left, Frank turned to Benno. "Keep an eye on him, Benno. Make sure he's okay."

Benno grabbed his hat and hurried away with a quick "Sure, Boss."

Frank shuffled some papers in front of him. "Let's continue with our meeting," he told Mitch and DeLuca. "Let's look at these expenses and related income."

"Frank, we got to talk about your brother," DeLuca said. "It's something that's been needed to be talked about for a while."

Frank quit playing with the pages. "What do you mean?"

"Vince has been coming to the construction site. If he

sees anything that he doesn't like, he yells at the workers. He scares them. Sometimes he shoves them around—like he owns them. Then they quit."

"How long has he been doing this?"

"More recently—the last few months or so. He's got a thing for the decorator—that Lila woman."

Frank smiled, remembering her lush curves and long, wavy black hair that she incessantly ran her elegant hands through, stroking it as if it were a small, pampered pet. "Well, I can understand that."

DeLuca continued with a serious face. "If Vince tries to force himself on her, she'll cause a big stink. We can't afford that right now—we'd have to pay her off big-time."

"You think Vince would do that?"

"C'mon, Frank. You know how he is. He can't stand to not get his way in any situation. It drives him crazy. Look at what happened just now."

Frank rubbed his face with both hands. "What do you suggest?"

DeLuca looked at Mitch. "What do you think, Mitch?"

"Can you talk some sense into him, Frank?"

"I don't know."

Mitch looked over at DeLuca. "Maybe you can talk to him, Tony. You're the oldest. Maybe he'd listen to you."

"I could try," DeLuca said. "But here's the thing. What if I fail? We got to have a backup plan."

Frank saw with clarity what he must do. "I have to be the one to talk to him. There's no other way."

"When?" the two other men asked in unison.

"This afternoon or tonight."

"Just remember," DeLuca said, "Vince sleeps all day. Then, he starts drinking as soon as he wakes up. He drinks before he goes to the beach for night deliveries, then he's there all night. You got to get to him before the drink does."

"Okay. I can manage that," Frank said. "Let's adjourn

for now."

Silently, the two men gathered their hats and left.

At four that afternoon Frank walked up the steps to the front porch of Vince's small bungalow. He rapped on the doorframe. Sweat dripped down his backbone, and even his feet felt too thick for his shoes.

No answer. Frank rapped again with increased force.

After a long pause, the door cracked slightly. "You visiting?"

"Social call, brother."

"My ass."

Vince opened the door. He stood in his T-shirt and baggy trousers. He was barefoot and need a shave.

Frank stepped inside and sat in the chair Vince waved at. The small living room smelled stale, as if it hadn't been aired out in a long time. Vince sat in another shabby chair.

"I hope I didn't wake you up, Vince."

"What's going on, brother?"

"We're worried about you."

"Who's 'we'?"

"All of us."

"What you worried about?"

"Your temper."

"Is that all?"

"Face it, Vince. Our whole business rests on you. You know we couldn't survive without your protection. You and Benno scare everyone off."

Vince sat back in his chair, his legs splayed out in front. Frank was too jittery to sit back, and he wondered if Vince noticed. Vince noticed everything.

"If me and Benno protect all of you guys and our business interests, it seems to me that you'd be a little more grateful."

"What else do you want, Vince? More money? A

better place to live? You make the same amount of money as I do, but I'm building a new place. You could do the same."

"That's not what I'm talking about, and you know it."

"What are you talking about?"

"You think you're better than me. I can see—"

"No, I don't."

"Sure, you do. You think your fancy rags and hobnobbing with those country-club people makes you something other than a crook. You think that your hands are clean from the killing I do to protect our business. But you know what, Frank? You're a killer just like I am."

Frank stood, heat rising in his entire body until his head wanted to explode. "You're the killer, and you enjoy doing it," he yelled, his body shaking. "I'm not like you, and I'll never be like you."

Vince sat calmly and didn't say a thing.

Frank raised his hand and pointed at Vince's chest. "You can't control yourself. If you keep killing people you're going to bring down our entire house."

Vince wiped the sweat from his upper lip with a hairy forearm. "Do you wonder why our profits haven't gone up even though we added more slots? I keep track of all the weekly payoffs and what we bring in from each machine. Someone who works for us is skimming off the top. It's shit like that that's going to bring us down, not me killing someone who needs killing."

"Someone is skimming?"

"Yeah, you know why you can't pay off those debts to the guys in New Orleans? It's because you and me and Mitch, Tony, and Benno are being ripped off by some of our own."

"You're sure?"

"Yeah, I'm sure. And I'm going to catch them."

"No more killing, Vince."

"Look. Don't tell me how to do my job. I don't tell you how to do yours. I know you go to fancy parties, take out those pretty girls, and cozy up to their dads who run this island. Hell, your bedroom probably has a different girl every night while I'm slapping mosquitoes and hauling crates on the beach. But I don't tell you what to do with your dick or how to do it."

"Vince, that's not—"

"I watch your house sometimes at night, Frank. I know what you do."

Frank couldn't control the sinking feeling in his stomach. Was this Vince's way of saying he knew about Lisa? And what lies was Vince telling Lisa?

"Look, Carlucci Enterprises has to be able to afford those hotshot entertainers DeLuca wants for the San Francisco. What's his name—Bob Hope? You got to pay your debts. So I got to take care of whoever is skimming."

Vince glanced at a small clock on the painted mantel. "Time for me to pick up Benno."

They both stood. There wasn't anything more to say, was there? Frank walked to the door and left without a word.

CHAPTER THIRTY-TWO

Frank descended into an even deeper fog of worry after the conversation with Vince. Every day he expected Vince to erupt into more arguments, fights, or schemes to kill people "who needed killing." Every night he expected to awaken to Vince's raspy voice and pistol barrel at Frank's head. "Jig's up," he'd say. "I already killed Lisa, now it's your turn."

The only project that brought Frank relief was working on getting his house built—his dream home. Six months later Frank stood on the porch of his finished new house. He'd managed to float another loan and get the damn thing done, the urgency to complete it gnawing at his insides.

Surely, the good luck of the soon-to-be-finished San Francisco would propel profits forward and give him the life he had always imagined—servants, ironed tablecloths heavy with starch, a butler who shined his shoes every night and woke him up with steaming coffee in an ornate silver pot. And a beautiful, eager woman—Lisa—in his arms. Yes, that would be a good life. But after all the months of never calling her, she'd probably found someone else. Dames were like that.

But today, well, today was another story. The house was buzzing with preparations for an official housewarming. Frank had invited everyone, including the mayor, the governor, even Will Sheppard.

That evening, Frank welcomed everyone at the door as the valets ran to cars whose polished hoods and chrome extended for blocks. He lost his breath as Lisa stepped out of the passenger side of a smart little red coupe. She was even more beautiful than before—if that were possible. A long, white gown covered her, coming together in a series of soft pleats under her breasts. There was shimmery stuff—or was it just his eyes that saw her shimmering in the floodlights of the entryway?

As he watched, Vince put one possessive hand under her left elbow and guided her forward. Frank's insides grew queasy. What else had Vince possessed all these months?

Her baby-blue eyes were shining as he stammered a hello and other meaningless phrases. She extended her right hand and touched his extended hand. "Good to see you, Frank. Gorgeous house."

Before he could speak, Vince interjected. "You look like you never saw a beautiful woman before, brother. And we know that's not the case. In fact, Margaret—"

"Come in, come in. There's plenty to drink inside. Plenty good food."

Even before people started leaving, Frank was tired. His body felt brittle with worry. Vince was drinking heavily and slurring his words. Lisa remained a distant pillar of loveliness in that icy white gown and had been avoiding him all night.

As everyone stood in the entryway saying long goodbyes, Charlie Cannady, Frank's banker, assisted by his wife, swayed, having trouble finding his feet. In an explosion of goodwill, he hugged everyone over and over. On his last hug, he sloshed his highball down the front of Lisa's dress. He clumsily began apologizing, trying to wipe it away with his other hand.

Vince reacted immediately. "Get your paws off my girl's breasts." He sprung at Cannady as if in a street fight and wrestled him to the floor. Mayhem ensued. Cannady's wife leapt on top of Vince, hitting him with her purse. Lisa plastered herself against the wall, staying clear of flailing limbs and spilled drinks. Cannady kept repeating, "Sorry, sorry."

Frank felt as if the world were crashing in on him. He gave a hurried sign to Benno as he and other security guys tried to control Vince. Finally, they succeeded in walking him to another room out of the sight of everyone.

Lisa turned to follow, but Frank caught her hand. "I miss you, Lisa."

"How are you, Frank?"

"You're gorgeous tonight."

"You noticed?"

"I still love you."

"That's not what I hear."

"We need to talk."

Lisa shrugged and started to walk off to where Vince had been taken. Frank didn't let go of her hand and pulled her around to look at him again.

"Vince has been lying to you about me."

"He's not the only one. I hear the name Margaret come up a lot."

"Give me a chance to explain."

"Not now, Frank."

"This week, then."

She relented just a bit. "Okay, Wednesday. Ten p.m. Ocean Front at Fourteenth. My red coupe."

"I'll be there."

A strange sound emerged from outside the house. Was that a funeral hymn? Frank jerked his thumb in that direction and asked one of the valets who had run inside.

"There's a group of people outside singing, sir."

"Who are they?"

"Some kind of church people."

Frank walked outside the house. There was a small crowd that looked right out of Edgar Allan Poe. Long, dark coats enveloped their forms. All the women wore black head scarves and black gloves. Even the hymnals were black. Several held upright crosses of dark wood. Unsurprisingly, the tall figure of the Reverend Fickum stood in front. His voice rang out in thunderous tones. "The work of the devil will be stopped. God will revenge his own. Evildoers will burn in hell."

Frank stuck a finger in Fickum's bony face. "I've had enough of your stupid demonstrations, Fickum."

Fickum drew his scrawny height to its fullest. "You, sir, are threatening me." His entire body quivered as if he were a terrier on the trail of a rat. "I will not be intimidated. I will not give in to the forces of evil. I am doing the work of God." Each enunciated syllable exploded into Frank's face with a spray of saliva.

Frank reached inside his front jacket pocket, and Fickum exploded into a roundhouse punch that sent Frank sprawling onto the lawn and rolling into the street. Later, Vince would say that he thought Frank's life was in danger, and that he had seen Fickum reach inside his own jacket for a gun. Frank didn't know any of this. All he heard through the fog of his own surprise and pain was Lisa's long scream of "Frank" and a single gunshot. The worst news would come later—Vince had shot the wrong person, an innocent woman, and Fickum didn't have a gun inside his jacket.

Vince was charged with homicide. Just the opposite of what Carlucci Enterprises needed—more bad publicity.

Even worse, it took every dollar of Frank's resources to bail Vince out of jail on personal recognizance and a promise not to travel.

Frank took him home in the early morning hours. He refused to talk to Vince other than a terse two-word order: "Stay home."

Vince didn't even reply as he walked to his cold, dark bungalow.

At home, when Frank peeled off his tux and collapsed into cold sheets, he wondered about sending Vince to Cuba immediately. But running things on his own? Forever? If Vince left the States, he'd had to leave forever. Frank was trapped. Trapped and alone.

CHAPTER THIRTY-THREE

The next day was bright and sunny, a bit cold—as cold as a Gulfstream winter ever gets. Frank awoke early and went to his study with a heavy robe over his blue pajamas. The still-new leather chair behind the expansive desk creaked as he sat down. Light filtered in through gauzy white sheers between the heavy burgundy velvet panels. Bentley had already delivered steaming coffee and departed through the large doors into the hallway.

Frank buried his head in his hands. Later this morning he'd have to go to church. Everyone would look at him and smile, but what were they really thinking? That he couldn't control his brother? That Vince was a maniac? That Fickum was right about Carlucci Enterprises? At least the incense-laden Mass would provide a haven of tranquility for an hour or so.

The last thing Frank needed now was the added expense of a good lawyer for Vince. There had to be witnesses in the crowd who had seen what Vince had seen—Fickum reaching inside his coat, presumably for a gun. Besides, Frank could testify that he'd seen a gun on Fickum another time. What if Vince hadn't reacted and

Fickum had pulled out a gun to kill Frank? There was no doubt that Fickum hated Frank enough to murder him—despite being a man of God. Frank had seen hatred in peoples' eyes often enough while growing up—yes, that dead coldness in Fickum's eyes was insane hatred. Vince had probably saved Frank's life—except there was no weapon when the police got to Fickum. Was Vince lying or had the weapon been handed off to someone else?

Frank's desk phone rang. Who'd be crazy enough to call him so early?

"Frank," Vince said. "You up?"

"Hell, yes. How am I supposed to sleep with all this going on?"

"You seen the paper?"

"Why?"

Vince let a moment of lightness creep into his voice. "Fickum is going all out. And that fucking newspaper is letting him. You got to stop that."

Frank sighed. "We don't control everything on this island."

"We used to."

"That was before three murders in two weeks and the chopped-up body in the suitcase. Public opinion has turned against us."

"It'll turn back when people think about how many jobs we bring to the island, how many money-paying tourists are ready to blow their wads here. We're the biggest fucking employer here."

"Do you have extra security at all our locations?"

Vince snorted. "Of course, I do. We've been watching Fickum crank up people for a while. But listen, you need to pay Fickum a visit."

"Are you crazy?"

"Go see him alone. Offer to pay him off. Everybody's got a price."

"He may try to kill me again."

"Take Benno or one of the guys that he doesn't know.

But talk to him alone and offer him big money. Maybe he'd like an early retirement, brother. You know how tiring it is preaching the word."

"Just for you. But I'm tapped out of money. Can't take any more risks until the San Francisco is up and running."

"Well, here's the worst news of the morning, Frank. Fickum has hundreds of demonstrators at the San Fran's construction site. He says he's going to stop us from opening, and he has enough people to do it."

"Shit."

"Be your most charming, brother. I know you usually save that for the dolls, but today use it on the reverend."

Frank pushed his coffee cup aside. "Got it."

After Mass, Frank drove to Fickum's house—a tall, brick mansion just half a block away from his denominational church. Frank moved his gloved hands slowly on the steering wheel. He'd ignored Vince's advice to take one of the guys with him—he didn't know why. It felt like he needed to handle this alone.

He parked his car down the block and studied the brick house. Everything looked cold and sparkling this morning in the sun. Dead leaves blew across the wide lawn, and the bare branches of a vine scraped across the boards of an unpainted picket fence.

Frank rapped the front door with his knuckles. After a long pause, the door cracked barely two inches. A woman's pale face, framed by wispy brown hair, inserted itself partially against the crack. "May I help you?"

"I'm here to see the reverend."

The little church mouse of a woman smiled. "The reverend is holding services today, sir."

"Yes, I would assume so. But will he be home later this afternoon? I need to talk to him."

The kind brown eyes grew larger, and the door opened wider. The slight woman, in a washed-out gray dress, looked Frank up and down, from polished wing tips to camel overcoat and matching fedora. "You're one of the Carlucci brothers, aren't you?"

"Yes, ma'am. I am Frank Carlucci."

Her eyes darkened. "You're a sinner."

"Your husband thinks I am, yes." Frank tried one of his most charming smiles—one that always worked with women.

She looked at the floor and began closing the door. "I can't talk to you."

Frank quickly inserted his foot in the space of the door's opening. "It's really important that I talk to your husband today, Mrs. Fickum. Is he at home now?"

She pushed against the door and strained with the effort. She raised her voice and whimpered. "Please, mister. You have to go now. My husband will be upset. Please, go. Please, please."

As her voice rose, Frank turned to leave but was surprised to see a tall figure dressed in black striding up the sidewalk and onto the small porch.

"Stop harassing my wife, you scum."

Frank didn't have to try hard to remember Fickum's sneaky blow to his jaw. "Don't get too close to me, Fickum."

"You hoodlum trash. What are you doing bothering a good woman like my Sarah Jane?"

Frank gritted his teeth and forced a smile. "I'd like a private word with you, Reverend. Do you have just a few minutes to spend with me?" This had to be the hardest thing he'd ever done.

The preacher seemed mollified. He smiled his own version of a possum grin and invited Frank inside to the parlor.

They sat on either side of a small, chipped wood table. Fickum glowered at Frank and rubbed his restless hands up and down his thighs.

"We hope to settle this unfortunate misunderstanding soon," Frank said.

"Mr. Carlucci, the great state of Mississippi has, thank the Lord, laws which prohibit your type of sinful activities."

"Reverend, we are legitimate businessmen—"

"You may add lying to your list of sins, brother."

"We are legitimate businessmen who own numerous restaurants, clubs, and other types of recreational enterprises. We are—"

"Sinners," intoned the reverend. "I pray for your souls every day, brother."

Frank was getting nowhere. Maybe Vince's tactics were the only thing this idiot could understand.

"How much money do you earn annually, Reverend?"

"I beg your pardon?"

"You heard me, Reverend. Let's stop playing games. I'm here with a one-time offer."

"You spawn of the devil."

"One-time offer, Fickum. Carlucchi Enterprises can give you the opportunity to live somewhere else beautiful. Somewhere you and your wife would enjoy more than this little pea-sized island. You wouldn't have to work for a very, very long time. Doesn't that sound nice?"

"You treacherous son of Eve. You have the audacity to believe that the work of God can be put off? You think that the man of God can be purchased with blood money?"

Frank reached inside his left coat pocket and drew out a thick envelope. Inside rested his last reserve of cash. The stack of one-hundred-dollar bills that he had put aside for the next debt payment to the New Orleans guys. He opened the envelope and ruffled the money with his fingers. "Everything here can be yours, Fickum. But you have to leave Zapata in the middle of the night and go somewhere that no one can find you—not the newspapers, not the governor, not the church people from all over the Gulf

Coast you've fired up."

Fickum leaned back in his seat and crossed his bony legs at the ankles. "Get out of my house, Mr. Carlucci. Get out right now. You are desecrating us with your presence."

Frank closed the envelope and placed it back inside his pocket. "Very well, Fickum."

He stood, aware of the heat of his anger rising and his own hands opening and closing with the desire to punch Fickum and pay him back for the past soreness in his own neck and jaw. Instead, Frank forced himself to walk to the entranceway, where Mrs. Fickum waited to see him out.

"Good day to you, ma'am," he said when she opened the heavy front door.

She didn't reply, and Frank counted it as just one more snub from the overly pious household.

He had known all along that this effort would fail. They'd have to find another way to stop Fickum, but it couldn't include murder—not now. Too much publicity already in the works.

Frank drove to Benno's rental. Even though Benno shared in all the profits, he hadn't upgraded much from his one-room situation. At least now Benno had a stand-alone little wooden house. Frank hoped that he'd be awake.

Sure enough, Benno opened the door and motioned Frank inside. A little gas heater was roaring inside the fireplace niche instead of logs. Benno motioned Frank into one of the ragged upholstered chairs.

"What's up, Boss?"

"Tell me what you know about Fickum. Vince had you guys following him for a while, right?"

"Yeah, for a while. But not real close. We got too many other projects."

"Find anything?"

"He uses his church network to bring all these people to the island. He likes standing with his Bible and yelling them up."

"How many people does he have here now?"

"Around five hundred."

"So he really can stop the San Fran's opening?"

"I think so, Boss. These people are crazy against us. We can't kill all of them."

Frank almost laughed. "We don't want to kill them, Benno. We just want them to go away."

Benno picked up a dime-store china cup he'd been drinking from. "You want some soup, Boss? Chicken noodle."

Frank shook his head no. "We got to find a way to stop Fickum. If he's gone, then these people will just melt away."

"All he does is go to the church, to his house, to Jackson every once in a while."

"Jackson?"

"Yeah, to a bookstore. Religious books and stuff."

"Why doesn't he get that stuff mailed to him?"

"Never thought about it." Benno put down the mug and rubbed his strong hands together.

"If he's driving to Jackson, that's a lot of driving time. There's got to be something there to make it worth his while. Know what I mean?"

"I didn't think about it that way."

"Next time he goes, make sure we know what he does every second of that trip. Suspend anything else you're told to do, and follow him closely. We got to find something on him, and we got to find it real soon."

"Sure, Boss. If there's anything worthwhile, we'll find it. Don't worry."

Frank left Benno's, feeling a little more hopeful, even if it was a long shot. At home, he told Bentley to cancel all his other commitments for the day. He replaced the envelope in his private safe and went into the secluded master bedroom. He didn't know why, but a nap seemed like the only thing he wanted to do. Soft, warm covers. A pile of pillows, a couple of aspirin, and no dreams. That's all he wanted. No dreams—good or bad. Not today.

CHAPTER THIRTY-FOUR

The next day found Frank early at his desk determined to deal with the large stack of paperwork needing his approval. He had called off the usual meeting and again cautioned Vince to stay out of sight and away from the construction site.

Just as he had pulled a looming stack of invoices, purchase orders, and payroll requisitions toward him, the phone jangled.

It was DeLuca. "I'm at the construction site, and we can't move an inch. My workers can't even get inside."

"What do you mean?" Frank snapped.

"Fickum has hundreds of people here. They're standing shoulder to shoulder. Blocking our way in."

"Shit!"

"That ain't going to help," DeLuca said. "Maybe the newspaper is putting him up to this. You see the headlines yesterday?"

"You mean that crap about 'God's Preacher Against Crime.' Paints him as holy and us as violent criminals.

You'd think we did the Valentine's Day Massacre, not Scarface."

DeLuca chuckled. "Remember, Frank. It's harder to fight the 'good' people than bad guys. You and Vince are going to have to come up with another strategy. Give more money to your church or something."

"I can't fix this problem by throwing more money at it. Besides, Fickum's church ain't my church. Vince has already tried his methods, and you saw how good that worked."

"Think of something because, at this rate, we're paying for workers who can't get a lick of work done."

"Okay, okay. I'll think of something."

Two days later Frank was still trying to come up with a solution. Everyone in city government claimed he couldn't take the risk of bad publicity. The black-coated followers of Fickum sang mournfully while standing in the cold, and sometimes rain, and only seemed to enjoy their misery. Fickum was in his element, striding in front, pounding his hands together and yelling, pointing toward heaven.

By Wednesday evening, Frank wasn't even sure he wanted to see Lisa. But he drove to the ten p.m. spot. Her little red coupe drove up only minutes later, and he forced himself to walk over and smile.

Her pale countenance rose above her darker coat like a beautiful white rose, and his grin became genuine.

"Get in the car, Frank."

He walked to the passenger side and slid into the leather seat. "This is quite a baby you've got here, Lisa."

"Vince bought it for me."

"How are you and Vince doing?"

"You asked me to meet you to talk about Vince?"

Frank sighed. Nothing was easy this week. "No. I want to talk about us, Lisa. Remember, 'us'?"

"Vince and others have told me about you dating other women. I can't take that."

"Why do you believe Vince?"

"Are you doing it?"

"Doing what?"

"Are you sleeping with other women?"

"Not since you and I, you know, made love the last time."

"Why should I believe you?" Lisa's determined face didn't look like she even wanted to believe him.

"Because it's the truth." Frank grabbed her gloved hand and brought it near his face.

"Don't try your charm on me."

"Why can't you believe me?"

"Because even the women who help me with my girls home talk about you. Who you were seen with at the club, who you escorted to parties, how long you were inside one of those damn cabanas at the pool with one of your little girlfriends." Lisa broke into tears. "It's more than I can take, dammit. I'm the one who's in love with you, remember? I'm the one who's had your baby, remember? I'm the girl you don't call anymore."

Her shoulders shook, and her voice broke. She rifled through a small purse for a handkerchief. Frank reached into his back pocket and gave her his.

"Lisa, I'm sorry you feel this way. I don't call you because I never know if Vince is there or not. He'd kill us if he knew, remember?" Frank tried to keep his voice soft and gentle, although he felt like screaming. "I have to go out with other women—it's part of keeping my ear to the ground with their dads and brothers who run this island. But I haven't made love to anyone since you and I got together. How could I? We sealed the deal, didn't we?"

Lisa sniffled into the white square of hankie. "I thought we had, Frank. Then I hear all these stories. For months and months, those damned stories."

He reached out and touched her elbow. "The stories

aren't true, Lisa. Most of what I do is endless paperwork. I'm at the office late, almost every night. Our businesses are under a lot of strain this year—trying to expand. All our money is on the line, and now this screwed-up situation with the new club we're building. Plus Vince on bail."

She turned to look at Frank. Accusation burned in her eyes. "How come you don't come over late at night?"

"I never know if Vince might be there."

"You know his beach schedule."

"No, I don't. He won't tell anyone except Benno. Every once in a while, he might mention it in one of our meetings. But other than that, I don't know what time Vince'll be on the beach. You know how secretive he is."

"I can't stand missing you this way."

"Every night I only think of you and making love to you when I go to sleep."

"Unless you got some other woman there."

"Lisa, there's never another women there. You're the one who belongs in my new house and you'll be there one day. I promise it."

"How much longer?"

"Money's really bad for me. I got to save enough so we can have the lifestyle we like." He slowly took off one of her gloves and kissed her palm.

"Oh, Frank, you can't do that right now."

"Why not?"

"Because—"

A sharp rap on the driver's-side window startled them. The windows had slightly fogged up from their body heat. Lisa jerked her hand away and looked at Frank with wide eyes.

"Roll down the window, Lisa," Frank whispered..

She did, and the black shiny leather of a policeman's belt and holster appeared. The officer looked inside the car. "Evening, ma'am. Just making sure everything is all right here."

The officer peered at both of them more closely.

"Good evening, Mr. Carlucci. I thought I recognized your vehicle. How you folks doing tonight?"

"'I hope I'm not parked illegally," Frank said.

"No sir, you're just fine. Routine check," the officer said before tipping his hat and walking back to the patrol vehicle.

"Shit. Shit. Shit." Lisa said, rolling up her window. "Frank, all this is driving me crazy. I hate living this way. Sneaking around. Having to listen to stories about you. Never telling anyone that you're mine."

"Look, Lisa. We're making progress. No more backroom gambling for me. I'm trying to save money, but every time I turn around something goes south. Vince's bail. Those hotels I invested in over in Louisiana. The guys in New Orleans will kill me if I don't pay off their loan—I got payments every six months. Now this craziness with the San Fran."

"What about the San Fran?"

"The most holy Reverend Fickum has stopped construction with the hordes of followers he's bused in from all over the mainland. We're completely stopped. No one in the city—even the mayor—will help us out because of the potential bad PR. We got contracts with all the best entertainers in the industry. Even if there's no opening night, we got to pay tens of thousands of dollars to them."

"You're kidding!"

"I wish I were. Things are bad. Real bad."

"The mayor's wife helps me at my home for girls. She's a board member. I might be able to talk to her."

"You really think that might work?" Frank couldn't keep the hope out of his voice.

"I'm willing to try," Lisa said with a little smile. "Do you think that police officer saw you kissing my hand?"

"Probably not from his angle. But, you know, why would he think we're meeting late at night like this on the seawall in winter?"

Lisa smiled again. "I think I recognize him from one

time Vince was playing pool with a lot of guys at the Queen of Sheba."

Frank studied her face—first hopeful, then sad again. "We can't do anything about it now."

"I'll talk to her, and maybe she can persuade him to help you. After all, don't us women control our men?"

Frank placed his hand over her now warm hand on the seat between them. "Then it's a good thing that no one knows you're my woman because I don't want anyone else to know you control me."

She laughed. "I wish I did control you."

"You do more than you know."

Frank pointed toward the black sky over a very black ocean. "See the stars, Lisa? It's a paradise of stars. They're burning on us tonight to give us hope."

Lisa sighed. "I'm tired of looking at the stars alone, Frank."

With that, they parted. Frank watched the coupe's taillights recede into the distance. Nothing was easy this week. Nothing resolved. The long months had eroded their connection. He wasn't stupid; he could feel her slipping away. But there was no solution. It was like the tide in the black night ocean—you could feel it, but you couldn't stop it from flowing.

CHAPTER THIRTY-FIVE

The next few weeks brought no relief to Frank or to Carlucci Enterprises. Luckily, the thick envelope in Frank's private safe was ready when the New Orleans guys showed up on schedule one dark night. Every house in Frank's new neighborhood twinkled with Christmas lights and reminded him of the number of days until the San Fran's scheduled opening. Every morning brought DeLuca's telephone call, saying that his workers couldn't gain access to the site.

Then one early morning when Frank picked up the jangling phone, DeLuca's voice had lightened from its bland moroseness. "Frank, it's a miracle."

"What?"

"The demonstrators are gone."

"You're kidding me."

"Not one of them is here this morning."

"What about the reverend?"

"Not even him," DeLuca said.

"We can start working again? We might just make the New Year's Eve opening."

"We'll have to work day and night."

"I just paid five thousand dollars for those damn cut-glass doors you chose, so we'd better earn it back soon," Frank said.

Frank called Lisa immediately to thank her. He didn't know how she'd worked her woman's magic, but he knew it must have come from her whispering in the ear of the mayor's wife.

"Lisa, you did it! The protestors are gone," he said as soon as she answered.

"Thank you so much for calling, but I'm not interested in a new washing machine," she said with brisk efficiency.

"Lisa, it's me Frank."

"Yes, I understand that you have a special deal right now, but I already told you I'm not in the market."

Frank realized that Vince must be there. Had he been there all night? "Thanks, Lisa. I love you," Frank said before hanging up. A voice—that's all he was. A voice on the phone full of promises and emotion. Vince was there in person—a real, live body—warm, passionate, willing to make love to her. Frank's body responded as he thought about making love to her.

But it didn't matter. He wasn't there, and Vince was. A voice couldn't compete. A woman needed more than a voice. She needed someone to watch the stars with her.

As DeLuca kept the workers and interior designer on track, Frank made sure enough staff was hired and food orders were in place. The chef de cuisine had been on hold, but was now told to get his kitchen ready and equipment tested. In the midst of all the activity, Vince continued his solitary waiting in his small house, although Frank had increasing difficulty persuading him that it was still necessary.

"C'mon, Frank, what do you think I'm going to do?"

"I don't know, Vince, and that's what worries me."

"I have to make sure security is tight for the new place. You know that. Plus, I still got to get rid of those guys who are skimming."

"We can't get rid of anyone right now. Not with your trial coming up."

"All you ever do is talk about how much money problems you got."

"Yes, and I still do, but we can't afford any more trouble right now. Lots of people are looking to take us down. What if those bozos in St. Louis quit killing each other and come for us again?"

"But can I at least look at all the security and make sure all the guys are trained right?"

"Go over there for the rest of this week, but don't you dare push anyone around or get with the Spanish lady. If you put your paws on her, she'll go straight to the newspapers. Guaranteed."

"I don't need her. I got all the female companionship I need. Just standing by," Vince said with a laugh. "You don't know who I sleep with, brother. You might be surprised."

Frank gritted his teeth. Everything with Vince these days was competition. Eternal fucking one-upmanship.

"Check in with me, and update me on how that security operation is running."

"Sure, brother. I'm glad to be on your fucking short leash," Vince said.

Frank slammed down the phone.

Days and nights of back-breaking work brought the San Francisco to readiness for New Year's Eve. Frank felt lines of worry and frustration etched into his face. Could this all pay off? Vince looked dapper in a new black tux and had even agreed to wear a small red rosebud in his lapel—one of Frank's signature touches.

A few hours before the opening, when DeLuca strolled by, Frank asked him for a quick rundown.

"Lombardo and his band are setting up," DeLuca said. "Kitchen has about a thousand people running around, and the chef is yelling like a Baptist preacher. Not a single waiter called in sick. Life is good."

Frank turned to his brother. "Vince, everything's squared to move the cash when we need to?"

"We been squared away for days."

"Every table is reserved," DeLuca added. "Some people flying in from Nevada. They even got all the spaces used up at the local airport for their Cessnas."

Frank couldn't keep his mind on having a good time. All he saw were dollar signs—how much the wrought-iron detailing had cost, the cut-glass vases, the glassware. God—this was driving him crazy. His mind couldn't let loose of the numbers.

"Does the main act like his dressing room?" Frank asked.

"Hell, yes. Fortunately, he's not one of them prima donnas. He was joking with the janitors in the back— keeping them in stitches. He's one hell of a funny guy."

"Good, that's at least one thing we don't have to worry about—our main entertainer being fussy."

People began pouring in around eight. Most of them were already sloshed from private cocktail parties earlier. The women were dressed in floor-length gowns, and the men wore black tuxedos. The elegance of the place and the festive night had become the perfect backdrop for wave after wave of beautiful women with their escorts. Margaret, in the middle of a crowd of her debutante friends, waved to Frank and blew him a kiss.

Around ten, just as Frank was finally beginning to relax, Lisa arrived. He hadn't called her since the washing machine call. She was wearing a light blue gown that accentuated her eyes. A short coat of white mink draped her shoulders, and a trio of sparkling star barrettes held back her wavy hair.

"Lisa," Frank said, "I'm so glad to see you."

She held out her gloved hand. He brought it to his lips and kissed it. He forgot to let it go.

"Oh, Frank," she giggled. "Let go of my hand."

"Never," he breathed through a smile.

"Vince is waiting for me," she said, pulling back from him.

"Too bad."

She leaned into Frank and whispered in his ear. "Vince found your handkerchief."

"What?"

"The one you gave me last time we met."

"So?"

"He saw the monogram."

Frank tilted his head back as if he were laughing, then leaned closer. "What did you tell him?"

She stepped back and laughed as if Frank had just told her the funniest joke in the world. "Oh, you are such a funny boy," she said and slapped his arm with the long gloves she had just removed.

Vince walked up from behind Frank and pulled Lisa into his chest. "Good to see you, doll-baby. Is my brother teasing you?"

Frank winked at Lisa. "Don't repeat that preacher joke tonight. Might not be appreciated in this company."

Lisa's laughter tinkled, and she put her free arm around Vince as he escorted her into the dining room.

Frank knew he wasn't going to be able to eat a bite, but he walked to the table reserved in his name for special guests and sat down. The mayor's wife was adjusting her husband's tie but they both paused to hug Frank. She pushed her breasts into his chest for a long, long time. "Congrats," she said, squeezing his hand. "You have outdone yourself."

It was going to be a hell of a night, and he was going to have to keep grinning the whole time.

CHAPTER THIRTY-SIX

During the next few days Frank worried endlessly about the monogrammed handkerchief that Vince had found. He didn't dare call Lisa to find out what excuse she had manufactured. Really, it didn't matter what she had told Vince—the crucial, and unpredictable, thing was whether Vince believed her or not.

Luckily, the crowds continued to flood into the San Francisco every night—Carlucci Enterprises barely had enough guys to count the cash at the end of each shift. If only their luck held out, Frank might be able to get rid of some of the crushing debt that gave him ever-increasing headaches and a sour stomach.

Margaret called him almost every night before bed. "Oh, Frankie-boy, why are you keeping me waiting so long? Your little bearcat is lonely. Come over, and let me relieve your stress—just the way you like it."

Some part of Frank wished that making love were all he needed for his stress. But that wasn't it, and he couldn't even explain it to himself. He needed Lisa's gentle touch.

Weeks later, Benno called Frank's office late in the afternoon.

"What's up, Benno?"

"We got your reverend for you, Frank."

"You're kidding."

"Nope."

"Where are you, Benno?"

"Jackson. Just like you said—there's got to be a damn good reason to drive hours on two-lane asphalt roads. He's got a sweetie here. A big-tittie sweetie."

"Can you get photos?"

"Don't worry, Boss. I got it all planned. The next time he hightails it up here, we'll get some good photos. He won't be causing Carlucci Enterprises too much trouble after that."

"That's a load off my mind. You know that fool still holds rallies downtown outside of Lisa's place. He still stirs up people to harass us."

"These photos will put him out of business. Don't worry."

"Good work, Benno."

As the short Gulfstream winter eased into an early spring, one morning Benno strolled into Frank's office. With a careful gesture, he placed a large brown envelope on Frank's spacious desk.

Frank glanced up, momentarily irritated at being disturbed. Seeing Benno, he managed a smile. "What's this?"

Benno rubbed his forearms under a light jacket and grunted. "Insurance. Reverend-type insurance."

Frank quickly grabbed the envelope and tore it open. Inside were nine-by-twelve glossy black-and-white prints of the most Reverend Fickum and a dark-haired younger woman. Both were reclining naked, although the reverend's trousers were wrapped around his scrawny ankles. Her dress was crumpled on the floor in a heap.

Benno chuckled. "Just like I told you—she's a big-tittie dame. Runs a religious bookstore in Jackson. She and the reverend treat themselves to a backroom romp every time he goes to replenish his supply of religious pamphlets and Bibles."

Frank studied the different shots of the surprised couple. "Do they know who took the photos?"

"They know I took them, and anyone on the island knows I work for you and Vince."

"You didn't say anything to them, did you?"

"Naw. They were so surprised when I jumped out of a packing crate in the back room that they couldn't speak. That's why there's so many photos of them looking wide-eyed and horrified. They never suspected me and the boys had been following him."

Frank smiled for the first time in a long time. "Good. We'll save these for when we really need them. Meantime, the reverend can stew in his own juices, wondering how and when we're going to use these. Too bad we can't put them on the front page of that newspaper that loves to quote him."

Benno smiled. "Wouldn't that be perfect? Maybe I could become a photographer for the newspaper—you know, in my spare time?"

They both laughed, and Frank placed the negatives and the black-and-whites in a special folder in his safe. Just like Benno had said—insurance. The very best kind of insurance.

CHAPTER THIRTY-SEVEN

The months rolled by so quickly that Frank couldn't keep track. He saw Lisa infrequently and only from a distance, although she remained a bright spark of hope in his mind for that distant day called "the future." He made sure to send her large contributions for the place she had established for wayward girls, and she always sent a thank-you note in scrawling blue ink to his house. He tried to believe that the "Love" at the closing of the letter really meant that she still loved him, but he didn't know. Some kind of wall had come up between them. A wall he was too exhausted to climb. But he was proud that the newspapers had begun writing her up as a "pillar of the community" and a "generous, untiring volunteer."

The expensive lawyers Frank hired for Vince used every tactic to delay the trial—it would help people forget and make it easier to pick an impartial jury in town. Vince swore and cursed but maintained a low profile. Vince's one ongoing complaint to Frank was that he needed to "take care" of the guys stealing from them internally. Frank always nixed the idea. They all trusted Benno, and for now that was enough.

On the second anniversary of the San Francisco's opening, Carlucci Enterprises hosted a big celebration. Frank arranged for all the main players to sit at his table—Vince, Mitch, DeLuca. Benno would run operations while they ate and drank with guests.

DeLuca brought his wife, Lucy, who looked regal in a turban and floor-length satin gown. Vince, of course, brought Lisa, who barely smiled at Frank and pointedly ignored him.

A top-name star entertainer regaled the crowd. "You know, I've enjoyed visiting your lovely island," he began. "When I accepted this job, I was mostly looking forward to staying with Frank Carlucci in his new home."

Everyone laughed.

"Well, actually, it's not that new. But the bedrooms are still in two different neighborhoods. In fact, I've been there a week, and I still haven't found Mr. Carlucci."

The crowd roared.

"The servants tell me just to follow the trail of underwear. Here's one of the ones I found." The comedian flourished a red-and-white candy-striped pair of boxers in the air.

Even Frank laughed at the thought of such outlandish shorts.

His second set was done, and drinks were flowing again when a loud pounding at the front doors startled everyone. Vince jumped up and gave his boys a sign. They immediately ran to the gambling rooms in the back. Dealers and craps-table men began bagging paraphernalia and cash.

This was a knowledgeable crowd when it came to illegal gambling, and they all took to the dance floor to begin the close dancing that would slow down the state troopers as they pushed and shoved to get to the gaming tables.

Frank's entire table stood up expressionless. It had happened so many times—these unexpected raids. But none of them could bear to stay as they had in the beginning. No, it was too heartbreaking to see the damaged furniture, confiscated equipment, the broken glassware and mirrors. The police always did more damage than was necessary.

Without a word, those at the table walked swiftly through the kitchen to waiting cars the boys had brought around. So much for an anniversary party.

"You guys want a ride home?" Frank asked.

Vince didn't answer but climbed into the back seat.

Lisa paused, then joined him. "This just can't keep up," she said. "They raid more and more often. What's going on?"

Frank shrugged his shoulders in a "who knows?" gesture. Vince said nothing, staring out the window on his side.

"This is costing me a damn fortune," Frank said.

"What do you mean, 'costing you'?" Vince asked.

"Your job is to scare everyone," Frank said. "My job is the numbers, and the numbers ain't that great anymore."

People parked along the street seemed to enjoy watching the official state cars with their flashing lights. It was gridlock, and no one cared.

Lisa leaned across and interrupted. "Calm down, you guys. Leave it for the morning."

Vince placed a large hand on her shoulder and pulled her back against the seat. "Shut up."

Frank jammed on the brakes. He jerked the car out of gear and opened his door. He walked around to Vince's open window. He brought his right index finger to Vince's nose and enunciated every syllable. "If I ever see you hurt a woman, I promise I will make you sorry."

The Carlucci Betrayal

"Yeah, you're Mr. Nice Guy but you ain't got a special dame like me. I ain't got to go to the country club every time my balls are full."

Frank tried to open Vince's door from the outside but it was locked. "I'm going to whip your ass," he yelled as he jerked the door handle over and over.

Lisa grabbed Vince's arm as he tried to open his door from the inside and swung her legs across his lap. "Please, he didn't mean it. Let's just go home. It'll be different in the morning."

Vince waited until Frank got back into the driver's seat. Then he took Lisa's hands off of him. "Don't you ever tell me how to treat my girl, Frank."

"You have no right to treat Lisa that way."

"She's mine, not yours. I can treat her any way I want. You ain't man enough to make it any of your damn business. C'mon, Lisa, we're walking home."

Lisa climbed out of the back seat. She took off her lovely satin heels one by one and grabbed Vince's thick hand for the long walk home.

Frank didn't say a word.

CHAPTER THIRTY-EIGHT

"We got to close down the San Francisco," Mitcheletti yelled at the other faces around the table at the Derby. "Not a table standing. They destroyed every long bar and all our cut-glass doors. Every piece of glassware."

"Shit," Frank said while Vince and Benno maintained a stony silence. DeLuca drummed his stubby fingers on the white tablecloth.

"We better think of something," Frank said. "FDR plans to repeal Prohibition."

"Yeah, and it looks like he'll get fucking elected," Vince said. "That idiot Hoover ain't popular."

Frank ran one hand down his face. "What'll we do, guys? Gambling brings in the most cash. But when we rebuild every few months, net profits are zero."

All heads turned as Benno spoke. "I have an idea. We need a place that can't be easily raided."

"Go on," Vince said.

"We need to build our own island."

Frank shook his head. "We don't have the money."

"Why not build a club at the end of a very long pier? We control access."

Vince's eyes narrowed. "That's fucking brilliant, Benno."

"What do you mean?" DeLuca squinted at Vince.

"Think, Tony, think. We build a hundred-yard pier, then put in several access points with thick doors the troopers can't easily force open. By the time notice is given by our security guys, and the police get to the club, everything is hidden." Vince, in his excitement, was speaking faster and faster. "That's it. That's fucking it!"

"Where's the equipment hidden?" DeLuca asked.

"Remember Cuba, old man?" Vince said.

DeLuca pointed at his own head. "This old head ain't as stupid as you think, sonny boy."

Vince sat back in his chair. "In Cuba, they had a spring-loaded system in the walls. Dice tables, roulette wheels—they all had hiding places. That Kraut that Carlos bragged about designed it. As long as they get plenty of beer and money they don't care what they build," Vince said. "Check it out, brother—you're the brains of this setup, or at least you think you are."

Frank smiled. It had been a long time since Vince had teased him without underlying meanness.

"Speaking of changing times," DeLuca said. "I got to talk today about something." He paused and looked around at each face at the big table.

His glare stayed on Vince. "Vince, I got to bring up something."

Vince's stony eyes stayed on DeLuca, but Vince said nothing.

"You're on the edge, Vince. That incident at Frank's housewarming was completely unnecessary. The governor? The attorney general? Our banker? After those three killings?"

Everyone at the table held their breath. No one ever told Vince anything unless Frank okayed it. And Frank never did.

"What do you mean, old man?"

"I mean you might want to retire from Carlucci Enterprises. Move on down the road. Find another group that needs your skills."

With a roar, Vince leapt across the table, his hands reaching for DeLuca's thick throat. "You goddamned Wop. Didn't you see that banker rubbing Lisa's breasts?"

Everyone else leapt into action as DeLuca struggled against Vince's iron grip. Benno poured two large pitchers of iced water on Vince's head, then placed a sopping napkin over Vince's nose and mouth. Benno and Frank fought to pull Vince off DeLuca and drag him into the next room.

Vince snarled and fought, breaking a glass coffeepot over Frank's head. Finally, Benno got Vince in a headlock and squeezed until Vince stopped struggling.

Frank ran into the other room and asked Mitch how DeLuca was doing.

"He's pale and coughing, but okay."

"Ambulance?"

"No, I'll take him home."

Frank returned to Vince's side. "You okay?"

The shards of glass that Frank hadn't had time to brush off his shoulders fell onto the floor.

"That fucking Wop. How can he think such a thing?"

"You need to calm down, Vince. Same thing I've been telling you for months."

"I'm tired of hearing all that—from you, from Lisa, from fucking DeLuca now. Nobody's going to take my part of the business. And that includes you, Frank."

"I don't want your part of the business. I just want you to calm now. We got a trial to get through. You got to stay out of jail."

Frank asked Benno to take Vince home. Vince's grumbling about the cold shower he had received echoed in the elevator as Frank called staff to clean up the mess.

Sitting on a powder keg was getting old. Real old.

In the cool green corridors of the hospital, Frank's footsteps echoed as he strode to the ER the next morning. He had gotten a call from DeLuca's wife—Tony was dead.

"Lucy, what happened?" he said as he grabbed her cold hands.

"He was shot. Downstairs in the library."

"Were you there?"

"I was upstairs asleep." She broke down, and the tears thickened her voice. "I slept through the whole thing. My sweet husband murdered in our own house and I slept through it." Her voice dissolved into keening, and Frank instinctively reached into his back pocket for a handkerchief.

"You have any idea who did it?"

"It was Vince, wasn't it, Frank?"

"Vince loved Tony."

"But they had a big argument yesterday," she said as she sniffled.

"I was with Vince all night, Lucy."

Her eyes opened wide as she searched Frank's face. "Are you sure?"

"Vince calmed down and was going to apologize to Tony today," he said and patted her hands. "Let me go talk to the police."

"Thank you. You've always treated us right."

Frank stood and walked into the ER. Tony's body, on a gurney, loomed large under the sheets. A police sergeant stood by writing in a lined tablet.

"Good morning, sergeant."

"No morning is a good morning," the officer said with a big grin. "What can I do for you, Mr. Carlucci?"

"Tony was a business associate of mine."

"I understand there was an argument yesterday with

Mr. DeLuca and someone in your organization. That right, Mr. Carlucci?"

"It was a minor affair."

"I'm just the responding patrol supervisor, but Homicide will be in touch." The officer made a point of returning to his notebook, concluding the conversation.

Back home, the first thing Frank did was telephone Benno. "Meet me at the office in thirty minutes."

"Sure, Boss."

Frank began soon after Benno walked in. "What do you know about DeLuca's shooting?"

Benno's eyes bugged out. "DeLuca shot?"

"Last night."

"You got to be kidding, Boss. Who would shoot Tony?"

"What time did you leave Vince's?"

Benno stared off in space. "About nine."

"You didn't stay all night?"

"I didn't need to. I only stayed until Vince was calm. How was he shot?"

"In the head. At home."

"Any witnesses?"

"Nope."

Benno sighed. "Too bad. A witness could clear Vince."

"You really think he didn't do it?" asked Frank.

"Not his style. Besides he had calmed down."

"Sometimes Vince holds a grudge for a long time," Frank said.

"That's true. But Vince liked DeLuca, and he knew the old man's contacts were important. "

"Okay, Benno. I'll talk to Vince later."

"Sure, Boss. You'll feel better when you do."

Once the elevator doors had closed on Benno, Frank allowed himself a long sigh. There was never any relief. Never. One thing went well, then twelve things went wrong. This was what people called the "good life"? He shrugged, and the small cuts on his forehead from the coffeepot tugged at the skin around them. This was the life he and Vince had chosen on that fateful day in Jakesberg. Nothing could change that decision—especially now.

CHAPTER THIRTY-NINE

A few hours later Vince watched Frank stride down the sunny sidewalk to his car from Vince's little bungalow. Damn Frank, having the nerve to ask him if he'd killed DeLuca. Who in the hell did Frank think he was? Didn't he know anything about his own brother?

Vince shook his head and walked into the bedroom. Sunlight came through the dusty blinds. He kicked balled-up socks away from the small floral rug at the head of the bed. Something was going to have to change. Frank was always on his case, always bitching about something. Sure, Frank had brains, but sometimes too many brains made people too nervous. Just now Frank had said he had a killer of a headache and was going home for the rest of the day.

Vince reached across the bed and dialed Benno's number.

"Hey, Benno."

"Yeah, Boss."

"We got to visit. Come over."

"Sure, give me ten."

Vince barely glanced up when Benno walked through the front door, opened to catch the early springtime breeze.

"What you got on those two guys stealing from us?" Vince began.

"I thought you weren't interested in them anymore."

Vince snorted with contempt. "I had some other things to sort out. But now it's time to take care of them."

Benno's steady eyes surveyed his face.

"What's the problem, Benno?"

"You heard about DeLuca?" Benno asked.

"I heard."

"Who do you think did it?"

"I don't know but we better beef up the security on everyone left—Frank, Mitch. You and me don't need extra security."

Benno grinned.

"The two stealing from us," Vince said. "Today's their day."

"How we going to do it?" Benno asked.

Vince became even more thin-lipped. "I've been planning it for a long time. After you told me how they do the switch. Still at six o'clock rush, right?"

"Right in front of the main-floor elevators at the Derby."

"Okay," Vince said. "This is how we're going to do it."

Vince had Benno tell Sal and the other guy to come to the cotton warehouses at ten. The gloom of night kept good and bad things hidden at that dark end of the island.

Vince waited inside.

The two men walked inside the wide door, and Benno closed it behind them. Vince was waiting high up on one of the stacks of bales. This was going to be like shooting pigs in a pen.

Benno rolled the huge doors shut. The idiots should have known it was an ambush.

"Assholes," roared Vince as Benno slipped on the lights inside so the men would be blinded.

Before Vince pulled the trigger, Nyman yelled, "Vince, don't do it."

Surprised, Vince held off. "Why not?"

"I got info you need."

"Sing it."

"I know who killed Tony."

"Who?"

Nyman jerked his thumb toward Adder. "He did."

Adder exploded in vigorous denial. "He's crazy. He did it."

Vince lowered his gun. "How'd you know it was me going to kill you tonight?"

Sweat dripped off Nyman's face. "We botched it at Tony's. We had a buyer for his papers—the details of expansions and bank accounts. We never intended to kill anybody."

Adder's quiet resignation lowered his voice. "Yeah, I knew you'd figure it out one day."

"Who was your buyer?

Both men looked at each other. Nyman spat. "Chicago."

Vince blasted each with his shotgun. Their bodies crumpled into lifeless heaps on the scarred cement floor.

Vince lowered his gun. "That's for Tony, you bastards."

Benno looked at Vince. "Guess we got two problems handled tonight, huh, Boss?"

"They're just more saps who needed to be eliminated. They bought your story?"

"They thought they were meeting Frank to discuss moving up the ranks."

"Fools. Should've known that Frank would never set his prissy feet and handstitched shoes in a place like this."

After the night's business of two more men dead inside the historic Civil War warehouses, Vince went to the Club. He grabbed his drink with the melted ice and walked out front. He'd always honored his early promise not to bother Frank with the details of taking care of business. After all, business was business. Numbers was Frank's specialty; protection was Vince's. Now everyone in the organization would get the message: Don't fuck with the Carlucci brothers.

CHAPTER FORTY

Zapata Island, Mississippi

Months later Mitch lumbered into Frank's office and slammed a folded newspaper onto Frank's desk. "Look at the headline."

Frank flipped it open and read, "Prohibition Ends."

He continued reading the first few paragraphs. "We knew it was coming," he said.

"It could put us out of business, couldn't it, Frank? You know, maybe I shouldn't say this, but I still miss Tony." Mitch looked tired, and his voice almost cracked.

Frank paused from his paperwork and looked up. "I do too, Mitch. But at least we gave him a big send-off. Remember that line of black Caddies? They couldn't even fit all the cars into the cemetery's parking lot."

"You ever talk to Lucy, Frank?"

"I call her almost every Sunday after church. Sometimes I escort her to Mass. They were married almost fifty years."

Mitch absentmindedly reached to an inside coat pocket for a candy bar, then stopped himself. "Sometimes I wonder what will happen when I die."

"Why do you think about that?"

"I'm not a young guy."

"Mitch, you're as young as you feel. C'mon, none of us are going to live forever. But hopefully, we'll just get some little piece of heaven while here on earth."

"I don't know," Mitch mumbled.

"No need to be so morose. Get everyone here at four, and we'll see what we have to do. Those bastards—repealing Prohibition."

Frank could see and feel each person's worry as his office filled. Vince's shoulders were tensed up and scowl lines marked his face. He chewed on an unlit cigar. Benno sat next to Vince, as usual. But even Benno's normally unruffled countenance was filled with new worry lines. Mitch was chewing on a chocolate bar before he even entered the room.

Frank felt wilted, but he was determined not to let it show. He'd gone home at lunch and spent some time alone in his favorite room—the library. In the pleasant shade generated by long windows with blinds and surrounded by all the rich gilt of leather bindings, he could think clearly—much more clearly than here in his office. He'd made some decisions.

"Thanks for coming, guys. I thought we should talk together about the end of Prohibition."

Vince spoke up first. "What do the numbers say?"

"We are overextended," Frank said. "The construction on the new place has been delayed, as you know."

Vince slapped the table. "Sometimes it's like we can't get anything going in the right direction."

"But the numbers from the slots are good, and profits are up at the Derby," Frank said. "That new system Benno figured out for money transfers gives us delivery at the bank a day earlier than before. That means we can leverage bigger cash accounts quicker—always a good thing."

Benno spoke up. "Is there any place new we can put slots?"

Mitch shook his head. "They're in filling stations, every grocery store—big and small, auto garages. The only place on the island without them is the churches." He paused and looked at Frank with a small smile. "Maybe you can speak to Father Patrick about putting them in the back of the cathedral?"

"What about the other numbers, Frank?" Vince asked.

"People love to gamble. The backroom games at the Derby alone sometimes bring in thousands in a few minutes. But here's the deal—we can't increase the percentages."

"Do we have slots in the whorehouses?" Frank asked.

Vince exploded into laughter. "Guys don't go to cathouses to play the slots."

"Look, we have to expand business. We need those frigging machines everywhere," Frank said.

Benno and Vince looked at each other. "Okay, brother. We'll see about an expansion," Vince said.

"Next thing," Frank said. "It's time to take on the Reverend Fickum."

Smiles left everyone's face.

"What the fuck do you mean?" Vince said.

"Let's tell the lawyers to quit delaying the trial."

Vince stood up as if uncertain what to do next. "Are you fucking crazy, brother?"

Frank kept his tone light and conversational. "Here's my reasoning. We need your name cleared. The island is a small place, and since all that happened, we've been stalled at City Hall. Think about it—delays in building permits, delays in building inspections, delays, delays, delays. Each delay costs us big.

"In addition to all that, we know that we'll win against Fickum because of these." Frank slid the large brown envelope with the photos Benno had taken across the table to Vince.

"What are those?" Vince asked.

"Look and see."

Vince tore open the envelope and spilled the photos on the table. Fickum's thin penis rose from pubic hair in every shot. Vince snorted. "That's one ugly guy."

Frank smiled. "And he'd be even more ugly on the front page of the newspaper."

Benno's face lit up. "It was uglier in person, believe me."

"Does Fickum know you have these, Frank?" Vince asked.

"He hasn't seen them."

"They're our insurance, right?" Benno said.

Vince turned slowly to Frank. "So how do these relate to my trial? Fickum doesn't need to testify against me for me to get convicted. He swore in his deposition that I shot the old bat."

"No, he doesn't. But public opinion is a fickle thing. The prosecutor's office and the mayor, the governor—all of them just want to get re-elected. These pictures can sway public opinion. We'll only use them when and if we need them."

Vince slowly sat down. "The trial's going to be touch-and-go. It's going to disrupt business for weeks, maybe months. Can we afford the expense?"

"That's part of why we need slots in every available building in this city," Frank said. "We also need to review all our procedures at the Derby to make sure we're not paying extra expenses. Mitch—look at our cash procedures. Let's figure out ways to be more efficient, more budget-wise. We can do it, guys. We just need to push harder for a while."

Vince looked at Frank. "There's other rackets we can run—extortion, dope—"

"Forget it." Frank's voice rang with finality. "We ain't that dirty."

"How long do I got to decide or are you deciding for me?"

Frank stood to end the meeting. "I'm not deciding. You are. Tell me tomorrow, and we'll go from there."

"I need some time alone. I'll tell you tomorrow."

Later that night after quite a few Scotches on the rocks, Vince still didn't know what to do. He drove to the seawall, parked his car, and decided to walk. It was dark and almost deserted. The black water rushed toward the shore in white-topped waves and receded back into the ocean. The salty breeze never stopped blowing.

Vince would never admit it to anyone, but his nerves were getting frayed by this looming trial. Yeah, the trial those expensive lawyers had been delaying because that's what they were paid to do. But wouldn't it be good to get the trial done and over with?

He drove along the seawall and found himself on the street of Lisa's new house. A lamp illuminated the front room. He parked parallel to the sidewalk and walked to the front door.

Vince pounded his fist on the doorframe. Within seconds, Lisa opened the door, and in one quick breath said, "Hello, Vince."

"You got company, babe?"

She laughed, "Don't be silly. Come in." She turned and walked into the room.

Vince's body responded to her cute ass underneath the swishing dress as her heels echoed on the floor. "You're looking good, babe."

She sat on the couch and turned to face him. "What's going on with you these days?"

"What have you been doing?"

"The home I run for girls keeps me busy."

"You still doing that?"

"I'll do it my whole life—that's how much it means to me."

"I'm glad to hear it, babe. Glad to hear it."

"You haven't been over in a long time, Vince."

"I ain't been anywhere in a long time. Fucking Frank told me to lay low. The only place I've been is my own house."

Lisa sighed and briefly put her right hand over her eyes. "Look, I'm supposed to meet a girlfriend in fifteen minutes. I can't talk too long."

Vince stood. "Let's go into the bedroom." He moved to where she sat and pulled her hand, placing his big lips into a smooch on the back of her hand.

She stayed seated.

"C'mon now, Lisa."

Her eyes blazed up at him. "You're drunk, Vince Carlucci. How dare you come over here for the first time in months and tell me you want a quickie."

"You ain't my girl anymore?" Vince's anger flared, and he grabbed her face, his strong fingers on either side of her cheeks forcing her to look up at him. "Whose girl are you now, dammit? Whose?"

He threw her back on the couch. Lisa sobbed, pounded her hands into the cushions, and then sprawled on the couch.

He hated the sound of a woman crying. He turned around and walked quickly to his car. "I can guess whose fucking girl you are, Lisa. And you're going to be sorry."

He flung himself into the car and screeched away. No one had any answers, not even him.

CHAPTER FORTY-ONE

Once again, Frank was at the hospital. A sobbing Lisa had called him this time—Mitch had been shot.

Lisa sat outside the emergency room, huddled against the wall with her arms wrapped around herself when Frank arrived. Tears ruined her makeup, and she looked distraught and lost.

"Oh, Frank, I'm so glad you're here."

"How's Mitch?"

She began crying anew. "He's dying."

Frank pushed open the emergency room doors and was struck by the brittle glow of white lights on the shining metal and glass bottles of the apparatus, beds, pieces of equipment.

One of the nurses saw him and lifted her tired eyes. "Oh, Mr. Carlucci, right this way. Quickly."

Frank followed the nurse to Mitch's bedside, where three doctors were working on him.

Frank stood by quietly, then finally placed a hand on Mitch's shoulder. Mitch's eyes opened, and he looked at

Frank.

"Mitch, who did this?"

"Don't know."

"We'll find him, don't worry."

Mitch's eyes went to Frank's side. Lisa had come up silently behind him. "You guys are my family—you know that, don't you?" Mitch said.

Lisa reached over and placed a small hand along Mitch's face. "We love you, Mitch."

"I'm leaving you."

Lisa's sobs increased. "No, Mitch."

Frank took Lisa into his arms as she wailed and sobbed uncontrollably. Her shoulders heaved and without even thinking he kissed the top of her head as she turned into his chest to weep. "It's okay, baby. It's okay."

As he held her, the curtains parted, and Benno walked in. He took in Mitch's still corpse in one swift glance and turned to Lisa and Frank.

"What's happened, Boss?" he asked as Frank and Lisa parted.

Frank reached into his back pocket for a handkerchief for Lisa. "We don't know exactly."

She hiccupped and said in a low voice, "The police said that it was a burglar."

"That doesn't make sense," Benno said. "Somebody after goods doesn't stay around to murder. Vince'll figure it out. Is he on his way?"

Lisa lifted her shoulders. "We haven't called him yet. Can you call him, Benno?"

Benno looked at Frank, then at Lisa. "I see."

Frank felt the absurd need to say something, but he didn't know what to say. "Lisa called me, and I came right down. I wanted to talk to Mitch before he died to see if he knew who did it. We haven't had time to call Vince."

Benno looked over at Mitch's bulk on the gurney. The sheet was gradually becoming redder as blood soaked into it from the wounds. "I'll go by Vince's house."

Benno turned, opened the curtains, and left quickly, disappearing into the ER's bright chaos.

Lisa turned to Frank. "Can you walk me to my car?"

"I'll be glad to."

Frank took her elbow, and they slowly walked through the medicinal-smelling hallways to the rear parking lot.

Lisa broke the silence. "I can't believe that Mitch is gone." She sniffled into Frank's white handkerchief.

"He's been with us since the beginning."

She smiled through her tears. "And always eating those crazy candy bars."

Frank also smiled. "Breakfast, lunch, and dinner. And every time in between."

As they reached her car, Lisa turned to Frank, suddenly serious. "Do you think Vince killed Mitch?"

"What?"

"I'm not kidding, Frank. Vince could do it."

"Vince loved Mitch," Frank said, almost too quickly even to his own ears.

"You haven't heard Vince rant and rave about respect. About how you and all the guys don't respect him enough. Don't give him enough of a cut for what he does."

Frank couldn't believe what she was saying. "Are you sure?"

"Sometimes Vince scares me."

"What do you mean?"

"Like earlier tonight. He came by—he wanted...he wanted me to make love." She laughed. "No, he wanted sex."

Frank's blood boiled.

"He gives me money all the time." Lisa's face turned from sad to angry. "But this time, I told him no. I thought he was going to hit me. But he didn't. He left."

She bowed her head. "I get tired of being the girl you both come to for sex, Frank. How many years has this gone on?"

Frank was too tired to explain everything again—not

on a night when he'd just lost Mitch.

"I'm still trying to save up money for us, Lisa. But every time I get ahead, some kind of shit happens. Losing the San Francisco. The trial. Tony dead. Prohibition ending."

"Vince is too much on the edge now. I never know what he'll do. Sometimes he calls me just to yell insults. He might have killed Mitch. He might kill you or me. You've got to get us out of this alive."

She turned back toward her car to end the conversation. Frank opened her door for her. She sat and handed back the handkerchief. "Let's not get your monogram in my house again. There was hell to pay last time."

He took the damp square of fine linen and folded it before he placed it in his back pocket. She drove off without another word.

Not for the first time, the weight of the world descended on his shoulders.

CHAPTER FORTY-TWO

The next morning dawned rosy and pink with the colors spread across a peaceful ocean that in no way mirrored what Frank felt. As he pulled a tiny red rosebud through his jacket's lapel, he thought about what he had to do today— pick a coffin for Mitch, confront Vince about what had happened last night, try to figure out how to continue operations with half of his trusted crew now dead. On top of all of that were the questions that he couldn't ask: had Benno suspected anything between him and Lisa last night? Did Lisa have another boyfriend? Would Vince hurt Lisa?

Frank sat at his desk in the upstairs Derby drinking coffee and looking at the early edition of the newspaper. Vince and Benno stepped out of the elevator—both looking like they'd been up all night in wrinkled shirts and dirty shoes.

They sat down with grim looks. Frank pushed some cups at them and extended the coffeepot across the table.

Vince poured and pushed the pot to Benno. "We got

some info, Frank."

"Go ahead."

"The guy who shot Mitch was from the Chicago mob," he said, glowering at Frank beneath dark eyebrows.

"How do you know?"

"Someone who owes me," Vince said, "shared some information."

"Are you sure?"

Vince almost spat out the words. "Police chief's badge."

Frank wrinkled his forehead. "What are you talking about?"

Vince looked over at Benno. "Remember the police chief that let the St. Louis guys come across the bridge for us—a few years back? The sonofabitch double-crosser?"

Frank creased his brow deeper. "I don't remember that incident."

Vince drank his coffee in one big gulp. "No wonder you don't pay me more, brother. You don't know half of what I do, so you don't know what I'm worth. All you remember are those damn parties you go to."

"Tell me about the chief's badge."

"It was a little, what do you call it—memento—that Carlucci Enterprises sent back to St. Louis. Sent it back in a nice-wrapped cardboard box with certain other artifacts. Mitch's killer was bringing it back to us—trust me on this. I know how these guys think. St. Louis goons aligned with Chicago to take us down."

"So where does that leave us now?"

Vince looked at Benno, then back at Frank. "It means we got some important business to take care of, brother."

Frank sighed.

Vince glared at Frank for a few seconds before speaking. "Let's push for the trial—like you said yesterday. Get it over with."

"We can't do that now. I can't run everything by myself."

"You still got Benno."

"I still can't do it. I've got no one on the money like Mitch. No one for the construction project." Frank's chest closed up tight. "I can't do it, Vince, especially not without you."

"We got to do it, Frank. I thought about it all last night. And that was before I found out about Mitch. If we don't get that damn club-at-the-end-of-a-pier built, then we're not going to have the cash to fight off these bozos from Chicago. Chicago is organized even though Capone's in jail. Nitti runs them, and he's good."

Vince softened his tone. "C'mon, Frank. The lawyers are expensive, right? My name not being cleared is expensive, right? Us not being able to expand is expensive, right?"

Frank knew that Vince was right. Where was the light at the end of the tunnel?

CHAPTER FORTY-THREE

Frank's telephone call the next morning to the offices of Esq. James Waring III in Atlanta, Georgia, brought Vince's desired results. Mr. Waring's office stopped the protracted legal maneuverings to delay the trial. Frank wasn't sure any longer it was the best course of action, but Vince was right—the lawyers were costing Carlucci Enterprises thousands weekly. With the end of Prohibition, the organization couldn't afford this much longer—especially with construction not even begun on the proposed new club.

That afternoon Frank drove to the seawall to look at potential sites for the new club. It was a temperate winter day, and the temperature was cool enough for Frank to keep his coat on as he walked on the broad sidewalk. People who knew Frank smiled and waved as he strode the sunny expanse. He tried to turn his thoughts to happier times—surely, they would come someday. On some magical day, Lisa would be his forever. He'd get to play catch with his son, Randall. Maybe, the kid liked baseball, as Frank had in earlier, innocent years.

Frank ran his fingers through his hair to smooth it down after the breeze had ruffled it. *I need a woman's touch.*

Then, the large, beautiful house that he'd worked so hard to afford would be filled with laughter and bright lights. Not like now, when he arrived home every evening after working late and the only lamp that burned was in the entryway. A solitary green lamp that Bentley switched on at dusk.

Lisa was drifting away bit by bit—he felt. Could he stop it? Frank didn't know. Did he have the energy to try? Frank didn't know that either. How do you keep a woman interested in you when you can't make love to her or give her presents?

A few months later Vince got his wish—the trial date was set. Preparations swung into high gear with more court-ordered depositions and high-pressure meetings with the lawyers that often ended with Vince in a rage, stomping out the door and driving off with squealing tires.

The night before the trial, Frank drove to Vince's small house and knocked on the door.

"Can I come in?" Frank asked.

"Why not?"

Frank walked inside to see the same dusty living room with the same tired upholstered furniture.

"You want a drink?" Vince asked.

"Yeah, pour me one, brother."

Vince paused. "You don't drink—remember? Don't want to be like Dad, huh?"

Frank laughed once. "Tonight, I'm drinking."

"Whatever you say." Vince poured a short Scotch on the rocks for Frank before refilling his own.

"Here's to you, brother," Frank lifted his glass to clink

against Vince's.

Vince sat in the other chair without saying anything.

"I was remembering what we decided when we left Jakesberg," Frank began. "You know, we've really done pretty well for ourselves."

"We could do better."

"Have you thought of what might happen if the verdict, you know…doesn't go our way."

"Yeah, I've thought of that a lot."

"We've got to win in court," Frank said. "Otherwise, we're out of business."

"We'll see."

"What do you mean?"

"Don't rush me, brother. I've been doing some sniffing around. Don't worry so much. You're a natural worrier, you know that?"

Frank forced another gulp down his throat. "I don't see how you drink that stuff."

Vince stirred the ice cubes in his glass with one thick finger. "It takes a real man to drink Scotch, brother."

It was time to go. Probably a bad idea to come over. Just some sentimental stuff he had been thinking about that first conversation in the barbershop in Jakesberg. They'd been in this together at that point—equals. Both excited and challenged by the chances they had to take to make it big. Back then, Vince had done whatever Frank had told him to do and nothing more. Now, who knew—really—what Vince did?

"Okay, Vince. I just thought it'd be good to have a drink together before the trial starts. I wanted you to know that I'm all with you in this. Backing you a hundred percent."

Vince raised his dime-store glass in a mock salute. "Thank you so much, Mr. Frank Carlucci. Please sign the guest book on the way out."

The next morning Frank took a chance and called Lisa to ask if she needed a ride to the courthouse. To his surprise, she said yes. But she seemed distant and preoccupied when he picked her up, and they barely talked in the car.

At the courtroom, they squeezed in to sit directly behind the defendant's table. Vince was well dressed—for Vince, that is. Vince's white shirt was starched and clean; his suit pressed and new. He even had new shoes that were spit-shined. Matching socks.

Frank had no doubt that Waring was behind the clothes. Waring, the best criminal lawyer in the South, was dressed in a brown, double-breasted suit with suspenders and a plaid bowtie. He radiated the benefits of a good diet.

Waring spoke in a low voice into Vince's right ear, but Vince shook his head no and scowled deeper while spinning his chair from side to side.

Benno came in and managed to slide into the row with Frank and Lisa. As the prosecutor walked in to take his place, Benno leaned over to Frank and whispered, "Hutchins hates Vince."

Finally, the bailiff announced the judge, and everyone stood for the Honorable Matthew Markel.

The judge raised his eyes to glare at everyone packed into the courtroom and rested his gaze on the district attorney and defense lawyer.

"Today we have the State of Mississippi vs. Vince Carlucci on trial for homicide that occurred on December 2, 1932, at 818 Spreading Oaks Drive, Zapata, Mississippi, Harrison County.

"Mr. Vince Carlucci, you are charged with homicide in the matter of the shooting of Mrs. Dolores Dixon on December 2, 1932. How do you plead?"

"Not guilty," Vince said.

"The prosecution will proceed with the opening

statement," Markel intoned.

The district attorney stood and turned to face the jury. "Your Honor," he bellowed, "it is a well-known fact that Mr. Vince Carlucci is part of the criminal enterprise that has long brought illegal liquor and gambling to our fair city. Mr. Carlucci's criminal activities keep honest people scared in their homes at night—"

"Objection, Your Honor." Mr. Waring jumped to his feet. "This is unsubstantiated hearsay. Jury will be prejudiced to hear my client called a 'criminal.'"

Markel pounded his gavel. "Sustained."

Hutchins continued, "I will prove beyond a doubt that on the night of December 2nd, 1932, the already drunk Vince Carlucci, known for his violent temper, in a fit of uncontrollable anger shot and killed Mrs. Dolores Dixon, a decent and God-fearing citizen who was peaceably and legally protesting the Carlucci curse in our community." His volume rose. "I will also show you the evidence of the gun that Vince Carlucci used with unforgivable recklessness that night.

"You will be convinced beyond a reasonable doubt that this man"—Hutchins strode over and stood in front of Vince—"was the out-of-control criminal, oh, excuse me, the out-of-control 'individual,' who shot an innocent third-party, completely indifferent to the consequences of his actions and disregardful of the safety of others."

Waring's turn was next. He rose slowly and adjusted his suspenders over his prominent belly. His glasses were already halfway down his nose, and he peered over them at the waiting jurors. His tone was fatherly and confiding, as if he were talking to a younger man on the back porch. "Folks, I have some important information to give you today and every day of this trial on behalf of Mr. Vincent Carlucci. Information that I think you'll see proves that he didn't intend to shoot Mrs. Dixon. Information that will reassure you that the milk of human kindness flows in his veins the same as it flows in yours—mostly especially when it comes to protecting the life of his beloved brother—just as you'd do, folks. Just as you'd protect your own kin.

"But's here's what's important, folks. The absolute most important thing is that you give Mr. Vincent Carlucci a fair shake. Think about it, folks." Waring walked to a thin man with almost no teeth seated near the end of the jury box. Waring pointed a finger in the man's face. "Sir, what if you were known to drink a little too much on Saturday nights? And, what if, on a Saturday night somebody that no one saw ran his car through a neighbor's rose bushes? Would it be fair to you for all the other neighbors to accuse you of running through those rose bushes just because they 'assumed' you were known for getting drunk on Saturday nights?"

The man shook his head vigorously. "Sure wouldn't be fair!"

Waring smiled. "That's right. It wouldn't be fair at all. And that's what has happened to my client, Mr. Vince Carlucci. Just because he's lost his temper through the years—and who in this courtroom hasn't lost his temper in the past ten years? Just because sometimes he's gotten a little too drunk—and who in this courtroom hasn't had one or two drinks too many in the past ten years? Just because there's a mob of rioting protestors outside who would string my client, Mr. Vince Carlucci, to a tree if they could, just because these protestors are exercising their American right to freedom of speech—is that a reason to sentence my client to the rest of his life in prison? Think about it, folks."

The judge instructed Hutchins to call his first witness.

Mrs. Mary Lynn Potter walked to the witness box. Her heels echoed on the wooden floor with certainty.

He established that Mrs. Potter had been on the scene the fateful night, and that she had been one of about a hundred protestors gathered by Fickum.

"Do you recognize anyone else in the courtroom as someone who was there that night?"

She pointed at Vince. "He was there." Then she pointed to Frank, "He was there too."

"Please identify the first man you pointed to."

"Vince Carlucci—everyone knows him."

"Please tell us what Mr. Vince Carlucci did that night."

"Vince Carlucci had a gun—a small black one—and he shot Mrs. Dixon."

"How far away from Mr. Vince Carlucci were you?"

"About six feet."

"What were you doing when you saw the defendant shoot Mrs. Dixon?"

"I was running away."

"In what direction?"

"I was running toward Elm Street from the front entrance of that other one's—Frank Carlucci's—house."

"What was Mr. Vince Carlucci's demeanor?"

"He looked like a wild bull—angry, frowning, and bellowing. A raging wild bull—uncontrollable."

With that, it was Waring's turn to question the witness.

Waring didn't vary from his soft tone and confiding manner. "Mrs. Potter, I am Jim Waring, Mr. Carlucci's attorney."

She shifted in the witness chair and raised her chin. "I know who you are."

"You stated that you saw Mr. Vincent Carlucci point a gun at Mrs. Dixon?"

"He sure did."

"You also said you were running away—correct?"

"Yes, but—"

Interrupting her, Waring continued in his purring voice, "You saw Vince Carlucci point his small, black gun at Mrs. Dixon, you heard a shot—while you were running away."

"I didn't want him shooting me!"

"So, if you were running away from Frank Carlucci's

front porch, your back was to Mrs. Dixon and your back was to Vince Carlucci, am I correct?"

"It had to be him," she sputtered. "He's a no-good criminal—everyone knows it."

"Hearsay," snapped Waring.

"Sustained."

Waring continued. "Now, Mrs. Potter, please answer the question. Did you see Vince Carlucci shoot Mrs. Dixon?"

"No."

"Mrs. Potter, what was the lighting on the night of December 2, 1932 outside of 818 Spreading Oaks Drive, Zapata, Mississippi?"

"It was dark. At night."

"How dark?"

"You heard me—dark."

"Were there any gas or electric street lighting?"

"No."

"Any bonfires or other fires to give rise to bright illumination?" continued Waring.

She squirmed in her seat and eyed Waring. "No."

"How well do you see in the dark, Mrs. Potter?"

"I see just fine," she sniffed.

"What age are you, Mrs. Potter?"

"Irrelevant," intoned Hutchins.

The judge looked at Waring. "What's your point, Counselor?"

"I am only seeking to establish the age of this witness in order to give the jury additional information to assess her ability to see in the dark, Your Honor."

"Answer the question, Mrs. Potter."

She gazed balefully at Markle in his pristine black robes, then back to Waring. "I am sixty-eight."

"How long since you had an eye examination, Mrs. Potter."

"I don't recall."

"Five years? Ten years? Twenty years? How long

since a competent eye doctor examined your eyes to make sure you could see in daylight and in darkness, Mrs. Potter?"

"I told you I don't remember."

"Thank you, Mrs. Potter. That will be all."

Waring sat down.

Then, Hutchins requested his next witness—Mr. John Rasmussen—an elderly man who ambled to the stand using a cane and almost fell into the witness chair.

"Mr. Rasmussen, were you present at the home of Frank Carlucci the night of December 2, 1932?

"Sure 'nough."

"What were you doing there?"

"Singing."

"Singing?"

"We wuz singing hymns."

"Did you see Mr. Vince Carlucci?"

"He was crazy mad."

"What did Mr. Vince Carlucci do that night of December 2, 1932?"

"He pulled a gun and shot Mrs. Dixon. I saw him do it."

"Did you see anyone else that night with a gun?"

"Only hoodlums carry guns."

"Please answer the question, Mr. Rasmussen."

"Nobody else had a gun."

"How do you know nobody else had a gun that night?"

"Ain't seen one."

"So you are saying that just because you didn't see another gun means no one else had a gun?" continued Waring. "There are suit pockets, pants pockets, shoulder holsters, plus some folks carry a gun in the small of the back or in an ankle holster. You know, I've even seen gentlemen carry a gun inside the front of their underwear—my apologies to the ladies present to have to mention such a private detail. I'm guessing you couldn't see in any of these places, correct?"

The old man eased himself deeper into the witness box.

"Answer the question," directed the judge.

"Yep, you're right," responded Rasmussen reluctantly.

Waring inserted pudgy fingers into the watch pocket of his vest and strolled closer to the jury box. "Do you have brothers or sisters, Mr. Rasmussen?"

"Three brothers and a sister. I'm the eldest."

"Do you love your brothers and sister?

"Sometimes."

Several people in the courtroom snickered.

"Has anyone ever tried to kill one of your brothers or sister?"

"Not that I know of."

"If someone tried to kill one of your innocent brothers or sister, and you were present, would you stop that murderer?"

Hutchins leaped to his feet. "Irrelevant. Calls for witness to make supposition."

"Sustained."

"You say you are the oldest brother. You understand the particular love that younger ones have for the eldest—just like my client, Vince Carlucci, had for his older brother Frank. Would one of your young brothers or sister try to stop someone trying to kill you?"

"Lennie laid out an old sow with a two-by-four upside the head when the pig tried to stomp me when I was a little mite."

"So your brother—out of natural brotherly love—stopped an unexpected act of aggression by a murderous sow intent on killing you. He stopped the vicious pig out of brotherly love, didn't he?"

Rasmussen grinned. "Weren't my brother. Wuz my sister. She had a good arm on her."

"Thank you, Mr. Rasmussen," purred Waring.

For three long weeks, the lawyers examined and cross-examined people who had been there that night. Waring's strategies were consistent: stress the unexpected aggression of Fickum's reaching for a gun and build a reasonable case for Vince's defense of Frank's life.

As the trial neared the end, Hutchins stated he had found it was necessary to call a witness he hadn't known about during discovery. The judge called both lawyers up to the bench.

"What's going on, prosecutor?" the judge demanded.

"Your Honor, I have new evidence that can only be verified by calling a witness that I didn't know about until today," Hutchins said.

Waring's face went from pink to white. The silence in the courtroom made it possible to hear every word the lawyers and judge spoke.

"You had better have an iron-clad reason," the judge said. "Proceed with calling your witness."

"Benjamin Everett Harrison to the stand."

Frank had never heard the name. Benno rose from his seat and walked to the witness box.

After the swearing-in, Hutchins began. "Please state your full name and place of residence."

"Benjamin Everett Harrison. 311 Crazy Horse Street, Zapata, Mississippi."

"Who is your employer, Mr. Harrison?"

"Carlucci Enterprises."

"What are your job duties, Mr. Harrison?"

"Kitchen stuff."

"Such as?"

"Cleaning, garbage, driving a truck."

"Is your job dangerous, Mr. Everett?"

"No, I wouldn't say that it's dangerous."

"Then why do you often carry a gun, Mr. Everett?"

"What do you mean by 'often'?"

"Let me rephrase the question. Do you recognize the gun that has been labeled Exhibit A over here on the table?" Hutchins asked.

"It looks like a .38 Special," Benno said.

"Have you ever seen this gun before the trial began?"

"I seen a lot of .38 Specials in my time."

Hutchins walked to the evidence table and picked up the tagged revolver.

"You don't recognize your own gun, Mr. Everett?"

"What makes you think it's mine?"

The judge spoke up. "You don't ask the questions, Mr. Everett. You answer them."

Hutchins's gaze bore holes into Benno. "This gun was registered in your name fifteen years ago in Biloxi, Mr. Everett. Did you give it to Mr. Vince Carlucci to carry?"

Benno remained silent.

Hutchins looked at the judge with raised eyebrows.

Markle cleared his throat. "Mr. Everett, you must answer the question or be held in contempt."

Benno was silent a few moments longer, then said, "I don't remember."

Hutchins walked to the jury box, then walked back to stand in front of Benno.

"What did you have for lunch yesterday, Mr. Everett?"

"Shrimp po-boy and a bowl of gumbo."

"And what was your professional name when you were a wrestler in 1925?"

"Big Benno."

"So, your memory works well most of the time, Mr. Everett? I find it curious that your memory seems not to work when it comes to guns and Mr. Vince Carlucci, your employer."

"Ask the question," Markle said. "Enough innuendo."

"Did you give this gun to Mr. Vince Carlucci prior to his shooting of Mrs. Dixon on December 2, 1932, on Zapata Island?" Hutchins asked. "The same Vince Carlucci who has already told us he's innocent and whose defense attorney could be planning to pin the murder on you, Mr.

Everett."

Benno sat stone-faced.

Vince stood up, yelling and banging on the wood table in front of him. "You cheapskate attorney! I'd never try to pin a murder on my best friend. What kind of guy do you think I am?"

Hutchins merely smiled as the bailiffs ran to restrain Vince.

"Yes, Mr. Carlucci. What kind of guy are you? You're the kind of guy who kills an innocent third-party with careless disregard with a gun you thought was untraceable."

CHAPTER FORTY-FOUR

Each day Frank picked up Lisa and drove to the courthouse. Benno joined them on the long, hard wooden bench as they formed the only set of supporters for Vince in the courtroom. At night, Vince stayed home, never visiting or calling either Frank or Lisa.

One evening as Frank drove Lisa home, she turned to him with tears in her eyes. "I think we're going to lose."

Frank placed his right hand over hers, cupped in her lap. "Why do you say that?"

"I just feel it inside. All the witnesses are against him."

Frank brought her cold fingers up to his lips and blew warmth on them.

"Frank, I hate to say this, but it might be the best thing that ever happened to Vince."

Frank waited a long time before he spoke. Finally, he said, "You think he needs some time off?"

Lisa pressed her lips together to hold in a sob.

Frank waited and offered her his handkerchief. As he

pulled up in front of her house to let her off, she sniffled and blew her nose, then handed the handkerchief back to him.

The sadness was so apparent in her blue eyes that it hurt him. "Don't worry, Lisa. Whatever happens, I'll take care of you."

She patted his hand with even sadder eyes that filled again with tears. "These winds have turned cold again. It's going to be a cold springtime, Frank."

He watched her wrap her heavy coat tighter, then walk down the sidewalk and enter her house. Her golden hair glowed in the streetlights. Why couldn't he tell her that he still loved her?

As the trial neared a climax, Frank called a meeting with Vince and Waring. For once Frank began with no preliminaries or small talk. "What's your opinion, Waring?"

"Hard to tell."

"That's not what I'm paying you for. I'm paying you for results—the results Carlucci Enterprises wants."

Vince remained silent, his eyes boring into Waring.

Waring pursed his lips. "The one witness that will kill us is Fickum. You've both read his deposition."

Vince leaned back in his chair. "He'd love to see me hang."

"Haven't you eroded the jury's confidence in what Hutchins and his witnesses say? All that brotherly love and protect your brother stuff," asked Frank. "No one who knows Vince and me could think he'd stand by and let me be gunned down."

Waring clasped his hands on the table and learned forward. "We're dancing on a tightrope. Could go either way."

Frank stood. "We ain't dancing any longer. We'll see

who remains standing when the music stops."

Vince watched Frank stride from the room, grabbing his hat and overcoat like an afterthought.

"So lovely to have had the pleasure of your company, Mr. Carlucci. Please call again for afternoon tea and cookies."

That evening Frank met with Benno.

"Hey, Boss, what ya need?"

Frank didn't smile. "We got any new employees that people around here don't know?"

"We got a kid from the Delta."

"What's he like?"

"Home-grown. Wet behind the ears."

"Can he be trusted with a special project?"

"He wants to be made—wants it bad. If not with us, then another family."

"He can't fuck this up," continued Frank. "Here's what he's got to do."

The following Sunday morning, a lanky freckle-faced kid with trousers a little too short sat in a back pew of Fickum's church the entire service. At the end, the kid waited for the crowd to disperse before approaching Fickum. Goodwill radiated from the kid's bright blue eyes. He extended a ham-fisted greeting and shook Fickum's hand as if pumping well water.

"I ain't never seen a preacher like you."

Fickum smiled slightly. "Where you from, boy?"

"My pappy and me farm us some land over near Eudora."

"What brought you to our lovely island, son?"

"I came here to find some good preaching, sir. I want

to get serious about following the Lord."

Fickum stood a little taller. "We hope that today's worship was edifying for you, young man."

"Yessiree, it's going to lead me to my salvation."

The kid lifted a worn bible. "This here's the only thing I own, sir. I been needing help with one passage. Could you enlighten me some?"

Fickum paused while the kid thumbed onion-skin pages.

"Yessir, I sure appreciate some right-minded guidance. My pap always says, "Ain't nothing more important than a good preachin' man."

The kid hefted the black book into Fickum's hands, already opened.

Sprawled across the pages lay a black-and-white photograph of Fickum and his nude mistress taped to a note in heavy block letters. "Don't testify."

Blood drained from Fickum's face as he choked out a strangled "Arghhhhh."

"That's what I thought," the kid said, grabbing the bible and slamming it shut. "I always wondered about the word 'vengeance' in Romans 12:19. Now I understand it right perfect."

He strode out of the church while Fickum remained stiff and white inside his billowing black robe.

A few days later Hutchins called his star witness.
"Reverend Elmer Starrett Fickum."

In a back row, Fickum rose and walked to the front. Frank's temples throbbed with the pressure. He involuntarily grabbed Lisa's hand.

Hutchins confirmed Fickum's identity and presence at the scene of the murder. After confirming that Fickum knew both Vince and Frank and could identify them, Hutchins continued, "Did you see Mr. Vince Carlucci, the defendant, shoot Mrs. Delores Dixon on the night of December, 2, 1932?"

"I cannot say," intoned Fickum.

Hutchins stood without moving. "Let me repeat the question. Did you see Mr. Vince Carlucci—"

"You cannot intimidate a man of the Lord."

Hutchins requested the judge direct Fickum to answer the question.

"You will answer the question, Mr. Fickum, or be held in contempt of court."

Fickum stood up in the witness box and raised one hand to point toward the heavens. "'Dearly beloved, avenge not yourselves, but rather give place unto wrath: for it is written, "Vengeance is mine; I will repay," saith the Lord." Romans 12:19, my friends. The Good Lord Jesus does not want our participation in a court of law—"

Markle pounded his gravel and gestured to the bailiffs. "You are not here to do anything but testify, Mr. Fickum. You are not here to preach. Step down if you refuse to answer questions."

Fickum's volume only increased. "God intends to punish the Carluccis, but He doesn't need my poor help. God is all-powerful. His vengeance will rain down—"

The two bailiffs reached Fickum and dragged him outside while everyone in the courtroom murmured and reporters rushed out to deliver the scoop.

Markle requested the two lawyers to meet him in his chambers and called for a recess.

Inside the judge's personal chambers, Hutchins barely contained his anger. "They bought him off or threatened him. Standard Mafia style. Those sons-of-bitches."

Waring remained calm. "The deposition of Mr. Fickum will have to be thrown out of the record."

"I insist that it remain," responded Hutchins.

"There's no way that anyone can now testify about the conditions under which that deposition was taken, now is there? For all I now, coercion was used. Or, maybe the reason Mr. Fickum refuses to testify in court is because the deposition contains lies? I will call for an immediate retrial and appeal if a deposition of a witness who refuses cross-examination was allowed to convict my client."

Markle eyed them both. "I'll see you two after the recess.

After several hours, court was back in session. Judge Markel looked at both attorneys long and hard before delivering his opinion. "The court orders that the deposition of witness Mr. Elmer Starrett Fickum be struck from the record. Please proceed."

Frank controlled every instinct his body had to shout, jump, hug or smile at the news. Surely, now, Vince would be home free.

You could hear a pin drop as the attorneys gave closing arguments. Frank thought Waring did a good job by building on the inherent uncertainties of the night especially with Fickum out of the picture. But, really, it was in God's hands.

The jury remained sequestered for an interminable five hours. Near the end, there was a fast series of notes exchanged between them and the judge. Finally, Judge Markle gave them permission to reenter the courtroom, now even more crowded due to the influx of reporters.

The judge delivered the news to the packed courtroom: a verdict of not guilty. There was a collective gasp. Benno jumped to his feet and yelled a victory shout.

Lisa began to cry, and Frank raised his arms in a victory salute as Vince turned around in his chair. Almost everyone filed out, but Frank saw a young pregnant juror hesitate, then walk over to Vince. They remained in conversation a few moments, and she wiped tears from her eyes. Before she left, she hugged Vince.

"What was that all about, brother?" Frank asked.

"You're never going to believe this. But that woman says she hit my parked car years ago. I barely remember it, but she says I took her to the hospital and gave her some money—she was out of work, and her husband was out of town. All I remember is her crying baby. Weren't you there, Benno?"

"I remember her, Boss. You got damn lucky."

"She must've been the hold-out juror. She can't talk about what happened in the jury room. But it had to be her." Vince hugged Frank, then turned to hug Lisa.

"You look fabulous to a now-free man, babe," he said into her ear. "Let's go celebrate."

Frank didn't know what to feel. Had he really wanted his brother to go to prison?

CHAPTER FORTY-FIVE

With the trial over, the brothers got back to business. Frank's brief closeness to Lisa evaporated in his need to distance himself from her and Vince's relationship, or what he imagined it must be like.

Over a year and a half later, he and Vince stood on the seawall, surveying their latest construction site.

Frank shielded his eyes from the glare with one hand, holding on to his hat in the stiff, hot breeze with his other hand. "Man, am I glad that German architect agreed to come to Zapata with his crew."

Vince watched the crew of deliverymen wheel in unmarked boxes on heavy-duty dollies. "You don't have the slightest idea how I guarded that damn equipment through Customs from Cuba all the way here. You have any idea of how much I had to pay in bribes both there and here to get it safely through."

"I'm going inside to talk to the architect," Frank said, turning to wave at a brunette in a snappy turquoise convertible.

"Anybody I should know?" Vince asked.

"The daughter of Phil Hardy, the city's head building inspector."

"You banging her?" Vince said with a smirk.

Frank counted to one hundred a couple of times as he walked down the pier to the Tahitian's entrance. The shade brought a bit of relief from the sun, although Frank could still feel his neck hot from Vince's insinuation.

The delivery crew was not allowed inside the room where the boxes were opened. Dozens of roulette wheels, dice tables, and slot machines had been assembled and now waited to be tucked inside spring-loaded hiding places constructed by the Germans.

The head architect, Hans Graf, had his blond head bent as he leaned over a large trapdoor in the floor. He looked up. "Good morning, Mr. Carlucci."

"Good morning, Mr. Graf, how are you this morning? I guess you miss your family?"

"Oh, the wife, she misses me. But I don't think about family when I work. This is different from men and from women, yes?"

Frank wondered if this was how it was. He knew when he was busy that he didn't think about Lisa. But at night or early in the mornings—those were the times he was lonely. Did she get lonely for him?

He walked around the place, marveling at the Germans' ingenuity: the five dice tables around the perimeter were hinged to flip up quickly into recesses in the walls that would then be covered by panels of Polynesian murals. Large trapdoors in the floor hid slot machines and roulette wheels. Rugs hidden in the freestanding primitive statues covered the trapdoors once they were closed.

As he walked through the various rooms inspecting what had been done and assessing what still needed to be done, Frank thought of DeLuca. If Tony were here, he would have supervised everything down to the last detail. Frank missed Tony's experience and good eye. More than that, he missed how Tony would think about something for a long time before speaking. His patience around the conference table in those morning meetings was sorely needed. Vince was always impatient with any kind of talking. This club had better enable them to retire. Frank thought longingly of the landscaped pool in his backyard that he never had time to swim in.

The Tahitian Room opened months later amid fanfare from all the major newspapers in the South. Hailed as the "Playground of the Rich," it was famous before it ever opened its doors.

Frank was too tired to sleep when he got home after the opening night. Had it gone well? Yes. Had its success in the face of the damn Depression's side effects been amazing? Yes. Despite the impending nationwide rhetoric about what was going on in Europe with Hitler's rise to power, the rich still wanted to play—and Carlucci Enterprises' specialty was giving them a place to have fun. High-powered fun. But he felt restless. He poured himself a drink and walked outside to sit by the pool.

The ice cubes swirled in the heavy crystal glass as he put it on the table beside his chair. The breeze was only slightly cooler—it was a part of the U.S. that didn't experience fall. What was wrong with him? He felt an unexplainable sense of impending doom. Wasn't everything okay? Vince was focused on security operations at the new place; Benno was Vince's steady, tireless sidekick. Mitch had been, well, not replaced, but certainly the organization had adjusted to both his and DeLuca's absence.

What is wrong with me?

Frank picked up his drink and took a large gulp, almost spitting it out as it burned down his throat.

This is why I don't drink.

CHAPTER FORTY-SIX

Toward the end of the week, amid all the chaos, Lisa telephoned Frank. It had been so long that he almost didn't recognize her voice immediately.

He waved some people out of his office and motioned for them to close the heavy door. "Lisa, how are you?"

"It's been a long time since we talked, hasn't it?"

"Yes." He could feel the hesitation in his voice and tried to control it, but he couldn't. He didn't know what she wanted from him, and it scared him a little.

She paused. Then she plunged ahead. "Listen, Frank, I'm sorry to call you but I need your help."

"Sure."

"It's Randall—"

Frank couldn't keep the fear from tightening his throat. "Is he okay?"

"Thanks to God, he's fine. But that's not the problem. He wants to go to Europe and enlist illegally."

"He's too young."

"I know he's too young—he's my own son, for

heaven's sake. He wants to lie about his age. He says the RAF takes anyone—they need flight crews and ground crews. I don't want him going overseas and being killed."

"Can't your cousins control him?"

"They're my aunt and uncle, Frank." Her voice grew steely. "I'm surprised you even remember you have a son."

Frank didn't need a conversation like this. His anger exploded. "Lisa, you don't know what goes on in my head every day and every night. How I've thought about playing catch with him, going to ball games like I always wished my dad had done with me.

"You never lower yourself to talk to me—even at parties. Even if we're standing next to each other. You're the one who doesn't care about me. You've got Vince, and I guess that's good enough for you."

There was no sound on the other end of the line. Frank imagined her standing in her house's cozy, little living room on the braided rug with the receiver in her small, white hand and her golden head bent toward his voice.

"Oh, Frank, I thought you didn't want to talk to me." He heard the anguish in her voice as she dissolved into sobbing.

"Lisa, Lisa, I depend on you to set the limits on what we say and do. I never know how close Vince is to finding out the truth. I never know if Vince is sitting on your couch. I figure if it's safe for us, then you'll call me or arrange a meeting. If you don't call, then I wait. And wait."

"Oh, Frank, it's been so damn long."

The need in her voice stirred Frank's heart. "Look, I'm up to my ears in alligators today. Can we meet for breakfast tomorrow? Really early? Let's figure out how to keep Randall safe. Let's clear the air between us. Okay?"

She controlled her sobbing, and he imagined her beautiful golden head nodding. "Okay, tomorrow morning early. Where?"

"Six. The Claw—West Beach."

A little lightness came into her voice. "I'll be there."

As he dressed the next morning, Frank looked out his window at the velvety blackness. Winter was a depressing season, wasn't it? He went to the deserted kitchen to trim a red rosebud for his lapel. Looking at the vase of rosebuds on the drain board, he decided to take the entire bunch to Lisa. The deep red would be smashing with her blond hair.

He almost missed the driveway to the Claw's parking lot in the heavy gray clouds of mist.

Lisa's car was already parked and empty. Frank rushed inside to find her sitting at the same table where they'd sat all those years before. That was a good sign.

He held the roses in a brown paper bag—the only thing he could quickly find in the kitchen. As he approached the table, he held them out to her.

"These are for you, Lisa."

A smile came to her face. "For me?"

"Just a little something."

She took the awkward package and looked inside. "Oh, Frank," she breathed, "they are lovely."

"Not more lovely than you, Lisa."

She laughed. "Don't start your charming ways on me, Mr. Frank Carlucci."

He took off his overcoat and laid it on a nearby chair. "You don't know how good it is to see you. You don't know. It's been years since we really talked."

He sat quickly and put his hands over hers on the table. "Every day is a rock fight for me." He paused. "Do you want to talk about Randall or us first?"

"Randall."

"What else do I need to know?" he asked.

Her bright face seemed ready to break into tears. "I don't know what to do. He won't listen to me."

"Can't your relatives control him?"

"He's sixteen now. Almost a grown man—or so he

thinks."

Frank pondered. It really felt wonderful to just sit here with his hands over Lisa's.

"This is what I've thought of, Lisa," he began. "Randall needs to come to Zapata to live."

"What?"

"You haven't seen him in years, right?" Frank swallowed the lump that formed in his throat. "And I've never met him."

Lisa's eyes rose to Frank's face.

For a moment or two, Frank couldn't continue. He gripped her hands—probably too tightly. "I know that I haven't been part of his life, but I've dreamed of doing that, Lisa. More than you could know. If he's here, I could be a good influence. You, too. Together we're a match for him. We'll turn his thinking around. Hell, I could arrange a job for him—something to keep his mind off enlisting while he finishes school and grows up some more."

Lisa looked at Frank with wide-open eyes. "I think it could work. Maybe. But what about Vince?"

"All Vince needs to know is that he's your nephew."

Lisa's eyes grew more reflective. "Give me some time to think about it."

"Does he have the money to go to Canada and find illegal documents to get to Britain?"

"I haven't the slightest idea."

"I've heard if boys can get to Canada, then they ship over to Europe and enlist under a fake ID and fake nationality."

She sighed. "I've got to decide today, don't I?"

Frank nodded and kept his hands on hers.

They ordered breakfast, and the waitress poured more steaming coffee into the thick china cups.

Frank took a deep breath. "What about us, Lisa?"

She smiled, but only a little. "I gave up, Frank."

Frank's throat closed up, and he couldn't speak.

"It wasn't doing me any good to be in love with you."

"But I'm still in love with you."

"Are you?" she asked. "What makes you think so?"

"You're the only woman I want; the only woman I need."

"Then how come I never see you or hear from you?"

"I told you—I can't tell if the coast is clear or not. I don't know your schedule or Vince's, for that matter. I don't want to make your life dangerous—if Vince finds out."

She took her fingers out of his hands and placed her hands on top his. "You'll always be my 'Little Carlucci.'"

Frank briefly wondered if everyone in the café would be spreading it all over the island that he'd met Lisa today for breakfast. If so, it'd get back to Vince that they were holding hands. Screw it, this was more important.

"Listen, Lisa, I want to be more than a happy memory for you. I'm a real man. I have real needs—I know, you've thought in the past that I just come to you for sex. But that's not what I need the most from you. I need someone who understands me—who wants to understand me. Someone who isn't just after the money she thinks I have."

Frank paused, struggling for words, then continued. "I've stayed true to you since I said that I would. I've hoped and prayed that you'd come back to me. But here's the deal, Lisa. If you don't want me any longer, then I need to move on. I need to find someone else."

Tears slowly filled her eyes, and she removed her hands from his. She pushed away the uneaten plate of breakfast. She turned to gaze out at the faint light appearing behind the fog and clearing it off. She spoke, not even looking at him. "I still love you, Frank, but I'm tired, and I'm scared, and I don't know what to do anymore."

He wanted to gather her in his arms and waltz around the joint's wooden floors. He wanted to shout from the highest rooftop. There was still a small chance.

Instead, he grabbed up the roses from the tabletop where she'd laid them and presented them to her in a bouquet. Quietly, he said, "One day, these are going to be a bridal bouquet for you, Lisa. One day."

Tears spilled down her face. She took one hand and wiped them away. He reached into a back pocket and offered his handkerchief. When she took it from him, she laughed. "You and your handkerchiefs. I think I have more in my chest of drawers than you have."

He tried to be lighthearted, but it didn't work so well. "One day the tears will be over, Lisa. That much I promise you."

CHAPTER FORTY-SEVEN

Back at his office, work engulfed Frank—just like always. In fact, this week in particular seemed to require every ounce of his wit and grit. But now, *now*, he had Lisa and Randall to consider—they were back in his life.

Late in the day Lisa called him. "I called Randall and asked him to come to Zapata," she said. "Yes, he said yes!"

"Do you think he'll actually come?"

"He's excited about finishing high school here and working too."

"I'll pick you up, and we'll go to the station together," Frank said. "What day will he arrive?"

"Late Saturday. But, Frank, let me think about it—I don't know that we should go to the station together. Vince'll be suspicious. I'll get back to you later in the week, okay?"

"Anything you say. And, Lisa—"

"Yes," she breathed.

Frank found himself choked up.

"What's wrong? Are you okay?"

Frank willed his self-composure to return. He slowly began breathing again. "Lisa, I love you. Please... I..." He couldn't finish his sentence.

She waited. For a long time, she waited. Finally, she said, "I love you too, Frank. I'll call you again before Saturday."

Frank stood there listening to the dial tone after she hung up, then he finally lowered the receiver into its black cradle. What was going on? He must be tired. Not sleeping so well. Something was going to have to change.

Frank's schedule was nonstop as the weeks wore on. But there were two people that Frank never forgot for a moment: Lisa and Randall. They were Frank's anchors amid construction details and Vince's rages at staff's mistakes and contractor errors.

One Friday afternoon a few weeks later, Frank decided to get away. Just as he was about to pick up the telephone on his desk and ask Lisa to meet him for a drink later, Vince walked into Frank's office above the Derby.

"Hello, brother. What's up?" Vince asked.

"Are we ready for the weekend?"

Vince flopped into one of the big chairs around the conference table. "Fickum's still stirring up shit—not just for us, but for Lisa too."

"Lisa?" For a second Frank thought Fickum must know about him and Lisa, but how could he? Frank just stared at Vince's cold eyes.

"Yeah. He has his protestors at her home for wayward girls—you know about it. Don't you donate money there?"

"What's Fickum doing?"

"Lots of those gloomy church people outside. Same thing they did at your house—singing hymns, carrying stupid signs. Her business is small compared to ours, and she can't afford to lose customers. Really, we can't either.

Those frigging people must rotate shifts between the Tahitian, the Derby, and Lisa's place."

Frank sighed. "I'll go see him this weekend."

Vince scratched the side of his face. "You sure?"

Frank's impatience rose, and he was warm all of a sudden. "I said I'd go, didn't I?"

Vince sighed and stood from the comfortable chair. "Sounds good, brother."

Frank watched as Vince punched the button for the elevator, then turned and left without even a backward look or a wave—typical Vince-style.

Frank no longer felt like meeting Lisa for a drink. But he did want to find out if she wanted him to go to the train station, so he called her an hour later.

"How are you, honey? Have you decided about the train station?" he asked when she picked up.

"I think it's best if Vince takes me."

Frank had figured that her answer would be a disappointment, but he still felt absurdly jealous that Vince would be the man at Lisa's side when Randall stepped off the train.

"Just make sure that Randall doesn't think—"

Lisa interrupted. "Vince just drove up. I got to go, Frank. Later."

She hung up quickly.

Frank found himself once again holding a phone whose only message was a monotonous dial tone. *Damn. Damn it all to hell.*

Sunday morning was cold and bright. Randall must have arrived last night. The Saturday night train. Frank dressed with absurd care even knowing that the visit to Fickum would be unpleasant. There was a chance—slight chance— that Lisa would bring Randall to church. After all, she knew that Frank always attended ten o'clock Mass at the cathedral. Frank wanted to look perfect—every detail matched in color and texture. A new tie, his new camel overcoat. The perfect hat. Impeccably shined shoes.

But no, Lisa and Randall weren't there. Frank lingered after Mass talking to friends—all of whom were full of concern for loved ones who had enlisted.

In the early afternoon, Frank drove to Fickum's parsonage, a two-story, dour building that radiated gloom despite the sunny day. Frank parked down the block and waited until he observed Fickum's long, bony stride from the church to the house. Then, Frank picked up the large brown envelope from the car's seat, opened his door, and walked to the house.

Fickum, himself, opened the door. His pious smile faded into anger when he saw who was standing on the porch.

Before Fickum could speak, Frank began. "Good morning, Reverend. I need to speak to you."

"Get off my porch."

"It's an urgent matter, Reverend."

Fickum drew himself up taller, his face flushed pink. "If you don't leave, I will call the police."

Frank gritted his teeth but maintained his smile. "It's cold out here, Reverend. I don't think your neighbors need to hear our discussion. Let's go inside. I'll only be five minutes."

Behind Fickum and to his side, the plump, aging face of his pale wife appeared. Concern was written in her eyes. "It's very cold this morning, dear," she said softly. "The furnace can't keep up."

With that, Fickum frowned at Frank, "Okay. You've got five minutes." He stepped aside and let Frank enter.

All three stood facing each other in the entranceway.

"Reverend, I think you and I should go to your study where we can talk privately," Frank said.

The wife's soft white hand rose to her throat above a high-necked blouse. "Is there trouble, dear?" A thin, gold band on her ring finger gleamed in the soft light.

"There's no trouble here, Sarah Jean."

"Reverend, I really think we should go to your study," Frank insisted.

"You said 'five minutes.'"

"Sir, if we could go into your study, I think you would be happier."

"I'll bring coffee," the reverend's wife whispered, turning back into another hallway.

Frank was ready to scream by the time they clumped down a short, dark passageway to Fickum's dusty study.

Fickum gestured to a couch, and Frank sat down opposite Fickum's prominent, bony knees.

"What do you want?" Fickum asked.

"Carlucci Enterprises would like to make a donation to your church, reverend," Frank began smoothly.

"We don't want money from sinners."

"Then you don't take money from your congregation?"

The reverend's eyes bore down on Frank. "They are not sinners like *you*, Mr. Carlucci."

"We would like to make a generous donation to your church by purchasing a new pipe organ to replace the one you have, which I've heard needs costly repairs."

"Blood money," the reverend intoned. "From sinners."

Frank drew the envelope to his lap. "For allowing us to make this generous donation, with the understanding that you will stay inside your church—rather than in the streets with your protestors—we will keep these photographs secret."

Frank drew out the glossy black-and-whites and passed them to Fickum.

All the blood drained out of Fickum's face, then rushed back, making his face so red that Frank thought he might have a stroke. Fickum hurriedly thumbed through shot after shot of him and his naked lover. He looked up at Frank and spit out the words, "You devil."

Fickum leapt up with a roar just as Sarah Jean entered the room holding a tray with a china coffeepot and cups and saucers for two. In the second that Frank turned away to look at Sarah Jean, Fickum grabbed his throat in an iron grip. Frank grappled with Fickum, and they both rolled over furniture and books on the dusty carpet, knocking over Sarah Jean with her tray of hot liquid. Frank finally dislodged Fickum's hands and managed to push the man away. But Fickum stood and reached inside his jacket, bringing out a small black gun.

Sarah Jean had been crawling on the floor whimpering. Her pathetic crying was a tragic backdrop to the scene until she came to the photographs. Then she stopped her sobbing. Her silence filled the room, and at that moment, she lunged for Fickum, her eyes wild.

Frank lunged at the same time. They both landed on the reverend, and he went onto the floor. The gun discharged, and, for a moment, Frank didn't know if he'd been shot or not.

He rolled off Fickum. Someone had been shot—but it wasn't Frank. Blood was pouring out of Sarah Jean's abdomen. Fickum threw down the gun and cradled his wife's head in his hands, sobbing and pleading. "Sadie, please don't die, please don't die. I'm sorry."

Frank quickly grabbed the photos and ran from the room, before Fickum's attention could return to him. As he rushed down the sidewalk to his car, smoothing his hair and brushing the dust from his coat, Frank heard one gunshot behind him.

In the next day's morning edition of the Zapata newspaper was the headline: Murder-Suicide at the Parsonage.

The sounds of Sarah Jean's whimpering stayed in Frank's dreams for a long time.

CHAPTER FORTY-EIGHT

A few days later Frank was still steaming that Lisa had asked Vince to go with her to pick up Randall. Vince didn't deserve to be the first man in Zapata to meet Randall. So Frank invited Vince for dinner at the Tahitian and suggested Vince invite Lisa, hoping Randall would also come.

"I don't know if Lisa will want a night out on the town," Vince complained. "She had that kid relative of hers come in on the train last Saturday. She might not want to hire a baby-sitter."

Frank almost had to stifle his chuckle. Vince didn't even know Randall's age.

"I thought you saw Lisa and the kid last weekend."

"Nope. I had other business."

"Well, tell her that we have some Dover sole flown in from England. Might not be able to get that for long," Frank said. "How about I make a reservation at eight o'clock for dinner, and if she needs to go home early for the kid, then she can leave right after dinner."

"Sure thing, brother. You save the table, and I'll get her there."

"You guys can bring the kid if you need to."

Vince rolled his eyes. "Me, eat with a fucking brat? I don't think so."

Again, Frank dressed with absolute care and attention. For Lisa's eyes, for Randall's eyes—if he was allowed to come to dinner with Vince. Bentley, as usual, had Frank's tux steamed and flawless—not a wrinkle.

As Frank snipped a red rosebud from a bunch in the refrigerator, he thought of how happy Lisa had been when he'd taken the bunch of roses to her in the paper bag. He would've like to have spread their wealth of soft petals over her naked body, then kissed them one by one, and gone on to kiss her warm flesh underneath them until he devoured every inch of her. *Whoa.* He couldn't be thinking this way when he had to work all night plus be cool around Vince. Good 'ole Vince with his eagle eyes.

Frank inserted the short, rigid stem of the rosebud into his lapel and walked into the mirrored dressing room to check each detail from every angle. Was his hair beginning to thin above his forehead? Too much worry. Too much shit always coming down the pike. How did you retire from being a crook?

Things were in full swing at the Tahitian when Frank arrived. Women in gaily colored dresses and matching pumps stood next to men in tuxedos as they waited to get in. Frank knew almost everyone in line and took the time to shake hands and welcome people back. The crowd was a little subdued, but they'd be ready to gamble, eat, and dance after a few drinks.

Inside, heavy glassware clinked as waiters delivered drinks to tables. No sooner than a guest pulled out a cigarette from a cigarette case than a waiter glided close and held up a lit cigarette lighter emblazoned with the Tahitian's logo. Frank did what he always did when on-duty. He checked with each section leader: the head chef, the head bartender, the emcee for entertainment, the head security guy, the head valet, and the head dishwasher. Frank had to find out who hadn't shown up for work, who was in training, who might need to leave early depending on the crowd. Problems were Frank's specialty and fixing them was his forte. *No wonder I'm losing my hair.*

About fifteen minutes before Lisa and Vince were supposed to show up, Frank checked to make sure his reserved table was perfect. Sure enough, a round vase of tiny red rosebuds sat in the middle of the table—just like he'd ordered.

At eight o'clock sharp, Vince and Lisa appeared at the club's entrance into the main dining room. Vince was on Lisa's left, but on her right was a young man with dark hair. *My son.* Frank went light-headed. Sixteen or so years ago, when all this began...

Lisa looked positively radiant. She wore a dark-colored two-piece suit of some sort. A little two-toned hat sat above her ear to the left. Each of her arms was entwined in those of her escorts. Randall looked wide-eyed and hesitant, but he stepped along with her into the room, as did Vince.

Frank was drinking in the details and forgot to move from the table to greet them. Lisa's laughing eyes found him. "This is no way to greet my long-lost nephew. Come get introduced, Frank."

She turned and placed a hand on Randall's left arm. "Randall, this is Mr. Frank Carlucci. Frank, this is Randall Cartright, from near Tulsa, Oklahoma."

Randall extended a large hand toward Frank. "I'm pleased to meet you, Mr. Carlucci."

Frank saw good signs in the young man's gaze: directness, a certain well-spoken ease despite his unfamiliarity with the place and people, deep brown eyes under dark brows.

"I'm pleased to meet you too, Randall. Why don't you all have a seat?"

Vince looked around as if to verify that his security guys were being alert. "I'll be back in a few minutes," he said, and rushed off toward the kitchen.

"You look lovely tonight, Lisa."

She took his arm and hugged him briefly. Whispering, she said, "Sweet roses."

Before Frank could reply, Randall blurted out, "Gosh, this is a great place, Mr. Carlucci. I've never seen a place like this."

"Thank you, Randall. My business owns quite a few places—restaurants, bars, a few other types of investments."

"Vince told me all about your and his businesses just today."

"He did?" Frank scanned Lisa's face for signs of distress. *What in the hell had Vince said?*

"Frank, why don't you tell Randall here about being in the restaurant business?" Lisa said.

Vince returned as abruptly as he had left. A drink sloshed in his hand as he set it on the table. "What are you drinking tonight, Lisa?"

"I think I'll have a glass of wine."

"Frank?"

"Me too."

Vince laughed. "Since when have you two become lightweights? If you want wine, the waiter can get it. I only walk to the bar for real drinks."

Frank turned his attention back to Randall. "Tell me a little bit about yourself."

"There's not too much to tell." Randall ran his fingers through his thick hair. "I grew up in a small town in Oklahoma. I've always done a lot of sports."

"Tell Frank about your trophies," Lisa urged.

"Well…it's not that big a deal. But I made state in two

sports last year: baseball and swimming."

Vince looked up. "How the hell you'd find enough water to swim in Oklahoma?" He raised the heavy glass to his lips and looked at Randall.

Randall glanced at Lisa before he answered. "Sir, we had a pool at the school and a community pool."

Vince smiled. "I like a kid who does sports. Healthy, right?"

Lisa began to sip a chilled glass of white wine brought by their waiter. "He's going to do sports here also. Frank, didn't you tell me the country club has a fabulous Olympic pool?"

Randall turned to Frank. "Olympic? I could really swim in a pool like that."

Vince slurped his drink. "Yeah, Frank likes to hobnob with the rich people. They're his specialty."

Frank ignored Vince's jibe. "Randall, I can get you into the club any time you want to swim. Just let me know."

Lisa smiled her thanks. Frank wanted to tell her *don't worry—we'll keep him too busy and too happy for him to even consider enlisting.*

Frank thought about toasting Randall's arrival, but what would Vince think? Instead, his toast was silent: *Thank you, Lord, for bringing my son to me.*

With dinner served, Vince lapsed into monotones, and Lisa and Frank carried most of the conversation. Frank hoped Randall was having a good time watching the floorshow and the elegant couples.

"Do you know how to dance?" he asked Randall.

"Yes, sir. I mean, no, sir. My girlfriend back home said all I do is step on her feet." Randall grinned. "But I think I do okay. I'm better on a ball field, sir."

"What's your position?"

"Shortstop, sir."

"That's a tough position, son."

"It's fast. I like that," Randall said.

"We've got some good ball clubs here. Maybe you'd like to go watch sometime with me?"

"Yes, sir. I'd like that." Randall grinned. "Maybe I could find me a club to play with."

"We'll do that, won't we, Vince?" Frank said, suddenly aware that they'd been leaving out Vince, who seemed sunken in a morose lethargy across the table.

"Sure, sure. We'll do that in our spare time." Vince drained his glass.

CHAPTER FORTY-NINE

One day late in the afternoon Vince received a telephone call at his office upstairs in the Derby. A gruff voice he'd never heard came loud and clear through the lines.

"Vincent Carlucci?"

"That's me."

"I am Phillippe Castrata," the voice said. "I am here from Chicago on a little vacation with my friends."

"How many friends?" Vince asked.

"Two of my closest friends."

"Carlucci Enterprises is honored that you are visiting us on Zapata Island. How do you like our island?"

"We are most impressed by everything here, Mr. Carlucci."

"What can I do for you?"

"We'd like to have a little discussion with you and your brother. A drink or two?"

"Why don't you come for dinner tonight at the Tahitian? Eight o'clock. I'll make sure my brother, Frank, is here."

"Good. We'll be on time. We can look out our hotel window and see the line of cars every night."

After placing the heavy receiver back in the cradle, Vince sat still, staring at the wall in front of his desk a long time. *These guys must think I'm stupid. You must think I don't know you killed Tony.*

Vince strolled into Frank's office. "You free tonight at eight?"

Frank's forehead creased. "Why?"

"We have a date with some guys from the Chicago Outfit."

"Chicago? Again? Why are they bothering us?"

Vince curled his lips back in what might be considered a grin. "Guess they wanted a little vacation spot to visit."

"Capone's out of commission. Who's running them now?

"Nitti's been the front man. 'The Waiter' Ricca is the real boss."

"What's going to happen at the dinner?"

Vince's narrow grin appeared once more. "We'll eat some delicious seafood. Hear what they have to say."

Frank flipped through a few more pages of his calendar. "I'm watching Randall's playoffs for regionals. I have to go."

"Don't worry, brother. I got everything under control. I've got a little surprise in mind for them."

Vince thought about his options. He called the Hotel Cortez, directly across the street, and asked for Mr. Castrata's room.

The same gruff voice answered.

"Mr. Castrata, this is Vince Carlucci. Listen, I think we should have a little preliminary meeting. You know, just you and me—at my house. Before the crowd at dinner."

"Mr. Carlucci, I am honored you have time in your busy schedule for a tourist like me. Where and what time?"

"In an hour. 123 Magnolia Boulevard. White house, yellow shutters."

A long, black limousine delivered Castrata to Vince's house. Two dark-haired young men with powerful arms and legs got out of the front and back doors. They opened the gate and walked up the front sidewalk to the heavy front door.

Vince watched their conversation with his own bodyguards at the front door. Finally, Castrata left the car and came toward the house in a beautifully creased suit of tan silk with matching shoes and a straw fedora.

Vince waited.

"Welcome to Zapata Island, Mr. Castrata," he said after Castrata came in.

Both men sat down.

Vince waited.

Castrata's raspy voice initiated the discussion. "The Waiter sends greetings."

"Yeah? Our greetings to him."

"We feel that the time has come for Carlucci Enterprises to become part of our organization," Castrata continued.

"Really?"

"It is apparent to us, after studying your organization, that you and your brother need some help expanding. Brothels, more numbers, extortion. The possibilities are endless."

"Really?" Vince said again, picking up an unlit cigar and placing it between his teeth. "Why do you say this?"

Castrata picked up a heavy silver cigarette lighter, placing it in front of Vince. "We've studied the way you operate, Mr. Carlucci. There are major expansions of business that you are missing entirely."

"Such as?"

"Narcotics. This is the perfect dropping-off place for narcotics from the South."

"My brother will never go for narcotics. He's too conservative."

"You could quadruple your income with that type of merchandise. That's what we've done. And that doesn't even include what a heavy expansion into prostitution and insurance fraud could do for your bottom line."

Vince picked up the cigarette lighter and ratcheted down the lever to create a long flame to light his cigar. While slowly puffing, he focused only on his cigar. Once it was lit, he finally spoke. "Frank won't okay that. That's why you're talking to me right now."

Philippe relaxed into the chair's cushions. "Can Frank be persuaded?"

Vince looked up. "I've always been able to talk sense into Frank."

"That's good, Mr. Carlucci. I'm going to trust your persuasive powers for right now. You can remind your brother that we have the long-term experience and personnel to get any job done. We can take your little enterprise here and build it into something respectable."

Vince stood. "See you tonight, Mr. Castrata. Eight o'clock."

Castrata seemed startled by Vince's abrupt close to their meeting. He slowly stood and gathered his briefcase from beside the chair.

"You guys are too small-time to run the kind of business we're proposing. You know that, and I know that. This is a one-time offer. Consider it carefully."

Castrata's bodyguards escorted him back to his car.

Vince exploded in a string of expletives. Keeping his mouth shut was a fucking hard exercise. But the payoff would be worth it. *I'm going to catch this Chicago cocksucker off-guard. He's famous for enforcement in Chicago, but he doesn't know me.*

Vince picked up his phone and dialed Benno.

"Get over to my house with Leon. Quick."

Benno and Leon sped to the Tahitian. Benno's thoughts were focused on the night's demands. He looked over at Leon. "Tonight is it. Tonight we show everyone how good we are."

The sound of women's laughter drifted in through the car's open windows, and a light Gulf breeze brought in the familiar smells of fish and sand, salt water and cotton candy. Leon's long, white fingers curled around the steering wheel, and he guided the car to the front of the line of cars waiting for valet service at the Tahitian.

Leon shifted a huge wad of chewing gum to the other side of his mouth. "It's a good thing you're pint-sized, huh, Benno?"

Benno looked down at his strong fingers, which had now worked for Vince in so many killings that he'd lost count. "Yeah, Leon. I'm pint-sized, but I always get the job done."

The doorman abandoned the car door he was opening and rapidly stepped to open Benno's door. Benno sprang out, ignoring the doorman's cheerful greeting, and rushed past the reception check-in and the front security guards. He ran into the private corridor that led around the dining room and casino to the executive offices. He unlocked and opened his closet and inspected his guns: two semi-autos, a Tommy gun, four .38 Specials, and a short double-barreled shotgun. With no hesitation, he grabbed the shotgun and double-checked it for the right type of shells. He also double-checked both the double-holstered handguns across his chest.

Satisfied, Benno closed and locked his closet. He

continued down the corridor to the exclusive boardroom and opened the door with caution. A long table was set with sparkling crystal, china, and silver. Dim lighting shone from the fancy chandelier above the center of the table. Only the faint sounds of the band intruded into the room. He stepped inside with his shotgun, closed the door, and took six steps to the long table. Then he bent down and climbed beneath the white tablecloth.

There in the semidarkness under the table, he looked at his hands on the smooth stock of the gun. That's one thing he had learned long ago: you always got to clean your guns after you use them. The faint odor of Hoppe's rose to his nostrils—an oily yet reassuring smell. The smell of competence. Yes, this would be his best job for Vince— his crowning glory of a job. This was the job that only he could do for Vince. A small-guy kind of job. What was it that Leon had said? Pint-sized? *I'll show you pint-sized.*

Sure, he loved Frank too. Frank was an all right kind of guy—smart with the numbers, smart with the babes. But Benno, well, Benno didn't need to be smart with the numbers or the girls. Benno just needed to protect Vince and get everything done the way Vince wanted.

The door opened, and Benno heard Leon's voice.

"Boss, we've been with these guys since they crossed the causeway. They never saw us."

"Good," Vince said. "Guess the Outfit's not as good as we've heard."

"The sheriff raised the drawbridge as soon as I asked him to. No chance any backup will get to them now," Leon added.

The phone on the side table rang, and Leon answered.

In a few minutes, the door from the hallway opened, and three men were shown inside the sumptuous room: Phillippe Castrata and his two boys. Castrata shook Vince's hands and directed his boys to stand outside the door.

Benno heard a cigarette lighter's ratchet and smelled

the strong aroma of a quality Cuban cigar.

"Did you convince Frank?" Castrata asked. "I need to know."

Vince tapped his foot twice, and Benno placed the front tip of the shotgun on the edge of Castrata's chair, right between his thin legs.

"Mr. Castrata, a double-barreled, twelve-gauge shotgun is aimed at your balls right now," Vince said.

Philippe jumped as Benno forced its metal into Philippe's crotch.

"I've tried dealing with the Outfit's interfering St. Louis asses before," Vince said. "And, now, what happens? He sends *your* interfering Chicago ass down here to persuade us to give up what we've built over years of hard work.

"You Chicago people understand only one thing—fucking force. Now, you're going to take my message back to your fucking brother, Mr. Castrata."

Benno read the slight relief in the man's leg muscles when Vince mentioned he'd be going back to Chicago.

Vince continued talking, and Benno saw him stand, feet planted in the carpet. "Call your men in, and tell them to lay their pieces on the table," Vince said.

Vince opened the door, and Castrata yelled, "Come in here, guys."

The two men came in quickly, followed by some of Vince's guys.

"Put your pieces on the table," Castrata said. "Do it now."

The men apparently hesitated, as Castrata yelled, "Do it!"

Through a small sliver underneath the tablecloth, Benno saw Vince's men unzip two large garment bags onto the floor.

Vince's voice directed Castrata's bodyguards to kneel inside the bags.

Vince's feet moved away from the table, as he

directed Castrata to place a phone call to his boss in Chicago. Benno heard the phone slam on the tabletop above his head.

"Tell your fucking boss that you and I are talking business. In fact, we're having so much fun talking business that I'm taking you out on a yacht for deep-sea fishing. We'll be back in a week with everything negotiated. That's when you need to be back, right? For the fucking Chicago Citizen of the Year Award Memorial dinner for your ex-boss?"

Philippe's hoarse voice replied, "Yeah, one week— the dinner."

"Okay, call him. If he ain't there, leave a message with somebody."

Philippe did as he was told. After the call, Benno saw Castrata's body twist in the chair. Exclamations of anger from Vince and Leon exploded into the room. One of Castrata's hands reached down to an ankle holster as he grabbed a gun and shot wildly. Benno got off a single shot from underneath the table. Castrata's body collapsed into his chair with blood gushing everywhere.

Underneath the table was silence. Dead silence.

CHAPTER FIFTY

Benno struggled out from under the table. His limbs were already stiffer than normal; his face creased in pain. Vince threw himself across Benno, holding Benno to his chest and helplessly trying to stanch the chest wound Benno had sustained.

"Benno, Benno," he bellowed.

Benno eyes glazed over. He coughed blood and grabbed Vince.

"Don't leave me. You can't leave me." Vince was both yelling and sobbing.

"Love you, Boss," Benno whispered. Then his eyes closed, and his arms hung limply at his sides.

Vince sobbed as he rocked Benno's small torso back and forth in his arms on the floor. Vince's boys maintained a steady focus on the Chicago mobsters.

No outcome could've been worse. Life without Benno was impossible to imagine. Every guttural sob of Vince's began deep inside his soul. For a while it seemed like the sobbing would never end.

Eventually, Vince regained control. He looked up at his boys and swiped one finger across his throat while nodding at the two Chicago boys kneeling on the black zippered bags.

Four bodies now decorated the carpet in the executive dining room. Only one body was carried in Vince's arms all the way to the funeral parlor.

There weren't too many attendees at Benno's funeral a few days later. But Vince sat in the front pew—stony-faced and devoid of any apparent feelings. On either side of him sat Frank and Lisa, dressed in black. A few of the boys came, although Vince had told no one except Frank when the funeral Mass would be. The archbishop presided, as Vince requested, and the gold threads stitched over the black funeral vestments glinted in the sharp-edged shards of colored light coming in through the stained-glass windows.

There were no pallbearers. Vince's orders. It was as if he couldn't stand to let anyone else inside the bottomless darkness of his grief. No one was supposed to touch Benno's casket but Vince.

Several times during the service, Lisa reached over to place a hand on Vince's hand. He didn't respond.

At the gravesite, there was no other sound other than the seagulls crying in the air above and Lisa's sobbing. Vince lifted the dirt in his palm over Benno's casket. It was as if he couldn't let go of the earth that would signal the beginning of Benno's burial.

They all stood waiting for Vince. When he turned his hand and released the dirt, his shoulders heaved convulsively. He raised his other hand to his eyes and pushed thick fingers over his eyelids as if that could stop the flow of tears.

Frank was wary of touching Vince. Finally, Lisa walked to Vince's side and whispered something in his ear. Frank saw Vince shake his head no. She whispered "okay," then walked back to the row of chairs a few feet from the open grave. Surely, she had asked Vince if he needed any help.

Lisa still cried softly when Frank walked her back to her car. Vince remained a solitary statue in a black suit at the gravesite even as the gravediggers moved in to shovel the dirt over Benno's full-sized casket—just like he'd always said he wanted one day.

"Are you okay to drive yourself home?" Frank asked Lisa.

She raised tear-filled eyes to him and nodded.

"Is there anything I can do for you?"

She sniffled and took a few deep breaths. "Frank, that could've been you."

Frank was silent.

"Don't you hear me? That could be you dead in that casket."

"I don't think so. I'm not involved in enforcement. Not like Benno."

"Let's get out of here, Frank. It's no good—all this waiting. And for what? More money?"

"I can't leave now. You know that."

She shook her head, smiled sadly, then looked at Frank. Without a word, she cranked up the ignition and slowly pulled out of the asphalt parking lot. No wave goodbye, no big speech. Frank couldn't see anger in her face, only grief.

Frank watched her drive away and told himself that no one would bother killing him. These days he didn't even carry a gun most of the time. Vince, maybe someone would want to kill Vince. *Not me—I'm not a violent man.*

CHAPTER FIFTY-ONE

Lisa hoped that Frank would somehow miraculously appear at her front door after the funeral. He hadn't. Didn't he know how much she needed him? Now everything was in question. Had Benno been the glue that held them all together? No, it couldn't be. She almost never saw Benno—hadn't seen much of him in years. But, but...his unquestioning loyalty, his rock-solid dependability, his strange yet perfect patience with Vince even during Vince's most horrible moods—the ones during which he would scream and curse and break furniture. Maybe Benno's presence was a kind of web, like a spider's web. An invisible but strong netting that held them all together.

The sound of a car pulling up in front of her house brought Lisa out of her reverie. *Oh, Frank, you've come!*

A car door slammed, and knuckles rapped on her front door. With a small cry of surprise and joy, Lisa ran to the door and opened it.

Vince stood there, hat in hand, still wearing the same suit he had worn during the funeral.

"Oh, Vince," she stammered, "how are you?"

"You got company, Lisa?"

"No, no one is here."

"Good," he said and pushed his way into the living room. "I need a drink."

Lisa stood by the front door, unmoving. "Sure," she said, forcing her feet to walk to the small cabinet under the kitchen countertop. "You want Templeton?"

"Sure, funerals are made for whiskey, aren't they? That's what the Irish say."

She brought him the drink neat in a small juice glass and handed it to him before moving to the couch across from his chair.

"You ain't going to join me?" he asked, looking at her for the first time. He swirled the brown liquid around the glass as if admiring its color in the sunlight streaming through the blinds.

"Randall will be home from school soon. I… I…don't drink before he gets home, and I fix dinner."

"Fine. I'll drink alone." He upended the glass and swigged the contents. He grimaced as if it burned. "I haven't had a drink since Benno…you know…" He placed the empty glass on the small coffee table in front of them both. "Another one. This time fill it up."

"Vince, I don't think that's a good idea. I mean, have you had anything to eat today?"

Regarding her on the couch, Vince reached and picked up the empty glass, then turned it back and forth in his strong fingers. "You trying to tell me that I can't have another drink?"

Lisa ran one hand across her forehead and gazed out toward the front yard. "It's just that Randall will be home soon and—"

"And what, Lisa?"

"And I don't think it's a good idea if he sees you here drinking and all, you know, in the afternoon."

"I don't care what Randall thinks."

"Vince, he's a kid…"

"Guys younger than him are getting killed every day over in Europe," Vince said, still examining the empty glass.

"I need to set a good example. You know, for my aunt and uncle's sake."

Vince walked over to where Lisa sat on the couch. He studied her face, then dug his fingers into her cheeks and squeezed hard. He directed her gaze upward to his face. "Right now, dammit. Right now."

With those few words, he lowered his right hand to his belt buckle, jerked it open, and started unzipping his trousers. With his other hand, he reached inside, pulling out his penis while the other hand on the back of her skull forced her head forward.

A voice came from the back door of the house. "Hey, Aunt Lisa, I'm home."

Lisa's eyes filled with tears, and Vince backed off. In the few seconds before Randall entered the living room, Vince zipped himself up and buckled his belt.

Lisa put her hand over her eyes and kept crying. She heard the curiosity and hesitation in Randall's voice. "Oh, hi, Mr. Vince. Aunt Lisa, are you okay?"

Vince's voice came out a little too loud. "Your aunt is still upset from the funeral, son. Why don't you see if she needs a drink?"

Lisa looked up. Randall's face reflected concern. Something was wrong, but he didn't know what. *Please God, keep him safe.*

Vince walked to the front door, retrieving his hat. "I'll see you later, Lisa. Hope you feel better."

Even after she heard the door close, Lisa didn't dare breathe. Somehow, somehow she had to hold it together.

"Auntie, what was that all about?"

"Vince is very upset about losing his friend. He just wanted to talk."

"You sure you're okay?"

"I'm fine, Randall."

Four days later and two thousand miles away a group of Chicago businessmen gathered to honor Al Capone, the Chicago Outfit's ex-leader, now out of commission but still respected. Members of Chicago high society mingled with many of the men who had worked for Big Al during the heyday of Prohibition. Things were different now: too many Feds, too many local citizens outraged by Big Al's violence and murders in broad daylight. But the myth? Yes, the myth that Big Al had fostered by large donations to charity, by soup kitchens during the Depression, by the handing out of favors and jobs and the occasional flashy piece of jewelry. Yes, the myth was alive and well, and tonight's testimonial dinner was important.

Big Al's brothers, still in town, and relatives of Al's wife were all in attendance tonight.

Paul "The Waiter" Ricca took a moment to pull Nitti aside. "Where's Phillipe, dammit?"

"He said he'd be back in time for the dinner."

"He knows how important this is," Nitti said, stopping for a moment to admire his good looks in the hotel's mirror.

A waiter passed with a tray full of champagne coupes. Ricca motioned him over and gestured to Nitti with his chin. "Grab two of them."

Both men stood with the wide-bowled glasses in their hands, scanning the crowd of new arrivals for Philippe. There were many first-generation Sicilians with their wives, but neither of the two men saw Phillippe.

At eight o'clock a waiter in a tux walked through the crowd, sounding a soft chime to signal that seating had begun in the large ballroom.

The six-course dinner proceeded with one notable absence at the head table—Philippe. Everyone drank plenty of wine and kept smiling as steaks were delivered, cooked to order, with herbs and garlic, doused with olive oil.

After dinner, as speech after speech rolled on, Ricca's face took on more of a frown. Something was clearly wrong. Philippe knew better than to be late when Ricca was waiting.

Finally, the highlight of the evening approached. It was time for the beautiful marble bust commissioned last year to be unveiled. This would be Big Al's full-sized tribute, to be ensconced at the union's headquarters. Ricca noticed that even the bishop seated at the head table took a moment out from dessert to look up with anticipation at the veiled bust that had been sitting on the small table in front of the podium all night—waiting for its moment of glory. A fitting tribute to one of Chicago's most successful businessmen.

The house lights dimmed. The emcee stood and said, "Ladies and gentlemen, we have come to the highlight of our evening. Our esteemed honored guest, Mr. Paolo Vallone, Chicago's mayor, will unveil the fine Italian bust as we all, family and friends, count down from ten to one."

Lifting his head to smile at everyone broadly, Vallone walked to the small table. Spotlights focused on the maroon satin drape over the bust. He yanked the cover off and kept smiling into the spotlights.

A few brief moments of silence gripped the crowd. Then a woman's ear-piercing scream rang out. The mayor looked down at the bust and saw the reality of what he had unveiled—half of a skull, sawed lengthwise with all its channels, brain matter, and bones exposed, floating inside a large bottle of clear liquid in eerie, horrifying serenity.

People rushed out of the room. Both men and women—some of them holding napkins to their mouths as their dinners rose in their throats—ran from the appearance of Phillipe's preserved half of a head.

Ricca stilled the bile rising in his throat. He walked slowly to the small table and looked closer at the jar. *Those damn Carluccis.* He motioned Nitti over and pointed one finger at the bottle. "That's our answer from Zapata Island."

CHAPTER FIFTY-TWO

With the attack on Pearl Harbor, events took an unexpected turn for Carlucci Enterprises The next week unraveled for Frank as many of his staff at the clubs turned in resignations to enlist. Frank was glad they were patriotic but worried he wouldn't be able to replace all the waiters, busboys, and cooks. "It's a good thing we were dishonorably discharged," he told Vince. "Otherwise, Uncle Sam might come looking for us too."

Vince looked glum and didn't reply other than to say that none of the security guys had quit—they all had criminal records and couldn't enlist.

Only later in the week did Frank think to call Lisa.

"Lisa?"

"Frank, are you okay?"

"How about you and Randall?"

"Oh, Frank—he is dying to enlist. What do I do?"

"He's too young."

"I know—damnit. He says he'll lie."

"Tell him you'll embarrass him in front of the

recruiting officer. Gosh, I don't know what to say."

"I got to go, Frank." Her voice was surprisingly firm. Unrushed. "Please think of something."

Frank pictured Vince striding up the front sidewalk of her bungalow. She would see him through the front room's venetian blinds, smooth her dress, and paint a fake smile on her face. Vince would pound on the front door, and she'd open it, still smiling. Then...Frank refused to think about it. Instead, he sat at his desk holding a phone line gone dead.

The next day Frank sat in his office waiting to leave for his next appointment—Rotary Club luncheon. It'd be good to be out of the office and in the historic Gallery—the dining room where Rotarians consumed excellent seafood under the stern stares of Civil War generals and pioneer prairie doctors. Damn good desserts there too.

The doors of the elevator opened, and Randall walked through. In the year and a half since he had been here, he had grown tall, with an athletic build and strong shoulders. He had just graduated from high school and already looked like an older college kid.

"Mr. Frank?" he began with a broad smile. "I know I don't have an appointment, but do you have time to talk with me?"

"Sure, c'mon in."

Randall sat in the chair across from Frank. He unfurled his winning smile and rubbed one hand along the top of his knee. "I sure appreciate you making the time to sit down with me. I know you're real busy."

"What's going on, Randall?"

"I just got turned down at the enlistment center. Something about my feet."

"Does Lisa know you went down there?"

"No, sir. I mean, she knew I wanted to do it something fierce. But she didn't know I went there today—not really.

If I'd told her, she would have kept me from going—you know how she is about me enlisting." Randall's voice dropped.

Frank sighed and hoped the noise didn't carry to the young man. Frank had promised Lisa that he'd keep Randall so busy and happy that he wouldn't even consider enlisting. It had worked for a time, but now it was obvious Frank had failed.

"Sir, I was wondering if—I know you know a lot of influential people hereabouts—I was wondering if you could pull some strings to get the medical board to let me enlist?"

"Are you sure that's what you want, Randall?"

"Yes, sir, I want to serve our country."

"This war could go on for a long time more," Frank said.

"Aunt Lisa enrolled me in coursework for next fall at the college, but I really want to enlist."

"What kind of courses?" Frank asked.

"Intro courses—business, maybe accounting."

"And the rest of this spring and summer?"

"Don't know. Most the guys on the ball team are gone." Randall lifted his shoulders in a helpless gesture.

"Why don't you come work for me?" Frank asked.

"Really? Could I do that?"

"Sure, why not? We need good-looking young men as waiters at the Tahitian. If you want, you can even help me with the books. You'd learn a lot more a lot faster than taking courses at the college."

Randall's face brightened with a broad smile. "Could you also see about talking to some of your friends on the medical board, sir? That's what I really want to do—go overseas and fight the good fight."

Frank studied Randall's face—its tanned outlines that all the cutie-pie girls seemed to notice, the brown eyes that now stared into his own dark eyes, the brow that wasn't creased by the wrinkles that now marred Frank's forehead.

Can I send my own son to be killed?

"Sure, Randall, I'll be glad to see what I can do. Meantime, go home, and tell Lisa that you'll be working at the Tahitian starting tomorrow. I'll call Jake. They'll measure you for the uniform and put you on the schedule for training. Would you like a ride over there? I'm on the way to Rotary."

Frank made the call before they left the building. Randall seemed more at ease, and just as Frank dropped him on the curb in front of the Tahitian, Randall turned back toward Frank after he stepped out of the car. "Thank you, Mr. Frank. I really appreciate your help."

Randall hesitated, but only for a second or two. "Is there something else I can ask you?"

"Sure, Randall. Shoot."

"Do you think my aunt is scared of Mr. Vince?" Randall nailed Frank's eyes with his own. The young man's intensity radiated across the front seat of Frank's car. This wasn't a coincidental question.

"What makes you ask that, Randall?"

"I can't put my finger on it. It's just a feeling I get sometimes when he's there."

Frank's heart sank, and his throat closed up. He had been assuming that Vince was never with Lisa anymore—not under any circumstances.

"A few months ago, I came in one afternoon. Everything was weird. I don't know why. Aunt Lisa was crying, and her face was real white. There were two pink spots in the middle of her cheeks. She and Mr. Vince had been alone before I walked in."

Frank thought all the long years since he and Lisa had made love that fated first time. How many times had Lisa told him that Vince was capable of killing all of them?

"Randall, would you promise me something?" he asked.

"Sir?"

"Promise me that if you ever again think that Lisa is

298

scared of Vince that you will get me. Can you promise me that?" Frank hoped his own fear and intensity wouldn't spook the kid.

"Sir, how do I find you?"

"Look, I'm only three places—my office, my house, the Tahitian." Frank dug out a card from his pocket and scribbled a phone number. "This is my private phone number at home. If you call me, I'll come right then."

Randall reached for the card and studied the handwriting before placing it in his shirt pocket. "Yes, sir, I promise."

They shook hands, and Frank left for the Rotary luncheon. He was supposed to be the guest speaker today, but for the life of him he couldn't remember what he was supposed to fucking talk about.

Oh, Lisa. Lisa, my love. What have I got us into?
And how do I get us out?

That same evening Frank's private telephone rang late, late at night. He was dozing in his pajamas, the fans on the ceiling moving the air around lightly. Frank, already in bed, was still thinking about the endless juggling required to keep food quality high during this damn wartime, and premium liquor at the bars.

Lisa was on the other end of the call, and she sounded upset.

"What's wrong, baby?" he asked.

"You know what's wrong, dammit."

The accusatory edge to her voice woke him up. "Are you okay? Is Vince there?"

"How come you worry so damn much about Vince? Why don't you ever worry about me?"

Frank sat up. This was going to be a long night.

"I worry about you all the time."

"Then why did you do what you did?" Her voice rang

clear in its vehemence.

Frank thought back to the day. What had he done wrong?

She continued. "I won't allow Randall to work at the Tahitian."

"Why not?"

"I don't want him mixed up with a bunch of crooks."

"You mean me?" Frank asked.

She didn't answer.

Frank had a crazy impulse to recite a long list to her of all his donations to the Church, to the soup kitchens, to that big plant after the fire, to orphanages. Shit, his huge donations for years to Lisa's own home for girls just released from prison.

"You like Vince's and my money, don't you, Lisa? We've supported you for years, and now you're telling me you don't like our business? You're fucking kidding me."

She didn't reply. In the background, Frank heard a deep-throated ship's horn.

"Where are you, Lisa?"

"Standing at a pay phone on the seawall. I can't call from the house."

"Tell me exactly where you are, and I'll drive over there and get you home safely."

"I've got my own car."

"Tell me where you are, and I'll be there in a few minutes."

Relenting, she told him the address, but Frank heard the reluctance in every syllable. He threw on khakis and a shirt, then grabbed the car keys.

He pulled up to the curb. Lisa's slender figure was wrapped in a light-colored jacket. She was wearing trousers—the first time he'd seen her in them.

She hesitated as if she didn't want to walk over to his car, but he was too angry to get out and open the door for her. *Crooks. She thinks I'm nothing more than a crook.*

Frank heard the door open, and she bent over to look

at him. She wasn't crying—she looked even angrier than he had imagined.

"Get in, Lisa," he ordered.

She pursed her lips, and then sat down. He gunned the engine and drove straight down the road parallel to the beach.

"Don't you think you can order me around like Vince does," she began.

"I thought you weren't seeing Vince anymore. That's what you told me."

"I can't control Vince any more than you can. Sometimes he comes over. Sometimes he doesn't."

Frank shifted gears and accelerated. "So I'm nothing more than money bags to you, huh?"

She didn't reply. Only the windshield and the whitish tops of the incoming waves received any attention from her.

"Dammit, Lisa. What's wrong with you?" Frank fumed.

"How dare you give my son a job?" She threw the words at him as if they were spears.

"Wait a minute, he's my son too."

"Not really, Frank."

Frank pulled over and parked. "What in the hell do you mean?"

"You're not around—not like a real dad. His real dad is my uncle in Oklahoma."

"I've been taking him to baseball games for the past year and a half—doesn't that count?" Frank asked.

She just stared out the window, refusing to talk.

Frank felt like forcing her to at least look in his direction, but that would be something crazy Vince would do.

"You don't care for me anymore, do you, Lisa?" Frank finally asked. It was the one thing, the biggest thing, he was scared to ask, but surely just getting a straight answer was better than these accusations tearing them apart, destroying the beautiful history that they'd had together.

Tears slowly ran down her cheeks.

"It's okay, Lisa. You waited a long time. Too long." Frank placed the car in first gear. "I'll take you back to your car."

He pulled up behind her waiting vehicle and walked around to open the door for her. She got out slowly, the trousers obscuring her beautiful curves. He didn't trust himself to hug her one last time, but instead took her right hand and brought it to his lips for a brief kiss.

"I'm going to miss you, Lisa. I'm going to miss you terribly."

She choked out a sob. Frank thought he heard a whisper from her, but he could have imagined it. If it was real, it said, "Me too."

CHAPTER FIFTY-THREE

The next morning was full of early golden light—real early. Lisa sat in her small kitchen lifting the percolator again and again until her stomach protested at the amount of coffee she had drunk. She dreaded seeing Randall's face at breakfast—his handsome face that looked more and more like Frank had looked when they had first met. Randall was growing up, losing baby fat along his jawline.

Why had she allowed Frank to leave like that last night? He'd seemed glad to be rid of her—maybe, he was. She shifted in the wooden chair and thought back to some of the good times between them—was all that gone now? What else did she have to live for?

She heard Randall's alarm clock in the tiny house. How was she going to confront him? He'd scribbled a note yesterday about a job from Frank but had already been asleep when she read it. *Damn Frank.*

The small house was soon filled with the sounds of Randall's preparation for his day—shaving, showering, all those masculine sounds that Lisa had dreamed of hearing

Frank make one day when they were married. That dream was now nothing more than a mockery of her stupidity.

Randall entered the kitchen, and Lisa's breath caught. He was the one thing that Frank and she had done well, wasn't he? A good kid, at least so far. He'd make someone a good husband.

"Good morning, Randall."

He replied in kind and sat at the table as Lisa delivered two hot fried eggs and buttered toast a few minutes later.

"Aren't you going to eat, Auntie?" Randall asked when he saw that she didn't have a plate in front of her.

"For some reason, I'm not hungry today."

As he gulped down orange juice, he looked at her and said, "I have something to tell you, Aunt Lisa. It's pretty important."

"About your note?"

"I went to enlist yesterday."

"You didn't." It was all she could think to say. There were a million things she couldn't say, didn't dare say. *Oh, God in heaven.*

"They turned me down," he continued. "Then I went to see Mr. Frank. You know, I needed someone to talk to."

Lisa could only stare. She smelled the aroma of fresh coffee in her cup. *Frank?*

"That's when he offered me the job as a waiter. Until those courses start in the fall."

"As a waiter?" she asked.

"I got measured for the uniform yesterday. It'll be okay for the spring and summer, won't it? That way I can help you with the bills." Randall's freshly shaven cheeks almost broke her heart. Her only son, her only child, exposed to danger? How much danger?

"I don't know, Randall. It's a fast crowd there."

"But you've eaten dinner there—I've been there with you plenty times. I promise I'll come straight home every night. It'll be a great experience for me."

She didn't know—could Randall stay free from danger for a few months before school started? The danger of enlisting, the danger from other mobster's guns, the danger of Vince recruiting him into enforcement?

Randall stopped eating and placed one of his large hands on top of Lisa's. "Auntie, I really want to do this. I admire Mr. Frank. Maybe I can get to know him even better."

"When school starts, you'll have to stop the job—you won't have time, you know," she said.

"It's just something temporary. For the warm months."

"Okay, Randall. Okay. Just for the warm months."

Randall grinned so wide it looked like he had swallowed the early-summer sun for breakfast. "You're the best, Auntie. The very best aunt a guy could have."

CHAPTER FIFTY-FOUR

Lisa walked along the seawall alone. As her eyes rose to the incoming waves of light blue reaching to white-sand beaches, she thought about the many times she and Frank had been together. What was it that kept them coming back to each other? Could it be just looks? She mused on the many other handsome guys who had asked her out over the years. No, good looks alone weren't enough for her. She liked brains; she liked a man who handled himself with calm assurance. Not acting as if he were always proving a point—like Vince with his instinctive swagger and volatile temper.

Slowly the sky deepened, and the sunset sprayed red-orange across the waves, beach, and seawall. Lisa kept walking. Would Frank take her back? And, if he did, what was she going back to—more years of waiting? More years of biting her tongue every time Randall called Frank "Mr. Frank" instead of "Dad." Yes, that's what it would mean—more years of loneliness, but more years of hope too. Lisa couldn't live without hope in some kind of future. She'd spent decades trying to give those prison girls hope in a future built on job skills. She had to have her own hope in a future even if it was a future built on unrealistic dreams.

Around midnight, Lisa drove to the Tahitian to pick up Randall from his first day of work. She arrived early and parked along the seawall. She walked to the entrance. In times past, the valets would have known her. And now?

Fortunately, Squid was on-duty—a face from the old days. His eyes sparkled with welcome, and he touched his arthritic fingers to his hat brim in a jaunty salute. "Good evening, Miss Lisa. We're mighty privileged to be seeing you tonight."

Lisa forced her face into a smile. "And good evening to you, Squid. Is my boy ready to leave?"

"There's still some tables in the back, Miss Lisa."

"Is Mr. Carlucci still here?"

"Mr. Vince is upstairs, Miss Lisa. I can ring and tell him you're here." Squid's words were interrupted by a laughing party of six who lurched out the front door and handed their claim tickets to Squid.

As Squid called a runner to fetch the car, Lisa overhead two of the ladies talking. "Did you see that new waiter?" one of them said with a giggle. The second woman grinned and swung her head around to see if the two men in their party were listening. "I'd like to have some bedroom time with him—wouldn't you?"

Lisa's anger flashed. How dare these hussies talk about her son that way?

The women's conversation shifted into quieter tones as their car was driven up to the portico. Lisa waited for Squid to open the car doors.

Once the car drove off in a fast gleam of polished chrome, Lisa looked at Squid. "I was wondering if Frank was still here. I'm supposed to sign some forms about Randall working here."

Squid's forehead furrowed. "Oh, Miss Lisa, he must've forgot. He left hours ago. Do you want me to call

Mr. Vince?"

Lisa tried to keep her face neutral. "That's okay, Squid, I can—"

"Well, here's my beautiful girl," Vince said, walking out the front door and planting a wet kiss on her cheek. "Come inside, and have a drink with me."

The smell of hard liquor rose from his mouth, and Lisa struggled to keep a smile on her face. "Thanks, but I'm just here to pick up Randall after his shift. I won't be here five minutes."

Vince placed one heavy hand on the small of her back and walked her into the club.

"Oh, Vince, I really appreciate it, but Randall will be finished in a minute, and I'm not dressed right, and—"

Vince waved the bartender over as he pushed her into one of the cushioned bar stools near a large mirror in the front dining room.

"What'll you have?" Vince slurred.

"Vince, I really can't—" stammered Lisa.

"Two martinis," Vince said to the bartender. Then he turned toward Lisa, "Where you keeping yourself? I been worried about you."

Lisa noticed that his words filled the almost empty room. It was like a cave—everything sounded louder. "Oh, I've been working hard. That home for girls keeps me busy."

Two drinks were set in front of them. The clear liquid sparkled in the room's festive lighting.

Vince raised his glass and toasted as Lisa picked up hers. "Here's to us, babe."

She gritted her teeth and hoped her face would not show her lie. "Here's to us, Vince."

He continued speaking after taking a long gulp of his drink. "It's not every night that my girl comes to see me at work." With that, he set his drink down and placed one hand on her thigh. Its heat almost burned through the thin fabric. How was she going to get out of this?

Vince reached for his glass again. "I'm happy to see you, Lisa. Real happy."

Oh, Vince, if you only knew.

He continued rubbing her thigh with his hand, and then reached with his other hand to her calf, beginning a soft caressing.

"We can go up to my office, Lisa. I got a couch."

Lisa set down her drink. "Listen, Vince, I really gotta go—I have a real early appointment in the morning."

Vince didn't listen, or, if he did, he didn't care. He moved his chair closer and began kissing the side of her head, her ear, and her cheeks while his hands roved up and under her dress.

"I can take care of you, baby. I know you want it," he whispered in her ear, his breath hot and slow.

"Auntie, my shift has ended," said a voice behind them.

Lisa imagined how she must look. *Oh, dear God in heaven.* Lisa reached under her skirt and forced Vince's hands off her legs.

"Randall, I've got that early appointment tomorrow. Let's leave."

She was too embarrassed to look at Randall's face. But she had heard the cold tone of judgment in his voice. His stiff posture as they walked out also betrayed his real feelings.

Vince stayed seated at the bar, a solitary dark-suited figure with a beautiful crystal glass in his powerful fingers.

Lisa had hoped to ask Squid to tell Frank to call her, but Squid was gone. All that remained in front of the elegant club were the stylish neon lights that would stay on all night.

They walked to the car in silence. The taste of the gin was bitter in Lisa's mouth. The truth? What was the truth?

Lisa slept late the next morning, awaking with a dull headache and a sense of sadness as if she had lost her only doll and was three years old again. Randall had already gotten up and made his own breakfast. He had placed a handwritten note on the center of the small kitchen table, letting her know he was going to play tennis at the club.

Coffee wasn't required for what Lisa knew she must do. After rinsing her face with cold water, she called Frank's office. His secretary answered. When Lisa asked to speak to Frank, the woman said she'd give him the message. Lisa didn't have to be told what this meant— Frank didn't want to talk to her. *Dear God in heaven.* This is what it all had come down to—messages left with a secretary.

The hole in Lisa's heart widened. For all these years, that hole had been filled with her love for Frank. Crazy love for Frank—against all the odds, against all common sense, against what should've happened but didn't, and against what shouldn't have happened but did—like her pregnancy, like Vince getting her initial note meant for Frank, and on and on. Despite his flaws and her flaws, his stupid love of money and fine clothes, and despite her own sense of decency and fear of Vince. Through all of this— they had made it. And now, now—it was all gone because she had called Frank a crook.

Wasn't this the truth, though? Shouldn't truth be the road to happiness?

For five days, every morning as soon as Randall left the house, Lisa called Frank's office and left a message for him to call her. All day every day, she waited by the phone. He didn't call. Finally, on the afternoon of the fifth day, she removed the receiver from the cradle and left it lying by the phone. If Frank called, he'd only get a busy signal. Damn him.

The next morning Lisa carefully planned what she would wear. She began with a long, hot shower after Randall was away from the house. She wore a pink suit with a small hat that curved around her curls. She picked shoes that showed off her slim ankles. Too nervous to eat, she drank black coffee. Before she left the house, she got down on her knees on the knotted rug beside her bed and prayed. Whatever happened would happen. All she had to do was to tell the truth—if Frank would let her.

Lisa drove to Frank's office at the Derby. In the good old days, Benno would have been downstairs, and they would have shared a laugh before he punched the elevator button for her. Mitch might have been downstairs with his paw around a candy bar as he crunched his way into an ever bigger girth.

The good old days were gone. Lisa sighed. All she had to do was to tell her own truth. She thought she'd found it in the excruciating five days that had just passed. Five days realizing that she was now on her own—without love—for the first time in a long, long time. The torch she'd carried for Frank was useless.

Things at the Derby had changed. A lovely but stone-faced young woman sat at a downstairs desk before anyone could approach the elevator. Her posture radiated propriety. But her movement inside the dress indicated a killer of a figure inside the expensive fabric's stitching. Could this be Frank's new girlfriend? Inside the smart tailoring that he loved?

Lisa stepped up to the woman's desk and smiled. "I'm here to see Mr. Frank Carlucci."

"Do you have an appointment?"

"No, I do not."

"Mr. Carlucci's schedule is very busy today."

Lisa smiled and brought her handbag up to sit on the polished wood of the secretary's desk. "I can wait."

The girl looked at Lisa, then at the handbag.

"I'll sit at the bar. Please tell Mr. Carlucci that I'll be waiting for an opening in his schedule."

"Your name, ma'am?" the girl asked.

"Lisa."

Lisa walked to the bar and looked at the pony racing results from the previous day on the high chalkboards. After two hours, Lisa walked back to the desk. "Has Mr. Carlucci been informed that I'm waiting?"

"Yes, ma'am," the girl said with a smile. *Yes, Frank would like a girl like this, wouldn't he? Prim and proper on the outside, and fiery underneath all the clothes.*

Lisa's pulse pounded at her temples. "I did not see you go upstairs to inform Mr. Carlucci that I was here. Nor did you pick up the telephone to call him. I do not believe that he knows I am here.

"Furthermore, I am walking to that elevator, punching the button, and going to see Mr. Carlucci—whether you like it or not." Lisa skirted the desk and did exactly as she had said.

The young girl didn't know what to do—this was one of the few times in Lisa's life that experience was in her favor.

The girl stood by her desk, mouth wide open and an ugly expression on her flawless face.

When the doors opened, Lisa stepped in, turned around to glare at the young woman, and punched the button for Frank's floor.

When the elevator arrived on the second floor, Lisa took a deep breath before walking out. Frank was looking at papers. Lisa spoke before he could raise his head. "Good morning, Frank."

He jerked his head up. "Lisa!"

"Yes, it's me."

"What are you doing here?" he said with a careful movement to push the pile of papers to the side.

"I have something important to tell you, Frank," Lisa began, but her voice choked up. This wasn't what she had planned at all. That elegant hussy downstairs. Frank looking surprised but not happy. The whole place feeling wrong and lonely without Benno and Mitch.

With Frank's coat hanging on a rack behind him, she

could see that he was wearing a shoulder holster over his ivory shirt with a small pistol in it. When had he gone back to carrying a gun?

Frank sat staring at her. He didn't speak; he didn't move.

Lisa regained her breath and invoked a short prayer to echo the one she'd said by her bed this morning.

"I only have one thing to tell you," she began. "Listen to me, and listen good. Because this is the most important thing I've ever said in my life—I love you, Frank. I will always love you. I'm sorry for what I said. I wish I could undo it, but I can't.

"Just please, please remember this—even if you forget me. Please remember that I loved you very much."

Lisa heard her own voice. It was almost like she wasn't saying the words herself. Where were they coming from?

Frank didn't do anything. He continued to sit still.

Lisa walked to the elevator and punched the button. She hoped against hope that Frank's voice would call her back. That his voice would have the old spark of happiness in it.

But he didn't. The elevator doors opened and closed. And Lisa rode the slow ride down, holding the corrosive sadness inside her chest.

Dammit, I won't cry in front of that stupid little girl.

But in her car…in her car, Lisa cried harder than she'd ever cried before.

CHAPTER FIFTY-FIVE

Summer rolled closer to autumn, and the days took on the monotonous quality of dominoes—one falling in line just after the one before it. Lisa resigned herself to Frank's silence, yet dreams haunted her with memories of the good times, her telephone chats with him as she sat in her small kitchen, or when they'd met at the Claw and he'd brought her tiny roses like red jewels. The times when she could count on his hunger for her body and his thorough, exquisitely thorough, lovemaking.

Lisa watched Randall mature before her very eyes—beyond a growth spurt, he was having a maturity spurt. His voice had deepened a few years before he came to Zapata, but now his shoulders broadened even more, and his eyes took on an increased ability for quiet regard and a deepened sense of empathy. Soon, she suspected, Randall would be gone. He had become a man in the humidity and heat of that Zapata summer as he worked his first job, played tennis every morning at Frank's club, and quit telling her everything—she could feel it.

Her nighttime prayer on the knotted rug by her bed was incessant: *Dear God, bring Frank back to me.*

Close to the end of Randall's first semester, one Friday he told her that he would be extra late getting home that night.

"What's going on?" Lisa asked.

"It's a party at a frat house."

"They let you off work?"

"Today I'm just helping Mr. Frank with the money in the afternoon."

"What time should it be over?"

"I don't know. I won't be too late because I have an early game tomorrow morning."

"You'll be safe?"

"Don't worry," he said with a smile. "I can take care of myself."

Lisa's head swiveled to see his expression after those words. Luckily, his open gaze and smooth brow belied any sense of arrogance or belligerence. A small shiver ran down her spine. For a moment, he had sounded just like Vince—he had sounded just like the gun-toting crooks he worked with.

She reached over and tousled his hair. "Okay, big boy, just be sure that you don't get into any trouble."

He laughed and shrugged off her hand. "I never get into trouble, Auntie. You know that."

Later that morning Randall tried to shake off the feeling of gloom that descended on him every morning when he ate breakfast with his aunt. She was trying to pretend that everything was okay. She smiled: she looked into his eyes when they talked. But something was different; something had changed over the summer. Everything seemed like an effort to her, and he rarely heard her laugh anymore. In a way, he was glad that she was out of the little house every afternoon when he came home to get ready for work. For him, life was good; life was exciting—college classes, helping Frank with the books and sometimes with the cash also, lots of good-looking girls at the club during the hectic nights when he worked, lots of even better-looking girls at the tennis courts every morning with long, tanned legs and shiny hair in curls.

Getting ready to go to the frat party, he took time to splash on cologne he recently purchased. It was cold and astringent on his skin—but in a good way. Was this how it felt to be a man?

Randall parked his car at the curb down the street from the frat house. Walking up, he noticed the heavy granite that went up two stories. Massive stone steps led to a spacious porch where people gathered with drinks in hand. Man, what a Frankenstein kind of place.

One of the guys yelled, "Hey, come on in. There's plenty of booze inside."

Randall ascended the steps, scanning for his friend Jon, a medical student and fellow tennis player. Several people parted so he could squeeze through. Just as he was sliding toward the front door, he spotted the most beautiful babe in the world. In the universe.

At first, she was in profile to him and talking to a tall guy. Then she turned. A heart-shaped face was framed with blond curls that blew slightly in the cool wind. Big brown eyes lit up when she saw Randall. In a voice that sounded to him like the voice of an angel, she spoke, "Where did you come from?"

Randall stepped toward her. "Oklahoma."

She laughed and pulled the hair out of her eyes. The tall guy placed a long thin arm around the girl's waist. "Let's go inside, Sophie."

She carefully extracted herself from his embrace. "Thanks, Gerald. I'm going to stay on the porch a while longer."

Gerald evaporated into the crowd.

She smiled at Randall. "You're an Okie?"

"I've been living here for a few years. Where are you from?" he asked. Man, how was he going to get his head on straight? When she looked at him, he couldn't think.

"Jackson."

She smiled at him again, and his heart lurched. Babes liked boys who could talk.

"Do you like Jackson?" he asked.

She laughed. "I've seen you at the Club, haven't I?"

"You play tennis too?"

The girl extended a hand. "I'm Sophie Sheppard. Pleased to meet you."

With embarrassment, Randall remembered his manners. "I'm Randall Cartright. I'm pleased to meet you too."

"I like your serve. Though I think you have a tendency to choke on the final point in a game, don't you?"

Randall laughed, reminded of all the times that had happened. "Yep—you got that right."

"I've watched you play."

With a question in her eyes, Sophie asked Randall how he'd come to be invited to the party. He explained his friend Jon's eager descriptions of how the medical students let it all out after the once-a-semester finals. "Yep, he said that it was like a pressure cooker releasing after the last day of finals."

Sophie raised a glass to her mouth and took a small sip. "Would you like a drink?"

"Could I get you something while I'm inside?"

She shook her head. "I'm on-call tonight. I'm just drinking water."

"Are you a doctor already?"

She smiled while cradling the glass in front of her. "I'm in nursing school. But I've been studying for days and nights, and I'm exhausted."

"You look perfect to me," he blurted.

Sophie gave him an appraising glance. "Slow down,

big boy."

Randall looked down at his feet, which had suddenly grown too large. Sophie's hand gently took his arm. "Can we go somewhere we can really talk? That Dixieland band inside is giving me a headache."

"Sure. Sure, whatever you say."

Disentangling themselves from the crowd on the porch, they walked down the sidewalk under the branches of huge oaks. Nesting night birds rustled and cooed overhead. A full moon rode high on the night's currents.

"Tell me about yourself, Randall."

"I'm in school at the college. Accounting. I work at the Tahitian—"

She exhaled. "Oh that place. What a bunch of crooks."

"Crooks?"

"Everyone knows those two brothers are gangsters from way back. My father has been trying to put them out of business for years." She shook her pretty curls from side to side. "They're smart, real smart. But he'll catch them one of these times, and they'll go to prison."

"Who is your father, Sophie?"

"Will Sheppard, the attorney general."

Randall couldn't think what to say. The most beautiful woman on the earth walking with him in the dim tunnel of old oaks under a full moon—and then, this.

"I guess I better take you back to the party, Sophie."

They stopped walking. She pressed closer to him and lifted her face to his. Wasn't this what women did when they wanted a kiss?

"You don't understand, Sophie. Frank Carlucci is my boss and—"

"Kiss me, Randall. Kiss me right now." She pushed slightly against him, the smell of her perfume an enticing invitation.

Their lips met, and Randall's cares drifted away. She pressed closer to him, and Randall felt the smooth mesh of their bodies in perfect conjunction. Every surface of him came alive. Oh, never had this happened, never before. Every pore of his body wanted her—forever.

She stepped back and reached one hand to his cheek. "I'm on call, and I've got to go now, Randy."

"But wait. Wait. I want to see you again, Sophie. How do I find you?"

"Nursing school. Sophie Sheppard."

"When can I see you next?"

She stepped into a red convertible at the curb. "Call me."

Randall stood transfixed, nailed to the spot on the cracked cement sidewalk, watching her shift into gear. The shapely outlines of her body in the dark sweater were visible against the light-colored upholstery. Shivers ran up his spine. What a body. What a smile. Had she just said he could call her? Man, tomorrow morning. Eight a.m. Yes, sir—eight a.m. Morning was never going to look as good as it would tomorrow.

CHAPTER FIFTY-SIX

Randall barely slept the entire night. Too much energy, too much desire to be contained in his body. The future seemed bright, full of a different kind of possibility. Sophie's soft lips had caused a thousand new hopes to rise in his imagination.

Thumbing a nickel into a pay phone at the college, he called the nursing school before his eight o'clock class. A receptionist informed him in a loud voice that Sophie Sheppard wasn't in. *Damn.* Randall lowered the heavy black receiver and walked into the classroom.

Finally, in late afternoon he reached Sophie. Her voice was full of sleep—husky and slowed.

"Hi, Randy."

"How are you, Sophie?"

"Tough night in the ward. Slept all day after my shift."

"Can I buy you a cup of coffee? Four o'clock?"

She paused. "Let me see if I can wake up by then. I've

got to be back at eight."

"I'd love to see you. Even for a few minutes."

She laughed. "Pick me up in front of the nursing school in an hour."

Driving to the old, ornate structure housing the nursing school and its dormitory, Randall was full of nothing other than his burning desire to see Sophie again. As he pulled up to the door, he was surprised to see her rush out and walk to the passenger side of his door. He'd planned to park, walk inside, and escort her to the car—like he'd been taught. Instead, all he could do was stare as she opened the door herself, sat down, and smoothed her wool skirt.

"Hi, Sophie."

Her brown eyes sparkled, and she dimpled. Yes, her smile was just as gorgeous as last night.

"Randy, we have to talk."

He pulled away from the curb. "Let's go to the Dot. I promised you a cup of coffee, didn't I?"

She placed her hands on top of the pleats of her plaid skirt and looked straight ahead. Man, this wasn't how he thought he'd be seeing her again.

Inside the diner they scooted into one of the shiny red booths and ordered coffees.

"Would you like something to eat, Sophie?"

She shook her curls from side to side and smiled. "I'm okay."

The coffee was delivered, and she placed her hands around the warm cup. "I've got to ask you something, Randy."

She paused and lifted those liquid brown eyes to look at him. "Why are you working at the Tahitian Room?"

"To earn money to help my aunt."

Sophie took a sip of her coffee.

"Why?" he asked.

"Some of the others I know said you're heavily involved in the, you know, money end of things."

"My major is accounting, Sophie."

Randall's neck was heating up. The sweater he'd worn all day had become too thick in this crazy diner.

Sophie twirled the handle of the heavy china cup from side to side in the saucer. "I can't be mixed up with anything illegal, Randy. Because of my dad—it would kill his career."

"If they were doing something illegal, wouldn't they already be in jail?"

She raised her head and spoke, emphasizing every syllable. "I thought I told you last night that they're smart. My dad has been trying to catch them for years."

"Sophie, I think you're jumping the gun. I like you; I want to spend time with you. The Tahitian is a part-time job for me. I'm not asking you to marry me, I'm asking you to, well, I don't know what I'm asking you to do, but I can't see how Mr. Frank figures into my love life..." He paused. Everything was wrong; everything he said and she said was jumbled up and stupid.

"Besides, Mr. Frank is a decent man—he gives money anytime the bishop or monsignor calls, or the mayor, or anyone else, pretty much."

Sophie didn't smile this time. Her face was no longer open and interested.

Could they get out of here and finish this awful conversation?

Randall raised his hand to signal the waitress for the bill. Sophie remained silent.

Randall drove her back, but she didn't immediately get out of the car. This time, he got out and opened her door, then escorted her to the front lobby.

"Sophie, call me when you sort this out. I'm not giving up my job." Randall looked away from her intense eyes, then back again, forcing himself to smile. He had a crazy urge to take her hand and raise it to his lips—just like the movie guys did when they said something romantic. Something final and courageous and bold. Instead, he held himself erect and still, unmoving and distant.

Sophie turned away, then back again. "Randall, I—"

He closed her lips with a soft kiss placed just above them, to the side. "Goodbye," he whispered. "Goodbye."

The long hours of that night became a mockery of his excitement of the previous night. The other night had been filled with Sophie's smiling face, with her easy laughter, with her curves and sleek, muscled legs. Tonight was full of the dismissal in her serious face and the hands that fiddled with the china coffee cup in an endless circle like the argument they'd had.

At the breakfast table Lisa questioned him about how bad he looked. "Just worried about finals," he said. From the long stare she gave him he could tell she didn't believe him. She didn't question him any further, though. That was good.

Months passed. Randall hoped that Sophie would call him, but she didn't. Gradually, hope faded. The days held the same kind of humid boredom as before that magical night he'd met her.

On the first night of spring break Randall showed up at the Tahitian early for his shift. First order of business was seeing Frank.

Frank's face broke into a big grin when he saw Randall. "It's almost time for us to be looking for baseball tickets for the season, isn't it?"

"Yes, sir. Mr. Frank, can I talk to you about something serious?"

"Sure, Randall."

"How do you know if you're in love with a girl?"

Frank got up from his big desk and walked to the conference table. He sat, got up again, and walked around the room, looking down at the carpet. "Love is a pretty big word."

"Yes, sir."

Frank raised one hand and covered his eyes as if he were tired. "I think it's when you can't get a girl out of your mind. She's there when you go to sleep and there when you're dozing in the morning."

Randall remained silent. Questions revolved in his head—the same ones that had been driving him crazy during the rainy, gray close of winter and now under the lighter skies of springtime's first attempts at warmer temperatures.

"You think you're in love?" Frank asked.

"I'm not sure," Randall said. "How else can I know?"

Frank sighed. "It's been a long time, Randall. It's hard for me to remember."

"Have you ever been in love, Mr. Frank?"

"Once. Only once."

Randall couldn't believe that question had come from his own lips. Mr. Frank was a friend, someone he could count on, but he was so much older, so appealing to the women—Randall heard flirty comments from women at the Tahitian all the time when Frank walked by in his tux with the red rose bud. How had Randall let himself ask that question?

"That's funny, sir. I mean, not ha-ha funny, but you know, weird-funny. My aunt Lisa says she's only been in love once too."

"You're in love when you ache for a woman, Randall. For her body, sure. But for a lot of other things about her too—her smile, the way she walks into a room, her voice on the phone. You miss her all the time. Sometimes you even miss her when she's right next to you, like when you're having an argument."

"I know about arguments," Randall said.

"That's too bad. Those are no fun."

"Yes, sir." Randall didn't know if he'd gotten what he

came for, but maybe it would be enough if he thought about it. "Thank you, Mr. Frank. I appreciate your time."

"Anytime, Randall. Anytime."

For months, one day was the same as the next for Randall. Then one night, while he strode down the long hallway into the front dining room, a tray with six seafood dinners aloft over his right shoulder, he heard a woman's voice behind him say his name.

He couldn't swivel with the heavy tray, so he stopped and waited. A tall figure in a beige gown with sparkles appeared before his eyes. A little heart-shaped face surrounded by blond curls smiled at him. "Oh, Randall, I am so happy to see you!"

He couldn't move. It was Sophie—more gorgeous than ever. She must be here with a date.

"I got to go, Sophie. Food's getting cold."

Her bright smiled remained, and she said nothing. He walked off, cursing his lack of words, cursing his lack of tact, and, most of all, cursing the red currents of happiness flooding his body just at glimpsing her. *Damn the heavy tray.*

Randall worked hard the rest of the night, but made sure he located the table where Sophie sat with five other people. There was an older couple, then two other younger couples, including Sophie. Thank goodness, he wasn't their waiter. He'd seen the kinds of things that sometimes went on under the long white tablecloths. If he'd had to serve food while Sophie put her hands under the table on her date, he would've gone crazy.

They were departing now, and he turned back to the bar, waiting for the bartender to finish placing seven Singapore Slings with their perky little umbrellas on a tray. A hand slid against his right elbow, and he turned. Sophie stood there smiling.

"Randall, it's good to see you." She reached to shake his hand, and a matchbook slid into his palm. She stood on her tiptoes and pecked his cheek. "Call me." She walked back to her group and left with them—joking and laughing.

Randall slipped the matchbook into his trousers without looking at it. At home, late after his shift, he allowed himself to peer at it. Inside, there was a scrawled number and one sentence. "I miss you." He fingered the cardboard embossed with the Club's logo and tossed it onto his nightstand before turning the light out.

The next morning, Randall called the number. After the fifth ring, Sophie answered.

"Randall, you free for breakfast?"

"I've already eaten and I'm on the way to classes."

"Oh." Her voice was small, noncommittal.

Randall laughed. "Wait a minute. I'm on spring break. We can meet as long as it's before I go to work at six."

Her voice brightened. "I owe you a coffee, don't I? How about we meet at the Dot? One hour from now?"

Sophie was already in a booth when Randall arrived. She looked tired. Guess she stayed up late with that guy from last night. *Damn.*

It was hard not to come under her spell. Those expressive eyes. The perfect pale skin.

"I've missed you, Randall."

"You have a boyfriend, don't you?"

She shook her head. "What are you talking about?"

"That guy last night."

"Pooh-George? He's my second cousin, for heaven's sake."

"Why were you going out with him?"

She tapped her nails on the hard surface of the table. "Randall, I didn't come here to argue with you."

Like Frank had said, you can miss her even when

you're sitting with her right next to you.

Was it love—thinking of a girl night and day, waking to her image in your mind, going to sleep at night imagining her body under yours? Frank had said it was love.

"Randall, I called and left messages. You never called back."

"I never got a message from you, Sophie. Where did you call?"

"The Tahitian. That's the only place I knew to find you."

"I never got a message."

She smiled but looked a little sad too. "Well, that certainly explains why you didn't call me back."

"Where does that leave us now?" he asked.

She slowly stirred her coffee. Raising her head, she looked into his eyes. "I've thought long and hard about our last conversation. You were right. We just wanted to get to know each other. My father and your boss shouldn't come into that decision.

"Do you think we can erase all the months of bad feelings and start again?"

Randall tried to find his mind, his heart. What would Frank do in this situation?

She looked out the window, then fixed those eyes on him as if she just remembered another stray thought. "That is, unless you are dating someone else now."

Randall pictured Mr. Frank sitting at his desk in the starched and ironed ivory shirts he special-ordered from Switzerland. Frank wouldn't back down. Randall had never seen Frank waffle—he was the only one who stood up to Vince or to the suppliers who occasionally muscled their way into his office to demand overdue payments in loud voices, their long arguments filled with cursing and threats. No, Frank would meet the situation head-on.

"I've spent months dreaming of you, Sophie. Months missing what I thought we might have between us. Crazy, how can you miss the future?"

Her eyes filled with tears, and she let go of a big breath. She brought one knuckle up to her lips as if to stifle a sob. "Let's try, Randall. I've thought of you a million times. Let's try."

Randall wanted to crush her in his arms, to feel her softness against his chest and place his hands on the blond curls that cascaded from her beautiful head. To cover her with kisses, to let his hope and desire and passion overflow from his heart to hers. He placed one hand over hers on the Formica tabletop. "I'm going to try my hardest, Sophie, because I want you to be mine."

CHAPTER FIFTY-SEVEN

Randall and Sophie slipped into a comfortable schedule of diner breakfasts after her all-night shifts. She looked tired each morning—her pale skin no longer luminous and the small hollows under her eyes a little swollen. Randall didn't care—it just made her more beautiful, more vulnerable.

He would listen to her stories from the long tedious nights of nursing—the people who slipped into death as if into the welcoming arms of a sweet, smiling grandmother and the people who clawed and clung to each ragged breath, as if to salvation itself. Sophie would shake her head and say, "I don't understand." Randall would just listen—he didn't have any answers to her questions. He thought that maybe, maybe, the best thing he could do was listen, then hold her next to his heart when she needed to cry.

Each night after working at the Tahitian he stood on the seawall in the heavy breezes to call her from a pay phone before going to his bed at Lisa's house. He grew fuller each day with Sophie's presence: her robust competitiveness when they played tennis on her days off, her sweet smile when she first glimpsed his face each day, her sadness when a patient she'd taken a shine to died.

As the tall bushes of azaleas unfurled their pale, frothy blooms in late spring, Randall became even more preoccupied with Sophie. He felt it happening. At school, his grades dropped. At the Tahitian, he began making mistakes taking peoples' orders. Sometimes at night his body would be so tense and full of Sophie's presence that it was tight as a bow ready to launch an arrow. He could barely lie down to rest with so much desire in his muscles. Sleep wouldn't come.

One morning at the breakfast table, Lisa was placing the eggs she'd just fried on his plate when she spoke. "Randall, what's that on your neck?"

Randall thought. "I've just shaven—I didn't see anything."

"Randall, that's a hickie."

Blood rushed into his face. "Auntie, I didn't see it when I shaved—"

"That's not the point."

He stood up to walk into the bathroom for a mirror. Lisa stopped him by taking his jaw in her fingers and turning it to the left. Her eyes blazed.

"Where did you get that, Randall?"

He sat, his legs abruptly too tired to stand. "I have a girlfriend, Auntie."

"It had better not be one of those hussies at the Tahitian. If Frank has—"

"She's not like those women at all. She's high quality—a real lady. And smart too—"

Lisa sat at the table across from him. "What kind of lady puts a mark like that on a boy?"

"Aunt Lisa, I'm not a boy anymore. Haven't you noticed? I'm a man now."

Randall's words were a slap across Lisa's face. He

hadn't intended them that way—not in the least. Somehow their message in the smallness of their kitchen at the round table they'd shared every morning for years now—that message came out with more force and vehemence than he'd predicted.

Lisa sat back in her chair. She reached for her coffee cup and raised it to her lips. Before drinking, she lowered it back to its saucer. She looked at him as if seeing him for the first time in a long time. "Oh, Frank—"

"Auntie, Frank has nothing to do with this."

That afternoon Randall showered and dressed quietly. Lisa was home but her bedroom door stayed closed. When he was walking through the living room, she came out and said, "You going to work early today?"

"I'm helping Mr. Frank with the money before my shift."

"Randall, you're lying to me."

"Come with me, and you can see what we do," he said with a stronger note of irritation than he wanted. Everything was so damn hard all of a sudden.

"You will not be smart with me, young man," she said with surprising steel in her voice. "You may not plan to live here much longer, but while you do you will respect me."

Randall nodded and sighed. "I'm sorry, Aunt Lisa. Today's a bad day for me. I apologize."

"Okay, Randall. Apology accepted." She smiled and kissed him on the cheek before he walked out the door. Did she mean it?

On the way in the front door at the Tahitian, Randall hoped for a smooth shift. Things hadn't been going well lately at the job. The messed-up orders, whole trays of dinners dropped in collisions with other waiters. No, he didn't have his concentration anymore. Would Mr. Frank regret offering him a job?

Surprisingly, Vince was sitting at the back bar with that fat lady—what was her name? The millionaire lady from far West Texas. The one famous for wearing dresses three sizes too small and diamonds ten sizes too big.

Randall waved at Vince as he strode down the hallway to Frank's office. The fat lady raised her face, put down a drink, and yelled, "Hey, cutie-pie, you come here."

Randall kept going, but he heard Vince's gruff voice, "Randall, step over. Join us."

The lady's eyes raked his body up and down as Randall walked up to the bar. "Vince, dearie, introduce me to this luscious piece of horse flesh."

"Randall, please meet Miss Ruby Rae Dalton, one of your many admirers."

Randall extended a hand. "Pleased to meet you."

A plump white hand with rings on every finger except the thumb grasped his hand with a surprisingly strong set of fingers. "Hello, darling, I'm Ruby. One of the favorite customers of the Carlucci Brothers."

"Yes, ma'am."

"You want a drink, darling? I didn't catch your name."

Randall was beginning to fear that Miss Dalton's boobs would fall out of her three-sizes-too-small dress. All that white flesh straining with every breath. Talk about disaster. "Randall Cartright."

She leaned toward Vince on the bar stool next to her. "Do you think we could have a private party with Mr. Cartright?"

Vince laughed. "You're drunk, Ruby. Randall is young—young enough to get plenty of young girlfriends."

Randall inched away, hoping to slip off Ruby's radar screen and into the safety of Frank's office.

Ruby winked at Randall. "Some other day, or night. Vince knows—I don't mind paying." Her hand descended to Vince's upper thigh.

Vince waved at the bartender. "Another round, George. And make them doubles." Then he turned toward Randall. "Picked up a lot of muscle this spring, haven't you? Work security for me whenever you want. Lot more fun than being a fucking piece-of-furniture waiter. Lots more money too."

"Yes, sir."

As spring's promise turned into Gulfstream summertime torpor, Randall convinced himself there was only one way his life could go—with Sophie. Throughout many sweat-drenched nights he tossed and turned trying to sort out the details. His degree—her career. His income—her income. Babies, no babies. House—apartment? He couldn't breathe a word of this to anyone, especially not to Sophie. He couldn't raise her hopes, then not be able to fulfill them. If he could only make more money, save more, get a little savings account going. Randall's insides churned whenever he thought about money and how he couldn't afford to marry Sophie—especially if he thought about the society she'd grown up in—debutante balls, cotillions, all that.

He'd signed up for summer school. Anything to hurry up his degree. His school schedule ate into the time that he and Soph would've played tennis, but Randall didn't care that much anymore. He had to finish his schooling. He could always make time later to keep up his body and the exercise it loved so much. Instead, he pushed himself to get up early and run on the seawall, then shower before meeting Sophie at breakfast. She started teasing him that they both looked exhausted now.

Randall tried to convey to Frank his sense of urgency about a degree without mentioning a future with Sophie, but Frank only reassured him that the experience he was getting from Frank's tutelage was better than a degree. What Randall couldn't say was "Dammit, Sophie is ahead of me. I'll never catch up."

Randall focused on what he might do to give Sophie a nice birthday. Her day was August 15. Right in the middle of the punishing dog days of summer. One afternoon, while he and Frank were poring over ledgers and orchestrating money transfers, he asked Frank what he would suggest to make the evening special for Sophie's birthday.

Frank looked up surprised. Randall hadn't mentioned a special girlfriend since that first day when they talked about love—months ago.

"So this is the girl, huh?"

Randall looked at the floor. "Her name is Sophie."

"You need to have dinner alone on her birthday. Some place really romantic," Frank said with a twinkle in his eye. "Some place really quiet. Where you can hold her hand."

"There's not too many places I can afford."

"Why don't you bring her here? I'll comp the dinner."

"Oh, gosh. Thank you, Mr. Frank. But it's never quiet here, and with me knowing all the staff—it might not be too, well, you know, romantic."

Frank laughed. "I didn't think about that. But why don't you bring her here for cocktails first? We can throw a little party in her honor. One of the private dining rooms, or we can close one bar for a couple of hours. You can invite who you want, and I'll comp that party. Then you two can go on your way alone for a romantic dinner."

"Really?"

"Why sure. I'd love to do that for you."

"That's great, Mr. Frank. It's a deal. I'll pay for as much of it as I can."

"Don't worry about that, Randall. Just don't invite two hundred people—otherwise, you'd put me out of business."

"No, sir, I wouldn't dream about it. And you'll be

there, right? I want you to meet her. She's my dream come true."

"In that case, I do want to meet her. I remember how that feels." Frank reached up to touch his red rosebud. "I remember how it feels to find your dream-come-true woman."

Randall waited for Frank to ask questions—who she was, how they had met, what kind of work she did, if any. Instead, Frank walked back to the table and pulled the ledgers closer. When he spoke, his voice sounded angry, and his eyes scanned the lined pages while his face maintained its perfect composure.

"Let's get back to work," he said.

CHAPTER FIFTY-EIGHT

The day of Sophie's birthday dawned clear and bright, as if Randall had ordered it personally. He hadn't told her about the evening's plans other than to say that he'd pick her up at six. Everyone else knew to be at the Tahitian's back bar before six. There'd be an element of surprise—enough to make it the best day of Sophie's year—a beautiful room of party-goers just for her. Flowers, white tablecloths, candles. The whole she-bang.

"So, I'm finally going to meet your girl tonight?" Lisa asked him that evening as he was shaving, the bathroom door open.

"You're going to love her, Auntie."

Lisa held up two dresses, one over each arm. "Which do you like best? The pink or the butter yellow?"

Randall canted his face to look at the folds of sparkling material. "I like the yellow, Auntie."

Lisa brought it up in front of her face and held it alongside her head. "Yes, it used to match my hair perfectly. Now there are just a few strands of gray."

Randall felt her eyes still on him.

"Will Frank be there tonight?"

"He's paying for all this."

"You and he must really get along," she said.

"I work close with him almost every day."

Lisa looked at him more intently. "Do you like him?"

"Mr. Frank is the best."

Lisa simply nodded.

"Way better than Mr. Vince," Randall added.

"You better stay away from Vince."

Lisa started to walk back to her bedroom.

"I might go to work for Mr. Vince," Randall said, lifting his chin to shave closer.

She turned sharply at his words. "Work for Vince?"

"I need the money," he said, sensing her change in tone. Couldn't he get out the door without another argument?

Lisa came to the bathroom's doorway and clutched both dresses to her chest. "Do you know what working for Vince means?"

"More money, for sure. Fewer hours."

"What do you need money for, Randall? You have a place to live here. I pay for your schooling."

Randall felt the sharp bite of his razor under his lip. Damn. Now he'd cut himself.

"Auntie, let's not argue. Not tonight of all nights."

She didn't quit looking at his face as he lowered the razor and tore off a small piece of toilet tissue to place against the cut.

"Okay, Randall. We'll talk about this later. Tonight is for good times for your girl and you."

Randall smiled, and the small wound stretched painfully. "Thanks, Auntie. I promise we'll talk about Vince's job offer tomorrow."

By the time Randall picked up Sophie from her dorm, he had forgotten the conversation about Vince. Other more important items crowded his mind: had the flowers been delivered to Sophie in time? Would she like the small restaurant he'd chosen for dinner? Would tonight be the night he'd ask her to marry him? His stomach was queasy every time he thought about proposing to her. Sure, she liked him; she wanted to go to bed with him—that much, he was also pretty sure of. But a lifetime commitment? What would she say?

He opened the heavy door to her building with ease and saw her standing in the small lobby. She looked ravishing. A long blue gown accentuated her muscular slenderness. A V-neck in front revealed a tanned collarbone. Her luscious brown eyes sparkled in the face he'd grown to love.

"Happy birthday, Sophie."

"Thank you for the flowers, Randy. They are beautiful."

"You're welcome, Soph. You look great."

She placed one hand in the crook of his arm, and they walked to his car. Had he ever been this happy? Not really, not ever. Her blue satin heels made a tiny but definite staccato along the cement walk, and his polished wing tips complemented their rhythm. This was how it was supposed to be. Different, but in harmony. Man and woman. His woman, and, oh, in his heart, he was hers, all hers.

He drove to the seawall, and they rode parallel to the sparkling, blue waves.

"I'm dying to know where we're going tonight, Randy."

"You'll see, Soph. It's all a surprise."

She put her hand on his right leg just above the knee. "Carefully orchestrated, huh?"

He prayed she wouldn't raise her hand higher. "Yep, that's me. Mr. Careful Orchestrator."

She giggled and removed her hand.

At the Tahitian, he handed his keys to the valet, who smiled broadly while another valet opened her door and offered his gloved hand.

At the receptionist's area, he checked them in while Sophie glanced around at the exotic vases and ornaments on the walls. Once they began walking down the long hallway to the club, she grabbed his arm and whispered, "You look so handsome tonight."

As she pulled closer he could feel her breasts on his arm.

As they entered the back bar, a crowd of people yelled "Surprise" and a wave of streamers and confetti descended from the ceiling. Everyone was clapping and singing.

Sophie pulled closer to Randall and said through a smile, "Who are these people, Randall?"

"My friends and family. Everyone's dying to meet you, Soph."

Frank was the first to come forward. "Happy birthday, Sophie. We are honored to have you here at the Tahitian." Frank's dark head bent forward as he shook Sophie's hand. "I'm Frank Carlucci, and Randall is one of my favorites." He glanced at Randall and slapped him on the back.

Sophie smiled and extended a hand. "Pleased to meet you, Mr. Carlucci."

Vince crowded forward with the awful fat lady squeezed into her habitual sequined toothpaste tube of a dress that was trying to force her upwards and out, boobs first.

Vince's slurred words rang out: "Hey, Soph, you've turned the head of Randall—that's for sure. Happy birthday! I'm Vince Carlucci, notorious brother of the handsome Frank Carlucci."

Sophie's eyes widened, but she extended a hand to Vince.

Fortunately, Miss Dalton managed to keep her mouth shut other than to wish Soph an enthusiastic and twangy "Happy birthday, darling." Then she toddled off to the bar stools with Vince.

The rest of Randall's friends crowded toward Soph and Randall. Where was Lisa?

As the crush of well-wishers moved to small tables with plates from the well-appointed buffet, Randall finally thought to ask Sophie if she wanted a drink.

"I'd love a glass of champagne," she said.

As he turned back from the bar, two coupes in hand, Lisa stood in front of Soph. They were talking and shaking their heads up and down as if sharing a joke.

He brought the glass to Sophie and handed his own glass to Lisa. "I see you ladies are doing fine without my introduction," he said with a smile.

Lisa turned her head. "I'm so glad to meet Sophie— finally. You've been keeping her a bit of a secret, huh, Randall?"

"I'll go get another of glass of champagne."

As Randall approached the bar, Vince waved him over. He pulled Randall to the opposite side from Ruby and placed one meaty arm over Randall's shoulders.

"Listen, kid. I'm ready to bring you onboard working for me."

"I don't know, Mr. Vince."

"Good money. Better than getting dressed up like a fucking penguin, smiling at people who think they own you because they can afford the price of a steak dinner."

"Aunt Lisa—"

Vince looked at him as if he hadn't heard her name in a long time. "What about Lisa?"

Randall didn't know what to say without pulling Lisa back into conflict with Vince. "I got to get her permission."

"She's not your fucking mother."

"I'll let you know. I promise, Mr. Vince," Randall said. "Right now, I have two ladies waiting for me to toast, and I don't have a drink. May I excuse myself?"

Vince waved Randall off. "Sure, kid. Just remember—good money, fast. Shorter hours. A little excitement."

Ruby leaned across Vince. Oceans of white flesh strained against the upper neckline of her dress. "You're looking very handsome tonight, Randall."

"Thank you, Miss Dalton." Randall deliberately didn't look at Ruby's plump hand working into Vince's lap. Man, these two needed to find a bedroom.

By the time Randall returned with his glass of bubbly, Frank had joined Lisa and Sophie.

"Let's sit down," Frank said. "I bet Sophie is ready to get off of her feet."

Lisa looked around as if to leave but finally murmured words that Randall didn't catch. At the table, Lisa drained her glass of champagne while Frank asked Sophie questions about her nursing.

Lisa waved over a waiter and asked for another glass of champagne. Frank directed all his attention to Sophie. She was far enough away that Randall couldn't even hold her hand. In fact, she kept both hands on the table—one around the stem of her glass and one holding her evening bag.

After a while, Vince strolled up with Ruby and sat at their table. Was that Lisa's third or fourth glass of champagne?

"Soph, may I get you a plate of hors d'oeuvres?" Randall asked.

Vince glared at Randall. "Tonight, you're not a fucking waiter. Call someone."

Lisa turned to Vince. "You will not speak to Randall that way."

Vince's eyebrows raised, and he clasped Ruby's white hand, bringing it to his lips for a wet smack of a kiss.

"What's wrong, Lisa? Jealous?" Vince asked.

Ruby patted his hand on the bar and rasped, "Oh, I guess she still likes you, Vince-baby."

Lisa's eyes darkened, and bright pink spots appeared in both her cheeks. "You are crazy."

Vince smiled and Soph stood up. "May I be excused?"

She walked to the hallway leading to the ladies' powder room.

Frank turned to Lisa. "How are you tonight?"

She smiled. "Thank you for doing this for Randall."

Frank continued looking at her, but Lisa looked down at the tablecloth and finally turned away. Randall heard her say something about the music.

"May I be excused?" Randall said.

As he stood and turned away from the table, he heard Ruby say to Vince, "It's time to go to your office, Vince. Momma's ready."

Randall found Sophie in the hallway to the restrooms. She was walking back and forth. The beautiful folds of her gown swished and swirled in response to her long, agitated stride.

"Sophie, are you okay?"

She turned with blazing eyes. "Who *are* these people, Randall?"

"What do you mean?"

"You brought me to drink with crooks and sleazeballs on my birthday?" she said.

Her words were as heavy as cannonballs, as pointed as bayonets.

"How can you say that about Mr. Frank? He's classy—as classy as they come on this island. And Aunt Lisa?"

She folded her arms across her beautiful chest and fumed. "Haven't I told you that my dad has been trying to put him in prison for years? He's a big-time gangster, Randall. Grow up, for heaven's sake—"

"Soph, that's enough. I brought you here because these are my friends, my family. Sure, Mr. Vince is rough on the edges—"

"And what about that broad he's with?"

"Soph, for God's sake. Let me finish."

She glared at him.

"I brought you here to give you the best night ever—
for your birthday. I wanted these people to know you and
love you the same way I do. My aunt Lisa loves me more
than anything—I know that. Mr. Frank is teaching me
accounting."

Sophie didn't speak.

Randall felt the nothingness of unspoken words engulf
them as they stood apart and angry in the long, carpeted
hallway.

"I've got to go to the men's room," he said and left
her in the silence.

That night Randall couldn't sleep. The events of the night
replayed endlessly in his head. What he had imagined as a
romantic evening had disintegrated into awkwardness and
ever longer silences.

For a while at the Tahitian, Soph's mood had
lightened. Some of his baseball pals had come over to the
table. She even drank one more glass of champagne.

As he and Soph left the Tahitian, Lisa had stayed at
the table drinking and talking with Frank. Neither one
looked happy. Vince and Ruby had long since disappeared
into Vince's office.

But over dinner, Soph stayed fairly noncommittal and
remote. She was polite enough to smile at his jokes and
respond to questions, but Randall knew her well enough to
perceive that her heart wasn't in it.

He escorted her to the dormitory, knowing that he
wouldn't kiss her goodnight. He couldn't bear to feel the
dismissal in her taut, closed lips. Those same lips that had
previously devoured every surface he gave to her.

How had everything gone so wrong?

He lifted her right hand to his lips. "Thank you for a
wonderful evening, Sophie."

She looked at him. "Liar." A faint smile appeared on

her face—that much he could see in the streetlight's glow.

"You're right, Sophie."

"Randall, what do we do now?"

"I don't know. It was a disaster. A holy disaster. And I tried so hard."

"Breakfast tomorrow?" she asked.

"No, Sophie. I got some thinking to do."

She placed one hand softly against his left cheek. "Okay. But there's one thing I need to do." She raised herself on tiptoes and barely kissed that spot under his bottom lip where he had cut himself shaving. "That little cut has been driving me crazy all night. It's been begging me for a kiss."

He let her walk the rest of the way to the door, open it, and go inside. The sparkles on her gown's long skirt trailed small spots of luminescence in the glow of streetlights. Gorgeous gown, gorgeous girl. His girl anymore? Who knew? Who knew?

CHAPTER FIFTY-NINE

Lisa was already up drinking coffee when Randall walked into the small kitchen the next morning. Her favorite pink dressing gown was wrapped around her, and she smiled when she saw him.

"Didn't go running this morning?" she asked.

"Didn't feel like it."

Lisa peered outside through the small window over the sink. Trees were bending against the breeze. "Bad weather's coming in. Probably good you didn't go. You might have gotten blown off the seawall in this wind."

She stood and hugged him. "Why don't you sit? I'll pour you some coffee?'"

Giving him a searching look, she pulled her robe tighter. "You and I need to talk, Randall."

He looked up.

"Frank and I talked a long time last night. There are some things you need to know."

"What's that, Auntie?"

She swallowed a long draught of her coffee and

looked up at him with a hesitant smile. "I can't tell you. But I want you to go talk to Frank. He's expecting you."

"Today?"

"Yes, the sooner, the better."

"Auntie, I got some things to figure out first. What's important to me is Sophie. She doesn't want to have anything to do with me because of, you know, because—"

"Because her father is the attorney general and Frank—"

"She says he's a crook."

"Talk to Frank. Give him the opportunity to tell you his side of the story."

Randall took one drink of the coffee in his cup. He rushed to the sink and spit it out. "I'm sorry, Aunt Lisa. That coffee's horrible."

Lisa shook her head. "I'm not surprised. I made it hours ago."

Randall sat at the table. "I got to go to Sophie first, Aunt Lisa. She's the most important—"

"Sophie may leave you, or she may stay with you, Randall. I don't know whether she truly loves you or not. But if she doesn't really love you for yourself, then you're wasting your time with her."

She smiled and crinkled her nose. "I've never given you advice on your love life before. Pay attention now, please. Go to Frank first. Give him a chance."

Randall left to shower and shave. He felt brittle to her, not at all like the pleasant, smiling young man of just a few days ago. Had last night put him in this mood? Of course, it had. On top of the disaster with Sophie not liking any of them, there had been Vince's disgusting actions, that ridiculous woman he was now escorting. The lies that enveloped them all in a thick fog of impossibilities and deceptions.

Outside, the winds howled all day while Frank waited for Randall, who didn't come. Frank didn't know if that was good or bad. It only delayed when they would talk. Frank tried to concentrate on his paperwork. For once, the phone calls that interrupted him were welcomed. Everyone was saying some bad weather was coming in, asking if Frank would evacuate, and on and on. The high seas outside his window churned.

Anything to take his mind off what he knew he had to do with Randall: he had to tell the kid that he was his father. That he'd failed him for decades by refusing to marry Lisa. That he'd placed money before their love, and his own personal success before the love of a good woman. That he had made her wait so long that she no longer wanted him.

Just before Frank left his office near four, he called Lisa.

"He didn't come by today, Lisa."

She exhaled and spoke as if tired already. "I was scared of that. He was upset this morning."

"What was he upset about?"

"His girlfriend. She must've dropped him last night."

"Why would she do that?"

"Frank, do you know who her father is?"

"Who is he?"

"Will Sheppard."

"Oh, shit. No wonder she was so unfriendly last night. Damn."

"You didn't know?" she asked.

"How would I know? I've never seen her before," Frank snapped.

"I told him that you deserved to tell your side of the story," Lisa said. "I told him—"

"Lisa, can we talk?"

"We are talking."

"No, I mean in person. Can I come over to your house?"

"Right now?" she asked. "Why, Frank?"

"Because I want to talk more with you—when I can see your face. I won't stay long."

Lisa agreed and put down the phone.

Outside, dark clouds scurried across the sky, and the date palms whipped their huge fan-like leaves back and forth.

Minutes later Frank's car drove up to the curb. Frank jumped out and ran to the front porch with his hand firmly planted on his hat.

How many years had he been coming to this same porch? He paused before rapping on the door.

Lisa answered his first knock.

"Frank, come in!"

The strong wind shoved him inside the front room. She helped him hang up his dripping raincoat.

Frank was first struck by how tired she looked. "Are you okay, Lisa?"

She smiled at him. "Do I look that bad?"

She still did that thing of reading his mind. "You never look bad. Bet you didn't sleep much last night."

"Not a wink," she said. "Have a seat on the couch."

"I didn't sleep either."

"Want some coffee?"

"Not really. Sit here, and talk with me, Lisa."

She lowered her slender form into the plush armchair across from the couch.

Frank remembered the night he'd made love to her as she'd sat on the side of that same chair. Her warm, shimmery flesh. His lips everywhere on her pale body. Each kiss bringing her into arching pleasure.

"How did we go so wrong, Lisa? I've been up all night trying to make sense of it all so I can explain it to Randall."

She didn't say anything—just looked away.

Frank anchored himself by looking into her eyes when she looked back. His nerves were jangling and jumping—

telling him to leave, to keep his mouth shut, to avoid the pain, to be done and gone.

"I can't figure it out, Lisa. We were so much in love. For years. Then we were broken up."

"I hurt you terribly, Frank."

"But didn't I hurt you too?"

Lisa reached across the coffee table and held one of Frank's hands in a warm clasp. "We both hurt each other terribly. We always forgave each other. I guess you finally ran out of forgiveness."

Frank sank into the blue wells of her eyes. As deep as he went he only saw sadness. A quiet, intense sadness. The same sadness he had glimpsed that first night when they talked on the swing outside of Marie's. No anger, no hatred—only sadness.

"But I could still love you, couldn't I? Maybe it's just buried under too much crap."

She put down his hand. "Do you have a shovel?"

He laughed. "Guess I'll have to go out to the toolshed in the backyard to see. Bet I can scare one up."

Lisa laughed too. "I almost don't care what happens anymore. I just know that I can't continue to live lies."

"You have to care."

"No, I don't, Frank. Maybe Vince will kill me, maybe not. Maybe Randall will talk to you, maybe not."

"Don't talk like that," he murmured, picking up her hand and holding it in both of his own.

"Although, I see that Vince has a new girlfriend, so I guess he's plenty busy. That's good, huh?" she said.

Frank smirked. "She's not a girlfriend. He only sees her when she's liquored up and gambling." He raised Lisa's hand to his lips and kissed it.

"Just like old times, huh, Frank?" she whispered.

He held her hand against his right cheek. "No, Lisa, it's not. But it does feel right."

She shivered, then looked at him. "Someone just walked over my grave."

All this was giving Frank the willies. The big storm barreling in. Randall and the talk they had to have. Lisa saying she didn't care if Vince killed her.

"I'm not going to let Vince kill you, Lisa. Don't even talk about it."

"How are you going to stop him?" she said. "He's stronger than you. And he's crazy. Probably better with a gun. There's no way to predict what he will do or when."

Frank ran his hand through his hair and tapped one foot on the floor. "Lisa, come stay at my house. There's security there all the time. At least I'll know you're safe."

"I can't, Frank. Randall will be coming home. I have to be here for him."

"Can you promise me that when he gets here, you'll both come to my house? Promise me that. Please."

She finally seemed to come alive. "Okay, Frank. I promise you that when Randall gets here I'll bring him to your house for the night."

Frank stood. "I'm going back to the Tahitian in case Randall comes to my office late. You have my personal phone number there? Call me if you need anything. Anything at all."

Lisa retrieved Frank's raincoat from the closet. Before he left, he hugged her and kissed the top of her golden head. "We're going to find that shovel together. Promise?"

She sighed. "Promise." But Frank hadn't felt any promise in the way she held herself stiff and remote during his hug. And when he tried to kiss her goodbye she only turned to offer him a cheek.

CHAPTER SIXTY

Frank drove back to the club in the driving rain, his car splashing sheets of water over the deserted sidewalks and seawall. When he walked into the long hallway he heard Ruby Dalton's loud, raspy voice.

"Vince, darling, I'm going to beat the pants off you."

Vince's throaty grumble was too deep and low for Frank to hear clearly, but he could only imagine. Those two must be rip-roaring drunk with only the bartender in attendance. Maybe a few other patrons who were trying to drink the storm away. If only life were that simple.

At his desk, Frank returned to his contemplation of the roaring sea. How many of his and Vince's secrets were buried down there in Davy Jones' locker? He couldn't tell Randall about all of that.

Ruby had been winning all afternoon. The storm had

brought her luck. The gin and tonics had brought her voice additional volume and her roaming hands additional audacity.

Vince watched as she pursed her lips before placing each card down. It was a simple game of Twenty-One, but she loved simple games with direct, quick outcomes. Her bosom heaved with each breath, and the wealth of white flesh stirred Vince. She was fat, but tonight she might be all there was. But not now, not until he'd won a few games and put her in her place. If he could hold off—that'd be good. He moved around in his chair to ease the strain in his crotch.

Next was his turn, and he laid down the card that would win him this round. Ruby laughed and drained her glass. "Okay, let's see how long you can keep it up." She moved tighter into the table so that her breasts were forced higher above the red sequined dress.

If no one else had been in the place, Vince would have leaned over and grabbed both those breasts and forced them out of the dress, then kneaded the nipples hard between his fingers. Ruby would have liked that—she liked it rough. Vince looked up at the bartender.

"Give us another round of doubles. Then pack it in for the night."

"Yes, sir, Mr. Vince."

Frank fidgeted in his office as the wind rose in volume. At first he didn't know if he was hearing a knock on his door. Then, it came stronger.

"Come in."

Randall's dark, rain-soaked head appeared. "Mr. Frank?"

The boy had lost the friendliness normally in his eyes. Even the way he walked was different—too erect, as if he didn't want to be here.

"Sit down, Randall."

"Yes, sir."

"There are some things I need to tell you, Randall."

"I already know."

Frank looked into the kid's eyes—there was nothing there. Empathy, sympathy, understanding—none of it was there. Instead, a wall of nothingness.

"What do you know, Randall?"

"That you're my father."

Frank felt the long breath escape his lungs. So many years of holding it all in. Years of unsaid words. Hugs that he hadn't been able to give; advice that was unspoken and unheard. The normal things that a good dad would do for a son.

"Who told you that?"

"Sophie figured it out. She says we look the same— too much the same. She said we even move alike and have the same hands, the same fingers. Something about a little quirk when we smile."

Tears came into Frank's eyes. Shit. He turned away from Randall's piercing gaze and dead eyes.

"Forgive me, Randall. I never wanted it to turn out this way."

"Damn you, Frank."

"Please, Randall. We didn't know what to do. We didn't want Vince to kill us and you."

Randall stood and turned to walk out the door. Then he stopped and turned back to look at Frank. "I'll complete my last shift working here tonight. I know you need the money counted."

The door softly closed. Frank considered following Randall into the room with the safe where he'd be working. No, that wouldn't be smart. Randall would have to come to some understanding on his own. Words wouldn't affect him right now. He was too hurt, too cut off. Frank turned off the lights in his office and sat back down with his head in his hands in the early darkness. It was past the time for solutions, wasn't it? Past the moment to ask for more time. Apparently, past the time when he could ask for forgiveness.

Ruby and Vince jostled each other as they swayed down the other hallway to Vince's office. Ruby reached up and rubbed her own breasts as she turned and offered them to Vince. "See these beauts. They're going to give you a swell time, Vince-dearie."

Vince put his arm lower around her waist and tried to steer them into the middle of the corridor. All he needed was Frank pissed tomorrow if they broke any of the exotic shit on tables along the hallway.

"Ruby, help me stay in the middle of this damn hallway."

She giggled, then reached down and removed her high heels. "This'll help. Momma's not too good in heels after a couple of drinks."

"Yeah, well, it was more than a couple, Ruby. More like a bathtub full."

She pursed her lips and blew him a kiss. "All the better to serve you, dearie."

They reached Vince's office and closed the door behind them. Vince kissed her with force, and she pushed against his body. Ruby turned her back to Vince. "Unzip my dress."

"We don't need that," he said, turning her around and forcing her to the couch.

"We got to take off Momma's beautiful red sequined dress."

Vince unzipped his trousers and pulled out his dick. "Kneel down, and give me a blow job. I'll sit here."

Ruby swayed. She looked at Vince's penis, then narrowed her eyes.

"No, I won't."

"You stupid bitch." He slapped her, but she remained standing. "What do you think I brought you in here for?"

Ruby advanced toward Vince with fire in her eyes. "Forget it. I can hire somebody to ball me without doing that. Someone that's not fat like you."

"Fat? Fat?" he yelled. Vince met her and took her by the shoulders and threw her on the couch. "You're so fat I'm worried I'll get hit by shrapnel every time you breathe in those damn sequin dresses."

Vince shook her by the shoulders. "I'm permanently scared your fat ass won't arrive at the train station on the same day your boobs do."

Ruby tried to sit up. Vince blocked her by sitting on top of her. He yanked off one of her fake eyelashes and rubbed it into her forehead. "Go look in the mirror, and see how stupid you look, Ruby."

Vince rolled off, and she finally stood up. Her eyes raked him, and she enunciated each syllable with surprising clarity. "Me? You think I'm stupid? No one is more stupid than you, asshole."

Vince sat down and eyed her. He didn't even bother slapping her again to get her to shut up. Not worth the trouble.

She pointed a finger at him. "You're so fucking stupid you don't even know that your brother has been screwing your girlfriend for years. You're so fucking stupid you don't even know that their kid works here every night of the week."

Frank? Lisa? It couldn't be.

The weight of the world descended on Vince's chest. His lungs quit working.

"Everyone on the island knows it," Ruby added. "You're the only one too fucking stupid to look in front of you."

Ruby tugged the neckline of her dress upward and straightened herself. She picked up the high heels she'd thrown on the carpet. Regal, for once, and quiet, for once, she opened the door without a word and walked out, the thick, black eyelash still on her forehead.

Vince sat stock-still on the couch trying to breathe.

Lisa sat a long time in the small living room after Frank left. The howling winds and driving rain were comforting, as if the entire world were coming to an end.

A car she didn't know came down the street and parked in front of her house. When she saw Vince get out, she picked up the phone.

"Frank?"

"What is it, Lisa?"

"Vince just got here."

"Shit. I'm on my way."

Vince pounded on the front door.

Lisa opened the door. "Come in, Vince."

Water drained down his clothing and puddled on the floor. He was breathing hard, and his face was pale. He opened his mouth to talk but no words came out.

"Yes, it's true, Vince."

A sound came out of his mouth that was part bellow, part scream, part sobbing agony. Lisa waited until it was finished.

"I'm sorry, Vince. I am so terribly sorry."

He reached and placed one meaty hand around her throat. "You're the only woman I've ever loved, Lisa. The only one."

Inexplicitly, tears rose in her own eyes, streaming down her cheeks.

He spoke again in a half-sob. "How could you?" His hand tightened around her throat, and he slapped her hard with his other hand.

She had no answer. She had been searching for years in her mind and heart for the answer. For a long time, the answer had been her incredible, searing desire for athletic,

handsome Frank, the debonair gentleman. That answer
hadn't endured through time. Had it been real love? Lust?
Who knew? She didn't. Not anymore.

"I guess it was fate."

He threw her across the room. "You bitch. That's not
a good enough answer. You took my heart and my money,
and all the while you were screwing Frank?"

Vince stormed through the room, swinging wildly and
smashing furniture, kicking everything in his way. His
anger matched the fury of the wind and rain outside.

A scream rose in her throat. When was Frank going to
get here? Could she survive until then? Would Vince kill
Frank as he drove up? Oh, God in heaven, don't let Vince
kill Frank...

"Vince, I'm sorry. You have no idea how sorry. Frank
and I stopped seeing each other years ago. We never saw
each other that much anyway. It was just—" She was
talking fast, talking to try to fill Vince's mind with other
ideas, to get him to leave sooner rather than later, talking a
blue streak despite the swelling in her face and mouth,
despite the sobbing that rose uncontrollably from her chest.

Vince stalked toward her as she stumbled over broken
furniture. "Vince, we didn't really make love. It was an
accident—only once."

He roared in rage. "I don't care how many times it
was. Once was one time too many. I trusted you. I trusted
you."

Vince reached her and slapped her down. He picked
her up again and pummeled her with fists and slaps until
she fell down. Then he kicked her in the stomach.

Lisa's body gave way to the punishment. "Vince,
listen. Frank is at the club. Go talk to him. Get your share
of the money."

Vince turned toward the door and snarled with
frustration. "Frank will not take my money. He took my
girl, but he won't get my money." With those few words,
he stumbled toward the front door and out onto the porch.

Faintly, Lisa heard his car's engine roar to life.

Thank you, God. Thank you for saving Frank's life.

Frank drove up to find the door wide open. The heavy rain obscured what was inside the house. *My God, let me be in time.* Vince's car was gone, but that didn't mean that he wasn't still here.

The living room was in shambles. At first, he thought Lisa was gone. As he carefully walked toward the kitchen, gun drawn, he found her crumpled behind the couch.

"Lisa!"

He cradled her head and freed one hand by re-holstering his gun.

"Lisa, darling." He bent down to try to feel her breath and was rewarded by a slight whisper of air into his ear.

"Vince knows. He wants. Kill you. Be careful."

"Where is he?"

"The Tahitian."

Frank found the telephone and dialed the operator. "Send an ambulance. Make it quick."

Frank leaned back over Lisa and caressed the one spot on her cheek that wasn't bruised or cut.

Her eyes fluttered open. "Am I going to die?"

He brought her to his chest and whispered into her ear, "No, my darling, I won't let you die."

She coughed. "Frank, I love you."

Tears rose to Frank's eyes for the second time in a night. He'd waited so long to hear her say it. "My darling, I love you too. Get well, then we'll be together, okay?"

She nodded a wobbly yes into his chest. A lightness that might be called joy came into his heart.

"Frank, where's Randall?"

"At the Tahitian."

"You got to save him from Vince."

"I can't leave you, Lisa. Not like this."

Through the storm they heard faint emergency sirens from an ambulance.

"I'll be okay. Save Randall. Our son. Save our son."

Lisa's blue eyes beseeched Frank with more eloquence than he could even put into words.

"Okay, Lisa. Promise me that you'll be okay until the ambulance gets here. Should only be a couple minutes."

"Go. Hurry. Vince knows everything. He'll kill him."

Frank carefully lowered her to the floor and stood up. He dashed to his car, thinking only one thing: if Lisa died, his own life was over.

CHAPTER SIXTY-ONE

The water was even higher in the streets. *Shit.* How had Vince been able to negotiate all of this? Waves dashed against the seawall and over it, forcing flumes high into the air. The sheets of rain were too dense for Frank's windshield wipers. With a jolt, Frank realized he had driven over the curb. He wrenched the wheel of the car back to find the street. Finally, he abandoned the car. Even with the wind, it would be quicker to run, and he was close.

When he opened the front door to the Tahitian, the wind wrenched it back on its hinges, and it careened wildly down the street. *Oh, damn.*

The long hallway loomed like a dim tunnel of death. Vince could shoot him easily there—if he was looking. Frank drew his gun and advanced down one side. The acrid smell of smoke was present. There must've have been a lightning strike or something in the kitchen.

Randall had said he'd be in the room with the safe.

Frank was betting that Vince would have gone there also—no reason to be in the bars or service areas. With the roar of the wind, there was no reason to be quiet.

The door to the money room was wide open. Frank heard Vince's voice.

"Don't move."

There was no answer.

"Put your fucking ass in the chair, kid."

Again, no answer.

Frank edged closer. The smell of smoke was stronger.

"What are you doing, Mr. Vince?"

"None of your business, kid. Sit down and shut up."

Frank looked through the door just enough to catch a glimpse of Vince stuffing packets of bills into a large leather bag.

"Can I leave, Mr. Vince? Lisa will be worried about me."

Oh, damn.

Vince stopped his feverish stuffing of money into the black bag and looked up.

"Lisa can go to hell."

Randall didn't reply.

Vince must've refocused because his voice was now lower and steadier. "I took care of Lisa; now I'm going to take care of you."

"I don't understand, Mr. Vince."

Thank God, the kid was trying to stall for time. But Frank had to figure out how to use the time. How could he be sure of his aim? His timing?

"This building is on fire," Vince said. The whole thing is going to go down into the waves. You will be in it— dead. Your pretty little girlfriend won't even have a corpse to cry over."

Frank stepped into the room with his gun raised. "No, Vince."

Vince looked to the door. Frank was gambling—just like always. But this was one gamble that he had to win.

"Vince, the person you need to kill is me, not Randall. Let him go—he's innocent."

Vince's face remained cold and unmoving. The small white candles that had been set up there—probably when the electricity went out—flickered. White tendrils of smoke had entered the room, and Frank briefly wondered if they all would go up in flames.

"Vince, I don't care if you kill me. But make it a fair trade. My life for Randall's life."

The building creaked in response to the storm. Was it swaying?

Frank looked at Randall. The kid's eyes were wide enough to show the whites. "Randall, get up and walk out of here. Now," he told him.

A sob escaped from Vince.

"Randall, leave us. This is between Vince and me."

The kid rose from his chair.

Frank spoke to Vince. "Thank you, Vince."

Vince yelled his next words at Frank as if they were bullets. "Why? Why? Why? Damn you."

The kid reached the doorway and passed by Frank without a look.

"True love, Vince. Lisa is my one true love."

Vince began sobbing, and his gun hand wavered. The smoke was now so thick that he coughed and choked. "You're not getting the money, Frank. You're not getting an ounce of it!"

"I don't care about the money, Vince. I don't care about anything."

Vince grabbed the money case as the flames rose behind him. Frank felt the intense heat.

Vince raised his gun and pointed it directly at Frank's chest. "Goodbye, Frank." As Frank dove toward the floor, Vince lost his balance as the floorboards gave way. With one arm clutching the heavy bag to his chest, Vince pulled the trigger, firing upward.

The searing pain of a bullet hit Frank's arm but something more painful occupied most of his attention— the sight of Vince disappearing through a massive hole in the wooden decking of the pier. Vince's scream echoed throughout the entire structure. In a flash, he was swallowed up by the wreckage and heavy seas. He had never turned loose of the black bag.

Scuttling out of the room, Frank tried to orient himself in the hallway. The smoke had engulfed everything in a cloak of impossibility. Not even vague shapes appeared.

A strong hand grasped his shoulder. "Frank?"

For a brief, terrified moment, Frank thought Vince had risen from the dead.

Randall's voice came clearer. "Frank, you okay?"

"We got to get out of here."

"Can you walk?"

"Help me up. I'm shot but I can walk."

Randall put a sturdy arm around Frank's ribs, and they half stumbled, half walked toward what they hoped was the exit. They could hear the timbers singing behind them as the fire consumed the fuel.

Finally, they made it to the sweet relief of the outside. They collapsed in a heap in the rain.

Randall spoke first. "You didn't have to do that."

"Yes, I did."

"I thought he was going to kill you."

Frank's arm hurt too much for him to smile, but he tried. "We got lucky, Randall. For the first time in a long time, we got lucky."

Randall straightened. "I got to get you an ambulance."

Frank nodded. "Your mom. We got to get to Lisa."

"Where?"

"The hospital. Vince tried to kill her too."

Randall began to shake visibly. "That's crazy. Why would he do that?"

"We hid our love all these years so he wouldn't kill us. We shouldn't have done it. I know we shouldn't have done it. Lisa and I agreed that I'd come here to save you. The ambulance was almost there."

Randall closed his eyes and bent his head. Frank

couldn't tell if there were tears or raindrops on his face, but he barely heard Randall say, "You two really love me, don't you?"

Frank placed his good arm around the kid's shoulders and brought him into his chest. It was beyond words. Beyond anything Frank had ever felt in his life. The love of a father for his son—it felt good even if just for this instant.

CHAPTER SIXTY-TWO

Lisa hadn't expected to wake up. She thought she'd be dead and in no pain. It was the pain that convinced her that she was still alive. Battered, but alive. A nurse hovered at her bedside.

The competent eyes surveyed Lisa's face.

"You don't remember me, do you?" the nurse said.

Lisa concentrated. "No."

"I'm Randall's girlfriend, Sophie."

"You don't like us," Lisa said.

A faint smile lit up the nurse's face. "That was a bad night when we met. Randall has convinced me that I was out of order."

The idea of her handsome son convincing this tall beauty of a woman that she was in the wrong was amusing. Lisa felt sure that if she laughed it would cause even more pain; she couldn't even smile.

"My son is very persuasive when he wants to be."

The nurse moved to leave the room. "Frank is here also."

Fear rose in her throat and clutched her guts. "Is he okay?"

"He's okay, just a little damaged, but they're fixing him up in surgery right now."

"Thank God," Lisa breathed. "Thank you, Father God."

After Sophie left, Lisa closed her eyes in relief. But she heard the door open again. When she looked, Randall stood there. Rumpled and red-eyed, he looked strangely different, strangely changed.

"Mom?"

Lisa's heart broke in that instant. Never before had she heard that word, and never before had she been aware of how much she needed to hear it from him, from dear sweet Randall—the kid she'd given away, then wept over for so many years.

"Oh, Randall, my dear son."

He rushed to the bed and clasped her hand. "It's okay, Ma. Really, it's okay. Frank's been shot—"

"Frank? Shot?"

"He saved my life, Ma. He saved my life."

Hot, salty tears flooded from Lisa's eyelids, but she was in too much physical pain to lift a hand to wipe them away.

"Are you okay, Mom?"

"I've been praying nonstop."

Randall stood at the side of her bed, and she felt his weight as he leaned across the white expanse of sheets to put a hand over hers.

"Just rest up. Sophie will take excellent care of you."

Frank was alone in his own hospital room dozing when he was surprised to hear a door open without a nurse calling out to him immediately. He looked up. Randall stood, hesitating, not approaching the narrow bed.

"Mr. Frank?"

Frank waved Randall closer. The kid looked rumpled and dirty. But he was walking erect and looked strong. He'd made a decision. Frank could see it in his posture.

"I want to thank you for saving my life, Mr. Frank."

"Randall, you're my son. How could I not do that for you?"

"I've asked Soph to marry me."

"Good for you."

"She said yes," Randall continued, squaring his shoulders slightly. "I'm going to ask her father's permission as soon as this storm leaves."

The planes of Randall's face reflected happiness, the faint glow of anticipation. Yes, he'd make her a good husband.

"Randall, have you talked to your mother?"

Randall looked down at his shoes. "Yes, sir."

"They're telling me she's okay. Is that true?"

"Yes, sir."

"Randall, I don't know if you'll ever be able to accept me as your father. I'm not going to push it. Forgiveness takes a long time. Trust me, I know—I still can't forgive myself for all the things I've done."

Frank paused. The tightening in his throat was strong and threatened to stop him completely. "All I ask." A sob rose and caught in his throat. *Damn.*

Randall's brow furrowed.

"All I ask is that you forgive Lisa. She didn't want to make love with me—that first time when we made you. I... I sort of forced her—"

"You raped my mother?"

"No, it wasn't like that. But I persuaded her because I was too selfish, too much—I don't know. I was stupid and horny and desperate because I thought she was the real thing. I'd never had anyone or anything real and beautiful and fine in my life. My whole life had been dirt and piss and ugliness."

Frank's eyes welled with tears. "I wanted—even just for a few minutes—to be together with the most beautiful, sweetest girl I'd ever met. I thought making love to her could take away her sadness, but all I did was cause more sadness for her—which wasn't my intention, but happened anyway."

Randall studied Frank's eyes. "I don't understand you."

"Most of the time I don't understand myself. All I ask is that you don't penalize your mother because I'm a dolt. I've been in love with her for years and made her wait. Years ago, I asked her to marry me, and she said yes. When we get healed up I'm going to ask her again. I'm praying that she says yes again."

Randall hesitated, then looked out the window at the brightness glaring off the ocean that had almost killed all of them so recently.

"You could say you were born out of our dreams and desires—the dream to be happy, the dream to be something better, finer, more genuine than we could be in daily life," Frank said. "You know, she was only about eighteen; I was barely twenty-one. We didn't make love again for a long time after that. But we made you that first time, and you carry all that's good, all that's hopeful about who we were trying to be. Don't hate us for that."

Randall shook his head.

The pain inside his chest was killing Frank—the sadness, the loss. His son slipping away. Like finely powdered sand leaking out of a closed fist. You could try closing your fingers tighter but when you opened it all the sand would be gone anyway.

"I've got to rest, Randall."

The boy's serious eyes swept down to Frank's bandaged arm. "Should I call a nurse, Mr. Frank?"

Frank forced his eyes open. "Don't call me 'Mister,' Randall. It breaks my heart."

The kid paused. "Yes, sir," he said, then turned and

left the room.

Frank closed his eyes. The tears ran hot and fast down his cheeks.

CHAPTER SIXTY-THREE

Several days later, when Frank could walk, they allowed him to go to Lisa's room. Dull-colored bruises disfigured her beautiful face. He didn't care—he was dying to see her.

"Oh, Lisa, my love."

The blue of her eyes was intense against the backdrop of white hospital sheets. A smile lit her face.

"Frank!"

He walked to her bed and placed a hand over hers on the thin blanket.

"I've been so worried about you, dear Lisa."

"Has Randall talked to you?"

"He can't forgive me."

Her smile faded.

Frank lightly squeezed her hand. "But don't you worry your pretty head. Maybe in the future. You know, maybe by our wedding?"

"Wedding?"

"Surely, you can't have forgotten that I asked you to marry me? Surely, you want to make an honest man out of me, my dear Lisa?"

"Are you serious, Frank?"

He stopped talking and wiped the smile off his face. "I'm ashamed of being a fool all these years. The money shouldn't have mattered to me. All those damn houses and custom-made suits—they shouldn't have mattered to me.

"I'm sorry it's taken me so long to realize what really matters—you, the woman I love."

Lisa withdrew her hand from under his and brought it to her face. She began crying, her chest heaving so hard that she coughed. Frank reached across the bed and leaned down to hug her.

"Oh, Frank—I love you too. Yes, yes, yes! I'll marry you," she said through the sobbing.

Frank's legs gave way underneath him, and he briefly hoped that a nurse wouldn't come in and find him collapsed on top of Lisa's slight body.

"Am I hurting you?"

"No, you feel so good, so right."

Half a year later, on a clear December afternoon, Frank stood in the vestibule of the church waiting for Father Patrick Linehan. He smoothed his suit jacket for the umpteenth time and looked down to make sure his white-rose boutonniere was still straight. He had their wedding rings in his inside pocket. Had he forgotten anything? They'd be a small dinner party at a restaurant he still owned—half his properties had been destroyed by the storm, just as the Tahitian Room had been. The priest had said the wedding had to be private, given that their son would be best man, but that was okay. It was the vows that mattered, not the guests.

The heavy door of the church scraped open. Randall walked in. He looked his usual athletic best in a black suit and stark white shirt.

"Thanks for being part of our wedding, Randall."

Randall walked to Frank and clapped him on the back. "Congratulations, Dad."

Frank thought his ears had made a mistake. Dad?

Frank pulled back out of Randall's hug and looked the kid in the eyes.

"Soph's been coaching me," Randall said with a laugh.

Frank's joy collapsed. The word had only been a rehearsed sop thrown at him. The coldness and disappointment must've translated into Frank's body because Randall stepped back and asked, "Are you okay?"

Frank couldn't keep his eyes from watering. He had hoped so much, hoped that this day might bring the three of them together finally and truly as a family.

Randall reached over and brought Frank close to him in a bear hug. "I wouldn't say it if I didn't mean it, Frank. I love you, and I love Mom. We're all together in this, and we're going to pull through—I know it."

Frank brought his fingers to his eyes and squeezed them shut so the tears wouldn't fall. But it didn't work. *Shit.* Randall reached into his rear pocket and brought out a white handkerchief that he gave to Frank.

"It's okay to cry, Dad. That's what Soph tells me—it's okay to let it all out."

After the ceremony, Frank and Lisa walked out into the bright daylight. Randall and Soph followed them to the brick courtyard in front of the church. A small diamond twinkled on Soph's finger—a sparkling promise of the future she'd share with Randall.

It was winter—as much winter as the Gulf Stream allows on the balmy coast. Frank had never seen Lisa look more beautiful. The ivory suit she wore hugged each precious curve in silk shantung. Her long legs were chastely covered in stockings and a longer hemline, but Frank knew their exquisite symmetry was there. The bruising had long since healed but Frank's feeling of protective love for her grew stronger every day.

Frank reached for her left hand—the one on which he'd just placed a gold band promising himself to her forever. He brought her hand to his lips and kissed the ring. "Now I can say 'Mrs. Frank Carlucci.'"

She smiled at him, brought his ring finger to her lips, and kissed it in return. "Now I've made an honest man out of you, Mr. Frank Carlucci. What are you going to do?"

He laughed out loud. "I'm going to enjoy it."

About the Authors

Robert B. Wilkins was born in Galveston and completed a medical degree at UTMB, where he was awarded the prestigious Ashbel Smith Outstanding Alumnus Award. While involved in his medical training throughout the U. S., he traveled internationally and visited casinos around the world. Those experiences were the impetus for the writing of The Carlucci Betrayal. Wilkins has also written the hit musical Galveston! The Vegas Before Vegas.

Sarah Cortez is the author and/or editor of thirteen award-winning books spanning the genres of fiction, memoir, poetry, and creative nonfiction. As a freelance editor, she brought to life ground-breaking anthologies focused on Latino/a and Native American crime writers. With a penchant for noir fiction (and publications of her own with Akashic Books), she is also a member of the Texas Institute for Letters, a fellow for the Dallas Institute of Humanities and Culture, and a member of the Dick Tracy Hall of Fame. She's a feature on American Trigger Sports Network television. Her careers as a writer, editor, and police officer come together in this book.

CPSIA information can be obtained
at www.ICGtesting.com
Printed in the USA
BVHW032330301021
620341BV00004B/14